THE RULES
OF FOREVER

Visit us at www.boldstrokesbooks.com

THE RULES OF FOREVER

by

Nan Campbell

2022

THE RULES OF FOREVER

ISBN 13: 978-1-63679-248-4

THIS TRADE PAPERBACK ORIGINAL IS PUBLISHED BY
BOLD STROKES BOOKS, INC.
P.O. BOX 249
VALLEY FALLS, NY 12185

FIRST EDITION: SEPTEMBER 2022

CREDITS
EDITORS: JENNY HARMON AND CINDY CRESAP
PRODUCTION DESIGN: SUSAN RAMUNDO
COVER DESIGN BY TAMMY SEIDICK

Acknowledgments

In writing this novel, I took to heart the old adage to *write what you know* and featured a teacher as one of my main characters. In my experiences as both a student and a teacher, I have witnessed teachers imparting countless tiny acts of ingenuity, compassion, tough love, and bravery. And all of those were in addition to meeting the objectives on the lesson plan every day. So first and foremost, I have to thank all the teachers who have taught me and all the teachers I've taught beside. In a country where very little value is placed on the profession, teachers truly are heroes.

Thanks to everyone at Bold Strokes Books, who made this new and exciting process easy and seamless. Thank you to Radclyffe for creating a company that champions and exalts the kinds of books I want to read and write. Thanks to Sandy Lowe for answering my novice questions with great speed and kindness, and taking even the most inane ones seriously. Thanks to Cindy Cresap for shepherding me through copy edits and the more technical aspects of publishing. And I must express tremendous gratitude to my editor, Jenny Harmon, for caring about my characters just as much as I do. She made the process absolutely painless, and I hope it wasn't too painful for her.

I would not have had the courage to complete this novel if not for the instructors and students of the GCLS Writing Academy. Thanks to Finnian Burnett, Anna Burke, and Karelia Stetz-Waters for their generous support and guidance. The members of my critique group were the first people outside my family to see any parts of this story, and their encouragement spurred me to keep going and finish the darn thing—untold thanks to Michele Brower, Cade Haddock Strong, Lori G. Matthews, and Rita Potter. Thanks also to my old high school buddy Michael Kardos for taking a look at some early pages and offering excellent feedback. I must also mention the time and effort expended by my mentor, KG MacGregor. She was kind enough to read the way-too-many words of my early draft and look for ways to improve it—twice!

I'm forever grateful to my parents for instilling in me a love for reading from a very early age. Trooping into the West Long Branch Library with my three sisters at least once a week during the summer to hunt down a stack of books to read at the beach will always be a treasured memory. Cathy, Betsy, and Sue are my biggest cheerleaders, and I share this achievement with them.

And finally, my wife, June, has been an unending source of love and support and I can't thank her enough for pushing me to make the changes necessary to complete this book. Words are what brought us together over a distance of nearly ten thousand miles, and words sustained us until we could bridge that distance. I've chosen to write happily ever afters for my characters because I'm living proof that they can happen, and I got one for myself.

Dedication

For June
My first and best reader

CHAPTER ONE

A nybody pick up on the extended metaphor in this poem?"
Cara Talarico sat with her five Advanced Placement English
Lit students, who'd formed a small circle with their desks. Their blank
faces gave her nothing. She waited and chalked up their low energy to the
oppressive steam heat from the ancient radiators in her Bronx classroom.
It made a crisp October afternoon sluggish and stifling. Her students' late
day listlessness couldn't possibly be attributed to the poem they were
reading because it was awesome, from the ingenious pen of her girl Emily
Dickinson. "Is anybody alive today? Should we read it aloud again?"

"Hold up, Miss. I'm looking for evidence," Yenifer said, pink
highlighter poised. Everyone dutifully started underlining random words.

"'I taste a liquor never brewed,'" said Rashard, ever the skeptic. "I
don't get it."

"How is it liquor if it's never, like, made into liquor?" Maritza
frowned at her paper.

Cara wasn't above leading them toward the light bulb. "Could she be
comparing something to the feeling of being drunk? Which, by the way,
I'm sure none of you have any idea what that feels like." That at least got
a covert smile from a few of them. "Miguel, what is she comparing in this
metaphor?"

"I don't know." Miguel turned doleful eyes toward her before he
looked back down at the page.

A flapping sound by the open windows jarred Cara from her seat
instantly. She grabbed the sweater she'd draped over her chair and snatched
a poster of common grammatical mistakes from the wall.

"Miss, a pigeon just flew in the window." Rashard gazed at it as if it
were a semi-interesting video on YouTube.

"Ladies and gentlemen, we have a guest today." Cara tried to keep
the tension from her voice. How many diseases could be transferred from a

bird to a person? The pigeon flew toward the ceiling, where it hovered for a moment before it descended and settled on an unused desk in the back of the room, as if waiting to hear what her students thought of the poem.

"Get it, Miss, before it poops on everything," Maritza shouted and backed away from their winged intruder.

Cara flapped her sweater toward the bird like a toreador and attempted to drive it back toward the window. "Miguel, take this poster and get on that side."

Miguel stood where he was directed and held the poster like a shield. Without being prompted, Yenifer took a position to Cara's left and waved her notebook toward the pigeon. As the others shouted unhelpful advice, the three of them triangulated their movements to herd the pigeon out, and slammed the windows behind it. Miguel loped back to his seat, but she and Yenifer watched at the window as it flew off into the blue afternoon.

"He just wanted an education, Miss," Yenifer joked.

"Wouldn't you rather have that life?" Cara kept a wistful eye on the bird as it grew smaller in the distance.

"I don't know. I've seen pigeons eat nasty old french fries out of the gutter."

"A valid point, Yeni." They rejoined the others, and Cara raised her voice. "Okay, bird emergency is over. Let's get back to the poem. I'll repeat my question: What is Emily Dickinson comparing to the feeling of being drunk?"

She surveyed the lowered heads and tamped down her frustration with the pigeon, the overheated classroom, and the open windows that had foiled her plan for a productive discussion today. A veteran teacher once told her never to try to teach with a bee in the room, but nobody had ever said anything about a pigeon.

"She's talking about flowers and nature and stuff," Fatoumata piped up, surprising since she was quiet and academically insecure. "Maybe she's drunk on that."

Cara gave her a wide encouraging smile. *Bless you, Fatoumata, for redeeming the final minutes of this class.* "You're on to something, Fatou. I would give you a thousand gold stars if I could."

Fatoumata rolled her eyes but then grinned proudly. Even seniors liked praise.

"Okay, we're just about out of time. Analyzing this poem is your homework, so remember Fatou's wise words as you work on your handout tonight. We'll discuss your findings tomorrow."

All five students immediately reached into pockets and book bags for their phones as their chairs scraped back from the desks.

"Please put the desks back in rows before you leave, and don't forget the due dates for vocab and independent reading." Cara raised her voice to be heard as the bell rang and her students began talking about things way more important to them than poetry.

Cara had ten precious minutes before her staff meeting started. Her phone buzzed with a call from her friend Lisa, her third today. "Hey, what's so important that you had to call during the school day? You know I'll return a text."

"I know, sorry," Lisa said. "I was getting seriously mad at you for not picking up but then I remembered school started again and I couldn't call you any time I wanted."

"It's the middle of October. I've been back at school a while now." Honestly, Lisa was a good friend but her spaciness was not cute.

"Yeah, yeah. Anyway, I knew you wouldn't see it on Facebook, so I thought I'd call to tell you. There's a post on the Perry Bidwell page. We're having a ten-year reunion!"

This required three phone calls? Cara tried to generate some enthusiasm for Lisa's sake, but came up empty. "Sweet."

"Sweet? That's all you have to say?" Cara imagined Lisa with her hands on her hips right now. "I would've thought you'd be all over this. Don't you want to go back and see everyone and let them know you're still crushing it?"

"Nope. Not all over it, and by no means crushing it."

"By any metric, you are."

"You mean the metrics that say broke New York City public school teachers with massive amounts of student debt are the definition of crushing it?"

"Yup, those metrics." Lisa's grin was almost audible over the phone. "You're going to come, right? Don't make me walk in there all by myself. We have to represent the day students. You know all the boarders will be there flaunting their Insta-worthy lives. I have to make them jealous with my bookkeeping job and my prewedding pregnancy."

"Excellent reasons for attending."

"I really want to see what everyone's up to now. Please say you'll come."

"I'll think about it." Except there was no room in her budget for the dressy clothes she'd need for an event like that.

"You have a month. It's right before Thanksgiving." Lisa started to singsong. "And I know you'll want to see a certain someone from our class."

"Who, Mrs. Keefe? You're right, I would like to talk to her."

"Not our English teacher, ya nerd. You know." Lisa paused for effect. "Your little crusharooney?"

"Crusharooney? Who the hell are you talking—oh." A vision of Cara's embarrassing, unrequited high school crush slotted into her mind's eye: beautiful, blond, and walking toward her in slow motion as harp arpeggios and choirs of angels sounded, wearing a pristine field hockey uniform, backlit by the sun with those golden tresses flowing behind her as if she were standing in front of a wind machine. Lauren Havemayer. "It was ten years ago, for God's sake. I haven't thought about her in years."

"Yeah, right."

"It's true." Although the speed and clarity with which her memory had returned was unnerving. "Who even knows what she's been doing all this time."

"Word on Facebook is she was living overseas but is back in New York now. You two are in the same city."

"Great, I'll look her up immediately. I'm sure she's waiting for my gay ass to call."

"You should. She's probably gay too. Wasn't everyone back in high school?"

"You weren't. Just because it's a girls' school doesn't mean everyone was a lesbo."

"I bet there was a lot of intrigue and romance among the boarding girls. What the hell else did they have to do?" Lisa took a breath. "I can't wait to hear what everyone's been up to. But you and Lauren, you're no-shows on social media. Everyone else at least posts somewhere once in a while. Why do I even want to go to this? I know what practically everyone is doing already. It's Facebook's fault. They ruined reunions."

"So we don't have to go?" Cara asked.

"No, we're going. Expect a paper invitation in the mail in the next few days. You'd better RSVP yes."

"I said I would think about it. I have to go, I have a staff meeting, like, right now."

"And think about what you're going to wear!"

CHAPTER TWO

Lauren Havemayer walked through the lobby doors of her temporary New York home and rummaged in her bag for keys.

"Ms. Havemayer?" Raoul approached from behind the concierge's
desk, a FedEx envelope in his outstretched hands. "This just arrived for
your father. Would you like to take it?"

"Sure, Raoul. Thanks." Lauren retrieved the mail and crossed the pale
marble floor to the bank of elevators at the rear of the lobby. After smiling
politely to an exiting neighbor, she stepped in and inserted her key for the
penthouse. As she was whisked upward, she sifted through today's mail
and caught sight of something from her alma mater, Perry Bidwell.

The elevator doors entered directly into her family's apartment. A
large flat crate, about five feet square, leaned against the console table. She
spied her father's briefcase next to the console table as she shrugged out
of her coat. "Dad?"

"In the kitchen."

Lauren found him seated at the island, working on his laptop with the
remains of a sandwich on a plate next to him. She handed him the FedEx
box. "Here you go. Delivery for Malcolm Havemayer. Is that the new piece
out there? When will it be uncrated? I can't wait to see it."

"It arrived later than scheduled, so they're coming back next week
to install it." He leaned over and kissed her on the cheek, keeping his eyes
on whatever business crisis was holding his attention. "Aren't you home a
little early today?"

"I had the meeting with the architect, remember?" Lauren opened
the envelope from Perry Bidwell. It was too early for their annual alumnae
fundraising drive. "What are you doing home?"

"I'm flying back to London tonight. How did it go with the architect?"

"Hmm." The invitation distracted her.

He looked up from his laptop. "What is it?"

"My ten-year reunion." The invitation landed on the counter with a
dismissive toss.

Her dad chuckled. "Time sure flies, doesn't it? I remember settling you in at your dorm like it was yesterday. Your mom thought twelve might be too young, but you took to it like a duck to water, just like I knew you would." He leveled a proud gaze at her. "You should go. Rebuild some connections. You've seemed a little lost since you've been back."

"It's only been two months." Lauren hadn't lived in the city since she was a child. It was going to take time to get into a groove. And while renewing friendships with former classmates might be a fun and nostalgic way to spend an evening, her job was her first priority. "I've got too much work to do, anyway."

Her father glanced at the invitation. "Not on a Saturday night, you don't. One night won't make a difference. Go, have fun."

Lauren grabbed a plum from the bowl of fruit on the counter. "I'll think about it. I'm going for a run before it gets dark." She collected the rest of her mail and the invitation. "What time are you flying out?"

"Wheels up at Teterboro at ten p.m. Be careful in the park."

"I'll keep my head on a swivel." She used the phrase he had repeated since she was a little girl.

He smiled and nodded. "Wait, what about the architect?"

"Oh, it went well. We're pretty much demolishing the kitchen and bathrooms and leaving the rest. He'll vet a few interior designers and general contractors and let me know."

"How long will it take?"

"Trying to push me out already, Dad? I thought you didn't mind having me here."

He spread his arms out in protest. "Honey, I don't even know why you had to get your own place. There's plenty of room here and I'm gone so much of the time. And it's so close to your job."

Pushing thirty and he still wanted her living at home? "I know and I appreciate it. You'll have me here for eight months, probably a year with how slow construction goes in the city." She put her arm around his shoulders. "I need my own space. You get that, right?"

"Yes, I get it. Now let me finish this email before close of business." He gave her a perfunctory half-hug and was already tapping at the keyboard as she walked away.

Lauren gazed at her alma mater's crest on the invitation envelope, curious about what her friends had been up to. She wasn't that fond of social media, and the only person she kept in sporadic touch with from boarding school was her former roommate, Sasha Weikert. She'd reach out and see if Sasha was going to the reunion, but even if she wasn't, Lauren would go. Her dad was right. She needed to renew some acquaintances and reinvigorate her social life. If New York City was going to be her home, she needed to put down roots.

CHAPTER THREE

Cara hurried through the doors of the best coffee shop in East Harlem and made a beeline for her former roommate, Samantha Cruz. "Hey, sorry I'm late." She plopped down in the chair across from her.

Samantha perched her glasses atop her long black hair and smiled, closing the folder in front of her. "Some things never change. What emergency was it this time?"

"No emergency. Homework Help ran long, that's all. Students were researching topics for their argument essays."

"At least they're coming for Homework Help."

"Only four, but it's better than none." Cara waved to Manny, the barista behind the counter. He lifted his chin at her and she nodded, confirming her usual order. She gave Samantha her undivided attention. "How are you? How's Hector? Are you still in the longest honeymoon phase in history?"

Samantha's expression became fond. "He's so good. This morning he brought me my coffee in bed with one of those little madeleine cookies."

"Bedside coffee on a weekday? Now that is love." Cara grasped Samantha's hand. "I wouldn't have been able to part with the best roomie I've ever had for anyone who treated you like less than seven-thousand-karat gold."

"That's a lot of karats, lady."

"He's got a lot to live up to."

"What's a lot of carrots?" A small porcelain cup and saucer were placed in front of Cara, the words *Café Mi Vida* printed in light blue lettering on its side.

"Thanks, Manny." Cara reached for the macchiato as if it were the staff of life. "Delicious, as always."

"Of course." Manny scouted the empty coffee shop for unassisted customers before he sat down next to Cara. "Speaking of carrots, I just saw the sweetest pic on Instagram of two carrots that had grown like they were hugging each other. It was mad cute. Love is love, you know? Even if it's carrot love."

Cara and Samantha grinned at each other. They were used to Manny's non sequiturs.

"Wait, I'll show you." He pulled out his phone and started scrolling.

"Aw, Manny, I miss you," Samantha said. "Can you please get a job close to my apartment so I can drink your wonderful coffee and listen to your words of wisdom?"

"I'm not leaving el barrio." Manny glanced up from his scrolling. "And what would Cara do if I left? She got so lonely once you fucked off to Brooklyn, I became her best Judy."

"It's true—" Cara threw her arm around his beefy shoulders. "We're besties now."

Samantha tilted her head. "I never noticed it before. You both have the same dark, wavy hair. You could be siblings."

Cara turned to Manny. "Mi hermano!"

"Hola, sis!" Manny laughed at the absurdity of it, but sometimes Cara felt like Manny was the little brother she never had. The gay, Dominican brother. "Look, here it is." He showed them the picture of carrots embracing, and Cara had to admit it was more touching than a photo of mutant vegetables had a right to be. The sound of the bell jangling above the door signaled the arrival of customers, and Manny jumped out of his chair. "Gotta go."

"I hope someday I'll find a carrot who loves me as much as those carrots seem to love each other," Cara said.

"If you want to find your carrot, you have to get out into the vegetable garden." Samantha looked at her shrewdly. "When's the last time you went on a date?"

"You know that's not my priority right now."

"Oh, right. The my-life-starts-at-thirty-five plan." Samantha blew a dubious breath. "Cutting your budget to the bone so you can pay off your student loans by the time you're thirty-five is nuts. And it's having a serious impact on your quality of life."

"You were smart and accepted that scholarship to Rutgers. I was dumb and went for shiny, shiny Princeton and took on a ton of debt. Who ever said eighteen-year-olds were qualified to make major life decisions for themselves?"

"Come on, you don't regret going there."

"No, I don't," Cara agreed. "I wouldn't trade it for anything. But I don't want to be paying off my loans for the rest of my life, so I'll live like a broke hermit for a while." Rent, groceries, and loans. Those were the only line items on her personal budget right now.

"But what about the things that make life worth living? Like finding someone cute and going out for drinks with her? You can be a little psychotically rigid when it comes to these rules you make for yourself."

"Psychotically rigid? Thanks, friend."

"All right, how else can I describe your single-minded pursuit of this arbitrary goal you've set? The teensiest bit unbending?"

"Okay, I'm unbending, but this is important to me. Anyway, I'm too busy advising clubs and staffing Homework Help to date. I need all the per session pay I can get."

"You're already working so hard at that soul-sucking school. Where's the trade-off?"

Cara ignored the question. "I miss you, Sam. I miss splitting a box of wine and mocking the Real Housewives with you. I miss trying to lure the bodega cat into our apartment with whatever random food we had in the place."

"Who knew cats loved McDonald's french fries so much?" They shared a smile. "I miss you, too. How's our building?"

"Good. The new tenants in our old apartment are leaving your mail on the ledge for me." Cara reached into her satchel for the bundle. "Would you please change your address? Or don't. At least this way I get to see you sometimes."

"I will." Samantha shuffled through the envelopes. "How's your place?"

Cara had moved out of their converted one-bedroom and into a studio upstairs, unable to bear the thought of living with a new roommate. "Best decision I ever made. It's a bit more expensive, but I'm tightening the belt in other areas."

"As long as you can afford to eat more than rice and beans." Samantha held up an envelope from Perry Bidwell. "What's this?"

"That, my friend, is an invitation to our ten-year reunion. We're officially getting old."

"Oh, yeah. Lisa told me. I can't go."

"Why not? We need you there for day student solidarity."

"I know, but work is going to be crazy. I have a huge case on the docket. I'll be swamped."

Cara conceded that was a good reason. "I guess I'll allow it."

Samantha looked amused. "So you're going?"

"I don't want to, but Lisa will have to go by herself if I don't."

"Why don't you want to go?"

"I don't know..." When Cara thought of the plans her teenage self had dreamed up, and how absolutely none of them had materialized, it became clearer why she wouldn't want to attend an event that asked her to confront her failures. "Just not feeling it."

"You're a good friend. Let's you, me, and Lisa get together after. You can tell me all about it." She looked at the calendar on her phone. "Say, the middle of December?"

"Sounds good."

Samantha gave her an evil smile. "I dare you to actually say something to Lauren Havemayer at the reunion."

Cara's cheeks got hot. "Not you, too. I already heard it all from Lisa." Had her teenage feelings really been that memorable?

"You should tell her about your crush. Who knows? Maybe she's gay and available. Get with her and you'll never worry about money again."

"Ugh. Shut up."

Samantha laughed. "I forgot how fun it was to tease you about her. You're still so defensive. At least try to get a pic of her for me. I bet you twenty bucks she's a Botoxed, plastic-surgeried freak, like one of the Real Housewives."

Cara sincerely doubted that. "I'll take that bet."

CHAPTER FOUR

L auren was instantly awake. A look out the window told her it was too dark to be morning. Her phone said three a.m. *Yikes.* It was months since she had returned from London, so she couldn't blame her sleeplessness on time zones anymore. She grabbed her robe and her phone, padded to the kitchen for a cup of chamomile tea, and took her mug out to the terrace.

The night was cold and clear and the moon was low in the sky, nearly full and shining. Lauren dropped onto one of the teak loungers, ready to contemplate her insomnia comfortably. For the city that never sleeps, it was awfully quiet on the Upper East Side tonight. The inky blackness of Central Park gave way to a few lighted windows in the distance, and Lauren cupped her hands around her warm mug in the stillness. After a few moments, contemplating insomnia became as boring as it sounded and didn't make her any sleepier. She pulled out her phone and texted a familiar number. *You up?*

Yeah. It's only midnight my time. Why are you?

Lauren didn't know. Her phone quickly rang. "Hey," she answered. "What's up?"

Her brother Preston's voice was a welcome sound. "You texted me. It's three a.m.—what's the matter?"

"Can't sleep."

"Why not?"

"If I knew…"

"The job?"

"No, the job is great." The most satisfying part of her life, in fact.

"Is it Dad? Is it a pain to live at home after all this time?"

"No, he's fine. He's hardly around, always traveling. And it's convenient to be so close to work." Living at home was temporary anyway. She was well on her way to true independence once her new place was finished.

"How's the social life? Reconnecting with old friends? Setting up a dating app profile?"

"Dating app?" Lauren recoiled at the thought.

"You have to jump back in sometime. You had an amazing city like London at your disposal and you wasted your last three years there by working yourself to death."

It was true. Saffron's betrayal had been traumatic, and work was the only thing that could distract her from heartbreak. It had been a hellish time, but here was her reward—her dream job in New York City. Her fresh start. Her blank page. Her new leaf.

At Lauren's silence Preston's voice turned serious. "Have you done anything social with anyone who's not Dad in the last seven days?"

She sipped her tepid tea and tried to figure out how to answer her brother's questions without sounding like a reclusive freak. "I'll admit I am struggling to get back out there. I'm still a little wary."

"About what? Dating? Being in a relationship? Sex? What?"

"Yes." Talking about this with her brother was a little weird, but she was more comfortable talking with him than with a therapist. "I mean, I don't want to become that strange old lady who announces her death with the smell that drifts out into the hallway, but I'm trying to not get hurt again. Even friendships seem risky right now."

"It's been three years and you don't even want a friend?"

Lauren didn't answer. Every time she thought about opening herself to friendship, she pictured Saffron's affable smile curdling into something sinister. Emotional connections seemed impossible.

"You need to be more of a guy about your relationships," Preston advised.

Lauren rolled her eyes. "I'd send someone a dick pic, but there's just one problem there, Pres."

"That's not what I'm talking about." He sounded insulted. "I've never done that in my life."

"Sorry. What are you talking about?"

"Emotions. A guy's not going to invest his emotions right away. He can see someone for a long time before feelings become a factor." The way Preston said *feelings* made them sound like bubonic plutonium. "You meet someone, go back to her place, etcetera, and then you're done."

"Etcetera, huh?" It seemed furtive, clinical. And he made it sound so easy. How was she supposed to not feel anything?

Preston elaborated. "You go out and bust a nut, get your rocks off, knock boots, do the beast with—"

"Oh my God, Preston, shut up! I get it, and could your euphemisms be any more dated?"

"All right, no need to disparage my euphemisms." Preston sounded part offended and part on the verge of laughing his ass off. "You get the point. Go right for the etcetera and ignore everything else."

"But..." Lauren hesitated to say this to her brother. "How do you do that? Not the etcetera part, the ignoring your feelings part?" Her heart was usually the first thing she gave away, and this last time with Saffron she barely got it back in working order.

"It's all about expectations. Make sure both parties are on the same page. That will help avoid hurt feelings."

Lauren had no idea what managing expectations had to do with not caring about someone.

"At least get back in the casual saddle. Three years is a long-ass time. Upload your profile somewhere. See what's out there."

"I don't want to use a dating app."

"I don't blame you. They suck, but how else are you going to meet people?"

"I have no idea." She let her head fall against the lounger, weariness catching up to her.

"What are you doing tomorrow night? Or tonight if we're being technical about it. There's got to be a queer club night or party happening on a Saturday night somewhere in the city."

"I'm going to my ten-year reunion for—"

"Perry Bidwell! Where my darling baby dyke sister first spread her Sapphic wings and tasted the love that dare not speak its name."

"Sometimes you really sound like a gay man."

"How do you know I'm not fluid? Any chance of rekindling an old flame?"

Lauren thought of the girls she had hooked up with in high school. Her experiences then seemed so free and innocent compared to recent history. "Not sure. I haven't been very good about keeping up with the PBSG crowd."

"Or the college crowd. Or the crowd from the Courtauld."

"Easy, Preston. I only just finished at the Courtauld. I haven't had a chance to not keep up with them. Give it some time."

"Well, that's my three a.m. sermon, over and out. I hope you heard me."

"I did," Lauren said softly. What had she ever done to deserve a brother like him? She tried to stifle a yawn, but Preston must have heard it.

"Go back to bed. We'll save talking about my personal life for next time."

"Thanks for the advice."

"You got it. Love you. Bye."

"Love you," Lauren said to the broken connection. She wandered back to her bedroom and slipped under the covers. Her brother was right. She didn't have to be looking for a partner for the rest of her life, just the rest of the evening. This was biology, not romance. She'd find some hot woman and ravish her and let herself be ravished. It was time to get back out there, to rejoin the socially active, so that she could then become sexually active. She'd never have to risk her heart again.

❖

"What time is Lisa coming to get you?" Cara's mom trailed her up the stairs as she headed to her childhood bedroom for a quick change into nicer clothes. One of the benefits of this visit back to her New Jersey home before the reunion was the pick-me-up provided by even a small dose of her mother's company. Some of Cara's anxiety about attending was relieved when she had stepped into one of her mom's infinitely long hugs at the Paterson train station. Plus, the bucolic campus of her old school was only twenty minutes away, so multiple birds and stones.

"Seven. But I still don't know what I'm going to wear." Cara belly flopped onto the bed.

"You didn't bring anything with you?" Her mom sat down beside her.

"Of course I did, but nothing is speaking to me."

"Well, that certainly would be odd if your clothes started talking."

"Joanne Talarico, did you just try to make a joke?"

"It's been known to happen." She poked around in Cara's bag. "There's nothing in here but jeans and a few shirts. Do you want to look in my closet for something?"

"No, Mom," Cara groaned. "We don't exactly have the same style."

"I don't know why you would think that. We are both education professionals. I have plenty of upwardly mobile duds in my closet that would look great on you."

"I'm really glad I came out early to spend some time with you, especially since you're not coming to the reunion, but if you ever say the phrase *upwardly mobile duds* again, I'll really start the emancipation process."

"That ship has sailed, honey. Long ago." Her mom went to the closet and flicked hangers aside in search of something. "I have an idea."

"Are you sure you don't want to come tonight? You usually love the reunions." Perry Bidwell School for Girls was one of the top girls' schools on the East Coast, and the only way she had been able to attend was because her mother was the administrative assistant to the head, and employees' children received free tuition.

"I do like seeing everyone again, but this is your reunion. I don't want you to feel uncomfortable with me being there."

"I won't, and I know you like to catch up with your favorites."

Cara's mom served as a sort of de facto mother figure for many girls who boarded at the school, and the yearly reunions were an opportunity for her to get updates on former students. She stopped searching through the closet and returned to Cara's side. "It's true, some of them need a little mothering now and then. I didn't think you minded."

"I didn't." Sharing her mom had been part of the deal. It was right there in the fine print.

"Those years—seventh to twelfth grade, my goodness—I know they weren't easy for you, but they were the best for me. I felt so lucky getting a glimpse of you in classes or walking across campus, being your brilliant self."

"My awkward, shy self, you mean."

"Maybe a little, at first," she allowed. "But then you joined practically every club and became more social and earned nearly perfect grades. I was so proud of you. Still am."

"I believe the only acceptable response here is aw, shucks," Cara said. She still basked in her mother's praise all these years later.

"And then we would go home together at five o'clock every day. I always felt bad for those girls we were leaving in the dorms."

Cara thought about the envy she had felt, the shenanigans she believed she was missing out on, the way the boarders seemed really tight with each other, while she and her fellow day students were kept outside of that circle. Ten years later, she only wanted to remember times of friendship and school unity.

Her mom returned to the closet and resumed her search for some outfit Cara probably had outgrown or hated. "I'm fine with not going. You girls like to catch up with each other, maybe talk with your teachers. Nobody comes to see the head's secretary. Nobody really cares about the head either."

"I bet at least ten of my classmates ask me about you tonight. They all loved you, and everyone knew where to find a tampon, some candy, or a sympathetic ear."

"Found it." She hid something hanging in dry cleaner's plastic behind her back and whipped it around with a flourish. "How about this?"

Cara grinned, her anxiety about attending the reunion abating. "Oh, Mom, I think you've got a winner. I hope it fits. I'd better call Lisa about this."

CHAPTER FIVE

L auren stood by the makeshift bar in the ballroom of Surrey Hall and tried to stay afloat among the memories. They had done yoga for P.E. sometimes in this room, and it still had that moldy gym mat smell about it. Two floors above, she had shared a room with Sasha, who had yet to appear although she'd promised to attend.

Everyone looked much the same. There was the addition of a slew of partners and spouses, which Lauren had somehow not been expecting. And baby pictures galore. Petra Morgan showed her evidence of three of her own already. There were a few baby bumps too, and one headed her way. When she raised her eyes from the bump, she saw it was a smiling Sasha, pulling a tall, handsome man behind her.

"I didn't know you were expecting, Sasha!" Lauren gently hugged her former roommate. "You look terrific."

"You look great, too! This suit makes you look nine feet tall, and cream is definitely your color. Gorgeous. So European. Meanwhile, I look—and feel—like an eggplant with legs." She presented her husband. "This is Colin."

"Hi, Colin, nice to meet you." Her grin masked a sudden embarrassment. "I'm still sorry about missing your wedding."

"It's fine. We didn't expect you to come all the way from England. Colin, heart of my heart, can you get me a sparkling water and another white wine for Lauren?" She steered Lauren away from the bar. "Let's sit. I should not have worn these heels. Now, who's here?"

"Most everyone, I think. It's a good turnout." They found some folding chairs on the perimeter of the room with a view of the action. The warm feeling of boarding school camaraderie stole over Lauren, absent for a long time but fitting now like a cozy sweater retrieved from the back of the closet.

"Lauren, come on. Even counting spouses, we're still missing a bunch. There's Ayumi. I guess that's her wife—look how they're practically attached at the hip. Oh, there's Petra. She's all over Instagram with her damn kids." Sasha's eagle eyes roved over the room. "The teachers are pretty well represented. I don't see Ms. Urwell or Mrs. Talarico, though. And I don't see Cara or Lisa or Samantha or some of the other day students either."

Lauren had forgotten about the day students. Her life had been centered around the drama and hijinks of her boarding friendships, but she now remembered the girls Sasha mentioned. They would probably show up later. At the moment, she needed to be a better friend. "How are you feeling, Sash? When are you due?"

"Late February. I'm trying to manage my stress. I read that online." Sasha didn't sound particularly stressed.

"You're in the middle of a surgical residency. How are you supposed to manage stress?"

"No idea." Sasha craned her neck. "Where's Colin with our drinks?"

There was a commotion out in the vestibule. Lauren could hear a chant rising in volume and enthusiasm.

"P! B! S! G!" repeated over and over and getting louder. Instantly, Lauren was hurtled back in time to victory on the field hockey pitch and boisterous celebrations in the locker room and on the away bus. It was all coming back to her now: "We're mighty! We're crazy! We're never ever lazy! We'll beat you! Defeat you! We'll even try to eat you! Gooooo Beavers!"

Lauren chuckled in remembrance. The Perry Bidwell Beavers. Unreal. Sasha had already gotten up and scurried toward the crowd of women. Lauren followed at a more sedate pace but was quickly embraced by her former classmates as they formed a ring around the two main chanters. Lisa Jankowski and Cara Talarico stood with their hands cupped like megaphones and bellowed the field hockey cheer toward the ceiling. Lisa had a faded PBSG sweatshirt on over her dress, but Cara appeared to be wearing her actual high school uniform, and boy, did she make it look good. Lauren suddenly felt her heart pounding. Everything went a little blurry around the edges as she beheld the magnificence of Cara Talarico in a ten-year-old school uniform, cheering away, eyes closed and smiling with joy.

The navy blue blazer with the school insignia over the left breast was too tight to button and left a few inches above her wrists exposed. The pleated plaid skirt would not have met regulations. It rode very high across Cara's thighs. Her white blouse had a few buttons undone at the top and framed the loosely knotted green polyester necktie all girls were supposed to wear. And Cara's glossy dark curls fell around her face in wild disarray, a feature Lauren felt sure she would have remembered from school.

Her eyes were still drawn to Cara, but her surroundings snapped back into focus as the cheer devolved into clapping and laughing and the new chant of "Bea-vers! Bea-vers! Bea-vers!" Lauren laughed at the incongruity of a bunch of grown women hooting and hollering like they were at a wrestling match, nostalgia and pride shining in their faces.

As Sasha returned to Lauren's side, she wiped tears of laughter from her eyes. "I'm so proud to be a Beaver."

Lauren smiled. "Me too." They turned toward the tapping on a microphone coming from the dais. Their head of school, Ms. Urwell, called them to attention as she had each day with morning announcements.

"Ladies of Perry Bidwell School for Girls, good evening," she said. "Welcome back. We're happy to see you here on our hallowed grounds again. You do us much credit as you carry out into the world the values that Lucia Perry and Penelope Bidwell began instilling in young women in 1906. It is with great satisfaction that I report the successes of your esteemed class, with members going into medicine, law, education, and government. We even have a representative in one of our greatest cultural institutions, the Metropolitan Museum of Art." Ms. Urwell caught Lauren's eye, and Lauren wondered how she knew about her new post.

"The administration and staff hope you have a wonderful evening," the head continued. "I'm told your valedictorian is not present, but perhaps your salutatorian, Cara Talarico, would like to say a few words?"

"Woo-hoo Cara! Speech!" Lisa Jankowski cried out and good-naturedly pushed her forward.

Cara mounted the dais and took the microphone from Ms. Urwell.

"Hello, fellow Beavers." Cara flashed a smile at the laugh she received. "I had to be convinced to come tonight, and although I've just arrived, I'm really glad I'm here."

Lauren was riveted by Cara and attempted to reconcile the earnest grind she vaguely remembered from ten years ago with this gorgeous drink of water with a head of hair that should be in shampoo commercials. Her smile was wide and welcoming, her brown eyes warm and lively. And the uniform. Lauren didn't know what it said about her that she was halfway to lusting after a woman who looked ready for Algebra class. It felt a little shameful, but she couldn't deny it.

Sasha nudged her. "Looks like you haven't changed," she whispered. "Still a beaver hound. Close your mouth. It'll stop the drooling."

"Shut up, Sash. I'm trying to listen here." If only Sasha knew how much Lauren had changed from the sexually free teenager she had been. Nevertheless, Lauren tried to compose her features into a less thirsty attitude. Cara Talarico had awakened impulses she had thought long dead and buried by her last relationship. Maybe she should resurrect her high school self. What was it her brother said? Find a nice girl, etcetera, move on. The more she watched Cara Talarico, the better that idea sounded.

"Being here on campus brings back loads of memories," Cara continued. "I'm looking forward to catching up with all of you, and talking with teachers and staff. You know, I'm a high school teacher now, and I can honestly say the experience we had here is rare. We had so many academic and extracurricular opportunities, patient and willing teachers, and counselors preparing us for the future. Not everyone has that." Cara paused, then looked like she wanted to wrap it up. "I'm just really grateful. Have a good time, everyone." She handed the microphone back to Ms. Urwell and stepped off the dais.

"She's a high school teacher? That's so sad," Lauren followed Cara with her eyes until she disappeared in a crowd of former classmates.

Sasha punched her arm. "Don't be a snob."

"I'm not! She's obviously smart, our salutatorian or whatever. She could be doing a million other things rather than teaching brats like we used to be." Lauren rubbed her arm. Sasha had fallen right back into that habit and Lauren did not appreciate it.

"What about Ms. Franciosi? If it wasn't for her art class, maybe you wouldn't be working at the friggin' Met. I bet Cara's doing that for her students. You should go over and thank her."

"Who, Cara? Why should I thank her?" *Maybe I should thank her for wearing that uniform. Wowza.*

"No, Ms. Franciosi. She's standing right over there."

"Okay, I will." Lauren moved in that direction, having lost all sight of Cara Talarico.

❖

"Cara," Lisa called. "The field hockey team is taking a picture. Get over here."

Reluctance made Cara's steps slow as she made her way to the group of women who posed informally. She was only on the team for one year and hadn't been very good. Lauren Havemayer watched her approach with a quizzical expression, as if wondering why they were waiting for her.

The evening had been fun, she had to admit. Everyone had been interested and curious about her life, both her day buddies *and* the boarding girls, and she enjoyed hearing about them, too. But being caught in Lauren Havemayer's crosshairs brought her insecurities roaring back. And that suit, white as Antarctica, was like a spotlight, so Cara knew her exact location all evening as she flitted among groups of women and easily conversed with everyone. Cara had avoided her, of course. There was no point starting a conversation now after all this time.

She took her place for the team picture. As somebody's husband juggled about seven iPhones, she could feel her smile mutating into something strained and fake. Her uniform blazer felt like a straitjacket, the skirt was just about cutting off circulation at the waist, and she needed a moment to take a breath. When the picture taking was finished, she made for the French doors to get some air, but rammed straight into a firm column of creamy, smooth fabric. Cara found herself staring into eyes that were keen, curious, and intensely blue. "Lauren Havemayer," she yelped. "I'm so sorry. Are you okay?"

"I'm fine." She put her hands on Cara's arms to steady her. "I don't think that was dangerous play, but we'll have to see what the ref says."

They were standing so close that Cara could see the tiny white line of a scar embedded in her left eyebrow. It had probably been there the whole time they had coexisted at school. And her hands. Were touching her. Cara's pulse thundered in her ears and her face burned.

Lauren Havemayer released her grip on Cara's arms but didn't move away. If anything, she stepped closer. "That was a field hockey joke, but I guess it wasn't very funny. How are you, Cara?"

Lauren Havemayer was trying to start a conversation, and Cara was as tongue-tied as she would have been at sixteen. She ran a hand through her hair. "I'm, uh…I'm hot, actually. I need to get some air. Please excuse me."

"I do, too," she said. "I'll come with you."

"Lauren," Petra Morgan screeched from across the room. "What was that place we went to in the city that time during break junior year? Lauren, c'mere."

She glanced in Petra's direction. "I'd better go shut her up before she starts broadcasting all my secrets at top volume. Maybe we can catch up later?"

"Sure." Blinking rapidly, Cara watched her walk away. She wondered who Lauren Havemayer was mistaking her for, because although she called her by the correct name, the few words they had just shared had been the longest conversation they had ever had. She felt a tap on the shoulder. *Oh God, what now?*

"You can take the girl out of the school, but not the school out of the girl." Her old English teacher Mrs. Keefe stood there with her husband, Coach Keefe.

Cara smiled, relieved to see such friendly faces before her. "Hi, Coach, Mrs. Keefe."

"You're a teacher now?" Coach asked. "I bet you're a good one. What subject?"

"English." Cara looked right into Mrs. Keefe's eyes.

Mrs. Keefe patted Cara's hand. "Welcome to the club."

"Actually, do you think we could talk shop a little? I have some questions for you."

"Sure. You don't mind, do you, Jack?"

"Not at all. I'll be outside."

Mrs. Keefe led them to an empty table near the decimated buffet. "What's on your mind, Cara?"

Cara sat and felt calmer now that she had something manageable to focus on. She could finally get some advice from someone she considered to be a master of the craft.

❖

As the evening wound down, Lauren wandered back to the folding chairs where Sasha had held court for most of the night. Colin sat on one side and Lisa Jankowski on the other. Earlier, Lisa had ditched her PBSG sweatshirt to reveal her own telltale bump, and she and Sasha were talking about episiotomies, whatever the hell they were.

Lisa turned to her. "Hey, Lauren, did you know that when you're pregnant you get hemorrhoids bigger than grapes?"

Lauren eyed the half empty glass of wine she'd been nursing all night and set it aside. "Gross."

"Not everyone does," Sasha said in her reassuring doctor voice.

Lisa laughed. "I'd better go. I'm becoming unfit for company." She gazed across the ballroom to where Cara and Mrs. Keefe were still deep in discussion. "But I don't think I'm getting out of here anytime soon, and I'm tuckered out. I'm supposed to drop Cara at the train station."

Lauren sensed an opportunity. "Where does she live?"

"In the city."

"Manhattan? Not Brooklyn or Queens, God forbid?"

"Yeah, not one of the derelict outer boroughs, Princess Havemayer," Lisa snarked.

"I can give her a ride." Lauren smiled at how this was working out. She wouldn't mind sitting next to that uniform for a little while.

Sasha glanced at her and muttered, "Once a beaver hound, always a beaver hound."

❖

Lisa bent down between Cara and her former teacher. "Hey, Mrs. Keefe, I'm sorry to interrupt you two."

Cara surfaced from their conversation to see far fewer people than when she began talking to Mrs. Keefe. She'd been keeping Lisa waiting.

"I found you a ride," Lisa said. "Lauren Havemayer is driving into the city. Better than taking the train, right?"

"That's great, Cara." Mrs. Keefe stood up and Cara felt bad for preoccupying her for so long.

"Thanks, Mrs. Keefe, you're the best. Tell Coach I'm sorry I kept you."

"Not to worry." Mrs. Keefe leaned over and squeezed her shoulder. "Keep chipping away. They might surprise you." She turned to Lisa. "And good luck with the baby."

"Thanks, Mrs. K."

Cara and Lisa watched her walk away.

"She's your teaching idol, isn't she?" Lisa asked.

"Best teacher I ever had. Who's yours?"

"Probably Coach. He was more of a yeller than a nurturer. I can relate to that."

"Says the mother-to-be." Cara grinned at her friend.

"Aren't you going to thank me?" Lisa poked her in her side. "Sharing a ride with the great Lauren Havemoney? This could have been your teenage dream."

Cara refused to acknowledge the frisson of anxiety that flared through her. "I'd better run and change. The three-inch safety pin holding this skirt together has been digging into my hip for the last hour. I guess I'll go a long way for a joke."

"It was a great idea. You were the belle of the ball. The pride of the party. No, the riot of the reunion!"

Cara rolled her eyes. "Okay, you can stop now."

CHAPTER SIX

Thanks for the ride," Cara said to Lauren Havemayer as they left Surrey Hall and traversed the lighted path to the parking lot. "No problem. I know I wouldn't want to take New Jersey Transit at this time of night." Lauren's smile was so friendly, Cara thought they could be on a first-name basis in her mind.

Cara pulled on her trusty peacoat to combat the late November chill, but Lauren strolled in only her amazing alabaster suit, an overcoat in the same shade thrown over her arm. She stole another look and noted how it clung lovingly to Lauren's body as if sewn by God's own tailors. Definitely not purchased from the sale rack at Macy's.

The silence between them lengthened as they approached Lauren's car, and Cara broke it with the most inane gambit ever. "This is your car? It's nice." The black Mercedes sedan was not quite what Cara expected, having the whiff of the undertaker about it. She had no idea what to say to Lauren now that they didn't have any classmates to fill in the conversational blanks.

"It's my father's. I don't have a car." Lauren opened the passenger door for her. After she settled into the driver's seat, she pointed to Cara's overnight bag. "You want to put that in the trunk? Or how about the back seat?" She tossed it behind her. "Is the uniform in there? That was a cute idea. You looked good in it." Her eyes roamed over Cara's jeans and coat before returning to her face. She gazed into Cara's eyes with an intensity that unnerved her, but then she smiled in a way that made Cara want to lean closer. "Really good."

"I don't have a car either." *Ugh. You have absolutely no chill.*

Lauren navigated through the campus and onto the county route that would lead them to the highway. The sepulchral silence inside the car was different from the rattling and whining of Lisa's aging Sentra. It reeked of luxury. Cara didn't think she could stand the quiet all the way back to Manhattan.

"What a night, huh? Who were you most surprised about?" Lauren interrupted Cara's escalating anxiety.

"I was surprised Lisa was so well-behaved, honestly."

"Yeah, she's hasn't changed at all," Lauren said. "Who did you least like talking to tonight?"

What a strange question. Cara couldn't think. "Maybe all those spouses I didn't know? That kind of small talk is excruciating to me."

"Me too."

"How about you?"

Lauren thought for a moment. "Probably Ayumi, who insisted on bringing up our little hook-up right in front of her wife. Who has that little tact?"

Cara did a terrible job of hiding her shock. "You hooked up with Ayumi?"

"Only for like five minutes during junior year when I was on a break with Petra."

"Petra Morgan? Who blabbed on and on about her husband and three kids tonight?"

Lauren nodded. "You didn't know about that? We dated most of junior year. She told me tonight she's bisexual, as if I couldn't figure that out. She started seeing a guy almost immediately after we broke up."

"Her loss." *Whoa.* Cara now had confirmation of Lauren's less than heterosexual status.

Lauren directed a quick smile at her as she flicked her turn signal to change lanes. "I certainly thought so at the time."

Cara let the news of her classmates' exploits sink in. "Wow, I had no idea. What else don't I know?"

"About the sexual shenanigans of our class? I could write a book." Lauren chuckled, then qualified, "Not just about me. There was a lot of bed-hopping going on in the dorms."

"All these bi-curious women sharing the same classrooms as me. I might've gotten some action so much sooner if I had known this." *Whoops.* Not the most graceful way of coming out.

Lauren took her eyes from the road, and her wicked grin set off a firecracker low in Cara's belly. "I knew it."

"Yeah? What gave it away?"

Lauren shrugged. "My gaydar pinged."

Cara needed some clarity here. "Are you bi?"

"Not interested in men," Lauren said breezily. "You?"

"Nope. I'm all the way over on that scale, the one named after that guy." Cara snapped her fingers and tried to remember his name.

"Kinsey?"

"He's the one."

"All the way over is a Kinsey six."

"I'm so gay I could be a Kinsey sixteen."

"Overachiever." Lauren gave her that sexy grin again, and Cara felt it down to her toes. "You didn't wear your hair like that when we were in school, did you?"

Cara smoothed a hand through her hair self-consciously. "No, I thought curly hair was embarrassing. I usually straightened it and wore it in a ponytail."

Lauren slapped the steering wheel. "I just remembered something! You, on the away bus after we won some match. You were standing in the aisle and lip-syncing 'We Are the Champions,' using your field hockey stick as a microphone. Your hair was all wild and coming out of your ponytail. God, you were cute."

"I'm surprised you remember that." Cara was glad her blush wasn't visible in the darkened car. "Back then, I thought the worst thing in the world was having Jersey hair." She shrugged. "Now I don't care so much."

"All that natural loose curl? It's gorgeous." Lauren took her eyes off the road again to gaze at Cara's hair.

This felt to Cara like the full court press of flirtation. Could her former high school crush be coming on to her right now? No, they were just talking. "I still wear it up at work." Cara snuck a look at Lauren's straight, shoulder-length hair in that beautiful shade of golden wheat. "In its natural state, mine is not very professional hair. I always liked your hair. It doesn't surprise me that you never changed your style. It's timeless."

"It's boring." Lauren was blunt. "But it's easy. And I started coloring it my senior year of college, but I'll deny it if you tell anyone." They both smiled at that, and the silence lingered for a minute. "So we like each other's hair. What else should we know about each other?"

"I have a question." Cara didn't think she would ever have this opportunity again. "Why don't we know this about each other already? Why was there such a divide between the day students and the boarders?"

Lauren was quiet, her profile thoughtful as she stared at the road.

"I mean, bed-hopping? I was clueless, and so were my day student friends, I'm sure. I'm thinking my experience was completely different than yours. Why that disconnect?"

"I don't think it was intentional," Lauren said. "We really bonded a lot in the evenings, when we were in our rooms hanging out, more than in class or during sports or whatever."

"I guess that makes sense." Cara adjusted her position in the car seat, feeling a bit warm. "It wasn't social class? Or family income?"

"No."

"I didn't pay tuition. Samantha Cruz attended on a scholarship. So did Lisa. Granted, not all day students were charity cases—"

"You weren't charity cases," Lauren interrupted. "We all deserved to be there. How we found ourselves at Perry Bidwell is not important. What matters is that everyone graduated and used their education to move on to whatever they imagined for themselves."

"For whatever we dreamed of?" *Oops.* Some sarcasm leaked out there. Cara unclipped her seat belt and twisted her body and felt the hot leather seat with the palm of her hand.

Lauren didn't notice, wrapped up in defending her claim. "Yes. You don't agree?"

Spoken like someone who had the wherewithal to make her dreams come true. Cara's experience had been much different. "I think it's more complicated than that."

Cara had to do something about her current condition. Parts of her were burning up and she needed relief. She braced her right hand on the door and her left hand on the console and lifted herself off the seat for a moment and then let herself sit back down. Then she did it again. And then again.

"What's wrong?" Lauren swung her eyes from the road to Cara's antics.

"I don't know. I think there's something wrong with your car. My, um, posterior is really hot."

Lauren barked out a laugh. "That's the seat warmer."

She poked at a button on the console and Cara felt immediate relief as the seat's intense heat faded. "Oh, thank God. I thought I was getting a rash or something, or a new disease called hot butt. That was so uncomfortable."

"Hot butt." Lauren guffawed. "Sorry, I must have been the last one to sit there. I turn it as high as it can go in the wintertime. I like a hot ass."

"You like a hot ass?" Cara laughed, too.

"Absolutely." Lauren directed that wolfish smile at her again, and this time Cara surrendered and let herself flirt back. It seemed inevitable.

"You have your own seat warmer on full blast?" At Lauren's nod, Cara said, "So you have an extra hot ass?"

"As hot as it gets."

Cara waited for Lauren to take her eyes from the road. When she did, Cara had her own flirty smile ready. Lauren's double take was worth it. "And now the rest of me is hot as well." Cara took off her coat and threw it in the back seat. She thought she heard Lauren mumble something. "What was that?"

"Nothing. So we're a couple of Kinsey sixteen Beavers with hot asses." Lauren chuckled.

"Go Beaves."

"Can you believe we were the Perry Bidwell Beavers? What genius came up with that idea?"

"What do you mean?"

"Using a beaver to represent a girls' school?"

"I still don't know what you mean." Cara kept her face blank.

"You know, *beavers*?" Lauren looked meaningfully at Cara.

"What about them?"

"Come on. You have to know…"

"Eager beavers? I think that was very appropriate for us. Or busy as a beaver? Perry Bidwell sure kept us busy."

"Cara—" Lauren stopped. She looked as if she really didn't know what to say.

Cara couldn't keep a straight face anymore. She burst out laughing, loud hoots that had Lauren staring at her in wonder, then joining in with peals of her own.

Lauren reached out to gently slap her forearm. "You're nuts. And a hazard to my fellow drivers."

"Your face," Cara giggled. "I don't think a more inappropriate mascot exists for a girls' school."

"Oh no? I've actually thought about this," Lauren said. "How about the Perry Bidwell Pussy Willows? The Perry Bidwell Bearded Clams?"

"Ha. I stand corrected." Cara felt so comfortable joking around with Lauren, she almost forgot she was speaking with her former high school crush.

"Do you remember anyone discussing the inappropriateness of calling our teams the Beavers back in the day?"

"Not really. We just accepted it. I guess we were a lot more compliant and unenlightened back then."

"And lacking in knowledge regarding sex slang."

But not lacking in knowledge about sex. At least for some Perry Bidwell girls. It sobered Cara, and she wondered why it bothered her.

"Oh shit." Lauren squinted into her rearview mirror, the upper half of her face drenched in bright light. She hunched over the steering wheel.

"What?"

"The cops are behind me. I have to move over."

Cara turned in her seat. A state trooper was right on Lauren's bumper, its blue overheads rotating but no sound of a siren. Was Lauren being pulled over? She maneuvered her car into the center lane, and the police vehicle roared past.

About fifteen seconds had elapsed, but the lighthearted atmosphere was gone. They were both quiet.

Lauren took in a breath and let it out slowly through her mouth, her hands white on the wheel. "I was only speeding a little."

"He just needed to get by."

"I'm a little shook."

"That would freak anyone out." Cara wanted to put a reassuring hand on her, but didn't.

"Could you do me a favor? Open the glove compartment."

"Why?" Cara was wary.

"My wallet's in there. Would you find my license and check the expiration date? I haven't looked at it in years."

Then it's expired, Lauren. The wallet was a velvety leather, and it felt intrusive to Cara to be pawing through it. She used her phone's flashlight to read the tiny writing on it. "You have to stop driving."

"Expired?" Lauren grasped the wallet on Cara's lap and shoved it in the pocket on the driver's side door.

Cara's nose wrinkled in a tiny fit of pique. She wasn't going to take anything. "By two years." She handed the license to Lauren.

"I haven't driven in a while. It's okay. I'll go under the speed limit the rest of the way."

She shook her head. "You can't drive on an expired license. There's a sign for a rest stop up ahead. You can pull over there."

Lauren glanced at her. "Are you serious?"

"It's the law. I have a valid license. If you don't mind me driving, I can get us the rest of the way."

❖

The car had been quiet since Cara had taken the wheel. She wouldn't say Lauren was sulking, exactly. Miffed was probably more accurate. Cara had tried to handle it with a minimum of fuss, and Lauren had been courteous in trading places and pointing out the features of the car, but the flirting was definitely over.

She couldn't deal with the silence. "So a new job brought you to New York?"

Lauren's manners seemed to kick in, and she responded agreeably. "Yes, I'm working at the Met."

"I heard you're a curator. Congratulations."

"Assistant curator," Lauren corrected her. "Thank you. It's literally my dream job."

"I'll bet. It seems like one of those jobs where a person might think: People get paid for doing this?"

"I'm lucky. But it's also really competitive and I worked really hard."

Cara didn't doubt that. "What's your area of art?"

"My specialty is a bit different than my job, which is in the European painting department." Lauren seemed happy to leave it at that, but Cara wanted to know more.

"And your specialty?"

"Female Impressionists. My dissertation focused on why they're so underrepresented."

"I didn't know there were that many. I can only think of one. Mary somebody? An American?"

"Mary Cassatt."

"Right, her. I'd like to read it sometime."

"You would?"

Cara was amused by Lauren's surprise. "Absolutely. I bet there are lots of people who would like to know more about women artists from that time."

Lauren twisted in her seat. She rested her back partially against the door and gazed at Cara's profile. "One of my long-term research goals is to create a comprehensive record of female artists, of all periods, who were talented and successful during their lifetimes, but whose reputations and worth never transcended their deaths like their male counterparts did."

Cara could tell Lauren was warming to her topic and had maybe forgotten a little of her earlier displeasure. She wished she could observe her as she talked about something she obviously loved. A smart, capable woman demonstrating her intelligence was the sexiest thing in the world. "Will you write a book? How will your research manifest itself?"

"I'm not sure yet. My greatest hope would be for the Met to invest in some of the artists I'm researching and exhibit them, but that is many years away."

"How do you get a museum to buy into your research goals? Wait, let me back up. How do you become a curator?"

"The short answer is I worked really hard in undergrad. I applied to some good internships and worked really hard at them, and got into a good PhD program and worked really hard to finish as quickly as I could."

Cara grinned and took her eyes off the road to glance at her. "Did you *work really hard*, Lauren?"

"Yes, I did," Lauren returned dryly, the smile in her voice just about the most alluring thing Cara had heard in a long while. "Okay, it's a simplification, but it's true, don't you think? Whatever your professional interest, you're going to have to work hard to beat out the other guy who wants it just as badly as you do."

That was true, Cara supposed, but Lauren discounted the advantage of her privilege. Money was no object to her career aspirations, and that was simply not the case for the majority of the population. "Where did you get your PhD?"

"The Courtauld Institute in London."

Cara was jealous. She had always wanted to visit London, visit anywhere outside the US really, but had yet to realize that goal. "How long did that take?"

"I moved to London right after I left New Haven, so about six years."

Cara knew from four years of teaching *The Great Gatsby* that New Haven meant Yale. What was it about Yalies that made them not want to refer to their school by its name? Or maybe that was just Lauren and Nick Carraway. "Didn't you have to get your master's first?"

"The master's and PhD programs were combined. It was pretty intense. I defended my dissertation in June and it's going to be published in *Woman's Art Journal.*" The pride in Lauren's voice was unmistakable.

"I'm impressed. Doesn't it usually take a long time to write a doctoral thesis?"

"Yeah, but I basically haven't had a life in forever. Like I said, I worked really hard."

"I believe you." Cara felt bad for teasing her earlier, then marveled at the fact that she was teasing Lauren Havemayer at all.

"It matters. You know that. You're a teacher, right? Where did you go to grad school?"

"My grad program was assigned to me."

"What?"

"I was a New York City Teaching Fellow," Cara explained. "I applied to the program, and they assigned me to a grad program in an area that had a need for teachers."

"Really? Where did you go?"

"Lehman College."

Lauren's silence told Cara she had never heard of the city-run public university even if she didn't say it.

"It's one of the CUNYs. I started teaching and grad school at the same time. They paid for my degree and got a brand-new teacher in one of the city's hard-to-staff schools in return."

"You started teaching before you got your degree in teaching?" Lauren's tone expressed how nonsensical she thought that was.

"It's the throw-you-in-the-deep-end method of teacher preparation. It'll put hair on your ovaries."

"I believe it. Where's your school?"

"In the South Bronx." Cara thought she knew what was coming.

"Whoa. It sounds like you started your career at the highest level of difficulty. Is the neighborhood safe, at least?"

"Safe enough." Cara was pleasantly surprised. Usually, a vigorous defense of where she chose to teach followed this disclosure, but Lauren seemed to get it.

"Did you always want to be a teacher?" she asked. "Wait, where did you go for undergrad?"

"Princeton. And no, I didn't always want to be a teacher, but I can't imagine doing anything else now."

"That's good," Lauren said. "That's how it should be, right?"

"I guess."

"What? Are you not happy teaching?"

"No, I am." There was no point dredging up ancient history. Best laid plans and all that. "It's just very hard work."

"I can imagine. No wonder you were talking to Mrs. Keefe. She was a great teacher. Were you getting tips from the Jedi master?"

"Trying to. She wasn't as helpful as I had hoped."

This seemed to bother Lauren. "She doesn't seem the type to keep her recipes to herself."

"That wasn't it," Cara said quickly. "I actually think she didn't know how to help me. She tried. I'm having trouble engaging some of my students. I have students who are far below grade level in reading or writing or both. I was hoping she might have some ideas, but engagement isn't really an issue at PBSG."

"Oh." Lauren was quiet.

Cara threw in some context for the poor woman. "Remember eighth grade English class? There was nearly a riot when George shot Lennie in *Of Mice and Men*. We were completely engaged. But at my school, we take anybody who shows up, no matter what ability level or how long they've been in the country. My kids really struggle."

"What grade do you teach?"

"Eleventh and the seniors who want to take AP Literature." A light bulb went off. "Hey, maybe you can help me."

"Me?"

"Yeah, it concerns your line of work. In the AP class, we work on poetry throughout the year because students need a lot of practice analyzing it. When we started the introductory unit, they were super into it because we analyzed hip-hop and pop music and they all brought in their terrible music and we picked it apart for literary elements, rhyme, meter, and all that."

"Careful, Ms. Talarico. Your bias is showing."

Cara glanced over to see Lauren slipping off her heels and curling up in the passenger seat like it was an easy chair in front of a fireplace. God, she was hot. "I kind of hate what's popular right now. Anyway, once we attempt anything older than, say, the last fifty years, their engagement level just nosedives. I know it's a lot harder for them to relate, but there won't be modern music lyrics on the AP exam, and they have to be ready for whatever the test throws at them. So when I was trying to figure out ways to develop their interest, I read about this lesson that used art to connect with poetry."

"Sounds promising."

"Do you know *The Fall of Icarus* by Brueghel?"

Lauren nodded in her peripheral vision.

"William Carlos Williams wrote a poem about it. We studied the story of Icarus. We discussed the painting and analyzed the poem, but not one of my five AP students showed any excitement at all."

"You only have five students in your AP Class? Is that typical?"

"It is in my school. There are very few students who want to take hard classes during their senior year at my school."

"That's a shame."

The Manhattan skyline came into view, and the Empire State Building was lit up in fall colors of orange, yellow, and red. Cara would never get tired of seeing it. "I mean, it's interesting right? You'd want to learn about it, wouldn't you?"

"What do you mean?"

Cara checked her right blind spot. "I try to meet my students where they are, but for any number of possible reasons, they weren't trying to meet me on the day we tried this. It doesn't seem like a boring lesson, does it?"

"Not to me. Using art as a gateway to analysis, any kind of analysis, is pretty brilliant. I'll do a little research about poetry and art, if you like."

"Oh, I just wanted to see what you thought. Would you really have time for that?" They were approaching the Lincoln Tunnel, which was blessedly free of traffic.

"Are you kidding? I love doing research. I wish more of my job were research. There's nothing better than the hushed silence of a research library or the dusty allure of a forgotten archive." She made it sound like the most fascinating of occupations.

"I never would have thought that about you." Cara didn't know what she thought about Lauren. She had absolutely no frame of reference except ten-year-old preconceptions.

"No?"

"I thought curators were busy trying to get rich people to donate their priceless collections."

"There is some of that, too. I haven't had to do it yet."

Cara maneuvered them out of the tunnel and onto the surface streets of Manhattan. "Where am I going?"

"Your place. I can drive myself back to mine." Lauren's voice warned Cara not to argue.

"Are you sure? I'm way up on 118th Street in East Harlem. I don't mind getting the subway from wherever you live."

"I'm sure. Just don't report me for breaking the law."

Cara felt her cheeks get hot. "I'm sorry. I don't make the rules."

"I'm kidding." Lauren put a hand on her arm, and Cara glimpsed eyes that were warm and forgiving.

The rest of the journey was quiet, and she was glad it was almost over. It was strange to feel so comfortable talking with Lauren, so different from the insecure schoolgirl she had been. "This is me on the corner."

Cara double-parked in front of her building, an admittedly shabby tenement with a bodega on the ground level. She got out and grabbed her stuff from the back seat. Lauren stood by the driver's side in her killer cream suit. "Thanks for the ride. And the conversation," Cara said.

"Thanks for driving part of the way." Lauren's smile made Cara feel like the flirting might be revived. "Do you want to get a drink or something sometime? I'm still trying to get on my feet a bit in the city and I could use some company." Lauren's gaze moved past Cara, and she turned to see two men outside the bodega, talking and laughing, their snapbacks pulled down low over their foreheads and their hands jammed into their pockets for warmth. "May I walk you to your door?" she asked, her eyes fixed on the men.

Cara grinned at the formality of her question. Was Lauren trying to protect her in her own neighborhood? *She is the cutest.* "It's okay. I know those guys. That's Rico and Manny. Rico works in the bodega. Manny deals drugs."

Lauren's expression flattened, and Cara realized she wasn't subverting Lauren's assumptions about her East Harlem neighborhood. She was being rude.

"That was supposed to be a joke. A bad one, apparently."

Lauren took a step back, and the distance between them seemed more than physical.

"Manny is a good friend of mine. He is my hookup, though. For caffeine. He's a barista. Anyway, yeah, text me, if you still want to.

We'll have a drink. Thanks again for the ride." As she gave Lauren her number, Cara wondered if she hadn't just ruined her chance at something interesting. Should she say how much she had enjoyed this little suspension in time, enclosed in the privacy of Lauren's car? Her teenage self would have likened it to winning the lottery. *Too late. You blew it.* She didn't turn around as she walked away.

CHAPTER SEVEN

Lauren sat on her bed with her phone in her hands. Her shared car ride with Cara had been on her mind for the last few days. Although their last moments together made her cautious, she couldn't deny she was intrigued. For the first time since Saffron, Lauren was attracted to someone who was funny and smart, and who ignited something in both her brain and loins. It was time to find out if Cara felt the same.

She had done some research, as promised, so she had a real reason to get in touch, but how should she initiate contact? She was extremely out of practice. It was just a drink, for God's sake. She took out her newly renewed driver's license and carefully angled her phone so it captured less than half the card—just her photo, really—and no private information. Then she texted it to Cara.

The reply came quickly. *Question: How come your pic looks like it came from Vogue while mine looks like it was taken at the Passaic County Dept. of Corrections?* This was followed by a series of ROFL emojis.

Lauren grinned. She could do this. *Want to meet up for a drink tomorrow after work? I'll share DMV photo shoot tips. Plus I have something to help with your poetry problem.*

I would srsly love that, but I can't. Going to NJ after school to help mom with T-giving. Cara added four turkey emojis.

T-giving? And turkeys? Oh shit. Thanksgiving was in two days? Lauren got up and searched for her father and found him in his library reclining on the sofa.

"Dad, are we doing anything for Thanksgiving?"

"We can if you want to. When is it? A couple of weeks from now, right?" he asked, not looking up from his tablet.

"It's on Thursday. The day after tomorrow."

"This week? Is it early this year? I'm supposed to fly to Hong Kong tomorrow. Maybe I can change it." He swung his feet to the floor and started tapping the tablet's screen in earnest.

"It's okay. I forgot about it, too. Don't change your plans. I don't even know if the museum is open. Maybe I'm supposed to work."

"I completely forgot, honey. We haven't had Thanksgiving around here in a while. You've been in London, and your brother is so busy..."

A quick search on her phone told her the museum was closed on Thanksgiving. An incoming text made the phone buzz in her hand.

Cara texted: *Are you gone for the weekend too? Maybe we could meet Saturday?* Two smiley face emojis.

Lauren replied: *After all those years in London, it kind of snuck up on me.*

Wait. Do you not have T-giving plans?

Lauren didn't reply, but more texts instantly followed.

Want to come eat turkey w me? (and my fam) More turkey emojis.

My mom is a good cook. You can watch a football game you don't care about.

Unless you care about football. Three football emojis.

And you get to come to NJ 2x in 1 week. Winky face emoji.

Lauren put her phone down. She could call Sasha and get herself invited to her Thanksgiving. Or just hang out here. Less than a minute later, her phone beeped again.

My mom says please come. She wants to see you! More turkeys, smileys and a car emoji.

Yikes. This woman liked emojis. And how had she talked to her mother that fast? Lauren wanted to sit in a dimly lit bar and drink a glass of wine with her, not say grace and chat with the relations.

"I'm sorry, Lauren. Want me to call Astrid? I'm sure her family would love to see you for Thanksgiving."

"I don't want to have Thanksgiving with your assistant, Dad." Lauren tried to change her delivery from testy to tolerant. "It's fine. I already have an invitation." Whether she would accept it was another matter.

"Oh, good." His relief was palpable. "Let's make sure we do something special at Christmas. Decorate the heck out of the Bedford house? Or we could open up the villa on Staniel Cay? Meet your brother in Utah?"

"Sounds good. I'll ask for the time off," she said and left the room. Socializing with Cara's extended family was not her idea of a good time. But how to decline the invitation gracefully?

❖

Cara sat in Café Mi Vida and looked out on a darkened Second Avenue. People on the street were hurrying to their destinations, but Cara wasn't ready to go back to her tiny studio apartment just yet. She picked up her phone. No new texts since the last time she checked five seconds ago. Her macchiato cup remained empty, and the pile of papers in front of her refused to grade itself. The nerve.

"You want another?" Manny called from across the room. He was wiping down the table where some older men from the neighborhood had been playing dominoes until one annoyed esposa called, leading to their protracted dispersal. During colder weather, Café Mi Vida didn't mind acting as a community center of sorts for the East Harlem residents, nor did it mind people like Cara who contributed little monetarily for the space they occupied.

"One is my limit. You know that." That's all she allowed herself even though she could have downed ten easily. Three perfect sips of Manny's macchiato was a luxury that made life bearable.

He sat down across from her.

Cara got a shock from his appearance. "Didn't you have eyebrows when I came in tonight?"

"I still do. They're just buried under glue and powder and foundation. It's slow AF so I'm trying a different technique."

"It looks good. Very believable. When are you going to do the rest of your face?"

"I'm working on it. It takes some big balls for a Dominican boy to paint herself like a woman."

"Understood. Let me know when you're ready to brainstorm drag names."

Manny nodded. "Why aren't you fiending tonight?"

"Fiending?"

"You know, grading like a fiend." He mimed crazily writing and making slashing marks with an imaginary pen.

"Distracted, I guess."

"You waiting for someone to hit you back?"

"No." Cara was *not* waiting for Lauren to text her back. She resisted the urge to look at her phone again.

Who was she kidding? Of course she was. There was never a question of whether to invite her. No one should be alone on Thanksgiving. But thinking back over their text exchange, she knew she had overdone it. She had been psyched that her obnoxious comment at the end of their car ride hadn't wrecked her chance to see Lauren again. But then she had to go and be way too pushy.

Manny gave her a look of disbelief. "Who is it?"

Cara surrendered, knowing he would get it out of her sooner or later. "An old classmate from high school. We sort of reconnected at our reunion and I invited her to spend Thanksgiving with my family."

Manny made a face. "Thanksgiving's a lot. I wouldn't want a new bae to see my family's type of crazy until we were secure."

"She's not my bae. I wouldn't have invited her, but she has no plans. I was trying to be nice."

"So you have your taking-care-of-people hat on for this? Then it shouldn't matter if she doesn't go to Jersey for turkey with your mami. And it doesn't explain why you looking at your phone like you waiting for Gaga's new album to drop."

"You're right, but there is some history."

Manny nodded like he knew it all along.

"She's my former high school crush, and seeing her again woke up some latent feels."

"That's something powerful right there. Remember Ricardo Abreu?"

"Haven't heard that name in a long time." Cara's smile was fond. When she and Samantha first moved into their building, Manny and his sprawling family lived in a two-bedroom on the second floor, and teenage Manny would invite himself over to watch *RuPaul's Drag Race* when he learned they had cable. She had spent many commercial breaks advising Manny on how to deal with his crush from Business Math. Now the tables had turned.

"That boy was so beautiful. Now he's a troll living off his baby mamas. My taste has improved, girl."

Cara's taste remained impeccable. "Lauren was the golden girl of our school—hot, smart, standoffish, but nice to everyone in a superficial way. She boarded at my school so I never got to know her very well. Boarders and day students didn't mix socially."

"I'm guessing she's not a troll now."

She looked at Manny helplessly and recalled how beautiful and stylish Lauren had looked at the reunion. "No, not a troll. She's a professional success now, has more money than God, and is so far away from my janky, front stoop, city employee world it's as if we live on different planets."

"She done made her millions already? And she's your age?"

"She comes from a wealthy family. I don't know if they actually produce anything, but it's the type of money that sways elections and influences legislation."

"I bet your little do-gooder heart is mad conflicted by that."

Cara didn't reply. She didn't have to. It was a bull's—eye .

"She sounds like Daisy Buchanan," Manny said. "Rich, beautiful, careless, and untouchable." He had gotten curious about *The Great Gatsby* while Cara worked on her lessons for the novel last spring. She gave him a copy of the book and they would have long discussions about it while she procrastinated her piles of grading.

"I guess she does." The assessment was maybe more unflattering than Lauren deserved, as Cara believed Daisy Buchanan to be one of the more despicable figures in literature.

"But you're not going to Gatsby yourself up for her."

"No. If she wants any of this—" Cara pointed her thumb at herself. "She'll have to accept me as I am. I will not become a shallow, bootlegging gangster for anyone. I probably won't hear from her again anyway."

Manny waggled his head. "It was just a crush? No action?"

"None. She was completely unaware of my existence back then, but seems interested now, I guess. Or seemed interested when she gave me a ride back to the city on Saturday. Now, who knows?" Cara shouldn't be disappointed. She was way too busy to add a potential time and money drain to her overburdened existence right now.

Manny's eyes widened. "The fabulous eggshell suit? The black Mercedes? That was Daisy? Cara, you got to get that."

"You noticed her?"

"Of course. You don't see white girls like her in this neighborhood very often. We ain't that gentrified. Maybe you should be happy she bailed on you. Like I said, Thanksgiving's a lot for whatever you got going with her."

"Which is nothing," Cara stressed. "I've got nothing going with her."

"Then hit her up after Thursday and set something up for another time."

Her ambivalence must have shown on her face.

"What? You don't want to get with her? Your high school crush? You should do it just to see what it's like so you can move on with that shit. I bet she's terrible in bed. I'm thinking Ricky Abreu is the worst lay in East Harlem."

She laughed. If she was completely honest, she definitely wanted to know what Lauren was like in bed. It had been a long time since she had felt that chemistry with anyone.

Manny pulled out his phone and scrolled. "Remember this?"

It was the picture of the hugging carrots he had shown her a while back. The unlikely image made her smile "Why do I love this picture of carrots so much?"

"Because it's love," he said. "When you look at that, do you see your Daisy Buchanan high school crush?"

She narrowed her eyes at him. "Before a few days ago, I hadn't thought of her in ten years. Why would I see her in this picture if you're telling me it's a representation of love? At most it's attraction, not love."

"Yeah, but this is the goal, right? Hang on." He bustled through the saloon doors into the back.

Cara started packing her things away. She slipped her silent phone into her pocket without checking it one last time.

Manny returned and thrust a color copy of the carrot image into her hands. "We just got new color ink for the printer. Take this home and put it somewhere you can see it. When you get together with Daisy, compare her with this picture. If she's not your carrot, put her back and find some other vegetable to love."

❖

Lauren entered the silent grand hall of the Metropolitan Museum of Art before the buzz of visitors commenced. As she ascended the main staircase, Tiepolo's *The Triumph of Marius* incrementally appeared. General Marius was triumphant in white and on horseback in the top right of the canvas, but Tiepolo meant for the eye to be drawn to the defeated Jugurtha, draped in red, in the foreground. The use of red to focus the composition was a marvel. But the day's agenda was packed, and she couldn't linger with Tiepolo or anybody else. She was already running late.

"Are you going to the planning meeting for the Pissarro exhibition?"

Lauren turned around as she checked that she had her notebook and phone. "Yeah, Felix, are you?"

"Yup, let's walk together."

Felix was another assistant curator who had been on the job about a year. They headed for the conference room adjacent to the American Wing.

"How're you settling in? It's been a few months now, hasn't it?" Felix asked.

"Since September. It's great so far."

"This is going to be a big show. It'll bring the crowds. People love the Impressionists. That's your wheelhouse, right?"

"Pretty much. Let me ask you, does any of the staff come in the Friday after Thanksgiving?"

"It's a big day attendance wise, since tourists are here for the parade and such, but the curatorial staff? I'd say about fifty percent take a vacation day. Why? Going out of town?"

They skirted a large group of tourists. "Just getting the lay of the land. Doing the work here is no problem. It's the institutional culture that's a bit harder to navigate. What are your plans for the holiday?"

"My boyfriend and I alternate visits to each other's family. It's his turn this year. We're roasting the turkey tonight and bringing it out to Mamaroneck with us. None of his family can cook for shit, but it's still fun. We usually get wasted and sing show tunes with his mom around the piano. What are you doing?"

Lauren had not responded to Cara's last text. She saw herself watching the parade on TV, moping around the apartment, and ordering Chinese. No drunken show tunes for her.

Thanksgiving used to be such a festive time when her mother and grandparents were still alive. The whole family would walk across the park the evening before to see the balloons as they were blown up for the next day's parade. There were usually lots of guests. Her mother was famous for extending invitations to people she knew would be alone. She always said, "Everyone should have somewhere to go on Thanksgiving." Now Lauren was the one with nowhere to go. Back in the States with a growing urge to celebrate the holiday, and her only invitation was from a woman she barely knew whose goodwill she had squandered. But maybe it wasn't too late. "I think I'm going out to New Jersey."

"You think?" Felix exclaimed. "Thanksgiving is tomorrow." They had reached the conference room. He held his badge up to the sensor and opened the door for them.

"Just have to confirm." Lauren held up her phone. "Go ahead. I'll be right there." She texted Cara: *Hey. Is it too late to accept your invitation? Sorry it took me so long to reply. I'm a bonehead.* All through the meeting she waited, but no reply came through. Cara had rightfully rescinded her invitation because of her poor manners. It was fine. She hadn't had Chinese in a while. She would call her brother, watch some Netflix.

It was midafternoon when Lauren's phone buzzed with a text alert, and the desperation with which she scooped it from her desk was something she would have to think about later.

Don't you work at the Met? I thought boneheads were the people who worked at the dinosaur exhibit at the Museum of Natural History! Three laughing emojis.

Then: *Of course! We usually eat around 3. Come anytime before that.* Cara added her mother's contact information.

Can I bring anything? Lauren exhaled with relief. She was celebrating Thanksgiving with a bunch of strangers and she was totally fine with that. In fact, she couldn't wait to go.

CHAPTER EIGHT

Cara's mother retrieved her largest pot, a sign that separating many pounds of potatoes from their skins was in Cara's immediate future.

The turkey was in the oven and it was time for the final push. Guests would be arriving in an hour. At the counter, her mom ticked items on her highly precise spreadsheet.

"After you're done with the potatoes, will you set the table?"

"Yup. How many?"

"With Lauren, it will be eight this year."

"Thanks for allowing me to invite her, Mom."

"Sure." She put her list down. "So she likes girls, too?"

Cara nodded. She told her mom almost everything about the night of the reunion, but not the sexual activity of the boarding girls.

"Any chance you two could…you know…" She began to chop an onion.

"What?" Cara was not going to fill in the blank. Her mother would have to come out and ask it.

"Date? Go out? Get together? Go courting? Hook up? I don't know what you call it these days."

"Certainly not courting." Cara tried to keep the disdain out of her voice.

"Is she single?"

"I think so. She expressed some superficial interest."

Her mother frowned. "Superficial how?"

"It was probably nothing. Anyway, it's not going to happen."

"Why not?" She glared at her. "I suppose you think she's out of your league, is that it?"

Cara was surprised at her mother's vehemence. "It's not that. First of all, I don't think she's interested. And second, she's richer than Beyoncé.

How am I supposed to relate to someone who's never known a moment of want?"

Her mom paused. "Are you saying you've known want? I know we've had some lean times, but there was always food on the table and a roof over our heads."

The guilt came swiftly. "I didn't mean to imply that I lacked for anything. Lauren and I live in two separate countries, that's all. Hers is a country of abundance, and mine is the country of the rest of us where the struggle is real."

"Want doesn't always come in financial form." She started chopping again. "When I remember that girl after her mother died, all the money in the world couldn't protect her from that."

"I'm actually surprised she's coming. She must have had better plans that fell through, or she's really hurting for company."

"Or maybe she liked being in *your* company. You haven't been out with somebody new in a while. Maybe she'll be good for you."

"Whatever, Mom. Just please don't embarrass me, okay?"

"When do I ever embarrass you?"

Cara rolled her eyes, feeling like a teenager again. Her mother usually did not embarrass her, but Cara was feeling anxious. She focused on the potato in her hand and took a settling breath. It was just a meal. Turkey and all the trimmings with Lauren.

❖

"Welcome." Cara met Lauren at the door and accepted a festive red shopping bag. "What's this?"

"Happy Thanksgiving. I stopped at Greenberg's yesterday on the way home from work." Lauren was smiling, her cheeks rosy from the journey from her car to the door. "I thought you might like some treats even though you said not to bring anything."

"What's Greenberg's?" Cara asked. "Let me take your coat."

"It's this great bakery I used to go to all the time as a kid." Lauren shrugged out of her overcoat, turning to Cara's mother as she came through the foyer. "Hi, Mrs. Talarico. It's so nice to see you."

"Hello, Lauren. Happy Thanksgiving. I'm glad you're here." She enfolded Lauren in a hug that lasted longer than Cara was comfortable with.

"Okay, Mom, let her go. She's not used to your hugs." As they separated Cara said, "There have been shorter ice ages."

"Actually, I do remember your mom's hugs. From school." Lauren looked shyly between them. "You were very kind to me back then, Mrs. Talarico. I didn't forget that."

"See, Cara? My hugs are legendary. You should appreciate them more. Come in and meet everyone, Lauren. Cara can do the introductions. I have to check on the celery casserole. We'll talk later, Lauren." She bustled back to the kitchen.

"Celery casserole?" Lauren asked.

"Traditional family recipe. It's better than it sounds."

"I like your socks." She pointed at Cara's feet.

"These are super special, and another tradition." Cara wore them once a year, deep orange with turkey legs printed all over them. They were her only nod to the holiday. She took in Lauren's silk print blouse and slim dark jeans tucked into luscious knee-high equestrian boots in a shade of brown that epitomized the fall, and wondered if she could get away with a hug, too. "You look fantastic."

"Thanks, and thanks for inviting me. All my family is thousands of miles away today."

"Consider mine a temporary replacement." Cara gritted her teeth. *What a dork.*

She led Lauren into a cozy wood-paneled room where all the seating was occupied by people watching football or gazing at smartphones. "Everyone, this is Lauren, a friend of mine from school." Cara pointed to each family member in turn. "That's Uncle Rick, Aunt Deedee, my cousins Tracy and Patrick, and my uncle Mike." There were friendly calls of hello and welcome, and Tracy looked up from her phone to rake her gaze over Lauren's outfit and wave.

"Hi, everybody," Lauren said. "It's nice to meet all the Talaricos."

Cara froze, and a hostile silence descended over the room.

Then Uncle Rick barked, "Bite your tongue, missy. We're McNamaras."

"Simmer down, Uncle Rick. It's an honest mistake." Cara said to Lauren, "Uncle Mike and Uncle Rick are my mother's brothers. My father hasn't been around in a long time."

"Oops. Sorry, everyone." Lauren looked mortified.

"Let's get you a drink. Anyone else?" Cara guided her into the kitchen, ignoring the chorus of relatives asking for beverages. "How about a glass of wine?" She poured two glasses of white.

"I'm really sorry about that." Lauren gulped at her wine. "Hopefully this will wash the taste of foot from my mouth."

Cara chuckled. "Don't worry about it. The real reason for his crabby mood is because he has to watch Dallas play Washington, two teams he hates."

"Why is he watching it then?"

"It's Thanksgiving. It's what he does every year. And he'll scarf his dinner down so he can hurry back in to watch more football he doesn't care about. It makes no sense."

Aunt Deedee sauntered through the kitchen and grabbed three bottles of beer from the cooler. "Don't let him bother you, honey."

Cara's mom looked up from the pot she was stirring. "Who bothered you?" She glared at Cara. "What happened?"

"Nothing," Aunt Deedee said. "Rick got a little feisty because Cara's friend called us Talaricos."

Lauren's cheeks went adorably pink. "I'm so sorry."

"No, I'm sorry, Lauren. My brothers' dislike of my ex-husband is no excuse for them to be less than civil to you."

"It's okay, Mrs. Talarico. I just noticed it smells amazing in here. Is there anything I can do to help?"

Cara hid a smile. Lauren was doing all the right things with her mom.

"That's so sweet of you. You can help Cara take the bird out of the oven. He's a big guy this year. Each of you take a side, and we'll let him rest before we carve him."

As they prepared to haul the roasting pan from the oven to the countertop, Lauren whispered, "Does your mom always assign masculine pronouns to your food?"

Cara handed her an oven mitt and grinned. "No. She named the celery casserole Francine."

"Cara!" Her mom scolded her. "Get him out of the oven. The little plastic thing popped out. He's done."

"Yes, Mother." She met Lauren's eyes and the two of them burst out laughing as they awkwardly hefted the turkey to the counter.

Cara's mom kept them busy until the meal was ready. Lauren helped her make the gravy, a two-woman task Cara was glad to relinquish. When they sat down, Cara was outmaneuvered and unable to get a seat beside Lauren, who was sandwiched between her mom and cousin Patrick. Uncles Mike and Rick sat at the heads of the table and talked about the game for the ten minutes they ate, then retired to the living room for more football. Everyone else ate more sedately and Lauren became the center of attention.

"Are you a teacher like Cara, Lauren?" Aunt Deedee asked. "Patrick, put your phone away for Chrissakes, we're at the table."

Lauren brought her napkin to her lips before she replied. "No, I work at the Met in the city."

"The museum? How nice. That must be very interesting."

"It is. I love it."

"What do you do there?" Cara's mom asked.

"I do research about art, write about it, take care of it, and figure out ways to show it to people."

Tracy inserted herself into the conversation. "I've been to the Costume Institute at the Met. I went to the show on punk and the one about fashion and technology. That one was weird." She added, "I'm into fashion."

Lauren nodded. "The Costume Institute is really popul—"

"I like your blouse. Where did you get it?" Tracy interrupted.

Lauren looked down at herself. "Um, I think I got this in London at a little boutique in Beauchamp Place."

"You've been to London? That's so cool. I want to go someday. Have you been to Paris?"

"Yes, I did some resear—"

"I'm dying to go to Paris. I want to see everything." Tracy swooned.

"Me too," said Patrick. "Like the Eiffel Tower. Did you go there? Up to the top? Have you seen *Rush Hour 3*? I just watched it again for, like, the twentieth time. Jackie Chan is the best."

Lauren was about to answer when Tracy interrupted again.

"I want to go to the Louvre and Versailles, and the Moulin Rouge. Have you been to all of those?" she demanded.

"Not the Moulin Rouge. I've heard it's pretty touristy. But I've been to the others." She directed her gaze at Patrick. "And I have seen *Rush Hour 3*. My brother loves Jackie Chan."

Patrick put down his cutlery and leaned toward Lauren. "What about at the end when he's fighting that guy and jumping all over the Eiffel Tower?" He mimed Jackie Chan's quick climbing.

"The best part," Lauren agreed. "And then when he hopped up and wrapped himself in—"

"The flag!" Patrick almost shouted. "That was amazing. I'm gonna do that someday. I'm practicing parkour."

Aunt Deedee looked confused. "You're going to do what, now?"

"Calm down, Pat," Tracy said. "If anyone's going to Paris, it'll be me, not you."

"Whatever." Patrick picked up his fork and pointed it at Tracy. "I bet I'll get there before you."

As Patrick and Tracy continued to bicker, Lauren glanced at Cara, amusement flickering in her eyes. Cara grinned back at her, unable to do anything else. She was too far down the table to have a conversation with her, but it felt like a quick moment of affinity before Tracy pulled Lauren into further interrogation.

Lauren had been so game throughout all of her family's weirdness. Even now, she was patiently describing to Tracy the city of Paris and its arrondissements while Patrick peppered her with Jackie Chan factoids. She had won them over completely.

The more time she spent with Lauren, the more she wanted to. They came from distinctly different worlds, but Lauren had easily transcended the differences with her family. She had no idea whether the reverse would be true, but she was open to trying.

❖

When the meal was finished, Mrs. Talarico announced that the cousins would help clean up and Lauren and Cara were excused since they helped before dinner.

On their way out of the dining room, Lauren stopped to linger over Cara's baby and elementary school pictures hanging in the foyer, but Cara took her hand and yanked her past them, pulling her up the stairs to her childhood bedroom.

"I figured you didn't want to sit with my uncles in front of the TV." She pushed the door but it stayed open by a few inches.

"You figured right."

"Welcome to the sanctified shrine to my adolescence, untouched since graduation." Cara flopped down on the bed and sat cross-legged with her back against the wall.

Lauren surveyed Cara's teenage refuge. The small, yellow-painted room was plastered with Perry Bidwell memorabilia, some of which Lauren recognized. She picked up the field hockey trophy on the dresser and waggled it toward Cara. "Senior year, huh?"

"Yeah. You may or may not remember that I was terrible at field hockey, but they still gave me a trophy."

With the exception of that memory of Cara on the bus, Lauren didn't remember her being on the team. Field hockey was Lauren's best sport and she had shared close friendships with most of her teammates, and it bothered her that she had no recollection of Cara. "You were a defender?"

"Uh-huh. Not like you, constantly running up and down the field and scoring lots of goals. But Coach Keefe did once tell me I led the team in kicked balls," Cara said.

This confused Lauren. "You're not supposed to kick the ball in field hockey."

"I know, but at least I did it better than anyone else. Where is my trophy for that?"

"Model UN, Geography Bee, Yearbook." Lauren read off the certificates that were tacked to the wall. "You participated a lot."

"I guess I developed my sense of self-worth through participation certificates. But let's be clear, the Model UN one was not just for participation. Samantha Cruz and I were awarded best delegation at the conference that was held at the actual United Nations in New York City." Cara's voice became extra boastful.

"The actual United Nations in New York City?" Lauren teased her.

"Mock me if you will, but we ran that conference. We were the Russian delegation, and we made everybody pass the stupidest resolutions. We proposed a resolution to build a six-lane bridge from Vladivostok to Anchorage, and it passed." Cara laughed, caught up in her memories. "Plus, Security Council."

"I don't know what that means."

"Russia was a member of the Security Council. We had power, baby! So much power," Cara held out her arms like that power was laid across them, physically weighing her down. "Sam and I were drunk with it. It was exhilarating. All the delegates were doing exactly what we told them, and we were on the same wavelength and it was like magic. It was like our minds melded in our drive toward world domination."

Lauren grinned at Cara's enthusiasm, kind of wanting to be Samantha Cruz in that moment. "Was she at the reunion? I didn't see her."

"No, she's working on a big case and couldn't spare the time. She's an ADA for Kings County."

"Are you still close?"

"We were roommates until she got married last year. I was a bridesmaid in her wedding."

Lauren nodded and began to prowl around the small room. She felt restless. She snuck glances at Cara and her sagging ponytail, with strands coming loose around her face. Lauren thought again of that memory of Cara pretending to sing her heart out on the bus. Her unrestrained exuberance, then and now, filled Lauren with a yearning to be seen as special to her, but she couldn't figure out how to move herself out of this state of acquaintanceship and into something that held the possibility of…what? Intimacy? Sex? Anything that led to Lauren running her fingers through Cara's delicious dark hair?

Discontented, she crossed to the large bookcase that dominated the other side of the room and examined the spines of Cara's books. "Gotta few books, huh?" *Duh. What a scintillating conversationalist. That'll really move the needle.*

"Yup. You are looking at all of my most treasured books from age three to eighteen."

"You were reading that early?"

"I didn't say I read them myself. There are a few faves from the very early days."

Lauren saw several picture books on the bottom row. She pulled one out at random. It was a well-loved copy of *Madeline* by Ludwig Bemelmans. She showed the cover with its illustration of the Eiffel Tower to Cara, then examined it for a minute. "I think I see Jackie Chan. It's either him or Patrick."

Her joke earned a snort of laughter from Cara, and it made Lauren feel like she'd won a prize.

"I think you've made a friend for life. We don't really indulge his Jackie Chan obsession."

"He sure is passionate. I'll give him that." She sat beside Cara and thumbed through the pages.

Cara moved closer and looked with her. "My mom read this to me three or four times before bedtime some nights. I'm surprised she didn't throw it away."

"I loved this one, too. Every time I had a stomachache, I told my mother I had appendicitis, like Madeline had." Lauren smiled at the memory.

"And I really loved that list at the end of the book of all the landmarks of Paris that were illustrated throughout the book." Cara reached over and flipped to the last page. Her finger trailed down the list as she read it. "Just like my cousins, I'm going to visit someday."

"You've not been?" Lauren inhaled while Cara invaded her personal space. She smelled of turkey and something lighter, citrus and floral and fresh. Lauren could breathe it in all day long.

"You know now that the Talaricos and the McNamaras are not big travelers, but that's just from lack of opportunity. I want to go everywhere, see everything." Cara glanced over at her. "Someday."

"You'll get there." Lauren could not take her eyes from Cara. She was about to propose they take a trip to Paris together when she realized how absurd that sounded. They barely knew each other. But Cara was gazing back at her too, and Lauren thought this might be her chance to move things to a more intimate level.

Cara inched even closer, and it was all Lauren could do not to touch one of those dark tendrils that had come loose from her ponytail. When they were centimeters apart, Cara said in a sexy voice, "You smell like gravy. It's inturksicating." She grinned wickedly at Lauren.

Lauren reared back, shocked, but she couldn't help laughing. "That was just terrible. You are so corny."

"You were sniffing me, Havemayer. I know I probably smell like onions or something, but I had to beat you to the punch." Cara leaned back too, still grinning at her.

So busted. "Do I really smell like gravy?" Lauren gave her armpits a conspicuous sniff. "Your mom had me working hard. Making gravy is stressful."

"Yeah, I was glad to give you that job this year. You stand there with the slurry in the measuring cup and respond like one of Pavlov's dogs when my mother shouts, 'Pour!'"

"I do think she gives herself the harder job though. It can't be easy whisking those drippings like a crazy woman."

"She is crazy, isn't she? But she makes damn good gravy. Not one lump."

They both laughed. Cara had diminished Lauren's embarrassment, but she had also cooled things down. It was awesome that Cara could make her laugh, but it also seemed like a way to put distance between them. They were sitting on her childhood bed, for God's sake, and her family was right downstairs. She didn't know what she had been thinking. Leveling up with Cara would have to be put on the back burner. "You know, I had noticed you smelled like turkey, but my exceedingly good manners prevented me from mentioning it."

"Mention away. We let it all hang out here." Cara's smile was sensual and warm.

Let it all hang out? Okay, then. Lauren took this as a sign. Front burner it is. How to maneuver this conversation back to the sexy? "Have you ever hooked up with anyone in this bed?"

Cara looked startled for a moment, then crossed her arms over her chest and lapsed back to her sardonic attitude. "No, why? Are you volunteering? I guess that's the cliché when people visit home on the holidays. I think *Saturday Night Live* even did a skit about it."

"Never?" Lauren was surprised by her answer.

"I was as pure as new snow in high school, unlike some people." Cara gave her a sidelong glance. "And when I finally caught up with everyone else in college, I wouldn't dream of bringing a girlfriend home and putting her through the McNamara wringer."

"You put me through the McNamara wringer."

"You're not my girlfriend, you're a friend." Cara said, her expression unreadable. "You stepped in it all by yourself. And believe me, it would have been much worse if I was presenting you as someone who had designs on me."

"Right." Lauren was chastened, but what Cara said now begged another question. "Do you have a girlfriend?"

"No, do you?"

"No, I told you I'm kind of starting from zero since I've moved back to the city. No friends, no attachments except my family. Well, my dad. My brother lives in California and I don't see him much."

Cara turned her body toward Lauren. "Yeah, but it's hard for me to believe that you have no friends. I mean, who wouldn't want to be your friend? Didn't you live in the city when you were a child? No family friends? And what about your friends from Perry Bidwell, and college friends?"

Lauren didn't know what to say when confronted with the evidence that she couldn't make a friendship or relationship last. She wanted to be honest with Cara, but she wasn't ready for this kind of nakedness.

Maybe being friends with her was all she should aspire to, and maybe she should try really hard to make it stick. Cara expected her to say something. "What can I say? I'm a miserable person."

"I don't believe it." Cara's response was immediate. "And I'm sorry for questioning you like that. It was really rude."

This was why she hadn't let anyone get close in years. Lauren scooted to the edge of the bed. "Maybe I should go."

Cara put a hand on her forearm. "Please don't go yet. I hate that I made you feel uncomfortable. And my mother would kill me if you left before dessert."

"Dessert? I couldn't. I'm stuffed."

"Look, I know I'm an idiot who fumbles the social graces. It's been a little hard for me to figure out where the line is with you. I know I've crossed it a few times. And spending time with my family isn't the most fun thing to do—"

"Cara, stop. I'm having a good time with your family. It's been a long time since I've been to someone's home and felt that family chaos and quirkiness and love."

"It's kind of you to express our particular family dynamic in such a diplomatic way," she said dryly.

"I mean it. If not for your invitation I would be sitting at home doing nothing. And even if I am a bit strange and can't help sniffing you, I'm having a good time with you."

Cara squared her shoulders and looked her dead in the eye. "I'm going to level with you. I had a tiny little crush on you in school. But before that makes you feel weird, I have to say the teenage me had a bunch of preconceived notions about you, and the present-day me is really enjoying getting to know the real, a bit strange, present-day you."

"You had—"

"Wait, I'm not finished. I feel like we could be friends. But I also think we should acknowledge this flirtation that's happening between us. Am I wrong? That's there, isn't it?"

When had Lauren become so bad at this? "I'm sorry if I've been pushy. I guess I was coming on a little strong."

"So you feel it?"

"Yes, I think you know I do."

Cara nodded and took a deep breath. "What if we see where this goes? I'm not looking for marriage here. I'm looking for light and easy, nothing too serious. We're both available, so why not give it a try? I get to satisfy my curiosity about my teenage crush and you get to sniff at me a little more. How do you feel about it?"

"You had a crush on me?" What Lauren was feeling for Cara right now seemed as if it could be categorized as a teenage crush, so they were even in that regard.

"Don't make me regret telling you. I wanted you to know in the interest of full disclosure." The tension in Cara's expression made Lauren feel bad.

"Here's my full disclosure: I felt an insane attraction to you from the moment I saw you in that too-tight school uniform."

Cara's posture slumped in apparent relief, and she nudged Lauren with her shoulder. "Perv."

"It would seem so." Lauren interlaced their fingers and gazed at how nicely they fit together before she looked back at Cara. "I'm not looking for anything serious either. I think we could have some fun together. Let's do it."

The warmth in Cara's eyes and her slow, pleased smile sent a flush through Lauren's body, and she hoped she wasn't turning red.

It was unbelievable how much she and Cara were on the same page. Lauren exhaled in wonder. "Are you always this direct? Damn, you're brave. There I was trying to figure out how in the world I was going to get in your pants and then you go having an adult conversation with me."

"Okay, slow down. The only person in my pants is me, at least for the time being." Suddenly, Cara froze, then whipped her head toward the door. She let go of Lauren's hand and put some distance between them. "Wow, that's so interesting. So you're saying it's physically impossible to lick your own elbow?"

Lauren eyed her in utter confusion.

Mrs. Talarico appeared at the door and pushed it all the way open. "Funny, Cara. Somehow my wiseacre daughter always knows when I'm about to enter her room. I could never get any dirt on her."

"Mom, try to lick your own elbow," Cara said, her voice laden with faux excitement.

"I just wanted to let you know dessert is ready, girls." She walked back down the hall, leaving the door open.

"Wait for it." Cara pointed a finger skyward. They heard the squeal of a floorboard as her mom approached the stairs. "How she can't hear that I'll never know."

"Such skills, and yet you never had any visitors," Lauren marveled.

"Come on." Cara pulled Lauren from the bed and back to family time downstairs. "How much you want to bet my mom is trying to get Patrick to lick his elbow right now?"

❖

Cara didn't eat much dessert. She skipped Aunt Deedee's traditional pumpkin chiffon pie, put a few of the cookies Lauren brought on her plate, and half-listened to the conversations happening around her.

Lauren's refined manners were evident as she laughed politely at something Uncle Mike said. Cara couldn't square her with the endearing, bumbling woman upstairs in her bedroom. It was so obvious Lauren was about to put the moves on her, and Cara was both amused and unnerved by it. That Lauren felt two meetings were enough to move them toward intimacy was flattering, but also way too fast. She believed Lauren liked her, and she couldn't deny her own attraction, but she intended on taking the slow local train to discovering what that meant, not the express.

It was almost surreal to have Lauren in the childhood home where she had spent many hours banking the embers of her teenage crush. Getting to know her as an adult, and to feel such a strong attraction toward her, meant she had to see where it would lead. She was incapable of doing otherwise.

Someday Cara wanted to have a grand passion and fall deeply in love with her forever woman, someone she would be with for the rest of her life, but it wouldn't be Lauren. For now, as she worked herself out of debt, she preferred to have fun and treat her romantic life with a light touch. She and Lauren could see each other, have some fun, some sex, and both feel satisfied with that.

They were so different, and while Lauren might not be bothered by slumming it in a lower middle class Jersey suburb for an afternoon, Cara worried about how she would fit into Lauren's life. But the existence of worries didn't stop her from wanting to see where their attraction went. Whatever she was embarking on with Lauren didn't have to include a reckoning of their relative class positions or income levels. She would compartmentalize her distrust of Lauren's wealth and simply enjoy her hotness for a little while.

Lauren's plate held only crumbs and she was refusing more coffee. She caught Cara's eye. "Do you need a ride back to the city?"

"Tomorrow is the traditional Black Friday shopping excursion with Mom. We get up early in search of deals." Cara liked that Lauren looked disappointed.

"Will you be shopping tomorrow, Lauren?" her mom asked.

"I have to work," Lauren replied. "I should get on the road to beat the traffic. Thank you, everyone, for a wonderful Thanksgiving." Lauren said good-bye to each of the McNamaras by name and followed Cara to the coat closet.

Her mother met them in the foyer with a bag of leftovers and pulled Lauren into another interminable hug. "You're a natural gravy-maker, Lauren. Come back next year, okay? You're always welcome."

"I'll walk you out." Cara opened the door for Lauren and followed her out.

"That seemed like just a heavier version of regular pumpkin pie to me. Why does your aunt call it pumpkin chiffon pie?" Lauren slung her coat over her arm and strolled down the driveway with Cara.

"Because pumpkin concrete pie was taken? It's a bit of a gut-buster."

"Yeah." Lauren patted her belly. "I don't think I'll be eating again for a week." She donned her coat but left it unbuttoned, then slipped her hands into her pockets. Her mouth formed an O, and she pulled something from her pocket. "I almost forgot." She handed Cara a postcard of Vincent van Gogh's *The Starry Night*.

"Oh, I like this painting."

"Everybody does. Turn it over."

Cara flipped the card to the blank side where Lauren had written "The Starry Night," Anne Sexton.

"Anne Sexton?" Cara frowned. "But this is van Gogh. She's a poet."

Lauren stood there, waiting for Cara to pick up the clue phone.

"Oh! She wrote a poem about it?"

She nodded. "You think your students know this painting?"

"I'm not sure. Maybe. Only one way to find out." Were those tingles she was feeling from Lauren remembering their conversation and delivering on her promise to help? No. Couldn't be. "I love Anne Sexton. I'll look it up and read it tonight."

"Maybe your students would find it a bit more accessible than Brueghel."

She slid the postcard into her back pocket. "Thank you. Will you help me with the painting? I think that's where my original lesson was lacking. I'm no art expert."

"Sure." Lauren seemed pleased. "I had a great time today."

"Me too. Thanks for schlepping all the way out here."

Cara stepped into Lauren's open arms. She slipped her arms beneath Lauren's dark coat and wrapped them around her waist. She pressed as much of her body as she could against Lauren's, and it felt like the shock of exposed wires touching. A warm feeling low in her belly began spreading outward to all her limbs. Her face was buried between the collar of Lauren's coat and her neck, and she could feel Lauren's pulse pounding against her cheek. "Mmm. Gravy."

Lauren laughed and tried to pull away, but Cara didn't let her.

"Hold on. I'm not finished yet." She ran her hands slowly down Lauren's back, from her shoulder blades down to her hips. Lauren relaxed against her and it made Cara feel almost giddy. She couldn't remember when a hug had felt so good. They settled into it, leaning against each other, standing there in the driveway, the heat building between them.

When they parted at last, Lauren spoke, her voice hoarse. "You're better at that than your mother."

"I'm going to ignore that extremely disturbing comment." Cara stepped back, but kept hold of Lauren's lapels, her gaze locked on Lauren's lips, wanting to press her own against them. When she raised her eyes to Lauren's, their deep blue color drew her in, but she saw hesitation as well. For all of Lauren's boldness back in her bedroom, Cara intuited that she was not as certain about the sparks flying between them as she might proclaim.

She dropped her hands from Lauren's coat and said, "I have a suspicion that my mom and Aunt Deedee might be watching from the window, so let's bow to each other like martial artists to really confuse them."

Lauren complied, her eyes mirthful, and they stood apart and bent at the waist before breaking out in giggles.

"Why are they watching?"

Cara shrugged. She doubted they were. "They want to be all up in my business."

"Family." Lauren opened her car door, but her eyes lingered on Cara. "Just one of many things to be thankful for." She got in and touched her fingers to her lips and blew Cara a kiss, and Cara nearly swooned at the sweetness of it.

She stayed in the driveway long after Lauren had disappeared, thinking about where the road they had now started down together would lead.

CHAPTER NINE

L auren poked her head into her boss's office about three minutes before their meeting was to begin. Helen Waters waved her in, phone to her ear.

"Sorry about that." Helen hung up and wrote something on a sticky note. "How are you, Lauren? How is the cataloging going?"

"It's great." She loved being up to her ears in the minutiae of the collection. "I'm really enjoying it, actually."

Helen smiled. "It really helps you understand what we have here, doesn't it? Are you ready to try something you've never done before?"

Lauren sat up straighter. "Of course. What do you need?"

"We're two years out and ready to start asking for loans for the Pissarro show. Our wish list is finished and I usually email the assignments for attaining the loans in the planning meeting, but I wanted to discuss it with you since you've never done it before. You read the policy, right?"

Lauren nodded. The Collections Management Policy was a lengthy and dry document that made for light bedtime reading.

"Good. That's your reference, but you'll shadow me once before trying it on your own." Helen pulled several documents from a folder in front of her. "We're hoping for loans from the Minneapolis Institute of Arts and the National Gallery in London. We've worked with both institutions before so I don't anticipate any issues."

Lauren nodded again.

Helen offered the folder to her. "The last request is from a private collection. It's right here in the city, but it might take a bit of finessing. I thought you might be the right choice for this one."

Lauren opened it and her stomach dropped at the name of the private owner—Genevra H. Winthrop. Now she knew why she had been tapped for this particular task. "I'll do my best."

Helen smiled. "Okay, keep me posted."

Lauren heard the muffled chime of a text alert as she walked back to her desk. It was from Cara.

Hey! Are we still on for tonight? Where should we meet? Three beer stein emojis.

She quickly texted back: *Yes! Corner of 76th and Madison. 6PM ok? That works! See you soon!* Four smiley emojis.

❖

On the corner of Seventy-Sixth and Madison at six p.m., Lauren was leaning against a mailbox in a luxurious-looking brown shearling coat, gazing at her phone as Cara approached. Before Lauren noticed her, Cara took a moment to appreciate her autumnal fashion, with her calf-length muted paisley skirt in shades of fall leaves and those delectable brown boots she'd worn at Thanksgiving.

Lauren looked up and smiled. "Hey, you."

Cara reached her side but left some room between them, still not quite believing Lauren was directing that smile at her.

"You look great. How are you?"

Cara looked down at her scruffy peacoat and gray corduroy jeans and thought she looked anything but great. She came straight from work and never tried very hard to dress to impress there. She thought this was going to be a casual drink. "I'm doing well now that it's Friday and school is over, but I wouldn't say no to something cold and refreshing. Where are we going?"

Lauren linked arms with her and led her to the revolving doors of an imposing hotel that anchored the corner with its pristine limestone facade. "Here. There's something I think you should see, and we can get a drink while you're seeing it."

"The Carlyle? I hope you haven't booked a room. Just what kind of girl do you think I am?"

"Relax. That will come later." Lauren's coy smile released a kaleidoscope of butterflies in Cara's belly. "Kidding." Lauren led them through the lobby to another door, completely black, her body obscuring the name on it as she held it for Cara to walk through.

It was a cocktail lounge, small in size and dimly lit, and the immediate impression was one of old New York opulence. The perimeter of the room was lined in rich brown leather banquettes with round tables fronting them. A man in a tuxedo played quiet jazz on the baby grand in the center of the room. Lauren chose a table in the corner and sat down, leaving Cara to slide in next to her so they were sitting at right angles to each other. There was a tall, slim menu standing beside the little lamp on the table, which Lauren placed next to her on the seat, out of Cara's reach. "This okay?"

Cara nodded and looked around. The ceiling was gold leaf and complemented the walls, which were covered in hand-drawn illustrations. "What is this place? Am I dressed appropriately?"

"You're fine. It's called Bemelmans Bar."

"Bemelmans? Like…" Cara paused. She now saw something familiar in the drawings on the wall.

"Ludwig Bemelmans. Look over there." Lauren pointed at the wall next to the bar, where two barmen were busy with cocktail shakers. "I think you'll see some old friends."

And there, replicated on the wall, was Miss Clavel and her twelve charges, including Madeline with her red hair. Murals covered every inch of wall space. Cara looked to her left and saw illustrations of a pond with couples rowing, parents and children setting their toy sailboats onto the water, a mom and dad on a bicycle built for two with their baby in the handlebar basket. It was all utterly charming. "I have to get a better look at these. I'll be back."

Cara didn't think the customers minded as she strolled by their tables and looked at the illustrations above their heads. She especially loved the drawings of nattily dressed animals of every species casually viewing humans in cages. While she took in the walls, she noticed the clientele: society women dressed to the nines, a few tourists with shopping bags from the Met and the Frick. How lovely of Lauren to bring her here after their conversation on Thanksgiving. "This is wonderful," Cara said as she returned to the table.

"I thought you might like it. I ordered you a drink. I hope you don't mind."

"Not at all. What's the story here?"

"Sometime in the forties, Bemelmans agreed to do the murals in exchange for staying in the hotel with his family, rent-free."

"I think the hotel got the better deal." A waiter in a red dinner jacket placed their cocktails in front of them, as well as some savory snacks. "Cheers." Cara raised her glass and Lauren did the same. The amber liquid tasted astringent and slightly sweet. "Nice. What is it?"

"A sidecar. I thought a place like this deserved a classic cocktail. Cognac, Cointreau, and lemon."

"It's delicious. Thanks for bringing me here." Cara finally stopped gazing everywhere but at Lauren and found herself ensnared by her eyes. She couldn't look away, and heat emanated from her skin. The atmosphere needed cooling. "Tell me about your day."

"Just a normal day at the office."

Cara scoffed. "Your office is unlike most in the city."

"As is yours."

"Mine is like thousands of offices around the city. They're just large and hold up to thirty-four students."

Lauren grimaced. "That sounds like a lot."

The last thing Cara wanted was to talk about school right now. "Let's talk about your work."

"Okay." Lauren rubbed her chin while she thought. "We're in the planning stages for a new exhibition of Camille Pissarro's work."

"Who's she?"

"Pissarro was a man, actually, an Impressionist known for *en plein air* painting."

"What's that?" Cara didn't know much about art at all.

"That's bringing all your gear out to the countryside and capturing a natural image outside in the moment."

"Oh, like Monet and van Gogh." Cara nodded and tossed a few nuts in her mouth.

"Exactly. At the end of his life, Pissarro was getting old and sickly and his eyes weren't that great, so in order to keep himself out of the elements, he would rent rooms in Paris that overlooked interesting city landscapes and paint them. He did several series of these locations in all types of weather and seasons, and we're amassing a collection of them to exhibit."

"You mean you're borrowing them from other places?"

Lauren nodded. "The Met only has three from this period."

"So what do you have to do?" She looked at her drink, already nearly depleted. "God, these are good."

"Yep, they are." Lauren flagged down a waiter and ordered two more sidecars, and then took a swig from her own glass. "Today my boss tasked me with arranging the loans for three paintings. It's something I've never done before." She laughed without much humor. "Actually, it's all stuff I've never done before. I'm twenty-eight years old and this is my first real job."

"Sure, but you've been educating yourself in preparation for doing this job for what…six years?" Cara thanked their server as he placed fresh drinks in front of them.

"Longer than that." Lauren lowered her voice and moved closer to Cara, sipping from her drink before continuing. "Ever since I started at the Met, I've been working on a theory, and today I got sort of a confirmation on it. I started studying art in the tenth grade. I loved everything about it, especially the late nineteenth century. I've known what I wanted to do since then and all the choices I've made with my education and research have been leading me to exactly where I am now."

"Working at the Met. Your hard work has paid off," Cara said, not sure where Lauren was going with this.

"But I'm thinking it's all kind of been bullshit now." Lauren's sudden gravity was at odds with the tinkling piano in the background.

"What do you mean?"

"All that stuff I said about working hard the other night? Bullshit. I think the only reason I got the job is because of my family."

"You mean your father pulled some strings?" This seemed probable. Cara found it difficult to believe Lauren hadn't been the beneficiary of nepotism at some point in her life.

"No, he promised he wouldn't get involved. I made him give me his word." Lauren gave her a surprised look. "Do you think he did it anyway? I hadn't even thought of that." She put her elbow on the table and rested her forehead in her hand. Her distress seemed genuine. "No, he wouldn't have."

Cara put a soothing hand on Lauren's back. She was sorry Lauren was upset, but was this honestly the first time the thought had crossed her mind? She tried to be supportive. "I'm sure you got it solely by your talent and drive." Maybe it was true. It probably wasn't.

"It was such a great interview. They loved my dissertation topic and totally agreed with me that the Met needed to be more inclusive of women artists, especially in the nineteenth century." Lauren seemed to be searching Cara's eyes for understanding, so Cara nodded in agreement although she wasn't quite sure why Lauren was bothered when she got the job she wanted. "I'm sorry. I didn't mean to have an existential freak-out in front of you." Lauren sat back and drained her glass.

Cara was surprised to see hers was nearly empty again, too.

"If not your father, what did you mean by your family?" She felt like she was missing a part of the story.

"I think I need another. You?" Lauren motioned for another round with a wave of her hand. Red jackets sprang into action. "I know this is going to sound unbelievable, but my family once had a history with the Met. My great-great-great-grandparents made a pretty large bequest to the museum about a hundred years ago, and I have other relatives who've made donations over the years, too."

Could she really be that naive? Of course she was hired because of her family history. How could Lauren think otherwise?

"And today I found out that one of the pictures my boss wants me to secure is in the private collection belonging to my great-aunt."

"They want you to use the family connections to get it?"

"Uh-huh, but what they don't know is that she and my grandfather had a falling out a long time ago and now our side of the family doesn't speak to her. He died when I was in college and the last time I saw Great-aunt Genevra was when I was about ten years old. Plus, she cut ties with the Met back in the eighties. How the hell am I going to get her to agree to loan us one of her paintings?"

Cara didn't know what to say. Honestly, this tale could be a novel, or a play, or a Lifetime made-for-TV movie at the very least. But even with her problems seeming to be so outside the realm of ordinary people, Cara didn't like seeing Lauren upset. The only thing she could think of to do was give Lauren's knee an inadequate pat. "I'm sorry about your grandfather."

After their server deposited another round, Lauren placed her hand on top of Cara's. "Thanks. He was a wonderful grandpa. I miss him a lot." With her free hand, she carefully raised her very full glass and downed about half of it, smacking her lips with gusto when she was finished. "I love these. I could drink ten of them."

"Me too." Cara took a big slurp as well. "You shouldn't feel bad that nepotism got you your job. It's practically the American way. I wish my students all had some rich ancestors to fall back on." She took another long sip and waited to hear Lauren's response. When it didn't come, she turned to see Lauren gazing at her with a combination of hurt and indignation in her eyes. Cara ran her words back through her alcohol muddled mind and realized how it sounded. Lauren tried to remove her hand from where it sat on top of Cara's, but Cara grabbed it and held it in both of hers.

"I can't believe I said that. How crass can I be? I'm sorry." *What the hell is wrong with me?*

Lauren added her other hand to the pile of limbs on Cara's lap and looked at her with watering eyes. "I hate money," she said with a vehemence that made her sound hoarse and desperate.

Cara was taken aback. "I'm not in love with it either, but you have to admit it comes in handy sometimes."

"Throughout my whole life, money has poisoned everything," Lauren said bitterly, her head drooping.

"Okay, I think we need some fresh air. Check please," Cara called to a passing waiter. "Let's take a walk and get some food and you can tell me more." She accepted the bill from the waiter and flipped it open, reaching for her wallet. "Holy shit! One hundred fifty-four dollars for three drinks?"

"Six drinks." Lauren plucked the billfold from her hands, stuck her credit card in it, and slapped it on the table. "I've got it."

"Can we split it?" Cara inwardly winced as she suggested it. It would put a serious dent in her weekly budget. Top Ramen for the next four days at least. She downed the rest of her drink. She sure wasn't going to waste it.

"No, I invited you here."

Cara said the first thing that came into her mind. "Goddamn money. It always ends up making you blue as hell."

Lauren reached for her scarf and raised her eyebrows at Cara.

"I don't know why I said that. A character from *The Catcher in the Rye* says something like it. I've taught it about five times. I have it practically memorized."

"Holden Caulfield. Ninth grade with Mr. Morrell. He was a rich kid from Manhattan, wasn't he?" The edge in Lauren's voice revealed her displeasure with Cara's comparison of her to the fictional character.

Cara now realized what the reference implied, but she hadn't meant to offend. "Mr. Morrell was from California." She smiled, willfully misunderstanding. "Don't you remember him always talking about tubular waves?"

Lauren smiled back, but it lacked warmth. "I remember really hating Holden Caulfield."

"Some of my students really do, too. They wonder why this privileged white kid causes so many problems for himself." Cara watched as Lauren signed the check and scribbled a tip in the allotted space. "I loved Holden, still do."

"Yeah? Why?"

"Because even with all his privilege, he was still a human being—just a fucked up kid trying to figure out how to grow up. And who can't relate to that?"

Lauren peered blearily at her for a moment. "You're nice."

Cara snorted. "And you're drunk."

❖

Lauren wasn't that drunk. She was buzzing hard, but not drunk. Cara had taken them to JG Melon, a burger joint a couple of blocks from the Carlyle. Lauren had completely forgotten its existence until the orange neon sign came into view. The tiny restaurant was packed but they managed to snag two seats at the bar.

Cara picked up a menu. "What are you having?"

"A cheeseburger. You want to split cottage fries?"

"Uh, yeah. Is that even a question?" She gave their order to the bartender.

"I used to come here when I was a kid with my family." Lauren took in the watermelon décor plastered all over the walls and the green-and-white-checkered tablecloths. "It looks exactly the same."

"I worked in a place like this in college. Low checks but high turnover meant a pretty good night's wages. Plus I ran my ass off so I never got the freshman fifteen."

"That must have been hard to hold down a job and go to school." Lauren never had to do that.

"Not only did I wait tables three nights a week, I also had a work-study at the library twenty hours a week." Cara shook her head. "But I got a lot of work done at the library while I checked out people's books for them, so it was good. It forced me to study."

"Did you have time for a social life?"

"Absolutely. Princeton is where I sharpened my time management skills. It's all about balance, right? I managed to have an excellent time in college while getting an excellent education. And I will be paying for it probably until I die. You're totally right about money. It seems to have a monumental bearing on every choice I make."

Lauren stiffened. They were back to money. She had hoped that embarrassing little outburst would be forgotten. "Hey, what I said earlier—"

"No, I get it," Cara interrupted. "Money and I are not friends. I'd like money to be my bitch, but really I'm money's bitch. Money is my landlord, prison warden, and fairy godmother all wrapped into one."

Lauren was not going to be drawn into a discussion about money. In her experience, it never ended well. She stayed quiet.

"Here's how I define my relationship with money." Cara seemed oblivious to Lauren's discomfort. "I imagine myself as the second son in an aristocratic family."

"The what?"

"Like from literature? I'm talking from a hundred years ago or more. First born son inherits, daughters get married off, and the second born son and any other sons after that get nothing."

"Am I supposed to understand what you're talking about?" As much as Lauren wanted to move the conversation on to a different subject, she was curious.

"Have you ever read *Howard's End*?"

"I don't think so. Maybe I saw the movie? Years ago?"

"Doesn't matter if you've read it. There's this character, Paul Wilcox, who is the second son of the Wilcox family—and they're super rich. His older brother Charles is going to inherit all the family wealth because that's how it was done back in those days. Paul has to leave home to make his own fortune. He can't marry because he can't afford a wife, and he can't even have a relationship because any woman who would get involved without the promise of marriage isn't worth having."

Now Cara had lost her. And why was she telling her this? "You're looking to get married?"

"No, the opposite." Cara gave her a teachery *Pay attention!* look. "Until I pay off my loans, I have to think of myself as seeking my fortune. Except I don't get a fortune at the end of it, I just get out of debt." Cara's *et voila!* gesture at the end suggested she had explained everything.

Back to money. Could they be done talking about this? Cara was gazing at her expectantly but she had no idea what to say. "So what happened to him?"

Cara frowned. "Who?"

"Um, Paul somebody?"

Disappointment flickered over Cara's features. "He's a total flat character. He gets the plot moving in the beginning and then returns at the end to be a jerk to everyone."

Cool story. Lauren was relieved when the bartender brought their burgers. Her mouth watered at the sight of them. That they were finished with this topic was an added bonus. "Oh, yum."

"So what are you going to do about great-aunt what's-her-name?" Cara seemed to accept the change of topic with grace. She placed a mass of onions and pickles on her burger and poured ketchup on it.

"I don't know. She's big on the charity circuit. Maybe I'll ambush her at an event."

"Let me know if you need moral support. I'll go with you if you want." Cara took a huge bite and closed her eyes in enjoyment.

Lauren stilled, trying to fathom where the kindness was coming from.

When Cara opened her eyes, she caught Lauren's stare. "What?" she asked with her mouth full. "Do I have ketchup on me?"

"No, that's really nice of you." She had let Cara down before, had barely been listening as she tried to convey something she thought meaningful, and here she was willing to extend a kindness anyway. As Lauren took a bite as well, she vowed to be more deserving of it. "Oh my God, that is amazing."

"Right?" Cara took a sip of her beer. "I mean, charity events aren't really my thing—meaning, I've never been to one—but I know it's probably daunting to go into one alone. And since you're friendless at the moment." She smiled and elbowed her to show she was joking.

"Yeah, I've been to a few and I can't imagine what it would be like without a partner. Small talk with strangers gives me the willies."

"Ah, you're doing all right with this stranger." Cara pointed to herself. "And I don't give a shit what rich people think. If anything goes wrong you can always blame it on me."

It was true they were new acquaintances, but Cara felt like the furthest thing from a stranger. "I've said it before and I'll say it again. You're nice."

"Shut up, you're embarrassing me. And don't say that near my students. I prefer them to think of me as a meaner Miss Trunchbull."

It was such an unlikely image, it made Lauren snort with surprise.

"Speaking of my students, what can I say about the van Gogh painting? The poem is great. So rich. I've got lots to say about that, but I stared at that painting for, like, an hour and all I could come up with is it's swirly."

"A technical term." Lauren laughed. "Ordinarily, I could refer you to our education department and they could definitely help you. But I have to tell you a little secret." She leaned closer to Cara. "It's at the Museum of Modern Art, not the Met."

"What? You gave me a painting that's not even at your museum?"

"I gave you nothing but a postcard and an idea."

"What am I going to say when I do this lesson?"

"Don't say anything. Make your students say it."

Cara frowned. "That's exactly what a teacher would do. Are you sure you're not a teacher?" She didn't wait for a reply. "But I still need to introduce it and give it some context, maybe provide a little background on van Gogh." She put her burger down. "Wait, I've got it. You can come to my class and give a presentation about the painting."

Lauren was dubious. "You want me to come and talk about *The Starry Night* with your class? You'll go a long way not to do some work, Lazy."

"No, I want my students to hear about it from a real art curator, not me, the art imposter. Come on, I said I would go with you to your charity event. It's an even trade."

"You already said you would go. Now you want to play let's make a deal?" But here was an easy way to repay Cara's kindness.

"Please? I'll give you this cottage fry." Cara held it up like it was a priceless gold doubloon.

"Fine, I'll do it." Lauren took it and hid a grin. "Now stop talking so I can enjoy the rest of this."

"Yay." Cara leaned over and wrapped her arms around Lauren's shoulders and shook her a few times.

Lauren, trying to hold on to her burger, awkwardly endured the impromptu embrace. With each shake Cara's nose crashed into Lauren's cheek and the contact made her shiver. Her senses were invaded by that light floral citrus scent of Cara's that immediately revved her engines. When Cara pulled away, the air crackled between them. Lauren's sex-deprived and booze-soaked mind leaped forward in their courtship and went to all sorts of X-rated places in the space of only a few seconds.

"When will you come?" Cara asked.

Lauren almost choked. She had no idea what Cara was asking. "What?" seemed the safest reply.

"When will you come to my school?"

"Oh. I'll check with my boss. Sometime next week?"

"Thank you." Cara leaned in again and kissed Lauren's cheek.

Lauren was warmed by that chaste little buss, but as she continued eating, she was now hyper-aware of every movement Cara made, like how she pushed her plate away and turned on her stool so her knee now pressed against Lauren's thigh. Cara leaned her elbow on the bar and held her glass, watching as Lauren kept herself occupied with her meal for a few moments longer before she too abandoned it in favor of a gulp of beer. Lauren repositioned herself so she and Cara were facing each other, one of Cara's thighs between her own. She put a hand on Cara's knee, her fingers drawn to the velvety texture of the wales of corduroy beneath them. She slowly dragged her hand back and forth over the ribbed fabric, entranced by its soothing suppleness and the warmth emanating from beneath it. An incongruous thought entered her head and she felt her cheeks flush.

Cara must have noticed. "What?"

"Nothing." She brought both palms to her flaming cheeks. "It's inappropriate."

"Hmm. Intriguing." Cara intercepted Lauren's hands as she brought them away from her face and rested them back on her thighs, this time with her own hands on top of Lauren's.

Time to be bold. Taking a page out of Cara's book, being direct, would put the idea of it out there, existing between them. Lauren locked eyes with Cara as she spread her fingers and sensually kneaded her thigh muscles through the fabric. "A thought popped into my mind when I touched you and your corduroy pants, a naughty one."

Cara took a deep breath in at Lauren's ministrations. "Do tell."

She leaned in toward Cara's ear, scratching her fingers over the fabric once again as she murmured, "Ribbed for her pleasure."

"You're getting turned on by my pants?" Cara laughed, but her voice took on a husky quality.

Lauren got a little further into Cara's personal space, her nose brushing her dark waves, tipsily embracing the silliness of her pickup moves. "Corduroy has never been so sexy."

"I don't think the condom makers had corduroy-wearing lesbians in mind when they came up with that phrase." Cara did not back away.

"I don't think the condom makers ever felt these thighs encased in corduroy." Lauren knew she was being ridiculous, and the way her hands were now wandering all over Cara's legs was bordering on obscene, but she couldn't stop.

"You have a unique seduction technique, but damn if it's not working. Do you want to go to my place?" Cara asked breathlessly.

"Yes, please." Lauren, not quite believing it had worked, reached for her bag and pulled her wallet from it.

"No, I've got it." Cara took cash from her front pocket and gestured to the bartender for their check.

They burst from the restaurant and hurried down the sidewalk. Cara took Lauren's hand as they neared Seventy-Third Street, slowing her progress. "Why are you walking south? We need to go uptown."

"I'm looking for a cab. I'm walking toward them." It made perfect sense to her.

"Lauren, look." Cara's head was turned toward the street they were crossing over. The residential street was lined with tall apartment buildings that were fronted by mature trees overhanging the street. Every single tree on the block was strung with bright fairy lights, wound into the farthest branches of each tree and creating what looked for all the world like a tunnel of sparkling stars, an enchanted wonderland on a random block on the Upper East Side. "Come on." Cara pulled them down the sidewalk farther down the block, then looked both ways, and led Lauren between two parked cars and into the middle of the street. She took out her phone and framed both of their faces with the fairy lights sparkling in the background. "Look at the camera."

Gazing at Cara under the glow of lights, Lauren found it difficult to turn her eyes from her. It was magical. She hadn't felt this way about anyone in a long time, but she had to be cautious. The physical attraction was overwhelming, but she had to keep things light. No emotions allowed.

Cara pulled her in with an arm around her waist and angled her head toward Lauren's. She depressed the shutter several times before slipping the phone back into her coat pocket. She looked into Lauren's eyes. "That's what's called commemorating a moment."

"What are we commemorating?"

"This." Cara brought her other arm up to encircle Lauren's waist and pressed her lips against hers. It felt like every synapse lit up at once, so immediate and intense was Lauren's reaction. She took Cara's face in her hands and savored the feel of her lips, so warm and soft and alive. Cara deepened the kiss, pulling her closer, letting her tongue explore Lauren's lower lip. Lauren's libido roared into overdrive and she opened her mouth, wanting more. She slid her hands up into Cara's hair, finally grasping those dark curls, something her fingers had itched to do since she had first laid eyes on her.

They both jumped at the blare of an angry horn. They shuffled to the side of the road and stood in the harsh glare of headlights as Cara motioned the car through with a sarcastic swipe of her arm. "By all means, come right through. Jeez, no patience for a little romance in this city."

Lauren attempted to recover, still a little stunned from their aborted kiss and her body's instantaneous detonation into flames. She wanted Cara. Of this she was absolutely certain. And Cara wanted her, too. But how was Lauren going to keep her emotions out of it? A precipice loomed before her, and she was about to step off.

CHAPTER TEN

Cara led the way up the four flights to her studio apartment, but left Lauren huffing in the hallway. "Hang on, let me just go in and give my place a lick and a promise." She left the door a few inches open and quickly tidied, throwing soiled clothes into the closet and pulling the covers up on her unmade bed. "Okay, come on in."

Lauren pushed the door open and turned three hundred sixty degrees as she took off her coat, and Cara tried to see the space as she would. Small and Spartan. A little shabby.

Bathroom to the right. To the left were a couple of cabinets and tiny-sized appliances that allowed the merest suggestion of a kitchen. A bed, some bookshelves, and a few other sticks of furniture pretty much filled the rest of the space. The walls were bare, except for a small, framed image hung on the blank wall facing the bed. It was the hugging carrots Manny gave her. She turned down the dimmer on the overhead light to set a mood. Which mood had yet to be determined.

"What is a lick and a promise?" Lauren's breathing had normalized and her mood seemed to perk up a bit. She had become quiet in the cab and Cara wondered if she was having second thoughts.

"You've never heard that phrase?" Cara opened her small refrigerator. "Would you like a beer? Water? Those are your choices, I'm afraid."

"Nothing, thanks." Lauren sat on the bed and leaned back on her hands.

"A lick and a promise is a saying of my mom's. It means to clean something up quickly with the promise of going back to do the job properly later." Cara sat down next to her. "And here endeth the lesson."

Lauren looked her in the eye. "I just want to make sure we're on the same page here. I'm not looking for anything serious. I'm not that great at relationships, and a few years ago I was in one that ended badly. Um, really badly."

"I'm sorry."

"It's okay. I'm over it now, but I'm not looking for anything long term or with feelings attached." Lauren grasped her hand and held onto it. "I want to spend time with you, have fun with you, etcetera." She looked at the bed pointedly. "I guess what I'm asking is, can we still be friends if we add sex to it?"

"So friend feelings are okay, but nothing past that?"

Lauren nodded.

"That's typically called friends with benefits."

"Are you okay with that?"

Cara was glad they were establishing ground rules. She appreciated guidelines, expectations, and structure of all kinds. If things between them ever got confusing or sticky or drama-filled, either of them could always refer back to right now when they were explicitly agreeing to the terms of whatever this turned out to be. "As long as we're being responsible and talking about our feelings, or lack thereof, I guess I should say that I'm in no position to acquire a girlfriend. Second son of an aristocratic family, remember? I'm fine with it."

Lauren nodded again. "Did I just take all of the sexy out of this?"

"All you have to do is touch my magical sexy corduroys again and we're back on track." Cara extended her leg across Lauren's lap like a dancer with a pointed toe. "Take off my shoe, woman."

Lauren laughed and complied, then ran her hand up Cara's trouser leg, letting it rest on her hip. "I do love me some corduroys." She leaned over and captured Cara's lips.

As they kissed, Cara felt an uncoiling in her belly. Lauren angled her face and deepened the kiss, and slowly and thoroughly moved her lips over Cara's. They lingered in the moment and Cara enjoyed the closeness and the building anticipation. She parted her lips and welcomed the brush of Lauren's tongue against hers.

As their kisses subsided, Lauren drew back and wound her fingers in Cara's hair, letting out a sigh. "I love your hair. I think I could kiss you for hours. This feels so good. You feel so good."

"Hmm, sweet talker with the compliments." Cara struggled to put a sentence together. Looking into those deep blue eyes was just as distracting as Lauren's kisses. "You don't have to keep trying to win me over, you know. You've already won."

Lauren's hands crept under Cara's shirt, traveling up to just under her bra. "Somehow I don't feel like I've won yet. Not quite at the finish line." She bent her head to drop a kiss below Cara's ear.

"They do say it's all about the journey." Cara lifted her chin and rested her hands on Lauren's shoulders.

"Yeah? Who's they?" Lauren murmured as she planted kisses down Cara's neck. She unbuttoned a few buttons of Cara's shirt and brushed her lips over her clavicle.

"They?" Cara was having a hard time concentrating on words when what Lauren was doing was so delicious. "Um, the sex…journey… people?"

Lauren pulled back and gazed at her with an amused smile.

"Should I shut up now?"

She laughed, pulled her sweater over her head, and finished unbuttoning Cara's shirt.

Cara allowed her to, drinking in all of the pale skin that had just been revealed. Then she tried to shed her shirt but, in her haste, had forgotten to unbutton the cuffs. She managed to get one hand free but the other was stuck. Frustration made her movements jerky, and Lauren bent to help. Cara tugged at the fabric with all her might and the button went flying as her hand shot out of the sleeve like a bullet from the chamber, smacking Lauren hard in the chest.

"Oof." Lauren lifted her head in surprise and crashed into Cara's nose.

"Ow!" Cara gingerly felt it with her fingertips.

Lauren rubbed the area above her left breast with one hand and held on to Cara's arm with the other. "What just happened? Did I do that?"

Cara tilted her head back, pinching above the nostrils. "I'm so sorry. I tit-punched you by accident. Are you okay?"

"I'm fine, just surprised. What about you? Oh, you're bleeding."

"It's okay, I'm prone to nosebleeds." She stretched to the nightstand for a tissue.

Lauren sat back and watched while Cara pushed bits of tissue up her nostrils.

"It's a hot look, I know. Back in a minute." Cara headed for the bathroom to clean up and dispose of the bloody evidence. Then she took a moment to collect herself. Lauren Havemayer, high school crush, recently returned from the oblivion of forgotten memories, was half dressed and on her bed, waiting to have sex with her. The strangeness of Lauren having been her crush notwithstanding, Cara couldn't remember the last time she was so attracted to another woman. She really wanted this. If they could manage to not knock each other out, they might have a good time tonight. She took a deep breath and left her tiny bathroom. Her heart sank when she saw that Lauren was still sitting on the bed but had donned her sweater again.

"Should we take this as a sign?" Lauren seemed ambivalent.

"A sign that all great sex starts with something swollen?" Cara sat down next to her. "Oh wait, that doesn't count for lesbians. Jesus, that was a terrible joke. I don't blame you if you want to leave." She took in Lauren's undecided expression and wanted to salvage the night. If Lauren left now, she had the feeling this opportunity would never return. "I'll understand if you think we've lost the spark, but I think we can get it back. Want to rub my pants some more?"

Lauren shrugged, smiling. "Couldn't hurt." She placed her hands on Cara's knees and watched while Cara removed her bra. She studied Cara's face. "It's not swollen, maybe a little red."

"Come on, Havemayer. My nose is not what you should be looking at right now. Way to give a girl a complex."

Lauren laughed. "Sorry." She made a blatant examination of Cara's breasts while she stroked Cara's thighs. "They're beautiful. You're beautiful."

"That's more like it." Cara's voice was huskier now. Lauren's gaze, coupled with the rhythmic motion of her hands, had brought her right back to pre-nosebleed levels of desire. She had to touch Lauren somewhere and slowly drew closer. "Heads up. I'm coming in for a kiss."

Lauren smiled up at her, flirty and welcoming. "I'm ready."

Their lips met and the kiss went from tentative to turbulent in a matter of seconds. They moved with an urgency that belied their earlier problems. Cara gasped when Lauren cupped her breasts and brushed her thumbs over them. Cara felt her nipples tighten into furled buds instantly. Lauren's tongue stole into her mouth and Cara was beginning to feel committed to seeing this through, and had to know if Lauren felt the same.

She pulled away and said, "What does your sign say now? Do you still want to abort?"

"Hell, no," Lauren growled.

"Then can I please take this off?" Cara plucked at the shoulder of Lauren's sweater. In response, Lauren lifted her arms, and Cara managed to pull it from her body without causing any more injury. The place above Lauren's breast was red also. She put her hand over it and Lauren immediately covered it with her own hand, drawing it down.

"It's fine, Cara. I'll survive." Lauren tilted her head. "Actually, maybe I won't if you don't touch me in a few more interesting places."

"Like where?" Cara smiled. "Earlobe? Kneecap? Big toe?"

Lauren laughed and nodded, and then reached back to unhook her bra. "Yes, them, eventually. Maybe start here?"

Cara simply stared at Lauren's beautiful naked torso for a moment before gently touching Lauren's flat stomach and the rise of her breasts, but she had to know how her breasts tasted. Suddenly she was pushing Lauren down against the bed and raining kisses on her chest while stroking all the skin she could grasp. She took Lauren's right nipple into her mouth, and she felt the intake of breath where her hand rested on Lauren's stomach. She circled the hard, pebbled peak with her tongue over and over. Lauren's breathy moans told her she was doing something right. After a while, she raised her head and raked her gaze all over Lauren. "So pretty," she breathed, meeting Lauren's eyes in a moment of pure intimacy.

Lauren sat up. "I want to feel all of you."

Cara retreated, creating some distance between them before shimmying out of her clothes. "Incoming," she said as a warning as she knelt before Lauren, who sat back and allowed Cara to undress her. She found the side zip of Lauren's skirt and stripped it from her but was confounded by the tights and boots underneath. They managed not to bash each other's heads as Cara pulled her boots off while Lauren pushed the tights down her long legs. Cara stayed there a moment with one of Lauren's riding boots in her hands, maybe falling in love with them a little bit right then. She couldn't resist running her fingers over the supple brown leather. She briefly wondered how Lauren would feel if she put them back on her now that her tights had been removed, but then rejected the idea as definitely too weird for their first time. She put them to the side and rested her hands on Lauren's knees, weighing her options. They could do several fun things right here in this position.

"No." Lauren divined her thoughts. "While I reserve the right to ask you to assume this exact position later, right now I want the full body treatment." She moved up the bed, her head resting among the pillows, and opened her arms to Cara.

Cara went into them, and the silky, soft warmth of Lauren's skin made her shiver. Her body reacted to the pleasant shock of it. Lauren moved her thighs against Cara's and nudged her nipples against her breasts. Lauren's stomach muscles trembled, in fact, her whole body trembled. "Are you okay?" Cara whispered.

Lauren made a sound that was halfway between a laugh and a sob. "So much better than okay." They rolled so they were lying on their sides, and Lauren's hands roamed everywhere.

There was a relaxing, a loosening of Lauren's limbs, that felt to Cara like a greater degree of comfort in their being together. Cara relaxed too and marveled at the lack of awkwardness that usually accompanied first encounters, especially after their inauspicious beginning. Lauren nudged her onto her back and straddled her, then bent as if to kiss again, but then she paused for a moment and simply gazed at Cara. Lauren was so incredibly beautiful looming over her like this. Cara reached up and brushed her fingers over her cheek.

Lauren kept her eyes on Cara's and reached to cover her nipple. Cara drew in a breath, expecting it but still not ready for how it felt, the rigid tip pebbling beneath the warmth of Lauren's hand. She raised her body to meet Lauren's mouth as it closed around her. When her hot, wet tongue rasped over Cara it sent jolts of electricity throughout her body. Lauren became preoccupied with her breasts and tended to them for many minutes until Cara couldn't stand the neglect of her other body parts. "Lauren, please," she gasped., She took hold of one of Lauren's hands and pushed it down her belly.

Lauren moved lower and situated herself between Cara's thighs. She glanced at her with a sly smile. Cara felt Lauren's fingers gently moving up her thighs, exploring, getting closer, and then Lauren lowered her head and her hot flat tongue swiped slowly and forcefully up her labia, the stroke ending just shy of her clit. Cara's whole body throbbed in anticipation.

"My God, that's good. More please," Cara urged her. She rose up on her elbows so she could enjoy the erotic sight of Lauren's head buried between her legs.

Lauren lifted her head, a lazy grin covering her features. "A lick and a promise."

"What?"

"A lick and a promise. I just realized how dirty that sounds." She lapsed into giggles.

Cara blinked. She liked the relaxed pleasure she saw on Lauren's face, but the timing of her little insight was killing her. "Seriously? You want to have a chat about this now? At this exact moment?"

Lauren seemed to realize how her priorities had wandered. "No." She crawled up Cara's body and resettled herself against Cara's torso, smushing their breasts together, looking her in the eye. "I wasn't sure how this was going to go, but it's great, and you're great. I'm really comfortable with you and you're getting me uncensored and a little random. I hope that's okay."

Cara instantly turned to mush. She wondered if her eyes had become little hearts as she gazed at Lauren's contrite expression. "Sure," was all she could manage in the face of all that adorableness.

Lauren blew a breath up toward the wispy tendrils that had fallen across her forehead. "And now that I've brought things to a lurching halt, do you want me to continue? I feel like we were just getting to the good part."

"Of course, I want you to continue. I was, like, seconds away from the good part."

"We're gonna get back there." Lauren grabbed Cara's face and gave her a long kiss. It had the intended effect of reigniting Cara's hunger for her. She smiled and said, "I have to deliver on the promise of that lick."

"That was absolutely terrible," Cara complained good-naturedly. "You owe me an orgasm for that. No, I want two orgasms."

"Coming right up."

"Oh God, with the puns now."

"Ha. I didn't even mean that one." Lauren's hand drifted down between Cara's legs, cupping her sex and squeezing in a commanding sort of way, causing Cara to take in a breath and hold it. "And you're going to lose count of the number of orgasms you're about to get."

Cara's skin felt like it was burning up and she grabbed on to the sheets.

Lauren slowly started to rub, moving her palm in concentric circles. Cara didn't know how she did it, but in a moment, she was back at the precipice, getting closer and closer to the edge. Lauren whispered, "Don't forget to breathe."

Cara exhaled violently and on the intake of another breath felt Lauren plunge two fingers inside her. "Yes," she hissed. Lauren took one of Cara's nipples in her mouth and her tongue rasped over it in the same rhythm with which her fingers moved. Cara clenched the sheets, her world distilled down to Lauren's hand and the way it was filling her up, and when Lauren's thumb caressed her just where all her nerve endings were screaming for resolution, it became all too much and she cried out and let go, her orgasm reverberating in what felt like every direction.

❖

Lauren watched Cara recover from orgasm one, wanting to gather her into her arms and revel in her lush femininity, but unsure where the intimacy lines were drawn after all their negotiations. She gave in and allowed herself to snuggle down next to Cara as her breathing returned to normal, her head on her shoulder, rubbing gentle circles on her belly. She had missed this. Not just the act of sex, but also the closeness, the cuddling, the warmth of a woman's body. How was sex not supposed to be intimate and emotional? She didn't know if she could do this. But then Cara gazed at her with a look of pure satisfaction and Lauren thought she could at least try.

"That was so good. Was that a strategy for drawing out the anticipation? It really worked." She grasped Lauren's butt and gave it a playful slap. "But it was pretty cheeky."

Lauren groaned. "Now who's punning?"

"Heh, couldn't help myself." Cara slid her hand over Lauren's ass, and it felt really good. She rolled Lauren onto her back and settled herself between Lauren's legs. She palmed Lauren's breasts, using her thumbs to caress her nipples. She took them between her fingers and rolled them and pulled gently at first, then a little harder as they grew firmer.

This turned Lauren on like nothing else and she started to breathe heavily through her mouth. "That feels amazing," she said, jerking her hips upward to urge some contact with Cara's body.

Cara trailed her fingertips slowly down Lauren's stomach and came to rest on her upper thighs, mere inches from the apex of sensation. She raised gleaming eyes to Lauren. "Now, observe my technique. I'm going to go down on you, and I will not stop to make conversation. I'm getting right down to business."

Lauren smiled. "I appreciate that."

But Cara must have had a different definition of what that meant, proceeding to draw Lauren out onto the knife-edge of release and leaving her to dangle for far too long. Lauren felt the lightest whisper of tongue against her clit and her pelvis involuntarily strained upward, craving more. But Cara withdrew, in total control now, her tongue a tool of torture that did not revisit her clit in favor of exploring every other millimeter of Lauren's core, alternating between firm, direct contact and barely there teasing that drove her insane with need. Cara would not be rushed, and just when Lauren opened her mouth to beg, Cara showed mercy and returned to her neglected clit and rewarded it for its patience, tongue swirling and lips enveloping her in a searing, wet heat.

"Oh my God, Cara," Lauren's body went rigid while her orgasm ripped through her. She lay there as the blood thundering through her veins slowly quieted, and she opened her eyes to find Cara, her arm propped on Lauren's belly with her chin resting on her arm, watching her with an expression Lauren could only describe as sweetly smug.

"See? When your mouth is too busy for chitchat, it's zero to orgasm in no time."

"I wasn't exactly starting at zero, you know." Lauren pushed her fingers through Cara's hair, loving the feel of it. The intensity of her attachment to this woman already seemed beyond what was safe. "Do you know how hot I get when I'm making you come? You're so beautiful and responsive, and you feel incredible. I was ninety percent there."

For a moment, Cara looked stunned at Lauren's words.

Lauren froze. Too earnest. Too much feeling for an encounter that wasn't supposed to have any. But was she not supposed to be honest?

Cara waggled her eyebrows. "So it's not my astounding sexual prowess?"

"You do have a masterful technique." Lauren said, relieved at Cara's ability to adjust the tone between them.

"Thank you. That's all I wanted to hear."

Lauren gave Cara an emphatic kiss. "Ready for orgasm number two?"

❖

Cara woke when she sensed Lauren sit up and swing her legs to the floor. The clock read just after three a.m. They had overcome the fits and starts of their first time and traded orgasms long into the night, and had only been sleeping for about an hour. Maybe Lauren was awakened by the clanging of the garbage truck dropping dumpsters back onto the pavement outside. "What is it?" she asked, laying a hand on Lauren's lower back.

"I have to go. I have an early squash game." Lauren reached for her skirt on the floor and shook it a few times to get the wrinkles out.

"Squash? Really?"

Lauren sighed and laid the skirt across her lap. "No, not really. That's a line from *When Harry Met Sally*."

Cara grunted in amusement and sat up against the headboard. "You don't need an excuse. You can go whenever you like. But if you want to go now, may I walk you to your door?"

Lauren turned to her in surprise. "That has to be at least a forty-minute walk. You want to walk me home?"

"Not really. I'd rather get some sleep, and you're absolutely welcome to stay. But it's late, and you offered the other night, so I want to return the favor. Should I get dressed?"

She scooched up the bed and sat next to Cara, flinging her skirt back to the floor. "I don't want to leave. I'm exhausted. And your bed is super comfortable."

"Then stay."

"I feel like if I stay, that's not a friend-sex decision."

"Who says?"

"I have no idea." Lauren's voice sounded frustrated. "I don't know what I'm doing. I've never had a friend with benefits. Have you?"

"No. I had a relationship once that turned into a friends-with-benefits situation, but I entered into it thinking it was love."

"Oh, that sucks."

"We grew apart. Then she joined the Peace Corps and broke up with me. I sometimes wonder if she joined the Peace Corps in order to break up with me." Cara shook her head. "She didn't have to go that far."

"Back in school, it was kind of understood we were only messing around. We called it dating, but it was more about whose bed you were going to sleep in. No one wanted to have a relationship or whatever, except maybe Ayumi." Lauren slid back beneath the covers. "I guess we were all friends with benefits back then. It feels different now."

"You know, I'm really glad I didn't know about you boarding girls' sex-capades."

"You didn't miss anything. It was a lot of fumbling around, if you want to know the truth. After high school, things changed for me. I haven't had many real relationships. Only two," she confessed. "Both were disastrous. So be forewarned—if I screw up sometimes, it doesn't have anything to do with you. I think it's because I don't have all that much practice with casual sex."

Cara put her arm around Lauren. "Come on, let's lie down. I'll be the big spoon." She snuggled in close, resting a hand on her waist, savoring how right it felt to have her in her arms. "If we're making confessions, I should tell you I was nervous about doing this with you."

"You were? I couldn't tell."

"I think I was nervous to be intimate with Lauren Havemayer, my high school crush. She was an idea of a girl who didn't exist. Sometime since the reunion, you became Lauren the person. I hope that doesn't make you feel weird."

"The girl I was in high school doesn't exist anymore anyway. All I know is that right now, I feel comfortable with you. And sleepy." Lauren pulled Cara's arm tight around her.

"We don't have to decide right now how to make this work. We'll figure it out as we go."

"Okay, sounds good." In minutes, she had drifted off again.

Cara nuzzled her face into Lauren's hair, breathing in the clean scent of shampoo and soap. Lauren was right about one thing—it did feel different. And after they smoothed over the bumps in the beginning, the rest of their lovemaking had felt anything but casual to Cara. She tried to put it out of her mind and rest, but it was a long time before sleep found her.

CHAPTER ELEVEN

L auren's Uber glided over the Willis Avenue Bridge and into the Bronx. It had been a week since she'd seen Cara, and their only contact had been the text messages that organized Lauren's visit to Cara's school.

The car negotiated a major thoroughfare lined with businesses and housing. Bodegas, check-cashing places, and hair salons occupied bottom floors of aging tenement buildings, and dollar stores and schools seemed to figure more numerously than on the Upper East Side. A working-class area with a few more bars across the windows and doors of the residences. Lauren saw the occasional colorful graffitied mural dedicated to a deceased resident, and some type of Latin music blared from a car window. Pedestrians went about their business in the chilly sunshine.

Lauren had only ventured into the Bronx for the occasional ball game at Yankee Stadium, but Cara's school was in an entirely different part of the borough and she had felt herself maintaining a heightened sense of vigilance. She was now relieved by the absence of the clichés of drug use and gang activity she had feared she would see, and ashamed for believing the worst of a neighborhood she had never visited.

When she arrived at Cara's school, she entered through monolithic windowless doors and was hit by that unmistakable school smell. Some things must be the same all over. She couldn't describe what it smelled like, but she knew instantly she was in a school. After undergoing a security check that was as thorough as the airport's, she was escorted to an elevator by a friendly security guard who gave her directions to the main office for Cara's school. She was surprised to learn there were three schools in the building.

Her stomach fluttered at the thought of seeing Cara again. Lauren hoped they could go out again after her visit with the AP students. This was the last class of the day, and it was Friday. Surely, Cara could leave after that. Isn't that why people became teachers? So their workday ended at three in the afternoon? She heard her name as she exited the elevator.

"Security let me know you were here." Cara jogged down the hall to meet her. Her hair was pulled back and she wore jeans and a black polo shirt with SBCP STAFF embroidered on the left breast. So cute and teachery.

Cara led her down the hall, eyeing Lauren up and down. As they walked, she said in a low voice, "You look fantastic. My students are going to be bowled over by you."

Lauren's outfit was all neutral tones of gray and black. She wore a soft heather gray turtleneck sweater beneath a darker gray herringbone tweed blazer with slim black trousers and high black boots, identical to her brown ones in all but color. She followed Cara into her empty classroom just as she heard a discordant recorded blare followed by youthful shouts and the squeak of sneakers on linoleum. "Have a seat here and I'll be back. I have to be at my door in the hallway during the period transitions."

Lauren sat at a grouping of six desks set up into a U-shape in front of the white board. She heard Cara's raised voice say, "I see you, Oscar, but I didn't see you during first period today." There were many more desks pushed away from the arrangement near the board. The walls were lined with bookshelves and posters, and a bulletin board with student essays pinned to it in the back of the room. It was bright, neat, and friendly, much like Cara herself.

Two girls came in together talking loudly until they saw Lauren sitting there. They clammed up and sat across from her in the opposite bend of the U. One of them pulled out her phone and took a picture of the white board. Another girl and a boy entered and sat down, writing the homework assignment Cara had projected onto the SMART Board into their notebooks. The boy observed Lauren. "You're here for the painting thing?"

Lauren nodded and was startled by the blaring of the bell again. It was an unpleasant sound more appropriate for a prison than a school. Cara reentered the room and closed the door.

"Good afternoon, people." Cara paused as she bustled by the desks to stand near the computer connected to the SMART Board. "Maritza, did you copy the homework assignment?" Cara said this to the only student not writing. She was also the one who had taken the photo.

"Yes," she said, flicking a glance at Lauren.

"Okay, good. You remember yesterday I said we would have a visitor today, right? This is Ms. Havemayer. She works at the Metropolitan Museum of Art."

"You can call me Lauren."

The students nodded and said hi. The door opened and another student came in.

"Sign the late log, please, Miguel," Cara said calmly, but Lauren thought she could detect a hint of exasperation in her voice. Miguel signed the log and took the seat next to Lauren.

Lauren wrote down his name, plus the other names she had heard, fashioning a seating chart for her reference.

Cara ran through the rest of their names for Lauren and then addressed the class. "Ms. Havemayer will help us analyze a piece of art today. You might remember the last time we did this, it didn't go so well, so I brought in someone knowledgeable to help us."

Miguel turned to Lauren. "You look like a professor. Are you a professor?" All the students waited for her answer.

"No, I'm an assistant curator."

"Ms. Havemayer has enough education to be a professor," Cara said. With a hint of pride in her voice, she added, "She recently earned her PhD in art history."

"How many years does it take to get that degree?" Yenifer asked.

"Four years to get my bachelor's, and then the master's and PhD was another six."

"That's just as long as it takes to be a doctor." The girl called Fatoumata seemed astonished by that.

"Technically, we should be calling her Dr. Havemayer," Cara said. "She's an expert in her field. She's earned it."

"You can just call me Lauren. Cara, I mean, Ms. Talarico, let's show them the painting." Lauren passed out color copies of the painting she had printed at work on placemat-sized card stock, the colors as vibrant as the original hanging on the wall at MoMA. "Has anyone seen this before?"

There were a few nodding heads. Rashard said, "It's van Gogh. It's my uncle's favorite. He has a tie with this on it."

"A tie?" Maritza sounded dubious. "Like a tie, tie?" She mimed a necktie down the front of her shirt.

"Yeah." Rashard was defensive.

"Isn't he the one who cut off his ear?" Miguel asked.

"What? Why did he do that?" Yenifer asked.

"Yes, Miguel," Lauren answered. "The artist is Vincent van Gogh and the title of this piece is *The Starry Night*."

Yenifer wrote this in her notebook. Fatoumata noticed and started writing, too.

"Why don't we start with the artist? Besides the fact that he cut his ear off, what else do we know about him?" Lauren surveyed the students.

"He also painted sunflowers," Miguel said. "And he was crazy. His brother had to take care of him."

"Is he right?" Maritza turned to Lauren. "How do you know all that?" she asked him.

"Because we saw the sunflowers in art sophomore year. You were in my class."

"We did? I don't remember that."

"Obviously," Miguel muttered.

Lauren took command of the conversation. "We can say with some certainty that he was mentally ill. We don't say crazy. He did enjoy a close relationship with his brother, Theo, and Theo tried to help him as much as he could, but ultimately, Vincent was unable to overcome his illness and committed suicide at the age of thirty-seven. Some say genius and madness go hand in hand, and it's possible van Gogh achieved his highly original work only because of his mental illness."

"How did he do it?" Fatoumata asked.

"Do what?" Lauren said. "Oh, he shot himself." Of course the students were interested in the more lurid parts of van Gogh's life story.

"Was chopping off his ear another suicide attempt?" asked Yenifer.

Lauren knew their curiosity needed to be satisfied before they moved on, but she didn't want to get into all the theories. "No, most historians agree it was a result of his illness, but the reasons for it are unclear. If we accept he was in the midst of a complete mental breakdown, perhaps in his mad rationalization, mutilating himself was the only thing that could alleviate the pain he was suffering."

Each student gazed at her with rapt attention. Cara slid onto one of the desks in the back, content to spectate as Lauren ran the lesson.

"That's what art is—the expression of emotion or ideas in a visual way. Sometimes it's beautiful. Sometimes it's beyond grotesque. Van Gogh was compelled to give the world this painting. Now we can try to figure out what he was trying to say with it."

Yenifer wrote furiously in her notebook.

Lauren paused to transition from talking about the artist to the art. "When I first started looking at art, I was given some advice. Look at the piece for at least a minute, more if you can, and let your mind relax, try and notice everything. A minute can be a long time, so force yourself if you have to. Then share what you've noticed with someone else. They will have certainly noticed something you haven't, and you will each learn from the other."

She waited a good minute or two. Rashard caught her eye and she nodded to him.

"That round part in the middle reminds me of a yin and yang symbol." Maritza raised her head and nodded at Rashard.

"And what does the yin and yang mean, Rashard?" Lauren asked.

Rashard struggled to put his thoughts into words. "It's like the connection of two things that don't go together?"

"Good. Now, we can't be sure this is what van Gogh meant when he placed that whirling entity in the exact center of the canvas, but it sure looks like a yin and yang symbol to me, too. Why would van Gogh do this?" She regarded the others, who gazed blankly back at her. "And remember, the beauty of interpreting art is that there is no right or wrong, there is only what you can back up with reasoning and evidence."

Fatoumata sat back. "You sound like Miss. She says that about every poem we read." She looked back at Cara, who grinned and wiggled her eyebrows at her.

"But why are there all those swirls in the sky? The sky doesn't really look like that," Yenifer said.

"And the moon isn't that giant or that yellow," Miguel countered. "So what? He's not being literal."

"True." Lauren glanced at Miguel, but leaned toward Yenifer, challenging her. "What do you think, Yenifer? What is he trying to convey by painting the sky that way?"

Yenifer considered the picture. "To me it looks like wind."

"Me too. I was going to say that," Fatoumata added.

"Yes! Movement." Lauren couldn't contain her excitement. "You can't see it very well from this two-dimensional piece of paper, but van Gogh laid the paint on really thickly with a palette knife to suggest texture and depth, and certainly that idea of movement. Now the sky is in motion somehow. What about the rest of the canvas?"

Rashard said, "The town at the bottom looks quiet and still."

"It should be," Maritza said. "It's nighttime."

"Why the contrast between the two?" Lauren asked.

"What's the deal with the trees?" Miguel said. "Why are they even there?"

"And why is the whole thing, like, blue?" Fatoumata chimed in. "The sky should be black."

"Not always," Rashard said.

There was a lull in the conversation. Lauren waited, curious about what they would say next.

After a moment, Cara spoke from behind them. "Symbols, people. We've talked about color symbolism. What did blue represent in *Gatsby*?" What do trees represent?"

Lauren, exhilarated, listened to the buzz of voices around her as the students started conjecturing about trees and the color blue. A push in the right direction and they were leaping to their own interpretations.

"All right." Cara reined them back in after a minute or two, looking at her watch. "Take three minutes. Sum up any important points from the discussion in your notebooks that might help with your analysis of the poem."

"What poem?" Rashard's wary expression amused Lauren.

"The one you are about to read. And analyze. And write an essay about." Cara slid off the desk and passed out copies of "The Starry Night," by Anne Sexton.

There was a murmur of dissension but only Maritza grumbled, "Always an essay in this class."

"I can add to that. How about revisions of your sonnet essays, too?" Cara shot back, warning in her voice.

The muttering stopped and they focused on the poem.

Lauren grimaced at Maritza in sympathy. Mean teacher. She looked up as Cara dropped a poem on her desk. The perceptive look on her face almost made Lauren bust out laughing.

"Should we read it aloud?" Cara asked into the silence.

"Just let us read it, Miss."

After a moment, Maritza announced, "The speaker wants to commit suicide, just like van Gogh. The first two stanzas end with 'I want to die.'"

"Go deeper," Cara said. "What is the imagery telling you?" She pushed a chair next to Yenifer's desk and entered the discussion.

Lauren took a mental step back and allowed their conversation to wash over her. Her gratitude to Cara for asking her to be here felt like a physical weight in her chest. She loved her solitary days in the archive, but being the catalyst for these kids flinging around their ideas about art felt absolutely amazing.

Before she knew it, that horrid blare sounded again and class was over. Desks screeched across the floor and were put back in rows. Cara called out reminders about homework and wishes for a good weekend as students exited. Miguel nodded at Lauren as he slouched out of the room. Yenifer approached with a shy smile.

"Thank you, Miss. That was really great." Her rolled up copy of the painting was held carefully in her hands.

"You're welcome, Yenifer. I'm glad you got something out of it."

"What museum do you work at?"

"The Met. On Eighty-Second and Fifth. You should come visit."

"I want to. I've only been to the Natural History Museum."

"Maybe Ms. Talarico could bring you on a class trip."

Yenifer's eyes lit up. "Yeah! That would be so great."

Maritza stuck her head back in the room. "Yeni, let's go." She cut her eyes at Lauren. "Bye, Miss."

Cara came over and gripped her forearm. "You were great. They were so into it."

It warmed Lauren from head to toe to be the object of Cara's admiration. "I guess it went pretty well."

"It was fantastic," Cara crowed. "That's what I wanted for the Brueghel thing. You are really good at your job."

"You're not too bad yourself, Miss."

"Thanks, Miss." Cara's eyes sparkled. "Don't ask me where the *miss* business comes from. It's a New York thing, I think. I try not to let it bother me, but sometimes it seriously bugs."

"Students in the UK call their teachers Miss and Sir. I heard them all the time in the gallery that was connected to my program."

"Huh. Who knew? I don't think it would ever fly at Perry Bidwell." She took Lauren's hand and squeezed it. "Thanks again for coming today. The whole lesson was terrific."

"You're welcome. Want to go somewhere and celebrate how terrific it was?"

Cara's face fell. "I wish I could, but I have a bunch of mock Regents exams to grade. I also said I would put in an appearance at happy hour later."

"It's okay. I shouldn't have assumed." Lauren's disappointment must have shown on her face.

"I'm really sorry. Do you want to do something after? I could be done around six or seven, and then we'd have the rest of the night." Cara's cajoling took on a seductive tone. "You deserve a reward for a job well done here today."

Lauren would wait all night on the promise implied in the husky timbre of Cara's voice, that playful look in her eyes right now. "Why don't you come to my place when you're free. I'll feed you dinner and then we can see what we want to do."

Cara took a step closer and lowered her voice. "How come this feels like I'm getting the reward?"

"Rewards are good, aren't they? For both the rewarder and the rewarded." Lauren held Cara's gaze for as long as she dared without dragging her into her arms.

"They all get a six," Cara blurted.

"What?" Lauren broke eye contact and reached for her portfolio with reluctance.

"That's the highest grade on the essay rubric. I'll just give them all sixes."

Lauren laughed. "That would definitely speed up the process."

"Come on, I'll get the elevator for you."

Lauren could wait the few hours for Cara to do whatever she needed to do. The prospect of having her company for the rest of the evening was more than enough to sustain her patience.

CHAPTER TWELVE

Cara ambled down one of the most pristine city sidewalks she'd ever seen. Lauren's address was high on Fifth Avenue with Central Park right across the street. Gajillionaire's Row. Everything was clean and quiet. Even the cars drifted down the street in a hush. Still several steps away from the entrance of a stately prewar limestone building, the doorman opened the art deco doors for her. She crossed the palatial lobby to the security desk and received a smile from the older gentleman standing behind it.

"Good evening. Which apartment?"

She frowned at the text Lauren had sent and its lack of an apartment number. "All it says is PH." Cara only realized as she said it that PH meant penthouse.

"Are you Cara?" At her nod, his smile grew wider. "I'm Raoul. Ms. Havemayer told us to expect you. May I see some ID?"

After the ID check, Cara followed Raoul to the bank of elevators. He inserted a key into the control panel to access the penthouse level, then left her with another smile.

When the elevator opened, Cara found herself inside Lauren's apartment. She took a cautious step into a spacious, high-ceilinged atrium and was confronted by a large piece of art hung directly across from the elevator. It drew her in, and her first impression was of comfort coupled with a feeling of intruding on a private and profound moment. Cara got lost in her examination of the work.

"Do you love it?"

Cara jumped and held her hand to her heart. "You scared me."

"Sorry." Lauren stood a few feet away, looking scrumptious in gray yoga pants and a baggy, navy, hooded sweatshirt featuring the Yale bulldog on the front. She leaned against the double-sized doorframe and gazed at the art. "It's my father's most recent purchase."

"Who's the artist?"

"Njideka Akunyili Crosby. She's from Nigeria but lives and works out of Los Angeles."

"It's so…" Cara was lost for words.

"Intimate?"

"Exactly."

Lauren moved to stand next to her. Side by side, they absorbed the work. The canvas depicted a Black woman sitting upright in a bed while a white man passively reclined against her. She held him with compassion and affection. And it was not simply a painting. What looked like photos and newsprint were layered within the composition. It looked like a collage but was really an image of a collage. Cara had never seen anything like it.

"Every day I come home and stare at it for a while."

"I would, too." Cara dragged her eyes from the piece to Lauren. Cara wanted to kiss her but felt shy and floundered for something to say. "Did you tell him to buy this?"

Lauren nodded. "I'm starting to advise him. This replaced a Francis Bacon he finally sold. I disliked it intensely." She gave Cara a confiding look. "Truthfully, it was downright ugly."

Cara giggled in surprise. "He buys stuff you don't like?"

"Let me take your coat and bag." Lauren stowed them in the closet. "Art is an investment to him. He calls it a class of asset." She mimed vomiting by sticking her finger down her throat.

"Isn't that how everyone thinks?" Cara didn't know much about art, but she did know that people wanted to buy low and sell high.

"Not me. My brain understands the function of the art market, of course." Lauren led Cara down a corridor lined with more art and into the kitchen. "But my heart wants beauty."

It seemed such a clean, straightforward declaration. Cara had respect for Lauren's forthrightness, if not a little jealousy of it. She was probably the only person Cara knew who had the freedom to pursue her heart's desire.

"There is undeniable beauty in that piece. It deserves to be seen and admired by many. How can a gold toilet or a dead shark submerged in a tank of formaldehyde compare to that work of exquisite splendor? Sit here." Lauren pulled a stool out from under the large kitchen island.

"I'm intrigued. There is a lot about what you just said that I want to address." Cara looked around the kitchen. Not only was it about three times the size of her entire apartment, it was also homey, comfortable and warm.

An array of copper and stainless steel cookware hung above the island. Aged, cream-colored rectangular tiles—maybe original—covered the backsplash and ran up two of the walls to the ceiling. The room had been renovated at some point and contained the requisite high-end appliances featured in all the Real Housewives' homes. At the far end along a bank of windows was a breakfast nook with a banquette upholstered in a pretty floral fabric and an oak dining table that could seat six.

"Before we start the debate, are you hungry?"

"Starving."

"Let's see what we have." Lauren went to the fridge and removed several plastic containers from its cavernous depths.

"Wait a minute. I thought you said you were going to cook for me?"

"I believe I said I would feed you." Lauren looked back at her with a grin. "If you took that to mean I would be doing the cooking, that's on you. Besides, you really don't want me to cook."

"You're feeding me leftover takeout?"

"God, no." Lauren's scandalized expression made Cara smile. "This is food prepared earlier today by the marvelous Paloma. She's been with my family since I was around six, and her cooking will knock your socks off. She's the best."

Cara stood on the rungs of the stool and leaned over the island while she looked into the containers.

"We have roasted brussels sprouts, braised carrots and parsnips, yum. Oh, here's some chicken Marsala. My dad loves this. And buttered farro. That's a well-balanced meal, right? Should I just make us a few plates?"

"Won't your father want the chicken? Should we save it for him?"

"He's out of town on business. Don't worry about him."

While Lauren assembled their meal, Cara inspected the creamy tiles laid in a running bond pattern on the wall adjacent to the refrigerator. She ran a finger over the smooth but imperfect glazing. It really did look old, and handmade. It was a traditional design decision, but there was something about its integration into the rest of the room that evoked a feeling of rightness in Cara. "Is this tile original to the building?"

Lauren looked up from her task. "I don't think so. The building is from the nineteen twenties. I think that tile is from the forties."

"It's in beautiful condition."

"This tile behind me is new." Lauren gestured to the backsplash. "When we redid the kitchen my dad insisted the new tile match the original. I think he drove the designer a little bit crazy."

The room was clad in more tile than was typical of modern kitchens, which could have seemed dated or old-fashioned to some, but Cara loved it. She moved to the backsplash and leaned in to inspect the cool, smooth material of the new tile. It looked and felt identical. When she turned around she thought she saw Lauren inspecting her ass.

"You have an interest in kitchen design?" Her eyes were now fixed on Cara's face.

"I love tile. My Instagram is filled with kitchen and bathroom designers and tile companies. A bit dorky, I know. It's my dream to own a home that has tile everywhere. Even my bedroom."

"In the bedroom? Why?"

"So I can enjoy it. Bathrooms and kitchens are rooms of utility. You make use of them, and then you go to some other room. I'll be spending a lot of time in the bedroom. What better place to enjoy it?"

Lauren's smile was indulgent. "Sounds logical."

Cara had probably exposed enough of her weirdness for the moment. "What can I do to help?"

"Will you open the wine? There are glasses in the cabinet next to the sink." Lauren passed her a bottle and a corkscrew. "How was happy hour?"

Cara glanced at the bottle. The label said Châteauneuf-du-Pape, but Cara didn't know if that was the winery or the type of grape. The bottle had crossed keys embedded in its green glass. It was French and probably expensive. "It was fun. We went to Iggy's on Seventy-Sixth. It's kind of a dive, but the drinks are cheap, and they have karaoke during happy hour."

"Never done it."

"How can you live in the world and not have done karaoke at least once in your life? You should try it. Live a little, Havemayer."

"I'm a God-awful singer. I don't even sing in the shower, so it's not something I would ever seek out on my own. I might go with other people if I were ever invited. To watch, not to sing."

Was that a dig at me? Did Lauren want to go with her to teacher happy hour? "The quality of your singing voice is not the point. You should have heard some of the off-key doozies performed today, mine included. It's just a way to blow off some steam and have fun."

"You sang?"

"Sure. I have a couple of go-to songs that fit my three-note range. Napkins? Silverware?"

Lauren handed them over. "What did you sing?"

"Backstreet Boys."

"Really? Which song?"

"'I Want It That Way,'" Cara said, as if it were the most obvious thing in the world.

"Of course." Lauren nodded and laughed. "I would have loved to have seen that. It's nice you do that with your coworkers."

"You don't do that at the Met?" Cara set the table and poured the wine.

"I haven't heard of anyone going for drinks. I'm still trying to figure things out there." Lauren brought their plates to the table and they sat.

She lifted her wine glass and Cara tapped it with her own before she took a sip. It unfurled over her palate with a luscious intensity unlike anything she'd ever tasted, bold in its fruitiness with something earthy and spicy underneath. It was a revelation. Where had this wine been all her life? Probably in some exclusive shop with lots of other things she couldn't afford.

She put her glass down and pushed it across the table so it was out of reach and focused on Lauren. Was she struggling to socialize at work? Cara wondered if they should talk about it, but she didn't want to embarrass her. And maybe it was a violation of their agreement. Would she be overstepping by bringing it up? Returning to their previous topic seemed safer. "Can we talk about the shark in formaldehyde?"

"Let's. I love a good shark conversation."

"The food is terrific, by the way. My compliments to, um…"

"Paloma."

"Right, Paloma." Cara skipped over the novelty of eating food prepared by a private chef and returned to the subject at hand. "Even though I don't know much about art, I have heard about the shark."

"Everyone has. That was Hirst's purpose." Lauren's disparagement was obvious.

"How is it art? I don't get it. He didn't create the shark."

"He didn't even catch it. He commissioned a fisherman to catch it."

"All he did was put it in a glass case filled with formaldehyde?"

"And he didn't even do it properly either. It started to decompose so he had to do it all over again with another shark. Although I guess we can't fault him for that because who knows how to preserve a dead shark?"

"I can fault him for that." Cara was indignant. "Why bother killing those sharks at all? Just so some rich guy could own it and call it art?"

"It's conceptual. He meant for viewers to create their own meaning from it."

"So he never has to explain it. That's convenient."

Lauren put down her fork and rested her forearms on the table. "Art is my business, so I have to be knowledgeable about it, and I could tell you about the last one hundred years of art, and how Marcel Duchamp submitted a urinal to an art show in 1917 and called it *Fountain* and changed the art world forever, but I really can't bring myself to care about it much."

Cara nodded in understanding.

"There's a place for that in art, where the idea is more important than the object, but it's not what I want to devote my life to. I may be unfashionable and prosaic, but the art I want to spend time looking at, thinking about, and sharing with others is almost always going to be technique driven, talent-based, and beautiful."

Cara let that sink in. Most of it made sense to her. "But not everything from before the last one hundred years is beautiful. What about Hieronymus Bosch? My uncle Rick had a coffee table book of his art that I made the mistake of opening when I was a kid. Gave me nightmares."

"Interesting." Lauren looked as eager as she did during Cara's class when she was coaxing Yenifer to think critically. "I would argue there is immense beauty in Bosch's work, even though much of it is monstrous and surreal. How else could a man who lived over five hundred years ago explain the consequences of immorality to a humanity that believed in a vengeful god? He was using his talent and technique to warn people away from the wages of sin."

"So context is everything." Cara wanted to fan herself. Lauren getting enthusiastic about art was incredibly hot.

"Exactly."

"You've convinced me. Maybe I should ask Uncle Rick if I could look at it again."

"Sorry, I get carried away sometimes." Lauren's bashfulness was beyond cute.

"Please, I love hearing you talk about art. But what you said before—in your line of work, it's considered unfashionable to appreciate beautiful things?"

"The market drives fashion, and that's not where the market is currently. The auctions are filled with conceptual pieces selling for hyper-inflated prices. Beauty is hardly considered in today's market." Lauren picked up her wine but didn't take a sip. "But who's to say how beauty will be defined one hundred years from now? Nobody was in love with *Starry Night* when van Gogh first painted it. Maybe Damien Hirst is just ahead of his time. If or when sharks go extinct, people may believe his work to be the most beautiful example of foresight the world has ever known."

"That's the most depressing thing I've heard today. You're such a buzz kill."

"I guess I am." Lauren seemed resigned.

Cara playfully nudged her in the arm. "I was kidding. Did your father buy that new piece in the hallway from an auction?"

Lauren sighed. "I know where you're going with this."

"Do you?" Cara was all innocence.

"You're about to point out the contradiction in what I said earlier. I realized it almost as soon as I said it. I was hoping you hadn't noticed. Yes, he bought it at Sotheby's."

The fact that Lauren knew where she was going did not deter Cara from making her point. "And the seller was another collector, not the artist, right?"

"Yes."

"So the profit from the sale didn't go to this Nigerian artist. It went to some other rich person, an art flipper, if you will."

Lauren nodded.

"And when you said that piece deserved to be seen by many..." Cara trailed off.

Lauren's wry smile had a pensive edge to it. "I know. It should be hanging in a museum so the whole world can see it, but instead it's hanging in my father's house where only a handful of people will get that privilege."

Cara moved closer. It was obvious Lauren was conflicted by the idea, and maybe annoyed with her. "Are you upset that I went there?"

"No, you haven't said anything I haven't told myself a million times. And my very weak justification is that it will likely end up in a museum some day, and my family is merely its steward for a little while."

Cara had made a tactical error. They were now physically closer than they had been all evening, but Lauren seemed far away from her.

"One of the reasons I wanted to curate on the institutional level was to contribute somehow, to maybe offset even just slightly what is currently happening in the art world, with so many people buying as investments and then storing their art in warehouses where absolutely no one gets to appreciate it. I'm not quite sure how to do that, though."

"I understand. I should have kept my big mouth shut."

Lauren drew back and looked her in the eye. "Don't say that. I don't want you to censor yourself, and I won't with you. We should be honest with each other."

"Good, because in most circumstances, it would be really hard for me to not tell you how I feel. It's kind of my thing. Let's shake on it." Glad for any opportunity to touch Lauren, Cara stuck out her hand and Lauren readily shook it. "Come on. Let's clean up and then you can show me your home. What else do you have that I won't see in a museum?" She deliberately caught Lauren's eye and let her see the playfulness in her own.

Lauren offered her a rueful smile. "How about we start with my dishwasher? I don't think we'll find that in a museum."

"I heard Damien Hirst is installing one at the Guggenheim."

The dishes only took a few minutes, after which they wandered through the expansive, well-appointed apartment as Lauren described the art on the walls. Cara recognized a Warhol and a Hockney in the formal dining room, and listened while Lauren geeked out over a smallish landscape which hung over the fireplace in what Lauren called the drawing room, as if she were living in Rosings Park. That one turned out to be by Edward Hopper.

They had traversed a wearisome number of rooms, many of them looking as if they had recently been photographed for *Architectural Digest*, cold and lifeless. The rest of the art was not familiar to her, and she dutifully admired them when expected to, but she had moved on to admiring Lauren: her finger as it sketched a shape in the air, her lips as she spoke about Cubism, and the outline of her thigh in those yoga pants. It was becoming harder to study the art when all she wanted was to gaze at Lauren.

The room they now entered seemed different. It was richly furnished, yes, but it was not a showpiece torn from the pages of a fancy shelter magazine. It felt comfortable and lived in, and the couch cushions were smushed on one side. Cara could see it was the best vantage point for watching TV. Magazines and mail were scattered on the coffee table and family photos sat on the baby grand piano. A room more private than public.

She listened with half an ear to whatever Lauren was saying about the Richter that hung on one wall and examined the photos on the piano. There was one of Lauren in her Perry Bidwell uniform and her parents in front of Surrey Hall on what must have been the first day of seventh grade, a near-panicked expression on poor twelve-year-old Lauren's face. Another framed photo showed teenage Lauren and a boy around the same age, taken on a ski lift, both of them wearing mirrored goggles and wide grins in the bright sunshine.

"That's my brother, Preston." Lauren looked over her shoulder at the photo.

"Handsome to your pretty," Cara said, then felt embarrassed by it. "I can't see your eyes, but I can tell you're super happy in this photo."

"Yeah, I have fun with him. I'll see him at Christmas. He lives in San Francisco and we'll meet in Deer Valley for some skiing."

"That sounds fun." Cara brought the picture with her and sat on the sofa. Lauren sat at the other end and straightened the pile of mail on the coffee table.

"Are you ready to make good on your part of the deal?" Lauren tossed an envelope at her.

"What deal?" Cara caught it. It looked like a fancy invitation.

"I help you with your class and you help me get in touch with Aunt Genevra."

"Sure, no problem."

"I did some research on my aunt and her charitable giving last year. I found a picture of her attending the Schermerhorn Foundation's Winter Gala on their website. There's no guarantee, but she might be there again this year. They were happy to send me an invite."

It was sad that Lauren had to go through all this subterfuge and couldn't simply telephone her aunt and ask for her help. "Why can't you just ask your father to intervene? This feud continued even after your grandfather passed away? Why didn't death let it die?"

"I don't know. It's just one of those weird family skeletons that nobody talks about."

Cara read the invitation. "A Winter Gala."

"Do you mind coming with me? It's December twentieth and it's black tie. I know that's not very convenient."

Cara paused. The formal dress code might present a problem. Then she dismissed it. She knew who to ask for help. "A deal's a deal. And let me say again how great you were today with my students. Thanks again for helping me."

"I'm the one who should be thanking you. I enjoyed it so much. Your students have quite a bit of personality."

"That they do." Cara got up to return the picture of Lauren and her brother to the piano. "I call them my treat at the end of the day. Some of my other classes are much more of a slog, but it always gets better during eighth period." When she returned to the sofa she sat closer to Lauren. "Would you have wanted to come with me to happy hour if I had asked you?"

Lauren looked surprised by the question, but quickly recovered. "If I had known you were singing Backstreet Boys, I definitely would have gone with you."

Cara smiled but pressed on. "You told me you were trying to get on your feet here. Would you like me to introduce you to new people so you can start making friends, widen your social circle? I mean, we're teachers, and we're all pretty much on a budget, but if you ever want to trade your remarkable bottle of red for domestic beer and drink specials, we can be lots of fun."

Silence. It was as if Cara had dropped her offer into a spinning blender, its meaning rendered an incomprehensible paste, if the furrowed brow on Lauren's face was any indication.

"What are you trying to say?" Lauren's voice held a razor's edge.

"Nothing. Just that there aren't any bottles of Chateau du whatever when I go out with my teacher friends." Cara had tried for flippant but certainly did not achieve it. The room filled with tension.

"Just spit it out, Cara. You're not talking about wine, are you?" Lauren's irritation was obvious.

"I am! You like expensive wine, right?" Cara dug herself deeper and her defensiveness increased. "Don't get mad. I was just trying to be nice."

"I have no fucking idea how much the wine cost!" Lauren blew up. "And don't tell me not to get mad. I'll get mad if I want to get mad."

"Okay." Cara threw her hands up. "Go ahead and feel your feelings."

"Now you're being patronizing. It sounds like you think I'm a snob who turns up her nose at drink specials and doesn't care to be around teachers, when I happen to like being around you, so why wouldn't I want to be around more people like you?"

Cara couldn't help yelling in her frustration. "Well, you're kind of intimidating, with the ginormous apartment, the private chef, the priceless art, and your many pairs of sexy boots in who knows how many different colors."

It could not be any clearer that this wasn't about wine.

"You think I'm intimidating?" Lauren said, hurt and disbelief coloring her tone.

Cara sighed, feeling chastened. "Let me rephrase that. You are not intimidating and you're not a snob, far from it. But all of this?" Cara gestured vaguely around the apartment. "It's a lot, especially for a scholarship girl from Paterson, New Jersey. I have a few adequacy issues."

"And you think I don't?" Her combative tone did not abate.

Cara took a moment to regroup. She moved down the couch, creating more distance between them. "Here's what I think: you're gorgeous, smart, accomplished, and rich. Why the hell would you want to spend time with me? You're also different than I imagined when I was crushing on you in school." She didn't know whether to keep going, but they agreed to be honest so she would just lay everything out there. "I like you. You're terrific, but I'm not that comfortable with your wealth and I'm struggling with how to deal with it."

Lauren didn't reply to that, she simply stared at Cara. She rose and walked to the fireplace, resting her elbow on the mantel and turning to face her. "There's that directness again."

"I don't know any other way to be."

"Is it a deal breaker?"

"Is what a deal breaker? My directness?"

"No, the wealth thing. Can we still be friends or is this something you can't get past?"

"Of course I still want to be friends, Lauren. But this is how I'm feeling. I guess my subconscious wanted you to know that. I'm sorry it came out the way it did."

Lauren exhaled slowly and returned to Cara. Instead of sitting on the sofa, she sat down on the coffee table directly in front of Cara. She leaned in, resting her elbows on her knees. "Most people like me because I have money, not in spite of it."

That's totally tragic. "I'm not most people."

"I'll say." Lauren looked away for a moment before returning her solemn gaze back to Cara. "So what do we do?"

Cara hadn't thought this far. She'd start with the obvious. "I don't have the financial means to keep up with a wealthy friend—"

Lauren broke in, agitated. "I'm not asking you to—"

"Hold on. Let me finish. I also don't have the right to tell you what to do. Agreed?"

Lauren nodded.

"Why don't we do this? When we get together, someone takes ownership. You pay for the da—I mean—times when you own them, and I'll pay for the times when I own them." They were not dating. Calling these dates was incorrect and hazardous, and Cara would do well to remember that. "For instance, you own this time right now since you asked me here and provided me with a delicious dinner and some invigorating conversation. Well, invigorating right up until we started arguing."

Lauren bit her lip. "I'm sorry about that. People have made assumptions about me all my life because of my family and it makes me angry. But I really don't want to argue with you."

Her look of contrition tugged at Cara's conscience. She *had* made assumptions. If she continued to let her biases overtake her manners and common sense, this would continue to be a problem. She needed to remember this moment and do better. "I don't want to argue with you either. Let's try to do as little of it as possible."

"Okay, that sounds very sensible. I agree to your proposal." Lauren extended both her hands and Cara took them, mirroring the sealing of their earlier agreement to be honest with each other. It was not like a handshake this time. It felt more like the grasping of something safe after encountering danger.

She hoped this would put an end to all the negotiating. The distance between them had slowly diminished as they talked, and their faces were now inches apart. The appraising way Lauren was looking at her, and the grin she was doing a poor job of hiding, made Cara lean in closer still. In an instant the atmosphere had changed from the relief of conflict resolution to the electric crackle of anticipation.

"You think my boots are sexy?"

Cara smiled. "Please. I had a dream about them two nights ago. Horses, cats, and grapes also figured prominently. How many pairs do you own, by the way?"

Lauren looked rueful. "Six. Brown, black, and brown-and-black, two pairs each, for New York and London. They're so comfortable. I needed them to match everything. I had them made when I was in England."

"Of course you did, rich girl." Cara patted Lauren's cheek and hoped her smile took the sting out of her words. She honestly didn't know if this was going to work, but until it blew up in their faces, she planned on having a good time. "I'm hoping this little détente now concludes the friends portion of the evening and we can start with the benefits? I've been dying to kiss you since I got here."

"Why did it take us so long? By this time last week, we'd already come at least two times apiece." Lauren rested her hands on Cara's knees and slowly moved them upward.

"Probably because we were sloshed on sidecars." Cara brought her other hand up so both were framing Lauren's face. She was almost panting and they hadn't even done anything yet. "At least there hasn't been any physical injury so far."

"There is that," Lauren agreed. "Let's stop talking now."

"Good idea." Cara surged against her and brought their lips together in a fierce affirmation of good ideas. She felt Lauren grab onto her hips and tug her closer, her tongue already begging for entrance past her lips. She slipped her hands under Lauren's hoodie, allowing them to creep up her sides, reveling in the warmth and smoothness of her skin. Suddenly she pulled back, her eyes accusing. "You haven't had a bra on this whole time?"

Lauren smiled dreamily, her eyes slow to open. "Took it off as soon as I got home. Always do." She took the opportunity to pull Cara's shirt over her head and remove her bra.

Their kisses became deeper and more languorous, and they touched the warm skin of each other's upper bodies. Somehow, Lauren had taken command of her will, and Cara was burning putty in her talented hands.

Lauren moved lower, her mouth getting closer to Cara's breasts. She hissed with dissatisfaction when her angle of approach didn't allow her to reach Cara's nipple, and she dropped to her knees and shoved the coffee table across the Persian rug with her foot. "I need more room."

It only took a minute or so before the slow and deliberate lashing Lauren delivered to Cara's breasts turned nearly unbearable. Lauren reached for the fly of Cara's jeans, but Cara was already there, slashing at the zipper and wriggling at the waist. Lauren ripped her jeans and underwear down to her ankles and tried to spread Cara's knees, but was stopped by her shoes and bunched up clothing. "Dammit."

"Remove my shoes, woman," Cara giggled, her hands on Lauren's shoulders.

Lauren laughed too and paused in her frenetic actions to give Cara a kiss filled with affection. "I like doing this with you," she said, and the smile she gave Cara was so radiant it stopped her breath. When the shoes and jeans were completely off, Lauren hunkered down between Cara's thighs. "My God, you are so wet."

Cara was about to answer when Lauren's hot tongue made contact, and she fell back among the sofa cushions. She grabbed at Lauren's head, holding on as she mindlessly shouted Lauren's name all the way to her climax.

❖

Lauren raised her head and gazed at Cara as she recovered her breath. With her eyes closed and one arm thrown above her head, tendrils of her raven hair escaping a now unkempt ponytail, Cara was a vision of wanton loveliness. Lauren's heart felt full almost to bursting. The relief she felt when their argument had been somewhat resolved led to this enthusiastic outpouring of sexual giving. Yes, it was fun and light, but it was helping Lauren feel like herself again, too. Cara had no idea how much Lauren needed it.

"You have a talent." Cara's afterglow lassitude only made Lauren want her more. As Lauren shed her yoga pants, Cara repositioned herself so she was recumbent on the sofa and grabbed a throw pillow to put behind her head. "Bring it in." She opened her arms and motioned to Lauren with her fingers, as if she were guiding a truck back into a tight spot, and Lauren brought her body into Cara, who enveloped her with open arms and legs so they were touching almost everywhere.

"I mussed your beautiful hair." Cara brushed a few wisps from Lauren's eyes. "I don't usually get so loud but, my God, woman, you have the tongue of an angel."

Lauren smiled.

"Could I have embarrassed myself a little more?"

"You gave me proof of a job well done."

"I think I gave your neighbors proof of a job well done, too."

"Nope. They're two floors away."

"Oh, right. Nobody can hear us in Havemayer House. We can screech away. And look how much we've improved. No women were harmed in the making of this orgasm."

"And I stayed on task," Lauren said.

"Did you ever." The smile Cara gave her was warm and contented. Cara's hand wandered over Lauren's chest, coming to rest over her right nipple where gentle fingers exerted minute pressure as she gazed into Lauren's eyes.

Lauren whined in frustration. "I'm really close. I bet if you'd suck on them I'd come."

"Challenge accepted." Cara maneuvered Lauren onto her back, her head sinking to Lauren's breast. Lauren wanted to hold on tightly, but her arms shot above her head to give Cara room. Then some fool knocked over a lamp. Cara moved lower, her belly resting against Lauren's pelvis as she used her tongue and teeth on first one nipple and then the other to drive Lauren crazy with want. Lauren strained against Cara, trying to douse the fire that was building within her. When Cara snaked a hand between their bodies, first one finger, then two, found their way into her center, and she set a short-lived rhythm. Lauren ground herself against Cara's hand until her orgasm hit her like a sonic boom moments later.

As Lauren came back to herself, her arms encircled Cara. They were both still for a little while. Then Cara said, "No fair. You were too quiet. But your heart is beating pretty loudly, so there's that. And knocking over the lamp was loud *and* unexpected. Extra points to you."

Lauren felt a giddy buoyancy in that moment. "You may not like being here in my home, but I'm really enjoying having you here."

Cara raised her head to look her in the eye. "I never said I didn't like being here. A person would have to be insane not to like this place. It's just not what I'm used to. And your presence here makes it infinitely less terrible." She paused for a second. "But you haven't shown me everything. Don't you have a bed somewhere? Let's go find it."

Lauren stood and put the coffee table back in position, picking up the magazines that had fallen when she kicked it away from the couch, then righted the lamp. Attending to these small tasks covered up any post-coital weirdness that might descend over them.

Cara lay there and watched her. "Do you ever do housework like that?"

"Like what?"

"All naked and hot? Maybe stretch up and use a feather duster on those high shelves? Bend over and buff the coffee table with such energy that your tits sway enticingly? You could invite me over to watch."

Lauren liked that Cara was good at glossing over the awkward pauses. "I can't say I ever do. Not when I know someone will be here to clean up after me eventually." She stood next to Cara. "Are you coming? Weren't you interested in seeing my bed?"

Lauren led them down a curved staircase to the lower floor of the duplex and into her bedroom. "This one's mine."

Cara nodded. "Bathroom?"

"Through here."

She handed the bundle of clothes to Lauren. "Back in a minute."

Lauren dumped their clothes on a chair. Her boots were still out from earlier in the day. She decided to leave them in view of the bed for Cara's sake.

"Lauren?" Cara called.

Lauren poked her head around the door. "What's up?"

"You didn't tell me you had a swimming pool." Cara stood staring at the admittedly very large tub in Lauren's bathroom.

"So it's a bit bigger than average. Sometimes we Havemayers like to have a little soak."

"Talaricos like to soak, too." Cara sounded hopeful.

"You want to use the soaking tub?"

The blush staining Cara's neck was visible in the bright lights of the vanity. "I don't have a tub at my place. I can't remember the last time I had a bath."

Lauren's answer was to lean across the edge of the tub and turn on the taps.

Cara clapped a few times in excitement. "You'll join me, right?"

"Sure." Lauren's answer was calm, but disquiet settled in her gut. She tried to ignore it.

"I didn't know wooden tubs existed." Cara didn't tear her eyes away from the tub. "Is it real wood? Where do you get a tub this big?"

"It's custom, I think. I'll get some towels." Lauren grabbed her pink silk robe and almost ran out of the room. When she returned, cedar-scented mist filled the air, and naked Cara sat on the edge of the tub with her feet in the water, twisting her hair into a lopsided bun.

"The smell is amazing." Cara reached out a hand, but Lauren avoided her. "Is it cedar?"

"It's Hinoki wood, like a Japanese cedar." Lauren removed her robe and stepped in, the heated water burning and soothing her feet at once. "Around the time I started attending Perry Bidwell, my parents were spending a lot of time in Tokyo, and my father really enjoyed the tradition of the soaking tub, so he had one installed."

"So it's not really a bathtub, is it?" Cara plopped herself down in the water and closed her eyes in obvious satisfaction.

"No, usually a person takes a shower before they get in the tub to soak."

Cara opened her eyes. "Oops."

"We're not that strict about it around here." Lauren refused to meet Cara's gaze as she lowered herself at the opposite end of the tub. She spread her legs so they wouldn't touch Cara's, her knees protruding above the surface like two tiny islands. When she turned off the taps, the silence that filled the room was deafening.

"Is something wrong?" Cara asked.

Lauren wondered if she should say what was on her mind or simply let it go. No, they had only this evening promised to be honest with each other. "I'm noticing how comfortable you seem to be in this bathroom that my family's wealth made possible."

Surprise rippled over Cara's features and she slowly nodded her head. "You're right. I'm a total hypocrite."

Lauren immediately felt bad. "No, you're not. Forget I said anything."

"You're absolutely right to call me on my righteous bullshit. I'm a tiny bit late to understanding that our disagreement earlier was my insecurities rising to the surface." She rested her fingertips on the water. "But that's my shit to work through. I'm sorry. I don't ever want to make you feel lousy."

Lauren looked away, reluctant to continue talking about this.

Cara grabbed Lauren's foot in both of her hands. "Do you feel like I'm taking advantage of you?"

"It's not that." Lauren regretted even bringing it up. She was so stupid sometimes. "As we've already seen tonight, the money thing is always this weird little hump I have to get over with new people. We don't have to talk about it right now." *Or ever.*

The silence lingered between them until it looked like Cara had come to some kind of decision. "Well, what can we do to fast-forward the evening to a place where we're relaxed with each other again?" She pulled Lauren's heel onto her thigh, pressing her thumbs into the ball of her foot.

"That," Lauren groaned. "Keep doing that. It feels so good." Trust Cara to figure a way out of the awkwardness again. Lauren just wanted things to be easy for a while.

Cara's eyes wandered as she continued to rub Lauren's foot. "It really is a beautiful bathroom. Again, I applaud your family's use of tile, and of course, the artwork is very original."

Lauren's eyes flicked up to the canvas that hung on the opposite wall. "You noticed that, huh?" The bathroom was clad in small mosaic glass tiles in varying shades of cobalt. The design went well with the modern wooden tub but contrasted with the modestly sized art piece above. It was a painting in oils of the Bethesda fountain and terrace in Central Park. At the bottom right were the initials LH.

"When did you do it?"

"Tenth grade, maybe? I couldn't get enough of the Impressionists, and I wanted to paint like them, out in nature. I made my mother buy me a portable easel and a wooden travel case of oils and I marched out to the fountain one day during one of our breaks from school and I tried to paint *en plein air*. In the wild and untamed landscape of Central Park."

"Stop. You did a good job. It's beautiful."

"You don't have to say that. It's deeply mediocre. It hangs in the bathroom for a reason." Lauren deliberately turned away from it.

Cara pinched her big toe. "Give your teenage self a break. It's better than most people could do."

She snuck another look at it. The one thing money couldn't buy—talent. *Jesus, Lauren. Do not go there.* "That's the piece that showed me I would never be an artist." *You went there.*

Cara frowned. "How so?"

After automatically treating Cara with suspicion minutes earlier, Lauren wanted to share something personal as an emblem of her trust. She wanted to believe Cara worthy of it. "I knew I wasn't that great at it, but I always thought I would improve. When I was painting in the park that day, this older man came over and sat on a bench nearby and struck up a conversation with me. He had a sketchpad and he was drawing the same view I was painting, overworking, torturing, generally making the mess you see here."

"I contend it's not a mess."

"And in five minutes, he had drawn something with such spirit and vitality, such life, something I realized I would never be capable of."

Cara brought both of Lauren's feet into her lap. She gazed at her with such an attitude of empathy that Lauren felt safe enough to reveal what she had never articulated to another person.

"I kept with it for a few more years, a couple of studio classes in undergrad, but I was only prolonging the inevitable. The ability to see something in my mind and transfer that vision to an external medium would never be mine. I had fallen in love with art, but it didn't love me back. And that crushed me."

"I'm sorry, Lauren."

"It was my first real failure, and it shocked the hell out of me. I had never failed at anything. That was the first time life took a swing at me."

"It must have sent you reeling, but you're still standing. I know it might seem like cold comfort, but you still love art." Cara leaned back against the smooth wood. "I wish I had known at the time. Maybe I could have done something, helped you out somehow. There I was, sitting in the same classroom as you, with no idea what you were going through."

"Who knows how our lives might have been different if we had become friends back then. I think mine might have been better."

"Mine too."

"It's odd that we moved in the same circles, like satellites in tandem orbits, but we never connected."

"It wasn't for lack of trying." Cara's laugh sounded self-conscious.

Lauren had no idea what that meant.

"My friends knew about my crush on you." She rolled her eyes. "I must have been so obvious. It's a wonder you never saw me mooning over you from across the chemistry lab."

"I didn't. I guess I was pretty self-absorbed back then."

"Maybe I did a better job of hiding it than I thought. But Sam and Lisa knew, and they would tease me all the time. I think it was their way of encouraging me to, at the very least, have a conversation with you. But I was too shy, too content to furtively watch you and dream about our hypothetical teenage love affair."

Lauren felt something clench within her at Cara's wistful delivery of that last phrase. "Where does the trying part come in?"

"Spring of our junior year. Do you remember reading *Pride and Prejudice* in Brit Lit?"

"Vaguely."

"Lizzie Bennett triumphed in the end. She found her happiness. It was annoying to me that a fictional character without much agency could achieve her own happiness, and there I was, accepting my fate as an invisible background player in the drama of your life."

Lauren reached under the water for one of Cara's feet and began massaging it.

"Ooh, that does feel good," Cara said. "Perry Bidwell isn't that big a school. You knew me. We shared classes, but you didn't *see* me. So I worked up a plan over the summer to throw myself into your sightline as much as I could as soon as school started again. God, this is embarrassing. I intended to join every activity you participated in, and that's how I found myself going out for field hockey senior year. Who plays a new sport in their senior year? Nobody, that's who. No wonder I was terrible."

"But your plan worked. I told you at the reunion that I remembered you singing into your hockey stick."

"Well, good for me. You noticed me. Once." Cara's voice was mild. "The plan was to join every activity you did over the course of the school year. You were bound to notice that odd girl who kept doing odd things in your presence, but guess what?"

Lauren instantly remembered. "I dropped all my extracurriculars once I got into Yale early decision. I don't think I even finished the field hockey season."

"You didn't. Coach Keefe lost his star player, but gained a champion ball kicker."

Lauren didn't know what to say. She had been dumb and selfish, but that was typical in the months after her mother's death.

"And then it was too late. I saw you in class but nowhere else. We graduated. I never got to be Lizzie. You were never Darcy. Or vice versa."

The water seemed colder all of a sudden.

Cara gave her a half-smile. "But it all turned out okay. What I learned from that whole unrequited crush situation was this: she who hesitates is a chump. I became more assertive and direct. I learned to ask for what I wanted. And when I got to Princeton, the first girl who caught my eye? I let her know and she became my first love."

If anything, Lauren felt worse with this disclosure.

"And now, all these years later, we're friends. A karmic boomerang, right? We're like Lucy and Ethel, if they fucked. Like Monica and Rachel, but doing it. Like Leslie Knope and Ann Perkins, if they—"

"I get it." Needing to stop her talking, Lauren lunged to the other side of the tub and threw herself against Cara, water sloshing over the side and onto the floor.

"Whoa, I think you found me, Nemo." Cara wrapped her arms around her. More of Lauren's skin was exposed to the air and she shivered. Cara reached over and turned on the hot water tap. "Should we put more hot water in? I think a third of it is on the floor now."

A minute or two passed in contemplative silence as the tub warmed again. Lauren tried to remember another clear memory of Cara from school but couldn't. She turned her body sideways and snaked her arm around Cara's middle, burrowing into her chest. Cara's chin rested on her head, and the weight of it felt good. "I don't understand how I didn't pick up on it."

"I would have been mortified if you did."

"Why didn't you just ask me about the homework in calculus one day after class? And then keep asking me?"

"I don't know. Actually having a conversation with you seemed impossible at the time."

"Maybe you should be thanking me. If your plan had worked, you would never have met the love of your life."

"I didn't say she was the love of my life. She was my first love."

"Was this the Peace Corps girlfriend?"

"No. This was a brief—I don't know what to call it—extended hookup, I guess. We were freshmen, and Starla transferred at the end of our first year because she couldn't hack it academically and didn't want to waste her parents' money."

"She got into Princeton and she couldn't hack it?"

"She'd led a sheltered life and majorly embraced her freedom. She spent so little time in class, her GPA just cratered."

"And her name was Starla?" Lauren couldn't mask her derision.

"I'm afraid so." Cara sounded a tad defensive. "What was the name of your first love?"

Lauren was silent. It would be churlish of her to refuse to share after Cara's openness. "Her name was Terri."

"Was this during college?"

"Yes, my freshman year, too. Like Starla, I got a little wild that year and constantly hung out at this club where all the queer people congregated. Terri was one of the bartenders."

Cara grunted.

"What?"

"Nothing. Go on."

"She was older, in her mid-twenties. Girls threw themselves at her left and right. She was hot and knew it, dripping with charisma."

"Sounds like a real charmer." Cara's tone was not complimentary.

"Out of all those women, she picked me. I was fully expecting to be her flavor of the hour, but for our first date she pulled out all the stops: flowers, dinner, a sweet kiss good night, the works. We saw each other most of my freshman year. She was sweet and attentive and sex on legs, and I fell for her like a piano from a ten-story window."

Cara didn't say anything, but squeezed Lauren in a way that felt protective. Perhaps she could sense what was coming.

"Toward the end of spring semester, she started talking about this plan to open her own club. She got me so excited about it that I actually offered to give her money for it. She was saved the indignity of having to ask me outright." Lauren scoffed at the memory. "I had to ask my father because I didn't get access to even part of my trust until I turned twenty-five. I wasn't there when he met with her, but he told me what he was going to do. He would offer her a choice: the money or me. If she chose the money, she would have to cut off all contact with me, and if she chose me, he would give her the money anyway, but she wouldn't know that until after her choice was made. He said I should know what kind of person she was, what her character was."

"And your dad was okay with this? Giving money to an older, possibly mercenary, love interest?" Cara asked with disbelief.

"Not possibly, definitely. He knew Terri wouldn't choose me."

"Damn, Lauren."

"I didn't believe it when he told me she picked the money. She still worked at the club for a few more weeks after she got the check, and I was a big old masochist and went to see her and she wouldn't even look at me. She was too afraid of voiding the terms of her agreement with my father."

"Another time when life took a swing at you. I'm sorry that happened. Nobody deserves that."

"It's part of the reason why I'm no good for anything long term. People don't see just me when they look at me. And trust is hard for me."

"With a chick like Terri in your past, I can see why."

Cara's lips press against her head in a series of gentle kisses. They felt soothing and tender, compassionate and concerned, and absolutely not what Lauren wanted right now. She turned in Cara's arms and rose up so she was half out of the water, kissing her with a furious intensity. Cara resisted for a moment before she melted into Lauren's onslaught, letting her dictate the pace, giving her complete control. Lauren's urgency subsided after a moment, and then Cara began to dominate the kiss, ravishing Lauren with her lips and tongue, grasping Lauren's waist and pulling her closer. When they separated several long moments later, Lauren looked into Cara's eyes and fairly growled, "Do you want me to fuck you here or in my bed?"

"In your bed."

"Let's go."

CHAPTER THIRTEEN

In the morning, they had a quick breakfast at Café Sabarsky, only a few blocks down Fifth from Lauren's place. It was on the ground floor of a German and Austrian art gallery that occupied a gilded age mansion, and it was what Cara imagined having breakfast in Vienna might be like. They sat in a bustling, old world, wood-paneled room in a velvet-covered corner banquette that looked out onto the street, drinking really strong coffee and eating ham and cheese and soft boiled eggs.

When Lauren put her coffee cup down, a bit of whipped cream clung to her lip. Cara was mesmerized at the sight of her tongue darting out to lick it away.

"I'm a little unclear about our ownership agreement," Lauren said. "Am I still the owner of this time since it's like a continuation of last night? Or does ownership expire at the end of the calendar day when said time was initiated?"

She wanted to give Lauren all the kisses for taking her time-owning idea seriously. Much as Cara wanted to be the boss of the rules of time-owning, something told her to let Lauren take the lead here. "I'm not sure. What do you think?"

"Maybe the time should end once we've separated from each other."

"I can agree to that."

"Good. What are your plans today?"

"I'm behind in my grading. I'm going to this coffee shop near my apartment to do that and some lesson planning. You?"

"I have an appointment at ten." Lauren checked the clock on her phone. "Actually, you might find it interesting. Why don't you come with me? It won't take long, and then I'll relinquish ownership of our time."

"Okay." She was enjoying being with Lauren, probably a little too much for a friend with benefits, and didn't want it to end.

Lauren gave her a tantalizing look. "Let's split a slice of Sachertorte before we go. I know it's totally decadent, but I still own the time so you can't refuse."

It was a chilly December day that was alleviated by powerful sunshine, and Cara lifted her face to the sky to absorb those warm rays as she walked with Lauren down Park Avenue. Her hands were in her pockets because she forgot her gloves, but every other part of her was warm and happy. They were only a few blocks below Eighty-Sixth Street when Lauren guided her into a corner prewar residential building. The building staff greeted Lauren by name as they breezed by them to the bank of elevators.

"Are we visiting someone?" Cara asked as Lauren hit the call button.

"Kind of." She pulled out her phone and checked for texts before sending one of her own.

"You're being secretive."

"Am I?" Lauren waited for Cara to enter before following her in and pressing the button for the twelfth floor.

The elevator was paneled in a dark-hued wood with mirrored insets. Cara studied the two of them in the reflection. Her schlumpy old peacoat at least hid the fact that she was wearing yesterday's clothes. Lauren was dressed casually too, but her jeans and sweater projected an image of cool insouciance rather than Cara's bedraggled, dirty, stay out look. At breakfast, Cara had not been able to keep her eyes off the pale gray boat neck sweater Lauren wore, and just managed to keep her hands from reaching out and caressing Lauren's clavicles, framed so perfectly by its neckline they seemed sculptural. The sweater seemed to invite touching too, looking soft and downy like the seed head of a dandelion before the wind scattered it. Now it was covered up by Lauren's trendy black parka, with its fur-lined hood and map of Canada on the sleeve, leaving Cara's grabby hands tamed for the moment.

Lauren's phone beeped and she uttered a sound of annoyance as she read it. "They're going to be ten minutes late. I knew this would happen."

Cara shrugged. She was now not much in a hurry to grade the vocabulary assignments of sixty lackadaisical eleventh graders. Pretending her life usually included fancy continental breakfasts and strolls down the toniest Upper East Side avenues with a beautiful woman at her side was much more pleasant.

They walked down a hallway and Lauren produced a key, opening the door for a unit near the end. She followed into an empty foyer and then through the living and dining areas of a vacant space. There was evidence of renovation in the form of supplies hidden under a canvas tarp and several dusty ten-gallon buckets nearby.

"Welcome to my new place. What do you think?" Lauren held out her arms and twirled, and her exultant voice echoed in the emptiness. It was as if this room was the top of the world and Lauren was standing on it.

"This is yours?"

Her smile as she nodded could have powered a small city. "I won't be able to move in for a while, but I will not always be living under my father's roof." Lauren grabbed her by the arm and pulled her into what had been the kitchen, now demoed. "We're knocking down the wall between the maid's room and the kitchen to make it bigger. Come see the bathrooms."

Bathrooms? Plural? For city living that was the height of luxury. "How many bedrooms?"

"Three. Do you like the floors?"

"Very much." Cara appraised the scarred herringbone-patterned wood floors, badly in need of refinishing. They were probably original to the building.

"There used to be this totally gross burnt orange wall-to-wall carpeting throughout, but look what we found under the plywood subfloor. Nice, right?" Lauren showed her the bathrooms, which had yet to see the sledgehammer. The smaller bathroom featured deep purple tile with black accents, probably circa late sixties.

"You're keeping this as is, right?" Cara kidded her.

"Not on your life."

The larger bath was a little less garish but equally dated, connected to an enormous primary bedroom with a fireplace at one end. The blackened brick inside meant it was functional, and Cara's mind went to cozy winter nights, lounging in bed and gazing at the fire. The other bedrooms were spacious and the numerous windows to the south and east meant tons of natural light throughout. It was a dream apartment. Definitely not as luxe as Lauren's family home, but certainly more than Cara would ever be able to afford in ten lifetimes. "It's beautiful, Lauren," Cara said sincerely. "I'm sure you'll be very happy here."

Lauren started to say something, but her phone rang and she apologized before taking the call. Cara wandered back to the living room, drawn to its postcard perfect view down Park Avenue. The window glazing must have been top notch. She could have heard a pin drop in the quiet room. No traffic sounds leaked into the space. A covered radiator fronted the window, and she leaned against it, steam heat seeping into her cold bones.

She wanted to be outraged at the excess of a three-bedroom apartment for a lone woman who had yet to turn thirty. She wanted to be furious at the notion that the price of this single apartment could probably fund the education of every senior with college aspirations who currently attended her school, but all she felt was a deep melancholy in knowing she would never belong here. Lauren and her wealth were so far removed from her quiet workaday grind, it was like something out of a fairytale.

It was dangerous to pretend like she had this morning that she belonged in Lauren's world. *Stay in your lane, Talarico.*

What was Lauren's purpose in bringing her here? Was she simply excited and wanting to share the attainment of one of life's milestones with a new friend? But that didn't exactly go along with all the personal stuff she had disclosed last night. Why would Lauren even want her here?

Lauren returned, pocketing her phone, and sat beside her on the radiator. She heaved a sigh, her features arranged in pleasant contemplation as she threaded her arm around Cara's and surveyed the empty room.

Cara nudged Lauren's shoulder. "Are you decorating this room in your head?"

"Maybe." Her wry smile told Cara she had nailed it.

"I'm curious. Why did you say you thought I would find this interesting?"

Lauren's contented expression faltered. "You don't?"

"No, I do." She backpedaled, belatedly realizing how impolite that sounded. "I was just wondering."

"You said you were into tile. My architect is coming with an interior designer who is bringing finishing options, some of which are tile samples for the kitchen and baths."

Oh.

"I thought maybe you could help me choose." Lauren lowered her eyes. "And I wanted you to see where I'll be living. It's more modest than my family home. It doesn't make you uncomfortable, does it?" Lauren asked this with such earnestness Cara couldn't glibly point out modesty was relative. It certainly wasn't modest compared to her shoebox in East Harlem. Besides, why would Cara's degree of comfort with her living situation matter to Lauren anyway? Being around Lauren suddenly felt impossible, but it felt equally impossible to be unkind.

She smiled and squeezed Lauren's arm. "No, it doesn't. It's a little large for your current needs, but I'm sure you'll eventually fill it up with loved ones: a wife, children, various furry creatures."

"No, the extra rooms will be a guest room for my brother and an office for me. No wife, no kids," Lauren's expression had gone flat.

"Not now, but someday," Cara reassured her.

"No, not someday. Not ever," Lauren said again. "I'd like to have good friends in my life, like what we're becoming, lots of friends. I've cut myself off from friendship for too long. But marriage? Nope. And no long-term commitment either."

It seemed absurd to Cara to deny that possibility completely. She had her own rules about when the time would be right for marriage. She wasn't ready now, either, but it was definitely something she wanted someday. She shifted on the radiator so she could get a better look at Lauren's face. "Do you mind if I ask why?"

"It's not for me." Lauren refused to meet her gaze. "I don't trust it. I also don't trust myself or my hypothetical bride."

Cara thought about that for a moment. "Does this have anything to do with your last relationship?"

Lauren gave her a look that could freeze lava.

"Never mind. None of my business."

"Sorry." Lauren looked away again. "It's my thing about trusting people again."

"Got it." *You don't trust your ex? Or you don't trust me?* She strove to thaw the chilly atmosphere to their warm camaraderie from earlier. "We'll have to get you some new friends, Havemayer. I'll put you down for the next teacher karaoke happy hour."

"I will not sing," Lauren warned her.

"Duly noted." Cara tried to think of other ways to broaden Lauren's circle of friends, but then it dawned on her what more friends for Lauren might mean. "You're going to thrive here in New York. You've got the hot job and the hot apartment, and pretty soon you're going to have all the friends you can handle."

It looked like it took some effort for Lauren to look her in the eye. "You're so nice."

To Cara, her praise felt damning and faint. Nice had never felt so depressing. "Just one thing: Could you please let me know if you extend your benefits to someone else? I may not have any experience with this sort of relationship"—she gestured between the two of them—"but I do know that I only have benefits for one woman at a time."

Lauren sat straighter as she caught Cara's meaning. "Of course, but the likelihood of finding someone else I want to share my benefits with is tiny."

"Don't say that. It's a big city. The very next woman you meet could be extremely benefits-worthy. You might want to benefit her all night long."

"I don't want to benefit anyone but you." Lauren's voice reflected growing irritation. "God, how many times must I say the word benefit in the space of a five-minute conversation?"

"Sorry I made us go there, but it's important to me that you know where I stand. I like clarity."

"For someone who's usually so direct, that was an awfully indirect way of telling me you want to be exclusive."

"I don't think I can make that kind of demand in this kind of relationship. I only wanted to—"

"Well, you just did, and I will honor your request, so can we please stop talking about it now?" Lauren snapped.

"Sure," Cara said lightly. She should probably go.

There was a knock, and Lauren opened the door to a man in a dark overcoat and a stylish woman in a parka that was identical to Lauren's, map of Canada patch and all. They both carried giant canvas bags into the apartment.

Cara stood a little apart from them as the architect made introductions, feeling off-balance from the pitch and yaw of their conversation. The woman was called Stacy Von Ocelot or something, Cara did not quite catch the last name. She was beautiful and put together and looked as if she would fit seamlessly into Lauren's life, far better than Cara ever could. Cara was so busy sizing her up that she almost missed her cue in the introductions sketch they were performing.

"This is my friend Cara." Lauren introduced her to Sheldon the architect and the ocelot woman.

Cara shook their hands and said to the ocelot, "I'm so glad Lauren will have the benefit of your expertise on this project." The slight emphasis she put on the word benefit was for Lauren only, but as she snuck a glance, she saw Lauren looked less than amused. "I'm afraid I can't stay. I'm sure you'll have a productive afternoon."

"You're leaving?" Lauren asked, but didn't seem surprised. "Let me walk you out." In the hallway, she watched Cara button up her coat. "I'm sorry I was impatient with you. I don't know what's wrong with me. I don't know how to do this."

"I don't either. It's fine. Everything will be fine." Cara saw Lauren's glum expression. "Hey, cheer up. You're about to do what I imagine is one of the best and most fun parts of home renovation."

"Are you sure you don't want to stay?"

"I'm sure." Cara was bummed not to be able to stay and witness a process she had only seen in home decorating shows on TV, but for her own sanity she needed to leave. "I have tons of work to do. Take pictures of the tile. You can show me later."

She grasped Lauren around the neck and kissed her soundly. "Your ownership of this time is hereby dissolved. I got next. Prepare to be wowed on a very low budget."

As she turned the corner that would bring her to the elevators, she looked back to see that Lauren hadn't moved. She was still standing in the same place with her hand on the doorknob, watching her go.

❖

Lauren was exhausted and hungry. Her meeting with Sheldon and Stacy had lasted for hours and she dragged as she walked up Fifth Avenue toward home. She was passing one of the most architecturally striking stretches along Museum Mile, which usually never failed to excite her, but now she barely noticed the Wright-designed Guggenheim or the Cooper Hewitt Museum housed in the old Carnegie mansion.

Contrary to what Cara presumed, Lauren did not enjoy making decisions today. Choosing a kitchen faucet was fraught with unknown pitfalls. Selecting a toilet paper holder seemed a monumental undertaking. Somewhere in between trying to decide between a basket weave pattern and hexagonal mosaics for the powder room floor, she wished she had not driven Cara away.

It was her own fault for getting testy. Cara's idea that she would find another friend with benefits was laughable, but what had surprised Lauren more was how intense her aversion to the idea of sharing Cara with someone else had been.

Cara had, in a very short amount of time, captivated her. That first blush of affinity had taken over and Lauren didn't want to be cautious. Her brain was telling her not to get addicted to the endorphins that surged when she was with her, but emotionally she wanted to smother herself in Cara. It reminded her of an enormous, beautiful, fragile, chocolate egg she had been gifted one spring as a child. The desire to gobble the whole thing up was strong, but so was the instinct to hold it close and protect it with everything she had. Nowhere was the idea of setting it on a shelf and treating it with the respect and care it deserved, for however long she deserved to have it.

These feelings for Cara—this craving to have her, this choosing to want—were the opposite of how she initially felt about her ex, Saffron. Where Saffron had pursued her, and Lauren allowed herself to be pursued. Active versus passive. There was a crucial difference. She compared Saffron to Cara in her mind's eye. They were as different as two women could possibly be. Should she tell Cara about Saffron? Could unburdening herself to Cara help explain her choices? Take away the obvious incomprehension in Cara's eyes when Lauren said she would never share her new apartment with anyone?

She stopped in her tracks on the sidewalk as the shame gripped her. The thought of bringing Saffron's betrayal back into the light for someone else to see was so humiliating, so degrading, it brought beads of sweat to her hairline even in the December chill. No, it was better to keep it tamped deep down in the bottom of her being, never allowed to surface again. And no matter how intense her feelings for Cara became, she had to remember that there was no future for them beyond friendship. They had both agreed.

Lauren passed a hand over her brow and resumed walking. She refused to let the past infiltrate this tiny bit of pleasure she had found. It had been so long since she had been swept up in feelings of desire and lust and affection, and she needed it right now. She needed Cara right now, and she was giving herself permission to have her for a while. It couldn't be forever, but just for now, she would let herself have this.

At home, in the kitchen while waiting for some of Paloma's food to heat in the microwave, she picked up her phone and scrolled through the images she took of tiles, wall coverings, and paint cards. So many decisions it made her brain hurt, and she had held off on making most of them. Cara said to take pictures, so she had. She switched over to her messaging app and added the images for the choices of powder room floor tile. *Hey. Which do you like better?*

She sat at the kitchen island and began to eat. Only a minute or two later, she got a response from Cara. *Basket weave, definitely.* Three thumbs up emojis.

And just like that, Lauren knew it was the right choice. The fact that Cara knew the first pic was called a basket weave pattern, something Lauren had not learned until today, made her smile.

Another text from Cara: *That's marble, not porcelain, right?*

Yes.

Looks great. Five smiley face emojis. *How was the rest of the day?*

Hard. Wish you had stayed. Was she too needy? *Could've used an expert.*

Lauren put her fork down and waited. And waited. It took longer for the reply to come this time, but it eventually came.

Still busy with grading. Shrugging emoji.

Lauren typed: *Just wanted to say sorry again about how I talked to you today.*

Not a big deal. I'm sorry I upset you. No emojis.

No. You didn't. Lauren wanted to see Cara. She couldn't help herself. *When will you be finished with your school stuff?*

Still have hours to go. Hard to concentrate. Frown emojis. Two of them.

Feeling reckless, she pushed for more. *Free tomorrow? Want to get together?*

Can't. I have plans.

Of course. Cara was a normal person with a normal life and plans that didn't involve Lauren. Then another text came through.

My turn for owning our time. Are you avail Saturday? Say 11AM?

Play it cool, Lauren. *Let me check my calendar.* She put her phone down and took two leisurely bites of her dinner, knowing she was absolutely free next Saturday. Then she texted: *Yes, I'm free.*

Great! Dress warmly. I'll pick you up at Havemayer House. Nighty night. Three sleepy face emojis even though it wasn't yet seven o'clock.

Lauren was dismissed. The chocolate egg wouldn't be devoured tonight, no matter how much Lauren wanted to gorge herself on it.

CHAPTER FOURTEEN

When Cara popped into Café Mi Vida on Sunday morning, Manny came from behind the counter even though there was a line.

"Hey, you're busy."

"Whatever, she can handle it." He gestured to Gisela, his weekend co-worker. "She did fuck-all yesterday."

"We didn't even get to chat, this place was so crazy busy yesterday."

"Yeah, Saturday and Sunday? We're going to have to move a hammock or something in here for you."

"I'm not staying today. I'm on my way to the subway and I'd much prefer your coffee to the bodega's. Plus I wanted to say hi."

Manny got started on her macchiato. "Where you going? Are you doing something with whoever you were thinking about yesterday?"

"What are you talking about?"

He didn't speak while the steamer gurgled and hissed. When he came back to her, Cara traded her cash for a to-go cup.

"Every time I looked over yesterday, you were looking out the window all swoony and romantical and shit." He put his hands on his hips. "It's Daisy, right? What's the tea? You two bang it out?"

She leaned in and gave him a kiss on the cheek. "A lady never tells."

"I wanted to tell you about how Calvin came by last night and how we hung out after closing, but I guess I can't now because a lady never tells."

Cara slapped his arm. "Calvin who you've been messaging with for the last two weeks? You met in person?"

"Yes, bitch."

"Okay, Manny. Tomorrow, we both spill." She took a bracing sip of Manny's macchiato. Today she'd be spilling to Lisa and Sam.

❖

Cara, Lisa, and Samantha were shown to their table at the Penrose, one of the more popular brunch places on the Upper East Side. Cara had never been there, and somehow Samantha, who now lived nowhere near this neighborhood, still knew the best place for them to meet. Once they were all settled and had ordered, Sam asked, "How are you feeling, Lisa?"

"Well, I have a sense of smell now like the bionic woman, I have heartburn all the time, retain water like a damn camel, and let's not talk about the constipation."

"The joys of impending motherhood," Cara cracked.

"Joys? Indignities more like." Lisa got a faraway look in her eye. "But then there's this." She grabbed Cara's hand and put it on her belly.

Cara felt the kick and looked agog at her two friends. "That's amazing." The kicking continued every few seconds, and Cara was surprised to feel tears welling in her eyes. Samantha rested her hand on Lisa's belly too, and the three of them sat there smiling at each other like a troupe of idiots.

"Okay, get your hands off me." Lisa flung their hands away. "It's like the nugget can sense when we're talking about him. He's going apeshit in there and he needs to calm down. He's going to be an attention hog, I just know it."

"A case of the apple not falling far from the tree, am I right?" Cara muttered to Samantha.

"I heard that." Lisa pinched her elbow, hard.

"So it's a boy?" Samantha looked at her Bloody Mary with something like joy as the server set it in front of her. "Did you have one of those gender reveal things?"

"No," Lisa said with scorn. "We don't know what the nug is, and we don't want to know until she shoots out of me in what will be the world's fastest and easiest labor."

"The power of positive thinking?" Samantha laughed.

"You know it. All I do know is the child will be a superstar at any sport where kicking is involved." Lisa nudged Cara. "Maybe it'll lead the field hockey league in kicked balls, Talarico."

All three of them said in unison, "At least I was good at something."

"So predictable, Cara," Lisa pinched her elbow again more gently this time.

"Tell me about the reunion," Samantha said. "Was there a good turnout?"

"Guess what?" Lisa grabbed Samantha by the forearm. "Cara found out the dorms were a den of lesbian iniquity. Or maybe I should say cave of iniquity. Some spelunking going on in Surrey Hall. We. Never. Even. Knew." She poked Sam's arm with each word, like tactile punctuation.

Samantha's eyes grew round. "How'd you find that out, Cara?"

Cara had been purposefully vague about her ride home with Lauren, but she had shared this gossip with Lisa. She hadn't divulged anything about their continuing to see each other.

Lisa answered for her, eyes nearly bugging out of her head. "Lauren Havemayer told her!"

"Wait. You talked to Lauren Havemayer? Explain. Immediately." Samantha had her interrogation face on.

"It's no big deal. She gave me a ride back to the city and we talked about how a bunch of the boarding girls got involved with each other."

"Did she participate? Is she gay?" Samantha asked, then looked at Lisa who was nodding vigorously. "Who was she with?"

"Ayumi Harada and Petra Morgan," Lisa whispered as if it were a deadly secret.

"Really? Petra Morgan has a husband and, like, twenty kids. I know this because they are a constant presence on my Instagram feed," Samantha said.

"I know. Who the Christ has time to be posting like that?" Lisa agreed.

Samantha shrugged. "Bisexual stay-at-home moms, I guess."

Cara thought they might just carry on talking about other classmates and she grabbed her water and drank nearly all of it in one go. She figured she would be talking about this today. Why was she suddenly so reluctant?

"So wait, Lauren Havemayer is a lesbian?" Samantha cut her eyes over to Cara.

"Yes. Who knew?" Cara said.

"You have to tap that, Cara. It's only ten years later. Fire up that old crush. Did you get her number?" Lisa playfully shoved her shoulder.

Cara could feel it happening. All her McNamara Irish blood was settling right below the skin of her chest and neck. Her complexion was probably changing color like she was a damn chameleon sitting on a tomato. But why? She wasn't embarrassed by what she was doing with Lauren.

Lisa leaned in. "Cara, what's wrong? Are you having an allergic reaction? But you haven't eaten anything yet."

"No, she's blushing, idiot." Samantha said. "Why, Cara? Why are you blushing?" Samantha looked like she was trying to remember what they were talking about before Cara changed colors.

"It's nothing, really," Cara mumbled. Betrayed by her body. She turned to a passing server. "Can I get some more water, please?"

"Oh my God!" Samantha shouted. "You slept with her."

Cara glanced at the surrounding tables. "Keep your voice down."

Lisa laughed with delight. "That is outstanding, Cara! That's got to be the longest conversion from crushing to copulating I ever heard. Somebody call Guinness."

"So are you guys dating? Why didn't you want to tell us?" Samantha asked.

"I don't know." Cara ran her fingers through her hair in frustration.

Lisa gave Samantha a look. "Was it just a one-night thing after the reunion?"

"No, she came to Thanksgiving at my mom's—"

"She did? Why?" Lisa interrupted.

"I invited her. Her family was out of town."

Samantha held a hand up. "Wait, was all your family there? Like your mean uncle who yelled at us for playing badminton too loud at your graduation party?"

"Yeah, he was there. He yelled at Lauren, too."

Lisa and Samantha laughed.

"So did you guys do it at your mom's house on Thanksgiving?" Lisa's interest turned salacious.

"No, we got together last weekend," Cara said. "And Friday."

"That's kind of quick for you, Cara. Are these booty calls or is it dating?" Lisa sounded suspicious. She exchanged another look with Samantha. Cara knew they were going to tag-team the information out of her.

"Two weekends in a row. That sounds promising," Samantha encouraged her, taking a different tack.

"Well, she has some stuff, and I have some stuff. I'm not sure it's worth pursuing."

They were all silent for a moment as their server laid their meals in front of them.

"Can you elaborate, please? What do you mean by stuff?" Samantha picked up her fork but kept her eyes on Cara.

"Well, you know my money stuff. I don't have two nickels to rub together. How can it possibly work? She's living with her father right now in a place that's probably nicer than the White House. And she just bought an apartment on Park Avenue that she's renovating. She showed me that yesterday."

"Where?" Samantha whipped out her phone. "What floor?"

"Eighty-Second and Park. Twelfth floor. I don't remember the building number."

"Yesterday? You said Friday." Lisa poured syrup on her waffle.

Cara felt her blush return. "It spilled over into the next day."

"This doesn't sound like a booty call."

She grimaced. "Not to me either. But we've agreed we are friends with benefits."

"Seven million," Samantha announced. "Three bedrooms, two baths, prewar doorman building. Damn, Cara."

Cara knew it would be in the millions but had no idea it would be that much.

"Why friends with benefits? Why aren't you dating?" Lisa was indignant. "Does she think you're not good enough for her?"

"I don't think that's it." She didn't want to violate Lauren's privacy. "She's really very sweet most of the time. And I think she likes me. She said she was attracted to me in my school uniform."

"Kinky. Cara wore her uniform to the reunion," Lisa told Samantha.

Samantha laughed. "Did you? Why?"

"Because I was too cheap to buy something new to wear," Cara said. "And that reminds me. Lauren invited me to this charity thing that's black tie. Any ideas for finding something to wear that won't bust my nonexistent budget?"

Lisa said, "I got nothing. I haven't worn anything formal probably since our prom."

Cara looked at Samantha with pleading eyes.

"You're too tall to fit into anything of mine, but I'm sure you can shop for something that'll work."

Cara's face fell. Shopping meant spending money she didn't have.

"Relax," Samantha said. "There are a few thrift shops we should try below Eighty-Sixth on Lexington. Can you think of a better place than the Upper East Side to get the castoffs of the rich?"

"We?"

Samantha grinned. Cara knew Sam could help. She had amassed a professional wardrobe on a shoestring and she always looked great.

"We can go when we're done here, if you want."

"You're the best, Sam. I don't care what anybody says about you," Cara said.

Lisa brought them back to the matter at hand. "Friends with benefits doesn't sound like you, Cara. Are you sure you're okay with that?"

Cara ignored her niggling doubts. "I'm surprised I hadn't thought of it before. It's a good idea. This way, I'm not investing time and money in dates that may or may not work out. I already know what I'm getting. And Lauren said this was the first time she was trying it, too."

"Oh, great. Neither of you know what you're doing. That sounds safe," Samantha said.

"There have been a few bumps along the way." The disquieting way they parted yesterday came to mind. "We're figuring it out as we go along."

Lisa leveled a frank look at her. "I'm glad you're getting laid, Cara, don't get me wrong, but you be careful with your gigantic little heart. You've been carrying a torch for her since the tenth grade."

"No, I haven't. *You* brought her up when you told me about the reunion," Cara said to Lisa. "I hadn't really thought about her since we graduated. I think she's pretty different than the girl she was back then, and I know I am not the same as I was when I was eighteen."

"True," Samantha agreed. "We've all grown up some, but Lisa's right. You have to protect yourself. I remember those booty call friends from law school when I just needed to get off so I could focus on the books again."

"TMI, Sam," Lisa said.

"All I'm saying is the intimacy can seem real, but it's not. And sometimes people want different things, which may change over time. Just keep checking in with each other to make sure you're both still on the same page, and make adjustments when it turns out you're not."

"Yeah, that's good advice, thanks," Cara said. "Now can we please talk about something other than my pitiful love life? How did your trial go?"

Samantha launched into a description of the defendant's antics and how they had in fact helped the prosecution, but Cara was only half listening. She toyed with her omelet, understanding the wisdom of her friends' advice about Lauren, but also coming to the realization she would not be following it. Lauren had essentially given their relationship an expiration date with her talk of rejecting long-term commitments. If she only had limited time with Lauren, she wanted to be all in. She wanted to feel all of the feelings, and if she covered her heart in emotional bubble wrap, it was true the lows might not be so low, but neither would the highs be as high.

Cara had entered every relationship with her whole heart, and she wasn't about to let the new words that defined this one stop her from doing that again. And this seemed like uncharted territory. What she was starting to feel for Lauren seemed deeper and stronger than what she had felt for other women, something entirely new in her personal experience. Limiting those feelings felt wrong, even if it meant she would be demolished by them when it eventually ended.

"Can I have some of these?" Lisa's fork was already stabbing multiple potatoes from Cara's plate. "The nugget steals my life force on the daily and I need more sustenance than an Olympic swimmer on race day."

Cara pushed her plate toward her. "Help yourself."

And when it was over, Cara could walk away telling herself she had nothing to be ashamed of.

CHAPTER FIFTEEN

*H*ey. *Sorry I'm a little late. Walking down 5th. 2 blocks away.*
I'm coming down. Meet you outside. Saturday had finally arrived. Lauren grabbed her coat and headed for the elevator. Out in front of her building, she saw Cara before Cara saw her. She walked quickly with her head down, her hands jammed in the pockets of her peacoat and the hoodie underneath bunched around her neck. And corduroys again, brown this time. The most adorable part was the Peruvian knit hat with earflaps she was wearing that covered up her dark curls.

When Cara raised her head, her preoccupied frown metamorphosed into a wide smile, and Lauren's heart jumped. They had texted some over the past week, but it wasn't the same, and not nearly enough. Her immediate need was to touch Cara. She barreled into her with a bear hug that threatened to knock them both off their feet, and Cara did her sneaky thing of sliding her arms beneath Lauren's open coat.

Warmth burbled up from deep within her. It felt good to have those arms wrapped around her, but she wanted more, and she wanted Cara to know it. Right there on the sidewalk, Lauren kissed her. Cara wasn't ready for it, but it only took a second for her to melt into the kiss. Lauren kept it PG-rated since they were on the street, but they could both feel its combustible potential. It was a shot across the bow, things-are-a-little-different-now kiss, a what-do-you-have-to-say-to-that kind of kiss. Lauren stood back to see what the reaction would be.

The smile Cara gave her was glowing. "I guess somebody missed me. What a warm welcome for such a cold, gray day."

Lauren could only smile stupidly in return. "This week seemed to go by pretty slowly."

Cara groaned. "Tell me about it. The kids are bonkers with only a week now before break. It was like trying to teach inside a taffy pulling machine. I'm glad to be with you now." She grasped the edges of Lauren's navy-blue duffel coat and opened them wide, eyeing her from head to toe. "You could not be better dressed for today's excursion. You're perfect."

Pleased, Lauren looked down at the turtleneck she wore under a thick woolen Irish fisherman's sweater. Faded jeans and Blundstone boots completed the outfit, and she felt ready for anything. "So you own the time today. What are we doing?" She put her knit beanie on and wrapped her scarf around her neck while Cara carefully did up the toggles of her coat as if she were a child, but the heated gaze she gave her when she was done was definitely adults only.

"We're getting on a crosstown bus." Cara said. "Have you eaten lunch?"

"Nope."

"Good. We'll pick up some food on the way."

They ended up in Harlem, in a neighborhood Lauren was unfamiliar with. Cara stopped at a deli and then it was a short walk to Riverbank State Park.

"How about lunch with a view?" Cara led her down one of several footpaths to an open area with some bare trees and benches.

The grass was still mostly green even with the onset of winter, and it seemed like a very pleasant space, but Central Park was closer. Why come all this way? Then they rounded a bend and Lauren knew why they were here. The Hudson River appeared in its grand, formidable glory before them, the stately George Washington Bridge to the right.

The sun came out from behind some gray clouds as they found a bench overlooking the water. Lauren sat near to Cara and closed her eyes, taking a deep breath into her lungs. Yes, it was cold, but there was nowhere she would rather be right now.

"So. How are you?" Cara asked.

Lauren opened her eyes and saw Cara squinting at her in the suddenly bright sunlight. *Happy.* "Hungry."

"I can fix that." Cara reached into the bag and pulled out two sandwiches wrapped in foil, handing one to Lauren. "New York's greatest sandwich—a chopped cheese."

"How can that be? I was born in New York City and I've never heard of it." Lauren unwrapped and examined it. "Is it a burger? Oh no, is it a cheesesteak?"

"Not quite either." Cara took a bite of hers and left Lauren hanging until she swallowed. "Seasoned ground beef chopped up with onions and melted cheese on a Kaiser roll. And, of course, lettuce, tomato and mayo to get your veggies in."

Lauren took a bite. "Yum. How do I not know about this sandwich? Is this a Harlem thing?"

"It started in Harlem, but you can get them in pretty much any bodega in the city now. It's actually a broke-people thing. They're cheap and filling." Cara handed her a bottle of water and some napkins.

"And delicious."

They lapsed into a comfortable silence, eating and gazing at the pleasant view. Lauren took off her gloves and made a note to herself on her phone. Cara nudged her with her shoulder.

"Dear someone-who-is-not-Cara. I'm on the ass edge of the island of Manhattan, bored out of my mind. Please come save me."

Lauren put her phone away. "Sorry. Just wanted to remind myself of something. I promise you, I'm not bored. Contented would be a better word." She leaned over and nuzzled Cara's cheek.

"I'm glad."

"Have you heard of the Hudson River School? It was an art movement in the mid-nineteenth century, pretty passé these days, but I remember reading about several women who were active during the period. It may be worth pursuing as an avenue of research."

"I'm guessing they painted the Hudson River?"

"And lots of other natural landscapes. There was one artist, Susie Barstow, who would trek out to these really remote locations to paint. She was a mountaineer, which was hard for women back then, because who wants to climb a mountain in those gigantic skirts they had to wear? If I'm remembering it right, she came up with this really outlandish hiking outfit with skirts that could be raised and lowered, and became known as this eccentric."

Cara was quiet for a moment. "I bet she was a lesbian."

"Probably." Lauren shook her head. "Imagine being gay back then."

"I think it's awesome that she did what she wanted despite the forces working against her."

"Society, the way it was a hundred years ago, you mean?"

"Yeah, absolutely that, but also whatever else might have stopped her, like a lack of education, or the money to support herself."

Lauren thought back to what she knew of Susie Barstow. "She was lucky. She could make it happen regardless of what society said. She was the daughter of a wealthy merchant and plenty educated for the time."

"Oh." Cara seemed to deflate a little. "Makes sense. She probably had the financial wherewithal to not care how she would be viewed by society." She took a bite of her sandwich and gazed at the river. "It isn't so much a factor anymore, is it? What society thinks of me seems like the least of my problems."

"What do you mean? What problems?"

"Ah, it's nothing. It just seems so much harder to achieve your dreams these days, you know?"

Lauren stayed quiet. It seemed like Cara had more to say.

"It's all I can do to get the bills paid every month and I'm only responsible for me. My mom never realized her dream, which was to become a nurse. I remember when I was little she filled out a bunch of applications so she could finish her bachelor's, but then my dad left. She had to work two jobs for a while just to keep us afloat. Things stabilized for us, especially after she started working at Perry Bidwell. But her dream died the day he walked out."

Lauren had never heard Cara speak with such bitterness. "I can't imagine how hard that must have been. How old were you when he left?"

"Nine. One day he was there and the next he was gone. He always wanted to play, ignoring my bedtimes and stuff. He was so fun and my mom was the perpetual buzz kill, with the brush your teeth and pick up that towel from the bathroom floor and no, you cannot have potato chips for breakfast. She did the work. He was never really a parent. And then he got tired of us. Of me."

Lauren could only listen with sympathy.

"I was so mean to her after he left. I blamed her. I went from being a good student to this little shit in the classroom. I got suspended for fighting. And when my mother picked me up, she wouldn't talk to me. She drove home in tears. I had never seen her cry before and it scared me to death."

Lauren's heart went out to that little girl. She put her arm around the adult version and drew her toward her, kissing her woolly hat.

"I still feel guilty about making her cry."

"You were nine."

Cara looked out at the river. "I stayed with him that summer while he was still attempting the joint custody thing. The two of us in a RV trailer in a campsite in Georgia. He'd leave me on my own for days at a time, and the towel stayed on the floor, my teeth were unbrushed, and I ate potato chips for all my meals because that was the only thing in the cupboard. Nine-year-old me couldn't do that for long. I would make these strict plans for myself to get through the day, like, I can only watch TV if I've cleaned the entire trailer and read something educational. Turned out I needed that structure my mother gave me."

Lauren squeezed her shoulder. Nine years old and developing ways to cope with her father's terrible parenting.

"My mother is a remarkable woman," Cara said. "She gave her love to this bullshitty, immature man, and then had to figure out how to compensate for his rotten DNA in raising me. It's like she made a deal with him to build a house, and she was in charge of the walls and roof and plumbing. He was in charge of the floors and electricity, but he bailed. How do you put that stuff back in retroactively?"

"Are you the house in this metaphor?" Lauren asked.

"Yeah, kind of terrible, I know."

"The house that is you is sturdy and strong, Cara."

Cara gave her a fake-looking smile. "Thanks. Finish your chopped cheese. It's getting cold."

Lauren put her sandwich on the bench beside her, squeezing Cara closer to her. "Seriously, you're the best person I know."

"It's been established that you don't know that many people."

"Ouch." Lauren laughed a little, but it smarted. Cara made a fair point.

"I'm sorry. This was supposed to be a fun day and instead I've dragged you into a pseudo therapy session against your will. And now I just insulted you."

Lauren ignored that. "What I wouldn't give to have an adult conversation with my mother."

Cara turned her whole body toward Lauren with distress written all over her face. "I can't seem to do anything right today. I'm sorry for going on about my mother."

"It's fine." Lauren crumpled the remains of her sandwich. "Your mom being awesome doesn't take anything away from my mom's awesomeness. It just makes me sad she's not around for me or Preston. There are times when I really could use her advice."

"I'll bet." Cara placed her warm hand against Lauren's cold cheek. "You must miss her so much."

"I do. My parents hid my mother's cancer for a long time. It made me so angry. They only told me how bad it was at the end of junior year, when it was impossible to hide the fact that she was so sick she hardly left her bed."

"Did they think you were too young to handle it?"

"I don't know, but I couldn't be angry with her. I was grateful for the time we did have during that last summer. Pres was home from Stanford, and it was like when we were kids, the whole family together, but there was this pressure, I guess, to stockpile memories for when she was gone."

"That must have been so hard."

"Yeah, it was." Lauren didn't want to dwell on sad memories. "Thanks for bringing me here. The view is spectacular. Lunch was great. Do you have anything else planned or are we going back downtown to warm up in the nearest bed we can find?"

Cara looked amused. "I should hope there is something else besides a bodega lunch with a view. I don't think we're ready for bed just yet."

"Hmm. Speak for yourself."

"Come on. We're going to get out of our heads for a little while." Cara pulled Lauren to her feet and led her in a new direction.

"What does that mean?"

"Instead of being horizontal, which will definitely come later in this time that I own, we're going to concentrate on staying upright." They walked briskly to another section of the park where a small group of people was lined up next to an outdoor rink that was sheltered by large fiberglass sails protecting it from the elements if not the cold. Lauren hadn't noticed because her head was turned toward Cara, but now she could clearly see that the people in line were exchanging their shoes for rented ice skates. "We need to get skates first."

"Ice skating?" Lauren stood on tiptoes. People were gliding through her line of vision beyond the barrier while spectators gathered to watch.

"Yup, and only five bucks each, a fraction of what it costs in Central Park. Are you totally opposed?"

"I haven't done this since I was really little. I think I'm going to be bad at it."

"That shouldn't be a problem. I know for a fact I'll be bad at it. We can be bad at it together, right?"

The hopeful note in Cara's voice drew Lauren out of her reverie. "I'm willing if you are."

After they were outfitted with rented skates, they hovered at the entrance to the rink. As Lauren's trepidation rose to an even higher point, she distracted herself by listening to Bono entreating his baby to please come home this Christmas. It was one of her favorite holiday songs.

Cara prepared to launch. After a tentative glide of about four feet, she turned back to Lauren with outstretched arms that said look how easy this is. And then came the flailing, the flapping, the frenzied running in place trying to maintain balance, and the inevitable fall as she landed hard on her butt.

She burst out laughing at the surprise of it, and crawled over to the wall, hoisting herself up, holding out a hand for Lauren. "We'll stay close to the wall for now, okay?"

Lauren cautiously followed her out onto the ice. Even though the potential for pain was likely, she was beginning to think she would follow Cara anywhere.

❖

After a lengthy return journey by bus and subway, Lauren was flagging even though it was only late afternoon. When Cara pushed open the door to her studio apartment, the aroma of cooking food assailed Lauren's nostrils, and she revived a little. "What is that? It smells delicious."

"I've had a beef stew in the slow cooker while we were gone." Cara reached for a pile of blankets on the chair. "Don't take your coat off. Follow me."

They went back out into the hallway, through a door at the end of the corridor, up a flight of stairs, past the fire door, which Cara propped open with a length of two-by-four, and out onto the roof. It was dark, but the city provided enough ambient light to see a motley collection of furniture, including a redwood bench swing that looked like it came from a summer resort in the Catskills and a rusty wrought iron table and chairs. Cara bent to plug an orange extension cord into an outlet and the roof was lit by many strings of lights that conveyed the feeling of being inside a cozy room with walls made of light. She was instantly transported from the chilly roof of a tenement in East Harlem to the interior of a starry, glowing egg of intimacy.

"Cara," Lauren said with wonder, but couldn't think of anything else to follow it with. Words failed.

Cara turned from where she was layering blankets on the redwood bench. "Do you like it?"

Lauren nodded. "It's magic."

She joined Cara on the bench and accepted the blanket she spread over their laps. Cara set the swing to a slow rocking motion with her foot. "It reminds me of our kiss on Seventy-Third Street, before we were so rudely interrupted."

"Yeah." Lauren took in their romantic surroundings for a moment more before settling her gaze on Cara. "You did this for me?"

"Well, no." Cara's rueful expression was beyond cute. "The lights have been up for a while now. Someone in the building fixed it all up so he could propose, and everyone loves it so the super lets it stay. It kind of cries out for a romantic encounter, right?" Cara spread her arms out to encompass the intimate surroundings. "No one will be crazy enough to come up here tonight in the freezing cold." Cara's eyes met Lauren's, a rare shyness in them. "I always hoped I would have a reason to use it for its intended purpose someday."

Wait. What? Lauren's heart rate tripled, her id spiky with happiness before her superego slammed down and informed it this was not allowed for her. "You're not about to propose to me, are you?" she said without thinking.

The light in Cara's eyes dimmed. "No, I was thinking more along the lines of a romantic seduction." But instead of moving closer and initiating the seduction, Cara abruptly rose from the bench, upsetting its trajectory and causing it to move crazily off-kilter for a moment. "You must be hungry. Let me get you some food."

By the time Lauren thought to ask if Cara needed help, she had already slipped past the fire door, leaving her alone. Lauren sank back against the bench and looked up at the cloudy, cold sky. Why was she constantly fucking this up?

❖

Cara brought two shallow bowls down from the cabinet and placed them a little too roughly on the counter, wincing at the slam of the porcelain connecting with cheap Formica. Anger made her clumsy and she needed to calm down.

Bracing her arms on the countertop, she dropped her head and concentrated on breathing long, steadying breaths. Friends with benefits was probably not for her. Compartmentalizing her feelings wasn't something she was used to, but that's what she had signed up for, and if she wanted to continue whatever this was with Lauren, she had to deal with it.

Christmas lights and making out. That was all this was supposed to be. Marriage had not been a thought in her head, but once Lauren had put it there, reacting so dramatically, Cara had only just stifled her own reaction. Anger was unacceptable. She had agreed to this.

But Lauren had surprised her in so many ways, with those glimpses of vulnerability and openness warring with her dogged declarations against anything lasting. From the very beginning, Lauren seemed so genuine. That hug and kiss on the sidewalk today had been so filled with exuberant honesty, such open affection. Cara knew it was real. It just didn't quite line up with Cara's idea of what a sexual friendship should be.

This was all super new. They'd only seen each other a few times. If Cara was hurt by the horror in Lauren's voice at the mention of a proposal at this early stage, then she should end it or try to be friends without benefits, although she didn't quite know how they would un-ring that bell, or if they even could.

She loaded a tray with everything they'd need for their meal and then ladled out two steaming bowls of stew, mentally preparing to head back up to the roof.

They wouldn't be deciding the fate of their relationship in the next five minutes. Cara closed her eyes for a moment and centered herself, letting the anger dissipate. *Go up there and have fun. We're friends. We're getting really good at having sex with each other. That's what this is.*

❖

Cara could see Lauren was uncomfortable.

"This stew is delicious," Lauren said with too much enthusiasm. "The beef is melt-in-your-mouth tender. I love it."

"Relax, Lauren. It's just a humble Crock Pot meal."

"What? It's really good."

"I'm glad you like it." She tried to be gracious. "I made a lot. There's more if you want it."

They lapsed into silence. She didn't know how to thaw the chill that now existed between them, and Lauren too seemed to be struggling with the swerve that being up on the roof had caused. Maybe she should just call an end to their time together tonight.

Lauren cleared her throat. "I'm sorry about what I said earlier. It's no reflection on you, believe me. My brain made the connection because of what you said about that proposal."

"Yeah, you were getting a little ahead of yourself there, Havemayer." Cara poured some more ale into their glasses. "I have a pretty good memory, and I heard you when you said you weren't interested in that kind of thing."

Lauren paused as she brought the spoon to her mouth. "You said you weren't interested either."

This must be that checking in with each other stuff Sam had mentioned at brunch. "I did say that, and I meant it. I'm not interested now, but eventually I will be."

"You have a timeline for when marriage is acceptable?" Lauren seemed to want to joke about it, but it wasn't a joke to Cara.

"I have a forty-six-thousand-dollar boulder named Sallie Mae that I have to get out from under before I can devote my attention to the dream."

Lauren gave her a blank look. "Who's Sallie Mae?"

She really is a rich girl. "Sallie Mae is the company that services my student loans."

"Oh." Lauren stiffened at the disclosure.

Cara couldn't think why it would bother her since she was the one with the loans. "I've already paid down about thirty grand, and I'm planning to have the rest paid off by the time I'm thirty-five. After that, I want it all: a relationship with a woman that will last forever, someone I can depend on and who depends on me, the proverbial house with the white picket fence and the dog in the yard, a passel of kids to keep us busy."

"Nice." Lauren's smile was brittle.

She might as well know what I'm looking for now. Lauren might even bail on their friendship without any more prompting than this. "It's a dream I have. I don't know how likely it is to come true. And I had always thought that whoever my future forever woman is, she'll have to be a lot younger than me because even after I've paid off my loans, it will be a long time until I'm financially ready to commit to someone. I'll be way past child-bearing years. She'll have to be the baby maker of the family unit. Can you see me? Fifty years old and hobbling around after my offspring with a cane in one hand and a tissue in the other."

In her mind's eye, Cara could see the home and kids and dog, and the woman beside her was Lauren. They looked so right together in her imagination—in love and happy, supporting each other through life's ups and downs. She shook her head to rid herself of the image. It wasn't going to happen.

Lauren had been gazing into her bowl. She looked up, shaking her own head a little. "A tissue?"

"To wipe my imaginary kid's imaginary snot."

"Ah," Lauren said, nodding. She picked up her spoon again.

"Sorry if that makes you uncomfortable."

"Why would imaginary snot make me uncomfortable?" Lauren gave her a half smile. "That sounds lovely, Cara. I hope you get your forever woman and all her accessories. You deserve it."

"Thanks." Her forever relationship had always been a comforting, hypothetical, someday, sometime thing. In all her youthful daydreams, she never once thought she might develop feelings for someone who wasn't driving toward the same life destination as she was, but there it was. All the wishing in the world wouldn't make Lauren want what Cara did.

"Not that I'm in any hurry for your status to change, but may I just ask: If this is what you want, why are you waiting? Shouldn't you be looking for the woman of your dreams now?"

"Well, the way it works is that I enter into this forever relationship without any debt."

Lauren let out a tiny laugh. "Is that the way it works?"

"That's the plan, yes." Cara put her bowl on the table. "I have to deal with my financial obligations sequentially. Doesn't seem fair to bring all that financial messiness into something that will potentially lead to more mess—like paying for a wedding or IVF. My parents constantly fought about money before their marriage ended. If I can eliminate that as a possible issue, I think my chances of success increase." Why did she sound like she was in a business seminar? Not very romantic.

"I admire your foresight—and your optimism. You know how I feel about long-term relationships, but there are people out there who could make them work. I think my parents' marriage was pretty great, a perfect example of what the institution can be. At least it seemed to be from where I stood. Strong and true and happy." Lauren's wistfulness broke Cara's heart.

"And you don't want what they had?"

"It's not in the cards for me." The flat finality of Lauren's reply made Cara flinch. She waited for Lauren to go on, to explain, but she stayed silent, picking up her glass and downing the rest of her ale.

"I don't understand, but you don't owe me any explanations." Cara tried to catch Lauren's eye, but she was looking away, staring up at the cloudy night sky. "If you ever want to talk—"

"I was used. I got burnt so bad I don't think I'll ever heal. That's all I want to say." Lauren turned and her face was like steel—impenetrable.

"Lauren, I'm sorry."

"It's okay." Lauren made a visible effort to relax. Her features slowly softened. "Could we go inside? My butt feels like a block of ice."

Cara tried to lighten the atmosphere. "Sure. You know all this outdoor activity was just a way for me to entice you into my cozy tiny bed for the rest of the night. Once you get under the covers, you won't ever want to leave."

"Was that the plan? You could have saved us a lot of time and brought us directly there. I can think of a bunch of things we could have done in your bed while we waited for the stew to cook."

"You mean I could have ditched all the planning I did? I'll try to remember for next time—sex is the priority." Cara tried to make a joke out of it, but it fell flat.

Lauren winced and put her bowl down. Cara was about to apologize for her glib words when Lauren said, "I know we haven't known each other long, but you have to know you mean more to me than just sex. I don't think you realize how good this has been for me. You've made me feel like I've joined the world again. Thank you for today. I had a great time." She held Cara's face in her hands and searched her eyes, the warmth of her palms scorching Cara's cold cheeks. "Am I being fair to you? Should we stop?"

"I don't want to stop." *Ever.* Cara realized this was true, but it scared her, and she didn't want to push for more than Lauren could give. "I'm not ready for forever yet."

Lauren kissed her and Cara felt a yearning, telegraphed through the softness and warmth of Lauren's lips. It was over too soon. She was surprised to see Lauren's eyes wetly shimmering with emotion.

"Whoever gets forever with you will be so lucky, but until then, is it okay if we still spend time together?"

Cara nodded and threw her arms around Lauren's neck, simply wanting to hold her close. She knew a hurting human when she saw one, and sadness was reverberating off Lauren in waves. It didn't help that Cara's emotions were close to the surface as well, and she couldn't stop the tears as she buried her face in Lauren's hair. They stayed that way until her roiling feelings receded, leaving Cara spent but at peace. "We're kind of ridiculous, aren't we?"

She felt Lauren's sputter of laughter as she nodded against her.

"Let's go downstairs." Cara didn't want the barrier of all their layers of clothes between them anymore. She needed to feel Lauren's skin against hers, the heat of her living, existing body telling her they were good together, at least in one way.

CHAPTER SIXTEEN

L auren opened her eyes to a perfect view. Cara was sleeping, lying on her back. Her hair, disheveled and wild, framed her face relaxed in sleep. One hand rested on her belly and the other flung out toward Lauren. Part of Lauren wished she would go on sleeping all day so she could simply watch her.

They had managed to lighten the atmosphere after the heavy talk during dinner and brought some laughter to Cara's bed. Lauren remembered Cara getting up at some point during the night to put the kitchen to rights. She had stowed the leftover stew in the fridge, and quickly washed the bowls and glasses before getting back under the covers. Lauren had watched Cara through half-lidded eyes as she attended to her chores in the nude, and she was aroused by the sight of her lithe body at the sink. When Cara returned to bed Lauren pounced on her with a renewed fervor. She scared the hell out of Cara, who thought she had been asleep.

Their first time notwithstanding, sex with Cara was the best Lauren had ever had, though she was reluctant to tell Cara this for reasons she didn't want to look at too closely. She also didn't want to think too hard about Cara ending things to look for her happily ever after with someone else. Just when she had allowed herself to revel in the pleasure of being with Cara, her conscience pricked her with reservations. At least there was time for her feelings to cool from her current desperate infatuation into something that didn't make her want to jump off a building at the thought of Cara dumping her.

Cara sighed in her sleep and turned away from her. Damn. It was so tempting to snuggle against Cara's back with its expanse of perfect soft skin. She sat up and looked around the small studio for something to distract her, but there wasn't anything except a framed picture of carrots hanging on the empty wall opposite the bed. It was centered on the wall, but so small and out of proportion with the space it was comical. Two carrots had intertwined as they grew to resemble one carrot hugging the other. Lauren wondered why it had earned such prominent placement.

Cara rolled back over and stretched. She opened her eyes and noticed Lauren was awake. "Morning," she growled in her sexy, sleep-saturated voice.

Just then, her alarm went off and blared a commercial for a car dealership before she reached over her and slapped at it with a vehemence Lauren found charming.

"Who sets their alarm on a Sunday morning?" Lauren still studied the carrots.

"I do, obviously." Cara raised her head to see what Lauren was gazing at. "You like my carrots?"

She scooted down so she was face-to-face with Cara, who shut her eyes again. "I do like them. They're endearing."

"I think so, too. They're the goal."

"What do you mean?"

Cara opened one eye, then closed it again. "You'll think it's stupid."

"Tell me."

"That's love right there. That's what it should look like." Cara got up and headed for the bathroom. "Be right back."

Just because it wasn't something she could have for herself didn't mean Lauren thought it was stupid. When Cara returned, Lauren asked for a toothbrush and used the facilities, too.

When Lauren reappeared, Cara was dressed in sweats and a T-shirt and was transferring dirty clothes into a laundry bag. Her own clothes had been halfheartedly folded and draped over the chair. Cara sat her down on the bed and went in for a leisurely Sunday morning kiss. Lauren savored the kiss, and drew her tongue across Cara's lower lip, asked for and was granted entry to Cara's mouth. Lauren fingered the hem of Cara's shirt and tried to pull it up before Cara stopped her and ended the kiss. "That concludes our time."

Her words registered and Lauren pulled back in surprise. "It does?"

"I have to do laundry. It's my Sunday routine."

"Do you have to do it right now? It's only a little after seven in the morning."

"The washers fill up fast. I should get there before eight if I don't want to wait."

"You go to a laundromat?" It was a stupid question, Lauren knew. Cara didn't answer. "Wait, what happens if we both don't agree about when our time is over?" Lauren had been imagining a lazy Sunday in bed with more sex and laughter.

Cara looked uncomfortable. "I don't know what you want me to say." "Wouldn't you rather stay here? We could get the *Times* and some coffee and hang out in bed. I'll read to you interesting things from the Arts section and you can get annoyed by the Op-ed page and complain to me about it." Lauren didn't know when she had last bought a physical newspaper made of newsprint, but the image was powerfully comforting and romantic to her.

Cara avoided looking at her. "That sounds wonderful, but I can't today." She stood up but Lauren grabbed her by the wrist and pulled her back down.

"Can you wait a minute and talk to me?" Sitting naked on the bed while Cara seemed to want to run out the door made Lauren feel incredibly vulnerable. "Okay. I understand if you have things to do today. I wasn't prepared for it. Can we get together tonight, or during the week?"

"Well, yeah. We're going to that charity thing on Thursday, right? I have it in my calendar." Cara grabbed her phone and opened the calendar app. "What time should we meet? And you haven't told me where it is yet."

"I thought we could get ready at my place and go together. Can you get there around four?"

"Four? I thought you said it started at seven. What will we be doing for three hours?"

Having sex. Getting ready. Maybe having more sex.

"I have Regents exam prep after school and that doesn't end until four. I could be there by five."

"Fine." Lauren watched Cara type furiously on her phone, as she moved scheduled items from Thursday to Wednesday. She guessed Wednesday was out now, but she wasn't giving up on seeing Cara more often. "How about tomorrow? Can we get together after work? You could come to my place or I could come here?" She knew she sounded needy but she didn't care.

Cara turned somber eyes to her and shook her head. "I told you I don't have a lot of money to spend on a relationship. I don't have a lot of time either."

Lauren frowned. "Not even for dinner?"

"I usually don't get home until eight or nine. Then I have a quick dinner and crash. I honestly don't have much left in the tank at the end of the day. I wouldn't be great company."

It sounded like an even lonelier existence than Lauren's. "I thought teachers went home at three o'clock every day."

Cara smiled, but it was without amusement. "Everyone thinks that. If I got paid for all the extra hours I work my loans would be a distant memory. Maybe some teachers in other types of schools can leave when the bell rings, but that's impossible at my school."

Lauren didn't know what to say. Cara sounded upset, but was it with her or with her job? She reached out to take Cara's hand, but Cara avoided her by standing up again.

"I've got to go. You can take your time and leave when you're ready. Just close the door behind you." She put on her peacoat.

Lauren had never seen Cara in a mood like this. There was a solemnity about her that was at odds with her usual, laid-back, dryly amused approach to things, and it bothered Lauren. "Wait, I'll come with you." She hurried to the pile of clothes on the chair and started dressing.

Cara scoffed. "You want to come to the laundromat?"

"I'll help." Lauren presented her credentials at Cara's dubious expression. "I know how to do laundry. I went to college. That's where people learn how to do laundry. I had to wear pink underwear for a whole semester, but I learned how to separate colors from whites."

"I'm a goddamn professional when it comes to doing laundry." She gave Lauren an appraising look. "You think you can roll with a pro?"

Lauren rolled her eyes and finger combed her hair. "Fine, I'll come and watch you be a pro at laundry. Do you have a hat I can borrow?"

Cara went to her closet and tossed her a purple painter's cap with branding from several AIDS Walks ago. It was hideous. She wanted Cara's cute Peruvian one.

"Where's your hat from yesterday?" she asked.

"Where's *your* hat from yesterday?" Cara answered.

Oh yeah. In her coat pocket. She put Cara's purple cap on and flipped up the brim. It looked ridiculous, but would serve the purpose of covering up her sex hair. "Are you ready yet? I've been waiting for ages."

Cara hoisted her bag onto her shoulder. "After you."

Lauren thought she detected a hint of a smile on Cara's face as they left the apartment. The last thing she cared to do was laundry at the ass crack of dawn on a Sunday, but she was willing to put up with a lot in order to see that hint of a smile.

❖

Cara dumped her clothes into a top loading machine, poured in the detergent, and spun the dial to cold. She couldn't be less interested in doing laundry right now, but she needed a moment away from Lauren. Under the cover of darkness, moving in concert between the sheets, she could ignore that they were in two different emotional places. In the light of day, under the harsh fluorescents of the laundromat, she was confronted by the direction her heart was leading her. Down a path Lauren did not want to take. All those concerns she had about Lauren's money were insignificant when compared with Lauren's aversion to commitment. She would leap at the chance to be with her for real, as devoted partners. But that didn't seem like it would ever be an option and she needed to keep that foremost in her mind.

Lazing in bed with Lauren and the newspaper sounded like absolute heaven. Spending every available moment with her was exactly what Cara wanted, but after their talk last night, it didn't feel like the safest course of action. She needed to compartmentalize. She had to locate a space inside herself and stuff into it all these burgeoning feelings that Lauren wouldn't welcome, and she couldn't do that with Lauren around.

After loitering at the washing machine and randomly swiping away at nonsense on her phone for a while, she returned to the molded plastic chairs where Lauren was waiting in that silly purple cap. An open tab on her phone reminded her of something. "Do you remember my student Miguel?"

"Sure. Bright but a little sullen?"

"That's him. He showed me this the other day." Cara gave her phone to Lauren. The browser was open to the main page of the Met's digital collection homepage and its current featured image of a Japanese woodblock print, *The Great Wave*.

Lauren nodded. "Hokusai. A perennial favorite. Available on coffee mugs and T-shirts everywhere, but most especially in the Met's gift shop. Shop early and often. Christmas is coming."

"Hey, *Starry Night* is on a million products, too."

"And for a very good reason. They're both masterpieces that speak to everyone, whether they love art or not." Lauren handed the phone back to her.

"He found a poem about it."

"He did? Good for him." Lauren elbowed her. "Good for you. Nice going, Teach."

"Thanks, but give yourself some credit, too. He wouldn't be interested if not for your van Gogh lesson."

"Okay, I'll take it."

"What do you think of me bringing the class to the museum so we could have another art-poetry lesson?"

"I think it's a great idea, but there's a problem. It's not available to the public for viewing."

Cara couldn't believe it. "But it's on the front page of your website."

"It's a popular image and it's good advertising, but this piece is extremely fragile. It was printed on paper, with all the brittleness inherent in an aged piece of paper, and the Prussian blue dye that makes it pop so vividly is prone to fading. It's almost two hundred years old. If it were left on constant view, its washed-out condition would only retain a fraction of its powerful resonance."

Cara grinned. "Even when you're giving me bad news, I have to say I love it when you start talking like an art history professor. Gets me pretty hot." She allowed her stare to smolder. Lauren flushed and sat on her hands. At least she had some hold over Lauren when it came to their physical attraction. It was better than nothing, she supposed, returning to the subject at hand. "Well, that stinks. I already told them we'd visit the museum."

"Let me look into it. Maybe I can arrange a private viewing."

"Really?"

"No promises. I don't know if it's even possible, but I'll try. If not, your class can still come visit. Maybe we can find some other poem-art combos."

"Thank you." Cara leaned over and kissed her cheek.

Lauren cleared her throat. "Don't mention it. Hey, are you hungry? Do you want to get some breakfast while we wait?"

"Not a good idea to leave my stuff unattended. People can be unscrupulous."

"You mean all the people who were supposed to be here doing laundry at eight a.m. on a Sunday?" Lauren pointedly surveyed the laundromat, empty except for an employee doing fluff and fold in the back.

"It's usually so crowded at this time. Maybe there was a party last night and everyone is sleeping in." Cara knew she was busted, but didn't try to explain. The real reason—wanting to be free of Lauren so she could process what she was feeling in private—wasn't for public consumption. "There's a bodega next door. Want an egg sandwich?"

"I'll get them. What do you want?"

"No, I still own the time, so I'll get breakfast. You wait here and guard my laundry."

"You said your time was over."

"I thought it was over, but you refused to comply. We're in a logistical gray area here."

Lauren stood. "It's not a big deal. Bacon, egg, and cheese?"

"And coffee with milk, no sugar, please." She let Lauren go. They had been heading toward a disagreement over who should pay, and she didn't want that during their time together. She didn't want to argue about anything with Lauren, and she could compartmentalize later. She only wanted to enjoy her for however long they could last.

❖

When Lauren returned, they ate breakfast, and Cara transferred her clothes to the dryer when the washer finished its cycle.

"Christmas is coming," Lauren said again when Cara sat back down.

"Yep, a week from Tuesday. It's not going to sneak up on you like Thanksgiving did, huh?"

"No." Lauren briefly thought about Thanksgiving at Cara's house. It seemed so long ago. "I'm flying to Utah on Friday night to spend it with my father and brother."

"That's great. I hope you get good powder. Isn't that what people say about a skiing holiday?"

"Yeah, do you ski?"

"No, that was the one club I did not join in school."

"Would you like to come with me? I could teach you. You could meet my family." Lauren didn't know she would be inviting Cara to spend Christmas with her until the words tumbled from her mouth.

Cara raised her eyebrows but said nothing.

She tried to sweeten the invitation. "It wouldn't cost you anything. We have a house in Deer Valley, and we're flying private. You would be my guest."

Cara's expression closed like a fan. "That's generous of you, but I can't. My mother would be crushed if I didn't celebrate with her."

Lauren entertained and then discarded the idea of inviting Mrs. Talarico as well. Too weird. "I want to at least get you a present. What do you want for Christmas?"

"My students to do their homework." Cara's response was automatic.

"I can't help you with that. What else?"

She was silent, but it looked like the wheels were turning. "Something green," she finally said. "An oaken forest in high summer. Or a rolling spring meadow. Put it right outside my apartment to give my eyes a break from the unrelenting gray of a New York winter. What do you want for Christmas?"

Lauren deflated. "I want an answer from you about what you want."

"I know you do, but I just don't need another fur coat." Her smile was playful.

The absurdity of the response made Lauren smile. "How did you know I was going to get you a fur coat?"

"I don't know. I'm psychic, I guess." Cara cozied up to her, wrapping her arm around Lauren's. "I have an idea. Let's exchange gifts, but they have to not cost anything."

"You mean I have to steal you something? Pick up something from somebody's garbage on the street? I don't get it."

"Hey, don't knock finding stuff on the street. I've found tons of things on the street: the chair in my apartment, a hair dryer, a picture frame. I even found a perfectly good broom one time. I still use it."

"Remind me not to sit in that chair. And a broom? How do you know it wasn't some poor witch's mode of transportation that you walked off with?"

Cara grunted in amusement and attempted to explain another way. "Let it be about the thought and not the price tag, you know? For instance, this year my gift to my mother is to make giardiniera with her over my break."

"Isn't that the disease you get from drinking bad water?"

"Ew, no, that's giardia. Giardiniera is Italian pickled vegetables. We spend the day chopping and canning. It's a big job. I'd help her do it anyway, but she knows my budget is pretty tight so she lets me get away with these kind of experiential presents."

Lauren tried to think of something that might work, something that would please her.

"It doesn't have to be like that. I don't mean to pressure you. How about this: it can be anything as long as you don't spend money on it. You can make something, or give me one of your own possessions. The one thing you can't do is go out and buy it."

"Okay." The idea was growing on Lauren. "Now, can I ask for one tiny pre-Christmas present?"

"Boy, you're pushy. What is it?"

Lauren spoke in a nervous rush. "Will you stay over Thursday night after the gala? I know it's a school night for you, and I know you're busy, but we won't see each other for a while after that, and it's not like the gala will be quality time with you, and I kind of need you in my bed at least once more before I leave, and I hope you know that I own the time on Thursday. It's my turn and I'm organizing everything and I—"

Cara silenced her verbal diarrhea with a quick kiss on her cheek. "Yes."

"Oh, good." Lauren relaxed.

"You're really cute sometimes, you know that?" Cara took her hand.

"Only sometimes?"

"Yeah, when you're not being pushy." Her indulgent look made Lauren grin like an idiot.

"Maybe I should go before you change your mind about any of this." She didn't want to let go of Cara's hand, didn't want to go at all, but Cara had tried to end their time together and she should respect that.

Cara didn't let go either. "Oh sure, promise to help me with my laundry and leave right before the tedious folding part."

"No, no," Lauren objected. "I said I was willing to help, and then you got all snotty about being a professional, and then I said, 'Fine, I'll watch,' remember? And believe me, I've been watching."

Cara kissed her again, laughing. "I was kidding, honey. You're off the hook. You're free to go."

Lauren didn't think Cara realized she had called her honey, but she heard it and it made her feel warm all over, right before it made her want to cry. "Okay, I'm going. See you Thursday." She jumped up and kissed Cara on the head and hustled out of the laundromat without a backward glance. If she didn't die from joy first, this friendship was going to kill her.

CHAPTER SEVENTEEN

L auren was getting ready for bed when Cara called. Called, not texted. Cara, who had never called before. By the time she had anxiously run through a mental list of terrible reasons why Cara might be calling, the ringing stopped. She quickly called back. "Cara? What's wrong?"

"Nothing's wrong."

"Why are you calling?" Was she canceling on the gala? Or canceling everything?

"You said you wanted to get together during the week and—"

"You turned me down."

"I know. I'm sorry about that. My days are pretty long."

"Okay, I understand." Lauren had only wanted to spend a little time with her. Maybe have a quick weeknight dinner. They didn't have to engage in multiple rounds of sexual congress every time they saw each other.

"But I didn't want you to think I wasn't interested in your, uh, day."

"You want to hear about my day?"

"If you want to tell me." Cara's upward inflection made it sound like a question. Was she nervous?

Lauren sagged down on the bed. Nothing was wrong. "My day was fine." There was a pause. Cara must have been waiting for more details, but Lauren didn't know what else to say.

"Let's start with an easy question. What did you have for dinner? I had leftover stew."

"I ate a ton of cashews when I came home because I was starving. Then I had a salad. This can't be interesting for you to know."

"It's all interesting. How's the museum?"

"Terrific. I made a new friend in the conservation department and she let me scrape rabbit skin glue off the back of a three-hundred-year-old canvas during my lunch hour. Hence, all those cashews after work." How boring could she be?

"A new friend, huh? Should I be jealous?"

Lauren grinned. "Yeah, you should. I'm totally hot for her. She's about sixty and told me all about her twin sons who are our age. Also, she has lumbago. So hot."

Cara laughed. "So you're into older chicks. I guess I never had a chance."

"When's your birthday?"

"May tenth."

"Mine's in September. Technically, you're an older chick."

Cara cleared her throat and said, "What day?"

"The eighteenth."

"Good to know."

"How was school today?"

"It was okay. Nothing as exciting as rabbit skin glue, though."

"Well, it is difficult to top something as life-changing as rabbit skin glue."

"We had a hard lockdown drill during third period. Those always scare the shit out of me."

"What is that? Why does it scare you?" Lauren was already dreading the answer.

"It's nothing. I shouldn't have brought it up. School was fine. The AP class is struggling with *Richard III*, as always."

"Cara, if it's on your mind, let's talk about it. Is that a drill for an active shooter?"

"Yes."

"Do you feel your school is unsafe?"

"No, I feel pretty safe. I think the students do, too. At least that's what they say on the yearly survey. But you never know what might happen on any given day." Cara's sharp exhale was loud in her ear. "I don't know what I would do if it ever happened."

"What do you mean?"

"I'm supposed to protect them, even the ones who act like buttheads on the regular. But what would I really do? Would I cower behind a desk or would I do something? I don't think I'll ever know unless I'm in that situation."

"And God willing you never will be." Lauren really didn't like the turn this conversation had taken. She had been scraping a damn painting while Cara was confronting her mortality. "Just for the record, if you ever find yourself in that situation, don't be a fucking hero, do you hear me? No one expects a teacher to take a bullet for her students."

"Okay, you don't have to shout. I'm sorry. This is not why I called."

Lauren hadn't realized she had raised her voice. "Then why did you?" she asked, now grumpy.

"Because I wanted to have an end of day wind down with my current favorite person, okay? Let's change the subject. What are you wearing on Thursday?"

Her grumpiness vanished and Lauren was charmed by the knowledge that she was Cara's favorite person. "I have a few things I'm trying to decide between. What color is your dress? I wouldn't want us to clash."

"I'm not wearing a dress."

"You know I love your corduroys, but they are simply not formal enough. Do you want to borrow someth—"

"I'm wearing a tuxedo."

Lauren was instantly intrigued. "Really?"

"Is that okay?" Cara waited for a reply. "Lauren?"

"Hang on, I'm not finished picturing this in my head."

Cara laughed again, and Lauren grinned at hearing it. Everyone's spirits had risen. "You're really good for my ego."

You're really good for my soul. Oh God, she needed to rein it in. "I can't wait to see you in it. You're going to look amazing in black."

"Oh, it's not black. It's sort of a dark blue, but the jacket has black lapels. It's not cheesy, I swear. Do you think I should wear my hair up or down?"

"Down, definitely." Sexy, sultry Cara in a tux, her hair a wild mane, she'd be beating the women off with a stick.

"What color are the dresses you're considering? I have to order your wrist corsage."

Lauren paused. Cara sounded serious. She couldn't be serious. This was another one of her jokes, right? She heard a choking sound, which turned out to be Cara trying to stifle her giggles. Of course.

"You are too easy, Havemayer." Her laughter was infectious. "I bet you're heaving a sigh of relief right now. Gee, how do I tell her wrist corsages are totally gauche, strictly high school proms and mothers of the bride? That's what you were thinking, right?"

Why couldn't she stop smiling? "I'm so glad you weren't serious. I don't know how I would have gracefully accepted one of those tacky things. I don't think I've ever seen one in real life."

"I have. I got one from my prom date. It was yellow roses and baby's breath."

"For our prom? Who did you go with?"

"His name was Brandon Cohen. He was a friend of Lisa Jankowski's boyfriend at the time. He was sweet."

"You went with a boy?" Jealousy reared up in Lauren over a kid who took Cara on a date ten years ago. She needed to get a grip.

"I did. I wasn't very secure in my sexuality back then."

"I didn't go to our prom." Lauren's voice softened as she remembered.

"I know." Cara matched her own voice to Lauren's tone. "I wondered why."

It was so long ago, Lauren could barely remember her reasons. "I think I was just over it. Over school, I mean. I didn't have anyone to go with, and I didn't care that much about it anyway. My senior year wasn't that great. I was still grieving my mom. I just wanted to get on with things. Make a fresh start in the fall."

"I'm sorry." Cara always sounded like she cared so much. "What did you do instead?"

"My brother had just come home from college for the summer and he came and picked me up. We went to a Yankee game in the city. He didn't know it was that night."

"A much better use of your time. The prom was the inevitable letdown it was meant to be." Cara chuckled. "You know, we had the prom in the ballroom at Surrey Hall, the all-purpose space for proms, rainy day gym class, and reunions, and I knew you lived somewhere on one of the upper floors. It didn't feel right that you weren't there. I had this idea at the time that you were up there in your room, and I wanted to go up there and bring you down and have a dance with you. Of course, that would have been impossible. I didn't know where your room was, and you would have thought I was some weirdo freak, and I was gutless, so I didn't even try, but it was a nice, John Hughes-ian fantasy to round out my high school days."

Lauren envisioned them in a transformed Surrey Hall, dancing, saluting the end of their school days in their teenage finery and matching cheesy wrist corsages. How different would her life be right now if she and Cara had connected at Perry Bidwell? She struggled to resurface from fictional memories and scrabbled for something to say. "We should go dancing sometime."

"Okay. Will there be dancing at this shindig on Thursday?"

"No, a cocktail hour and a dinner with speeches. And an auction." She tried to suppress a yawn, but Cara noticed it.

"Sounds like a fun time. I should let you go. We're both tired."

Lauren had to agree. "Thanks for calling." But she didn't want to hang up. "Good night."

"Sleep well."

"You too." Lauren was still smiling when she laid her head down on the pillow. She could get used to going to sleep every night with a smile on her face.

CHAPTER EIGHTEEN

Cara stepped out of the elevator and into the foyer of the Havemayer home. The Crosby piece was as magnetic and engrossing as ever, and she stared at it while she waited for Lauren to appear. She waited a few minutes with no sign of Lauren. Maybe she was somewhere near the familiar music Cara could hear, so she went to find its source.

The drawing room now featured a tall, elaborately decorated Christmas tree, and Cara paused by it before continuing her search for Otis Redding warbling a song Cara loved off to the left somewhere. She followed it into a room Lauren had not shown her on her last visit.

It was a mahogany-paneled library with heavily laden bookshelves on three walls. Many of the lower shelves held record albums instead of books, and there was an array of audio components sitting on a narrow table where Cara could see Otis's LP rotating as he implored her to try a little tenderness. An imposing desk stood at one end of the room and a well-used sofa perpendicular to that, but the room was empty of people. As Cara turned to leave, she heard two voices approaching, neither of which were Lauren's.

An older man entered the room followed by a woman who obviously was an employee. He stopped enumerating the list of items she was writing down when he saw Cara.

"Who are you?" the man who must be Lauren's father said, his voice one degree shy of a demanding bark.

"Malcolm, this must be Lauren's friend." The woman stepped forward, gazing at her with kindness from behind a pair of large horn-rimmed glasses. "I'm Astrid. May I take your things for you? I'll put them in one of the guest rooms. Lauren told her father you would be spending the night."

Cara gratefully surrendered her bags to her. "I'm sorry, I've come a little earlier than expected." She turned to Lauren's dad as Astrid made a quiet exit. "Hello, Mr. Havemayer. I'm Cara Talarico. I went to Perry Bidwell with Lauren."

"Cara Talarico." He repeated her name as if he were committing it to memory. "You surprised me. It slipped my mind that you were coming." He took her measure while he lowered the volume of the stereo. Lean and imposing, with short gray hair and sharp features that were nothing like Lauren's, he had piercing blue eyes that seemed to be the only genetic link they shared.

"I'm sorry for intruding. I was following Otis's voice."

He gave her a stiff smile and folded his arms over his chest. "Irresistible, isn't it?"

Cara nodded.

"How does someone so young know Otis Redding?"

"I guess the same way I'm sure Lauren knows about him. We have parents who enjoy his music."

"I see. Were you at the reunion, Cara?"

"Yes, I was reluctant to attend, but happy in the end that I went."

"I think Lauren felt the same."

"It's been terrific to see her again." She stood awkwardly next to the console.

"Please sit." Mr. Havemayer gestured to the sofa. "Forgive me, but I don't remember her mentioning you back then. I remember Sasha and Petra and a few other girls. They would visit occasionally."

"We weren't that close. This is sort of new." It felt like a job interview. Cara was subordinate on the couch while Mr. Havemayer maintained his power position by the desk.

"I see. What came after Perry Bidwell for you?"

"Princeton. I double majored in English literature and international economics and decided to become an English teacher."

"You preferred teaching to using your economics degree? Why?"

The judgment implied in his tone brought heat to Cara's cheeks. "I had my reasons." *None of which are your business.* Cara rattled off the rest of her résumé, now believing she was undergoing some sort of test.

Mr. Havemayer sounded grudgingly impressed. "Teaching is a noble profession, and doing it in the Bronx is not easy, I'm sure."

"It's not. Did Lauren tell you about the lesson she and I co-taught my students?"

"No."

Cara couldn't help gushing at the memory of Lauren's mastery over her topic in the classroom. "She was so great, Mr. Havemayer. She spoke about van Gogh, and got my students thinking and questioning, and there was genuine interest, which is really hard to accomplish with them. She really knows her stuff."

"What was your part of the lesson?"

"Lauren found a poem by Anne Sexton about van Gogh's *Starry Night*, which I facilitated an analysis of, but my students wouldn't have even been interested in the poem if Lauren hadn't primed the pump so well beforehand, so to speak."

"I'm glad to hear it." He braced his hands against the desktop, his posture becoming more open. "I'm grateful she's found something she loves to do."

"She's lucky."

His expression turned sharp. "You don't love what you do?"

"I do, but as you said, it's hard."

Mr. Havemayer looked as if he was waiting for her to say more.

She struggled to explain how she could feel equal amounts of enjoyment and disgust for teaching, and how she spent nearly every waking hour working, with only negligible financial rewards. "When I was interviewing for my current job, someone said something to me that I've never forgotten. He said my success as a teacher is never wholly dependent on me. In most jobs, if you work hard, you can be successful, but this is not true in teaching, particularly for the population I teach. I could give one hundred percent every single day, but if the students aren't able to do the same, that has an impact on my success. And we both know there are many factors preventing my students from giving their all on any particular day."

"So what do you suggest?"

Cara caught herself before she replied. "That's a long conversation, and I'm stepping down from my soapbox. I shouldn't be boring you with this."

He shrugged. "I asked. And I know your boss. We're friends, so if there's anything I can do to help…"

She frowned. "I'm sure you don't mean Barry Wedderburn, my principal."

"No." Mr. Havemayer chuckled. "I mean the mayor."

"Oh." Her frown deepened but she kept her mouth shut.

"I think I hit a nerve," he said. "You're not a fan of the mayor?"

"My mother says if I don't have anything nice to say, I shouldn't say anything at all."

"I think there's a movie that changed that aphorism forever. Now it's if you don't have anything nice to say, come sit by me."

"Mr. Havemayer." Cara put on a scandalized voice and tried to hide a grin. "I wouldn't have taken you for a fan of *Steel Magnolias*."

He shook with silent laughter. "One of my wife's favorites. We often watched it together." His smile was warmer than when they had first started talking. "It's okay. Say what you want to say."

Cara tossed circumspection out the window, her eyes blazing. "The mayor is a billionaire union-buster, sir. I am a proud union member. He's actively working against the middle-class rank and file in this city. The ramifications of that have not been felt yet, but they will if he succeeds in his plan to slaughter the city's unions."

"I was wondering where my plainspoken, ultra-direct friend was." A freshly scrubbed Lauren stood in the doorway, hair damp, feet bare, wrapped in her pink silk robe. Her eyes were locked on Cara like she was a snack to be gobbled up. "Astrid told me you'd arrived. Sounds like I got here just in time."

She shot an apologetic look at Lauren, then couldn't drag her eyes away from how infernally cute she looked. "I'm very sorry if I overstepped, Mr. Havemayer. I know you just said he was your friend."

"Not to worry. It was a pleasure talking to you." He smiled and moved to shake Cara's hand. "Have a good time tonight, girls, and Merry Christmas, Cara."

"Merry Christmas." Cara had no idea how this little interview had gone, but was glad it was over. She followed Lauren down to her room.

As soon as Lauren closed the door, Cara stepped into her arms and buried her face in her neck. The scents of Lauren's soap and shampoo, the warmth of her arms stealing around her, the brush of her lips against her hair, it all calmed Cara. Knowing how much Lauren's father meant to her, she hoped she hadn't screwed it up.

"So that's my dad."

"He's a bit intimidating," Cara murmured into Lauren's neck.

"Looked like you were holding your own." Lauren smoothed her hands over Cara's shoulders. "You're early." Before Cara could reply she captured her lips in a quick, searing kiss.

"I got stood up by my students so here I am. Funny, none of them showed up for exam review the day before break starts." Cara went in for another kiss, this one lasting longer than the first.

"Thank you, students." Lauren raised her chin as Cara diverted to placing kisses along Lauren's jawline, down her neck and onto her chest, her hunger for Lauren spiraling. Who was she kidding? Talking on the phone was good, but having Lauren in her arms was much better. She returned to Lauren's mouth and brushed her tongue across her lower lip, feeling Lauren's intake of breath as she untied the sash of her robe and slid her hands beneath the draping silk. Cara pulled her closer, grasping her hips with both hands, reveling in Lauren's skin, her taste, and her scent. "You feel so amazingly good."

"You have too many clothes on." Lauren unbuttoned Cara's coat and stripped it from her with a haste that bordered on frenzied. Everything came off and they stood just inside Lauren's room, getting lost in each other. Had it only been four days? Cara was becoming dependent on this, and a portion of her brain was banging a tiny gong in alarm. It went beyond pure sexual gratification. She had become needful around Lauren, and the depth of feeling she derived from their time together was unlike any of her sexual experiences before. Lauren had to feel it, too.

But it was annoying to think about that when all she wanted was to possess Lauren with her tongue. She took Lauren by the hand and pulled her toward the bed, practically throwing her down and crawling up her body. Bending over her, she lashed her torso with kisses, dragging her tongue up her belly to the underside of one breast, then covering its turgid nipple with her mouth. Lauren gasped and thrust her fingers in Cara's hair.

Cara was about to give the same attention to her other breast, but Lauren pushed her back and sat upright. Cara sat back on her haunches in surprise. "What's wrong?"

"Nothing. Come here." Lauren pulled her up to straddle her thigh and rest her weight upon it, and instantly reacted to her heat and wetness. "Cara." She gazed into Cara's eyes and the intimacy was almost overwhelming.

"You do that to me." Cara felt her pulse pounding in her clit. "Sometimes just by looking at you, I get wet. But I wasn't finished. I want to make you feel good."

"You do. You will. Let me go first."

It felt right to be facing each other. Lauren covered Cara's nipples with her palms, and Cara's breathing got shallower. She snaked her arms around Lauren's shoulders. "Look at us. Each trying to top the other."

"It's not that. I don't want control. I just want to give you your orgasm first." She gently pinched Cara's nipples.

"And I want to give you yours first." Almost as if she couldn't help herself, Cara bore down on Lauren's thigh and started to slowly grind against her.

Lauren giggled. "Are we seriously having an argument right now?"

"I think I just lost." Cara laced her fingers behind Lauren's neck and brought their foreheads together, her breathing now labored.

"And now you're getting ahead of me. Stop that."

"I can't." The friction between them was everything, alleviating the ache within her. "Keep doing that with your fingers," she said. "A little bit harder."

Lauren timed her not so gentle caresses so that they were the most intense just as the underside of Cara's clit slid against Lauren's thigh. The rhythm Cara set as she moved against Lauren slowly increased until her orgasm tore through her, leaving her a heaving mass of exposed nerve endings. "You're so good, you're amazing." She became limp in Lauren's arms, resting her head against Lauren's shoulder to catch her breath.

"I can't take much credit for that."

"It was all you." Cara plastered her chest against Lauren's, wrapped her arms around her, and held her until she was calm. They were both quiet, and to Cara it felt like they were suspended somewhere outside of real life, somewhere sanctified and precious. She wanted to preserve it somehow, but she also had a desperate need to taste Lauren.

She quickly tasted Lauren's mouth, but then gently pushed her down against the pillows and trailed her tongue between her breasts and over her abdomen. She separated Lauren's thighs with her fingertips and settled down between them, hungrily gazing at the most intimate part of her before directing her eyes upward. Lauren was staring back with an expression of bare need, and it made Cara want to give her all that she was.

She hooked her arms around Lauren's thighs and anchored her in place before she descended. Lauren shuddered as Cara's lips barely grazed her heated skin. Lauren was more than ready for her, as wet and juicy as a ripe peach, and Cara used her tongue to slowly explore her slippery, sensitive folds while avoiding the one place she knew Lauren wanted her. She could remain there, buried between Lauren's thighs, all her senses suffused with her, for approximately forever.

But that was probably too long for Lauren. "Cara," she pleaded. Her fingers reached into Cara's hair to urge her upward, while her hips slowly undulated.

"Mmm." Cara rested her mouth against Lauren's opening and the vibration of that single low note made Lauren twitch and groan. Cara relented. Her mouth and lips closed around Lauren, and it felt as if Lauren's whole body throbbed once and liquid heat poured from her as she came against Cara's tongue.

Cara stayed where she was and rode the crest of Lauren's orgasm along with her until she felt all of Lauren's muscles relax. She was a little blown away right now. Definitely a first when giving to her partner was just as satisfying as receiving. She rested her head against Lauren's thigh and tried to get a handle on her emotions. It was getting more and more intense, and Cara didn't know what might come tumbling out of her mouth in these tender and unguarded moments.

"Come up here." Lauren's fingers splayed over Cara's forehead, ruffled through her locks.

But Cara couldn't face her yet, didn't know what to say. She could usually find a way to keep things light and easy between them, but she was fresh out of ideas after her world had been rocked while she was rocking Lauren's. The compromise was to lift herself from between Lauren's legs and flop onto her torso. She looked into Lauren's half-lidded eyes and blurted, "I taste a liquor never brewed."

Lauren huffed out a laugh. "That's me? A liquor never brewed? That has to be poetry, right?"

"What can I say? Your pussy makes me feel drunk." Poetry was fine. Sure, it was embarrassing, but at least it wasn't unwelcome heartfelt declarations of feelings Lauren wouldn't return. Cara wiped her mouth against Lauren's belly in a lubricious display of naughtiness, feeling more at equilibrium. "Emily Dickinson. She's my favorite. I don't tell my students she was a lesbian, and the poem I let them think is about nature is really about her going down on her female lover."

Lauren's smile was tender. "Maybe you should, poetry girl."

"Nah, they can write their own paper about it in college and get a D from a homophobic professor." Cara scooched up so she and Lauren were face to face, lying on their sides. Her heart was full, but she wasn't on the verge of confessing any messy feelings anymore.

"I have to say, this pillow talk has really taken a turn," Lauren said. "Maybe you could go back to poetically extolling the virtues of my vulva?"

"Virtues of my vulva—love that alliteration. Okay, you want more poetry? Here goes." Cara rolled onto her back and thought for a moment. "There once was a woman named Lauren."

"Oh no." Lauren sat up on her elbow.

"You asked for it." Cara giggled. "Whose vulva was never called borin'."

"Would you look at the time? We need to start getting ready." Lauren flung the covers aside and headed for the bathroom.

It was just as well. Cara couldn't think of anything else that rhymed with Lauren.

CHAPTER NINETEEN

Lauren was still in her robe, putting her earrings on, dangly ones that complemented her updo, when there was a knock at the door. Cara stuck her head through, the shoulder of her tux visible. Lauren had been dying to see it since Cara had told her about it. "Come in, let me see you." She tried to mask the hunger in her voice and failed utterly.

Cara came through and raised her chin to meet Lauren's gaze with a mixture of confidence and defiance. She swaggered across the room runway style with hands in pockets. Her smile was full of sass as she struck a pose, one hip canted forward and arms akimbo. "Well?"

She looked so sharp, so gorgeous, but also so goofy with her Superman pose. The midnight blue suited her coloring, the jacket accentuated the line of her waist, and the tapered trousers exposed some sexy ankles. "I knew you would look amazing."

The tuxedo was incredible, but Cara had made an effort in other ways, too. Lauren didn't know what she had done to her hair, but there was an added luster that enhanced the curl. She also had applied a more dramatic style of eye makeup, and a deeper red lip than Lauren had seen her wear before. Lauren came close and raised her fingers toward Cara's lips. She didn't touch them, but she wanted to. "Your lips look so kissable right now. I mean, they always are, but there's something different, they look so good, so delicious, they…" Lauren trailed off, realizing she sounded demented.

But Cara looked pleased. "My friend Manny gave me some tips. He's great with makeup."

"How am I not going to kiss you tonight?"

"Who says you can't kiss me?"

"But I don't want to m—"

Cara stopped her words with a kiss, proving that there was no moratorium on her lips tonight.

Lauren took a half-step back. "You're lovely, Cara. I couldn't be prouder to have you on my arm tonight."

Cara lowered her gaze and thrust her hands deep in her pockets. "Thanks."

Lauren smoothed the lapels. "One thing." She ran her fingers over the placket of the white shirt, the pleats starched and crisp to the touch. Cara had left open two buttons at the top, but Lauren saw fit to open another. "Let's make this a little more cleavalicious."

Cara looked down. "Oh hello, new bra. I can see you. So will everyone else."

"Stop. You're perfectly decent. Nobody but me is allowed to look down your shirt. I won't let anyone get close enough to try."

"So protective of my virtue." Cara's smile was half proud, half naughty.

Sure, let her think that. "Will you help me with my zipper?"

"I didn't think this robe had one." She undid the sash for the second time that evening, this time revealing Lauren's black lace undergarments. Cara's mouth fell open. "Holy fuck, is that a garter belt?"

"You weren't supposed to see that until later," Lauren said, chagrined. "But now that you have, you can help me with the zipper *on my dress.*" Cara had spoiled the surprise, but Lauren was deeply satisfied by the way her mouth went slack and her eyes seemed unable to look away. Lauren had never been one to spend extravagantly on lingerie, but the time and money spent at La Perla last week was going to pay great dividends later tonight.

Cara held the robe open with one hand while the other dragged up Lauren's outer thigh. "You look unbelievable." Her voice was full of wonder. "What that bra does for your tits. And are these silk stockings? Do we really have to go? Can't we stay here in this room with you dressed like that? Preferably forever?"

Oh yeah. A fantastic investment. "Just think how great it will be when we come back here after you've been imagining what's under my dress all night. I know I'll be good and ready to tear that jacket off you."

"You make an excellent point. How can I help?"

She stepped into her dress. Cara zipped it up and stood back, allowing Lauren room to twirl in the floor-length, crimson silk dress with a very full skirt. The bodice was pleated with a halter top and a modest neckline, but it showed off her shoulders and neck with a fit that was exact and flattering. She looked to Cara for her reaction and was surprised to see her chin tucked against her chest, her eyes almost somber as they looked up through her lashes at her. She could swear she saw the gleam of a tear in Cara's eyes for a moment, but then felt she must have been mistaken when she looked again.

"You're beautiful." Cara kissed her lightly on both cheeks. She held Lauren's gaze, and Lauren had never felt so admired or desired. "You're just…stunning. Shall we go?"

Lauren grabbed her clutch. She nodded toward Cara's peacoat, carelessly slung over the easy chair in the corner with the rest of their clothes from earlier. "It's cold out. Don't forget your coat."

Cara wrinkled her nose at it. "I don't think I'll need it. Where's yours?"

"Upstairs." Would Cara want to borrow a coat? *Would I offend her by asking?* Best not, Lauren decided.

Astrid and Paloma came through from the kitchen, as if they had been lying in wait. Astrid was often around for her dad, but he had already left for an event of his own. Paloma was never here this late. She cooked during the day and was gone long before Lauren came home. "What are you two still doing here? It's late."

Paloma took Lauren by both hands and stretched them outward. "I wanted to see you all dressed up. You look so beautiful."

"You both do," Astrid said warmly. "I told your father I would take a photo of you."

Lauren smiled at these two older women who felt like family. They both seemed so happy for her and Cara. "Cara, this is Astrid, my dad's assistant, and this is Paloma."

"I've met Astrid. She saved me from your father thinking I was an intruder. Thanks for smoothing that over," Cara said to Astrid, then turned to Paloma, and stuck her hand out. "Hi, I'm Cara. I love the way you cook brussels sprouts. Lauren shared some of your cooking with me and I can't stop thinking about it."

"Anyone who compliments my food gets a hug." Paloma pulled Cara into her arms. "You're so pretty. Are you Lauren's girlfriend?"

"Paloma." Lauren tried to deflect her nosiness. "Cara is a friend."

"Just her escort tonight," Cara added.

"Such a shame. You look great together. And Lauren needs to settle down. She promised me babies and I'm not getting any younger."

"She did?" Cara looked surprised.

Lauren's cheeks reddened. "How old was I, Paloma? Twelve? You're going to hold me to that promise?"

"You were younger than that, and yes I am." She held onto Lauren's hand with obvious fondness. "Now stand back so Astrid can take the picture."

Cara took her phone from her jacket pocket. "Will you take one with mine, too?"

As the phones clicked away, Lauren turned to Cara and murmured, "Maybe you should have gotten that corsage. I feel like we're leaving for the prom."

"They care about you," Cara whispered as she smiled at Astrid. "I think it's really sweet."

They finally managed to get into the elevator and out to the waiting limousine. As they moved down Park Avenue in stop-and-go traffic, Cara scrolled through the pictures. "We look hot." She showed her phone to Lauren. "Not that I'm biased or anything."

"Objectively speaking, we do look hot." Lauren's nostrils got a fleeting whiff of Cara's scent. "Will you send me that? Will you also send me the picture from that night we got drunk at Bemelmans? From the street with the lights? I kept meaning to ask you for that." A few seconds later she felt her phone buzz from inside her clutch. She felt better for having them.

Cara smiled. "That was some kiss. I already knew I was going to sleep with you, but after that kiss, you could have laid me down in the street and had your way with me right there."

Lauren didn't know what to say. That kiss had a serious impact on her, like she was a piñata full of feelings that had just been smashed open—lust, yearning, and wonder pouring out of her.

"And each time since then, it feels more and more special. Weighted, kind of, with specialness."

Lauren stayed quiet. She brought Cara's palm to her lips and tried to draw strength from it. She couldn't speak, couldn't trust herself not to say something regrettable.

"It doesn't seem like the kisses of a friend. It feels like more." Cara's voice was soft and tentative.

Lauren gently returned the hand to where it had rested before, on Cara's thigh. "We're close friends."

Cara's expression was impassive as she looked out the window, and Lauren could sense she was letting it go, and she was relieved that Cara wouldn't press anymore.

There was silence for several blocks before Cara picked up her phone again. Lauren watched out of the corner of her eye as Cara typed, adding about ten heart emojis before firing off a message. Ten. Heart. Emojis. Cara had never included a heart emoji in any text she had sent to Lauren and she was overcome with the need to know who was receiving that text. "Who are you texting? Your mom?" It was acceptable for Cara to text heart emojis to her mother, no one else.

Cara paused to read a reply that had come right away. "No, Samantha Cruz. She helped me with my outfit. We found it at a thrift store and she hooked me up with a tailor. I sent her a picture."

Lauren supposed heart emojis to a close friend were allowed, but she had just declared the two of them close friends. Where were her heart emojis? *You're such a hypocrite.* "Tell her thanks from me. You should only wear tuxedos from this moment forward."

Cara snorted. "I'd love to know what my students would make of that. You can tell her yourself. She's having a New Year's Eve party. You could come if you want. Will you be back in town?"

"We're not scheduled to come back until New Year's Day." The holiday week stretched interminably before her, and the thought of her separation from Cara felt more and more unbearable.

Cara's phone chimed. "She says we both look hot too. See? It's unanimous. What did your dad say when you told him you were looking for your aunt?"

"I didn't tell him. I need plausible deniability. If we just happen upon her tonight, it's not premeditated, and it's not necessary to bring it up unless I find her." Truthfully, Lauren had almost forgotten the reason they were going to the gala. Finding her great-aunt and convincing her to allow the Met to borrow one of her paintings had been pretty low on her list of priorities lately. She had been so caught up in arranging a night out with Cara, playing dress up, and relishing the thought of owning their time at a fancy event in public. She took out her phone and navigated to the gala's web page from last year. "Here's what she looks like."

As Cara leaned in for a look, Lauren was intoxicated by her scent. It was a combination of her hair products and that citrusy floral perfume along with something indefinable. As surreptitiously as she could, she inhaled deeply to hold a part of Cara within her.

"A real grand dame type. I'll be on the lookout." Cara's eyes were intent on the phone's image. "And by the way, you are so not subtle with that sniffing business."

"I have no idea what you're talking about." *Dammit.* Why did Cara always have to call her out on her embarrassing behavior?

"Sure you don't." Cara's delivery was dry, but the smile tugging at her lips was fond and forbearing.

"I have to breathe, don't I?" Why was Lauren even trying to hide it? She buried her face in the place where Cara's shoulder and neck met and snuffled madly like a pig with a prize truffle while Cara laughed. Before she pulled back, she kissed Cara soundly. "Fine, I was sniffing you. You smell great. I couldn't help it."

Their limo began to slow. They had arrived at Cipriani on Forty-Second Street. Huge klieg lights straddled the sidewalk, and velvet ropes and security kept the horde back. Their driver joined a queue of cars slowly making their way to the entrance.

"There's a red carpet," Lauren said. "That's why we're not just getting out and going in. It's only society photographers, but it can be kind of a scrum with all the flashbulbs going off."

"Not interested." Cara's distaste was clear. "Is there another way in?"

Lauren didn't respond, speechless for a moment.

"Oh, do you want to go that way?" Cara said into the silence. "I'll hold your purse if you want."

"No, we don't have to. I thought a red carpet was something most people would want to experience."

Cara's sneer suggested this was the last thing she wanted.

"I went to a few of these events in London and Saff—I mean, my guest really enjoyed the attention and the spectacle of it. I'm surprised, that's all."

"Who is Saff?" Cara's eyes were steady in the shadowy light of the car.

Lauren pursed her lips, beyond annoyed that she had allowed Saffron to intrude on her evening with Cara. And of course, Cara caught it. Nothing got by her. "Saffron, my ex-fiancée." Lauren waited for the deluge of questions Cara would no doubt have after this admission, but none came. Instead, Cara's gaze softened and she grasped Lauren's hand. Maybe the word ex-fiancée implied enough to fill a book.

"Do I strike you as someone who wants to participate in the violation of her own privacy?" Cara looked out the window. "But if you want to run that gauntlet, and you need company in order to do it, I'll be there for you. Do you?"

"No, I never liked it. It feels invasive to me."

Cara nodded. "Okay, no red carpet. But know that I'm here for you. Whatever you need tonight, I'm your wingwoman, and I take the job seriously. You helped me out, and now I'm helping you out. We're going to get that painting for your exhibition. I've got you."

Lauren knew in her heart that Cara did have her. She was loyal, and Lauren had felt more with her in these few weeks than she ever had with Saffron.

Cara leaned toward the window, then pulled on Lauren's hand. "Let's go. I think we can sneak in the side there." She opened her door as the limo was still inching along, which forced the driver to come to an abrupt stop. She helped Lauren out of the car before the driver could react, and they walked briskly behind the backdrop that advertised the sponsors of the event, and where a line of fancily dressed people queued to have their pictures taken. Lauren still held onto Cara's hand as they ascended some steps and slipped through a door that was not thronged with handlers and hangers-on. Whatever the night was going to bring, Lauren felt stronger for having Cara by her side.

CHAPTER TWENTY

As Cara returned from checking Lauren's coat, she took out her phone and recorded a video of the floor as she walked back to where Lauren stood in line to register them. When Lauren's crimson dress came into view, Cara slowly tilted the phone upward to get a complete toe to head look at Lauren. She held the camera on her face and said, "Smile!" as a bemused Lauren watched. "Have you seen the floors here?"

Lauren looked down. "Is it tile?"

"Inlaid marble," Cara gushed. "So intricate. You never see this anymore." She barely restrained herself from getting down on her knees for a few close-up shots as Lauren claimed their table number and an auction paddle. She took Lauren's arm as they were ushered into the cocktail reception.

"Wow." Cara could see the space properly now, with a soaring ceiling at least sixty feet in height. The room was vast, and everything seemed to be encased in rich, heavily veined slabs of marble in hues ranging from almost black to rosy garnet to creamy white. They passed the main hall, where forty or so tables were covered with sumptuous linens and laid with fine china and crystal. As they walked by a low marble partition with signs every few feet that said "Teller," it clicked. "Oh! This used to be a bank."

"This place is gorgeous." Lauren snagged two flutes of champagne from the tray of a passing waiter and handed one to Cara. "Cheers. Thanks for being here."

"I wouldn't have missed it. Here's to us." A server approached. "Ooh, bacon-wrapped shrimp. Want one?" She grabbed two from his tray.

"Thanks. Let's do a circuit. The sooner we confirm Aunt Genevra is not present, the sooner we can get on with having a good time tonight."

They wandered toward a thicket of cocktail tables populated with older gala attendees. After some covert surveillance under the guise of idle chat and champagne sipping, Lauren squeezed Cara's arm. Cara directed her gaze where Lauren was looking and saw a regal, faded beauty of a certain age. The woman gazed at them and grasped the arm of the woman in a rather Bohemian outfit sitting next to her.

This must be the notorious Great-aunt Genevra.

Lauren took a deep breath and moved toward her. Cara followed.

"You are the mirror image of your mother," the woman said when Lauren stood before her.

"Hello, Aunt Genevra." Lauren looked serious and shy.

"Except for your eyes. Those are your father's. And your grandfather's."

"And yours," Cara said from where she stood half a foot behind Lauren.

"Aunt Genevra, may I introduce Cara Talarico."

Lauren's aunt glanced at her and nodded. "Won't you both sit down?"

Cara and Lauren took the two unoccupied chairs at the small cocktail table. Cara didn't know what formal fashion was supposed to look like for septuagenarians, but these two women couldn't look more different. Aunt Genevra was heavily but tastefully made up and looked as if she had arrived straight from a hair salon. Subtle plastic surgery left the planes of her face smooth and unlined, but her neck and hands gave her age away. Her blue sequined dress with matching jacket looked expensive.

The woman next to her seemed to wear her wrinkles with pride. The dark, velvety caftan she wore looked like the latest style for Ivy League commencement exercises. She wore no makeup and her more salt than pepper hair was worn in a braid under a slouchy beret of the same fabric as her robes.

"This is my companion, Barbara McDevitt." Genevra reached for the woman's hand and held onto it with what looked like a firm grip.

Cara, who was sitting between Lauren and Barbara, extended her hand to the woman. "It's a pleasure to meet you, ma'am." Barbara shook it with her left hand since Genevra hadn't let go, something Barbara didn't seem to mind. Her smile was a little roguish.

"Get a load of you. Ma'am. I'll never get used to that. Call me Barb. Everyone does." She cast an appraising eye over Cara and Lauren. "You two are together?"

Cara turned to Lauren, allowing her to answer. She was fully expecting to hear the friend appellation she had been given thus far and felt a swoop of surprise in her belly when Lauren lifted her chin and answered, "Yes."

"You were right, Gen," Barb said. "I guess it skips a generation, and I love the irony. Man, if Charles only knew about her."

Genevra was gazing at Lauren. "Your mother was an excellent woman. You must miss her terribly."

"I do."

"Do you remember coming to visit me?"

Lauren furrowed her brow. "I must have been ten or eleven. It was before I started at Perry Bidwell. We had tea. It was summer, but we had hot tea, and I wasn't used to that. You served these tiny, beautiful pink cakes and I think I ate too many of them."

"You were a little pig." Genevra said it with affection, but it still struck Cara as rude. She took Lauren's hand and tried to show support the only way she could. Lauren gripped it hard and pulled it into her lap.

Genevra turned to Barb. "Were you there?"

"I don't think so. I was probably working."

"Right," Genevra said. "Your mother got in big trouble for bringing you to see me. She knew she would, but she did it anyway."

"Why?"

"She didn't agree with what Charles did," Genevra said.

No one said anything. Cara had to ask, "Who's Charles? What did he do?"

"Charles is my grandpa," Lauren told her, then turned to Genevra. "What did he do, Aunt Genevra?"

"Your father never told you?"

Lauren shook her head.

Barb patted Genevra's arm. "Maybe we should save this for another time. Aren't there other things we can talk about? You haven't seen her in twenty years."

Genevra nodded. "How is your father, Lauren? And your brother?"

"They're fine," was Lauren's short reply. "I'd like to know what you mean about Grandpa." She looked so serious and worried, Cara wanted to put her arm around her, but she didn't.

Genevra looked over at Barb, who shrugged. "You know my last name is Winthrop," she began. "That's for David Winthrop, my late husband. He died when I was twenty-three."

Cara noticed Genevra and Barb exchanging looks. There was a story there.

"Charles stepped in to help execute the will after David's death. Needless to say, David's estate was sizable. Charles had me sign a bunch of papers that I barely looked at—" Genevra stopped abruptly and laid her hand on the table in front of Lauren. It had an ostentatious ring on every finger, including the thumb. "Don't ever sign anything without knowing what it is, Lauren. Learn from my gross ignorance."

"Okay, here's where I come in," Barb said. "Genevra and I met at a political rally downtown in front of city hall in 1972. We were both fighting for New York to ratify the Equal Rights Amendment and, long story short, we fell in love."

They looked at each other, and Cara could see their love was still strong after all this time. She smiled like an idiot at them, and they smiled back, but Lauren wasn't smiling.

"What did Grandpa do?"

"When he found out about us, he…" Genevra paused, evidently searching for the right words.

"Made things difficult," Barb supplied, and Genevra nodded.

"Because of my terrible misogynistic lawyer, Charles got wind of a large donation I was planning to give to NOW, and tried to take control of my finances."

"That's the National Organization for Women. It still exists, youngsters," Barb said.

"It was only because I got a new, better lawyer who actually fought for my interests instead of preserving the old boys' club mentality that I was able to hold on to my money." Genevra's tone had turned confiding, and Cara thought it was endearing. "The legal action caused a rift between us, of course, but Charles really couldn't stomach the fact that I was a lesbian."

"He was a homophobe of the highest order," Barb cut in.

Genevra nodded. "Our financial discord was a means to cut me off from the entire family. My only brother, without a backward glance or a moment's hesitation, severed all contact because I chose to love a woman. He robbed me of a relationship with you and your family. And that, Lauren, is the reason you don't know me or Barbara."

Lauren leaned forward. "I have questions."

"I imagine you do," Barb said.

Genevra turned to her companion. "Barbie, the cocktail hour is almost over. We need to put these ladies at our table."

"On it, dear." Barb got up from the table with a bit of effort. She held her hand out to Lauren. "Your table card, please?"

Cara jumped up as Lauren surrendered the card. "May I help?"

"Sit down, young lady. I'll be right back."

Cara watched her bustle away from the table, jeans and New Balance sneakers visible beneath her graduation robes.

"We have a table and invited several friends to help fill it up. It won't be a problem for a couple of them to move to your seats." Genevra spoke while she made an avid study of Lauren, who looked stunned by the revelation of her grandfather's shameful behavior.

Cara tried to change the topic from family laundry airing to the small talk they should have been engaging in. "I'm not familiar with the Schermerhorn Foundation, ma'am," she said to Genevra. "What cause do they support?"

Lauren ignored her. "Grandpa died almost ten years ago. Why didn't you get in touch sooner?"

For the first time, Genevra looked less than righteous. "You'll have to ask your father about his part in this, but I will admit to allowing my anger about this to color my judgment of you and your family. Barb convinced me I should try to reach out."

"So why didn't you?" At Genevra's confused expression, Lauren clarified. "Reach out."

"Well, I did. I am," Genevra exclaimed as Barb returned. "This is me reaching out."

"Oh boy," Barb said. "What did I miss?"

Lauren exhaled sharply and Cara hoped she could keep it together. "How are you reaching out? I looked you up and found your picture from last year's gala. I arranged to be here in order to find you. If anything, I'm the one who reached out."

"How do you think that photograph got on their website? Do you think I allow just anyone to take my photo?"

"So you started engineering this meeting a year ago?" Cara asked.

"No, that's preposterous," Genevra huffed.

"But that is when we found out Lauren would be finishing up at the Courtauld." Barb tried to be helpful.

Cara had a sinking feeling, and from the look on Lauren's face, she was beginning to connect the dots as well.

"We knew you had gone to Yale, but we lost track of you after that," Genevra added. "It was only by sheer luck that we found out you were studying in London. We have a dear friend who attended a talk you gave on Berthe Morisot's *Portrait of a Woman* at the Courtauld Gallery. When she mentioned it to us, I was thrilled to find your artistic interests aligned so closely with mine." Genevra's smile was almost tremulous as she looked at Lauren with a hopefulness that made Cara wince.

Lauren's pinched expression was a study in arrested indignation. "And the Pissarro picture?"

"Of course, you may have it for your exhibition, my dear."

Lauren was silent for a moment. Then she got up from the table and walked away.

Cara watched her go, then turned to Barb and Genevra. "Why can't any of you people pick up a damn phone?"

"What just happened? Why did she leave?" Genevra said.

"She feels set up, Gen. I told you this might happen." Barb was fatalistic.

Cara got up as well and collected Lauren's evening bag and auction paddle. "Barb, Genevra. It's been a thin slice of heaven."

"Wait," Genevra said. "Will you talk to her? Get her to come back?"

"Lady, I don't have that kind of pull." Cara looked behind her to where Lauren was disappearing around a corner. "And what would I tell her? Hey, I'm sorry your long-lost aunt manipulated your life, and robbed you of the opportunity to get your dream job on your own merit, but at least you can stay and have a nice dinner?"

Genevra gaped at her. "I didn't manipulate anything."

"Well, yeah, honey, you kind of did," Barb said.

Genevra turned to Barb. "You agreed it would be a good idea—"

"Why did you do it?" Cara interrupted. "Why was it so important to get in touch with Lauren now after all this time?" She watched as a silent conversation played out between the two older women.

"Just tell her," Barb finally said.

Genevra turned back to Cara and stated, "I want an heir."

Of course she did. She couldn't even with these people. Cara looked from her to Barb.

"Don't look at me, young lady. I'm not going to be her heir."

"Ask her to come back. I can explain everything," Genevra pleaded.

Barb gave her a table card. "Here are your new seats if you decide to stay."

Cara shook her head. "I'll try. Don't get your hopes up."

❖

Lauren would have collected her coat, but Cara had the coat check ticket. And she would have texted for the limo, but her phone was in her purse, which was now God knew where. Instead, she sat in front of a mirror in the empty women's lounge and listened to toilets flush and women gossip in the next room. How many women had sat where she was and cried? This venue was an expensive wedding factory, and here was the place where a bride cried when things went wrong.

She wasn't a bride and she wasn't crying. Right now she was more numb than on the verge of tears, and she really wished her mother was with her to tell her everything was going to be all right. She needed her mother to reassure her that she was an intelligent, accomplished person, capable of making her own way in the world, even as recent events might suggest otherwise. And then there was the news that her beloved grandpa was a homophobic dick who probably would have disowned her because she was gay.

Cara flung open the door. They had been apart less than ten minutes, and Lauren was too glad to see her. Cara strode across the small room and took the stool next to her, placing Lauren's clutch on the counter in front of her. She held on to the auction paddle and used it to fan her face. Lauren gazed at her reflection in the mirror. She really did look great in that tux.

"You're the smartest person I know."

Lauren scoffed. "Really? How do you figure?"

"Way back on our first date—no, scratch that—during our first time, at Bemelmans, you had your suspicions about your family meddling in your job. Turns out you were right." Cara gave a half shrug. "Smart."

That didn't make her smart, just mistrustful. Knowing she had been right didn't interest her now. "Why are you always so careful about not calling our time together dates?"

Cara stopped fanning herself and eyed her with apparent disbelief. "You just called us friends in the car. And that's what we agreed to be. Calling them dates goes against our decision to be friends, not two people pursuing something less…restrictive in its definition."

"You find our arrangement to be restrictive?" Lauren didn't know why she was forcing the issue right now with Cara. She might not like Cara's answer. Of all the weird shit happening right now, her volatile feelings for Cara were the least weird.

"The fact that you call it an arrangement should answer that particular question. But let's put that to the side. Your aunt wants you to come back. She says she can explain everything." Cara carefully placed the auction paddle next to Lauren's purse. "She also said she wants an heir."

"And that's supposed to be me?" Lauren sneered.

"I'm just relaying what she said. I feel like I've been dropped into the pages of a Victorian novel. Long lost lesbian relative bequeaths her fortune to the also-a-lesbian penniless waif, except wait, here's the twist, Oliver. She's not penniless. It's so Dickens. So Brontë." Cara's smile lingered. "Honestly? It's a tale as old as time."

"Oh, is it?" Lauren's spirits rose three-quarters of an inch. "Is it a song as old as rhyme, too?"

"Absolutely, Belle." Cara's eyes sparkled with merriment.

Lauren wanted to be swept away by Cara's playfulness, but it wouldn't resolve her current situation. "So I'm supposed to go back out there and listen to her outline her reasons for making me her heir?"

Cara shrugged again and the lightness in her dimmed a bit. The non-answer wasn't helpful, but none of this was Cara's problem. Lauren retrieved her lipstick from her clutch and reapplied. Cara watched her and mimicked the way she moved her lips. God, she was adorable.

"What would you do?" Lauren asked.

Cara's eyes locked with hers in the mirror. "It's your time and I'm your wingwoman. I'll do whatever you want me to do."

"I know that. I'm asking what you would do if you were me. Would you go back out there and talk to her about all this crap, or would you ditch this place and let me get lipstick all over your shirt collar in the back of a limousine on our return trip uptown?"

Two women passed by them and overheard what Lauren said, and Cara's cheeks pinked in a way Lauren thought delectable. They could be in her bed in about ten minutes if they got a good run of green lights.

"I'd stay and hear them out." Cara surprised her.

"Why?"

"Because they're your family, and they seem like they've had interesting lives. More interesting than mine, anyway. And you haven't been in touch in twenty years. Don't they deserve more than ten minutes of conversation between glasses of champagne?"

"But what about the underhanded way she used her influence to get me my appointment at the Met?"

"You don't know that." Cara didn't sound convinced herself.

"Seems pretty likely, though."

"Maybe you should consider it a compliment, that she was willing to go to so much effort to bring you back into her life." Cara's words were breezy. "And anyway, are you any less guilty than she is? You could have called her the same day your boss asked you to acquire the loan, but you didn't. You engaged in some skullduggery of your own and set a convoluted plan in motion just like she did."

That pricked Lauren's sense of sanctimony. "Okay, we'll stay, but I don't want to talk about any of the stuff Aunt Genevra told us tonight, or the Met, or the Pissarro painting, or anything like that. We keep the conversation light. I need to talk to my father before I wade into this topic again."

"See? Smart." Cara nodded her approval, and Lauren marveled at how good it felt to earn it. "And by the way, if we don't talk for twenty years, please just call me. I will make sure my number is searchable on Google or whatever replaces it."

She had a hard time imagining Cara gone from her life for a week let alone twenty years, but now was not the time to think about that. "You don't want me resorting to skullduggery? Here's a by-the-way for you: that was the first time I've ever heard a person use that word in conversation. There's probably a reason for that."

"Shut up. You loved it." Cara's tiny smile seemed to reflect both embarrassment and affection.

Lauren's spirits lifted completely as they exited the restroom and got back to the gala. The truth was, she did love it. She loved it a lot.

❖

There was a ripple of activity when Lauren and Cara approached the table in the cavernous main hall of Cipriani. Several older women got up and moved so the places on either side of Genevra and Barb became vacant. Lauren laid down the ground rules to Genevra, who nodded and grasped her hand in what looked very much like gratitude. Barb gave Cara an ostentatious wink and said, "Seems like you do have that kind of pull, young lady."

Genevra and Barb's friends were a fun group of salty broads who never let their glasses get to half empty. Cara encouraged their storytelling, and Lauren was quiet with an ever-present glass of wine in hand. She seemed to enjoy herself as she listened to their bawdy stories of queer New York City during the seventies.

When the auction began, Cara was astonished at how competitive the bidding was among rich, well-lubricated fools who seemed to want desperately to be parted from their money. It was after this that Lauren gave Cara the signal to go—a signal Cara had been dearly wishing for—since Lauren's state of sobriety had been breached and overrun by a disreputable gang of elderly society lesbians.

A few minutes later Cara caught Lauren's Louboutin when it fell from her foot as she dove into the back seat of the limo. She calmly followed her and nodded at the driver as he closed the door. She found Lauren sprawled across the back seat, with her eyes closed, head lolled against the headrest, and legs splayed across the interior.

"You okay, Drinky McGee?" Cara placed Lauren's coat and shoe to one side and scooted closer to her.

Lauren looked up at her blearily. "Yeah. Too much to drink."

"So I noticed."

Lauren pulled off her remaining heel and dropped it with a clunk. "Thanks for running interference. You really got those old school lesbos talking."

"Happy to do it." Cara had worked harder this evening than she had expected. She had thought she would be a benign observer to the antics of the rich and richer, and now she was glad they were both safely in the car and headed back to Lauren's place.

"I thought I was going to be miserable, but it wasn't terrible," Lauren said. "At least I laughed a lot."

"Yeah, those women were a ball."

Lauren rubbed a finger across her teeth and bared them at Cara. "So much red wine. Are my teeth purple?"

"No, you're fine." Cara smiled at Lauren's comical drunken expression.

"I do like red wine." Lauren sat up and began what Cara could only assume was singing, although it came closer to off-key bellowing. "Tale as old as wine, song as old as wine, beauty and red wine!"

"Whoa, I realize why karaoke is a no-go for you now. We'll keep you away from auditioning for any of those singing competition shows, too."

"Rude." Lauren snuggled into Cara. She rested her head on her shoulder and curled her arm around her neck. "But I forgive you because you're so sexy. You're my sexy breast fend. Best friend."

Cara yawned, allowing herself to set her level of vigilance one degree lower. "I'm pooped. I wish I didn't have school tomorrow."

"Sorry, baby. Do you want to go home?"

Her heart lurched at the endearment. "No, I'm fine going back to your place."

Lauren placed her thumbs on Cara's cheeks, pulling the skin down and gazing deeply and drunkenly into her eyes. "These eyes. They're goddamn beautiful is what they are. I want to fall into them like I'm the fat kid in that chocolate factory. Just float around in the left one for the rest of my life. Then, when I die, I'd jump across the bridge of your nose into the right one and there's heaven." After placing an imprecise, sloppy kiss next to Cara's ear, she slumped against Cara's shoulder and fell asleep.

Cara secured her arm around Lauren's shoulders. She couldn't deny the protective instinct that welled up in her for Lauren, and there was something that felt absolutely right about holding her this way. Her dedication to Lauren tonight was more than simply returning the favor of her classroom visit. She couldn't abide seeing Lauren upset or unhappy. This investment of her emotions in Lauren, with no collateral or guarantees, was utterly risky, but she couldn't stop herself and didn't want to anyway. She was all in, and would deal with the fallout when it came.

Wanting to preserve everything about this moment, Cara did it the only way she could think of—she pulled her phone out and took a photo of them. Lauren was too out of it to notice.

CHAPTER TWENTY-ONE

Thirty thousand feet above Middle America, Lauren sat across from her father in a plush leather captain's chair, watching him type with single-minded focus. A table had been raised between them, and their dueling laptops suggested a productivity that was in reality only one-sided. She hadn't accomplished anything since takeoff.

Her brain had been fuzzy when Cara woke her, and she couldn't exactly remember how her dress came to be hanging in its garment bag on the closet door. The T-shirt she wore over her sexy underwear meant her drunkenness had torpedoed plans for a hot night with Cara.

She had requested Cara stay with her last night and then hadn't even made it worth her while. In fact, Cara had taken care of her worthless drunken ass instead of collecting benefits. At a little after six in the morning, Cara had awakened her in the gentlest way possible. She pointed out the water and Tylenol she had left at her bedside and the wrapped gift box on the chair across the room and wished her a merry Christmas before bestowing a chaste kiss on her cheek.

Lauren had sat up and pulled Cara back down, drawing her into a good-bye kiss that lived up to the name. She had plunged her fingers into Cara's shower-damp hair and tasted mint on her lips. Enveloping herself in Cara had been the goal, so she could tide herself over for their days apart. She was in deeper than she intended, but where Cara was concerned, she couldn't help herself.

Cara had chuckled as she pulled away and said, "You give great good-bye, Lauren. I'll text you."

"Wait…" Lauren hadn't known what her next words would be.

Cara had waited, a tender smile on her tired face.

Vocalizing the desires that were still only half-formed in her head had proved too difficult when it felt like her brain had been encased in a layer of quick drying cement.

Cara had caressed her cheek with a warm hand. "We'll talk later. I have to go. Travel safely."

And now, a thousand miles away from Cara, Lauren still could not extract an ordered thought about what she wanted from her time with her. It was still a hapless, nebulous cream puff of doubt, with a rich filling of inarticulate longing, and a dusting of sexual need over top. And even though she suddenly felt the desire for something sweet, it was time to use her brain for more constructive endeavors.

"Dad?"

"Hmm?" He didn't look up from his laptop.

"What are you working on?"

"The residential side of the São Paolo project has hit a few snags with city government. I'm drafting a document for the lawyers." He gave her a quick smile. "Want to get it finished so we can have some fun on the slopes."

"Oh." Lauren watched as he continued to type. "Dad?"

"Yeah, honey?"

"How did Grandpa feel about gay people?"

He raised his eyes in surprise. "Why are you asking about that?"

"I have a reason for asking, and I'll tell you what it is in a minute. Could you please answer the question?"

He was silent for a few long moments, and Lauren began to understand that the quick dismissal of her fears she was hoping for was not coming.

"I could tell you my father was a product of his time and maybe he was scared of things he didn't understand, that he had a good heart underneath it all, but you're old enough to know the truth."

Lauren braced herself. She saw her father grapple with what to say next.

"You and Preston saw a side to your grandfather that no one else saw. He treated you both with a love and kindness I had no idea he was capable of. He certainly never showed me the same love, nor did he show it to any other family members, or the hundreds of employees who worked for him."

"But, Dad, this is Grandpa. Grandpa, who used to take us to Greenberg's for black-and-white cookies on Saturdays, who taught me how to play poker with M&Ms."

"He was great with you kids. To say I was astonished is putting it mildly. Your grandfather and I had a very different relationship."

"What do you mean?"

He struggled to choose his words. "He was hard on me."

Lauren sat back in her chair. "Dad…"

"He was a bully, Lauren. He bullied your grandmother, his underlings, and me. My solution was to ignore all the belittling comments and put my head down and do the work. It was the coward's way out. I never stood up to him." He snorted. "He tried to bully your mom, but she just refused. She always found a way to rise above his petty bullshit." His expression had equal parts pride and shame within it. "He had met his match with her. But she never stooped to his level. She just had this steadfastness, this unwillingness to compromise her beliefs. She was unshakeable."

Lauren was surprised to see tears welling in her usually stoic father's eyes. She reached across the table and took his hands in hers. "I miss her so much."

"I do too. Every damn day. She took on a lot when she agreed to marry into my family, but she made it look easy." He took his hands back and cleared his throat. "So you want to know how he felt about gay people?"

Their emotional moment was over. It was so like her dad not to dwell on morose thoughts, to push through the pain to return to a plateau of composure. "Yes, even though now I think I can guess."

"Do you remember coming out to your mother and me?"

Lauren was surprised by the question and had no ready answer. "Um, I can't think..."

"That's because you didn't, really." Her dad smiled. "The closest you came to making an announcement was when you were seventeen, home for a weekend from school. Petra was with you, and you proclaimed she would be sleeping in your bed and wouldn't need the guest room."

"I'm sure I meant for you to think we were girlfriends gossiping into the wee hours together." The thought of her teenage self blithely forcing knowledge of her sexuality on her parents was totally cringe-inducing.

"Yeah, we got that, honey." The duh was implied. "It was the way you couldn't meet our eyes, and the way you looked at Petra, like she was a life-sized piece of birthday cake you couldn't wait to devour."

"Dad! Gross."

He laughed while Lauren made retching sounds. "After you and Petra left the room, your mom gloated over getting confirmation on a claim she had made years before." He gazed at her in a knowing way. "Seems to me I saw a similar expression on your face recently, perhaps when a certain someone and I were talking about education?"

She didn't rise to the bait. "What did Mom mean?"

"She saw it in you very early. Beginning when you were seven or eight, she would mention it every once in a while, the possibility that you might be gay."

Lauren's mouth dropped open.

"Your first-grade teacher, what was her name?"

She instantly recalled. "Mrs. Marks."

"You told Mom you were going to marry her."

"I did?" Lauren remembered having strong feelings for Mrs. Marks and being inexplicably nervous about giving her a hug at the end of the year.

"That wasn't a smoking gun, of course, but little things kept coming up, and she would point them out to me: your obsession with the Pussycat Dolls, your brief but intense fascination with my neckties, how you would tomboy-out with your brother and his friends when he'd let you play roller hockey in the park with them."

Taken individually, it wasn't much, but as a body of evidence it was more indisputable. Thinking back, her obsession with the Pussycat Dolls had almost nothing to do with their music. "Was Mom bothered by it?" Lauren suddenly felt tense.

"Not at all. She thought it was fine, the most normal thing in the world." His reassurance made her deflate with relief. "She was doing it for me."

Lauren furrowed her brow in confusion.

"She was preparing me. Grandpa loathed gay people, and unfortunately, she thought it might have rubbed off on me."

"Did it?"

Her dad looked uncomfortable. "I'll admit to having possessed knee-jerk opinions about gay people before you were born, but your mom forced me to confront them, and I realized nothing I had previously believed was grounded in fact. It was all prejudiced nonsense." He looked down and then back at Lauren. "It shames me that your mother thought there was even the slightest possibility any of your choices would alter my love for you. They didn't then, and don't now. They never will."

Tears welled in Lauren's eyes. They had never talked like this before, and she wondered why that was so. "I saw Aunt Genevra at the gala last night," she said.

"Ah." Her dad nodded slowly. "Now it begins to make sense."

"I have a confession to make." Lauren told her father about the Pissarro exhibition and how she had stalked her great-aunt.

"How did she look?"

"Fine, I guess. I recognized her from a photo on the foundation's website. I never would have known her otherwise. It's been almost twenty years since we've seen each other."

He shook his head. "She was at the funeral."

"She was? I'm surprised. She seemed pretty bitter about Grandpa."

"Not that one. That bridge was well and truly burned. No, she was at your mother's funeral."

"I don't remember that." It wasn't surprising. The day was mostly a blur. It had been a searingly hot day in July, the leaves drooping like the effort it took to remain attached to the trees was too much. Her clearest memory was watching a mailman and a bicyclist collide on the sidewalk while her family waited for the limo to take them to the funeral service.

"She was, and Barb too. They were very gracious. Said some very nice things. Now that I think about it, they probably came and went quickly to avoid seeing your grandfather. It probably took some nerve for her to come." He looked out the window. "I regret I never reached out after Grandpa died. I should have. The number of Havemayers is dwindling, and family should stick together."

"Then why didn't you?" Lauren didn't want him to feel bad, but she wanted to know.

"I don't have any kind of an excuse." He rubbed his hand over his face. "I could barely function after your mother died. Then Grandpa died and I had my hands full keeping the company on an even keel." He smiled without any warmth. "If I didn't, I know your grandfather would have a few choice words for me if I ever saw him in hell."

Lauren reached across the table and took his hand, for once seeing him not as her father, but as an adult man who was still dealing with the crushing disappointments life had handed him. If the incessant pace at which he still worked was anything to go by, her father was still using it to fill up the emptiness her mother's death had left.

"I failed you, your brother, and Aunt Genevra, and I'm sorry. I should have done better by you all." An uncertain look, followed by a grimace passed over his face. "You said it had been twenty years since you had seen her?"

"Yeah, almost. Mom took me to Aunt Genevra's for tea when I was around ten."

"I remember. Your mother and I had a huge fight about it." He gave her a guilty glance. "Of course, your grandfather heard about your visit— he seemed to have spies everywhere—and he read me the riot act for not controlling my wife and making her toe the family line. I couldn't understand why she would go out of her way to upset him like that."

"Why did she?"

"She never told me why. But now, with the benefit of hindsight, I can hazard a guess."

"She wanted to piss off Grandpa?"

"No," he said with a chuckle. "She knew his anger would come down on me, so it had to be worth it. I think your mother wanted you to see there were women who were living differently than the traditional nuclear family. And here was an essentially married lesbian couple in your own family. I think she wanted you to see their example, to know what your life could be like."

"I had no idea. Barb wasn't there. It was only Aunt Genevra, and she was pretty intimidating."

"Well, you were ten, and I'm sure your mother thought this would be the first of many visits. She probably thought she was laying the groundwork for the future when you were more certain of who you were. And if her assumptions about you were wrong, then no harm done. You had simply gotten closer with members of your own family."

"And there were no more visits because she was obeying Grandpa?"

"She was obeying me." He looked ashamed again. "I asked her not to do it again, and she said okay. It's only now that I'm putting it all together that I'm realizing what I took away from you."

"It's all right, Dad. I turned out fine, don't you think?" Lauren's smile was tentative.

"Of course. I couldn't ask for a better daughter."

She allowed herself a moment to think how her life might be different if Genevra and Barb had been guiding influences within it. How witnessing a strong same-sex union might have impacted her romantic decisions and self-worth. It was something she would never know, and there was no use dwelling on it. "I think Aunt Genevra may have pulled strings with the Met to get me my position."

Her father looked at her with shock. "Why would she—how did she—"

"She says she didn't, but there are a few too many coincidences lining up for it not to be a possibility."

"I'm sorry, Lauren. I know you wanted to earn it on your own." He patted her hand. "You don't sound sure about it, though. Could she be telling the truth?"

Lauren didn't know, and didn't know if she should even pursue it. She loved her job, felt she could do some good in it. It couldn't be over before it had barely begun. "She might. But think about it. Hypothetically, she asks someone from the board to lunch. She wouldn't even have to ask. Just the mention of a niece finishing her PhD would be enough. That, and the unspoken prospect of her own enormous collection glinting in the sunlight for someone to pounce on."

Her dad tilted his head. "That may be true, but any institution is going to take notice of a résumé with the Havemayer name on it. That's just a fact, and it has nothing to do with your aunt. I respected your wishes when you told me to butt out—"

Lauren protested. "It wasn't like that."

"I know. I understood where you were coming from, but you're a Havemayer. It's a legacy that comes with privileges and drawbacks, whether you like it or not."

She nodded. Both were completely familiar to her.

"Maybe it was your aunt, or maybe someone over at the Met has a long memory and remembers the Havemayer bequests, or maybe you impressed the hell out of them at your interview and really did get there on your own." The pride in his voice was unmistakable. "Your brains and talent are what's going to keep you there. What does it matter as long as you're adding value and flourishing?"

Before Lauren could respond, Ralph, their flight attendant, approached from the fore of the plane. "The captain wanted me to advise you we've begun our descent and should be on the ground in about a half-hour. May I remove the table?"

During the remaining flight time, Lauren ruminated on all her father had said. What she had feared was an insurmountable family divide seemed only the inertia that came with the passage of time. And even if Aunt Genevra had meddled in her career, her father had put her potential actions in perspective. Lauren wanted to get to the bottom of her aunt's involvement in acquiring her job, but she also owed it to her aunt, and her parents, to try to renew their connection.

Switching her phone from airplane mode as they taxied to the private hangar at McDonald Field, Lauren received a text from Cara. *Your ginormous present arrived. Call me when you get a chance.* Three Christmas tree emojis.

She texted back: *Just landed. Is it too late to call in an hour?*

Nope! Two thumbs up emojis.

❖

Unlike their tree in New York, the tree in the Utah house was real, and the living room smelled like a pine forest. Coming to Utah for Christmas had been a family tradition for many years, but had lapsed when Lauren and Preston had gone to college. It was nice to be reviving it this year. She said good night before retiring to her room, grabbing Cara's present on her way up the stairs.

It was after one a.m. on the East Coast and she promised herself she would keep it brief with Cara as she settled under the covers. She smiled at Cara's groggy hello. "Were you sleeping?"

"Dozing. How are you feeling? How was the trip?"

"Fine, I had a good talk with my dad. How was your day?"

"Eh, school was okay. Everybody was just waiting for dismissal. Nothing got done. Then tonight I met up with some old school friends I hadn't seen in a while. That was fun."

"Oh? Anyone I know?"

"No, some of my Princeton friends returning home for the holidays. We make a point to get together when there's a bunch of us around."

"Sounds like fun. What did you do?"

"Hung out in a bar in the East Village, chatted. Then I ate a dollar slice—two, actually."

"Big spender."

"Ha. Rico caught me when I got home and told me a delivery came for me to the bodega. Then he helped me carry it up the stairs. The thing is huge."

"I'm sorry. I didn't remember it being so big."

"At least four-foot square. It looks like a piece of art. Is it art? I'm kind of wondering if you abided by the gift-giving rules."

"I did!" Lauren sat up, indignant.

"Okay, my mistake. I guess I'm feeling a little insecure about my present."

"Don't, I'm sure I'll love it. I have it right here. Should I open it?"

"Go ahead." She sounded resigned.

"I've got you on speaker and I'm putting the phone down for a second." Lauren made quick work of the wrapping paper and opened the box to find the framed image of the hugging carrots from Cara's apartment. She laughed. "Thank you, Cara. I love it."

"Believe it or not, that picture means a lot to me."

"And now it means a lot to me, too." Lauren gazed at it for a moment, then leaned over and propped it on the chair next to the bed. Affection for Cara and her simple gesture of togetherness rose in her. "Are they supposed to be you and me? Lauren Carrot and Cara Carrot?" She giggled. "Cara Carrot. That's cute."

"Hmm. Maybe."

"Okay. Open mine."

Lauren waited while Cara removed the extensive packaging. Sounds of tearing and dragging preceded Cara's low, "Lauren."

"Do you like it?"

"I adore it, but it's too much."

"No, it's not. Describe it to me."

"Wait. You don't know what it looks like?"

"I do, but it's been a while. Tell me."

"Okay, hang on. I'm going to set it on top of the bookshelves so it will be the first thing I look at when I wake up in the morning. Now that the carrots are gone, the wall is empty."

"That's where I imagined you could put it." Lauren waited for Cara to come back to the phone.

"Okay. I'm sitting in bed. I can't take my eyes off it. I want to be inside it, it's so beautiful. Should we FaceTime so you can see it?"

"No." Lauren snuggled deeper into the pillow, gazing at the framed image of carrots. "Talk to me."

"It's serene," Cara began, her voice dreamy. "Summertime, but the sun and sky are pale. In the distance are lush green rolling hills, woodlands, and a silvery river feeding into an amorphous lake. The foreground is an unfurling field of white flowers—daisies, I think—that stretches so far into the distance the individual flowers merge into a carpet of white. And I can almost hear the insects buzzing around us, and the crunch of dry grass under our feet, the pollen dusting my fingertips as I brush them over silky petals on our way to that cool, inviting river."

"Sounds about right." Lauren sighed with contentment. Was it unreasonable to think Cara's plural pronouns included her?

"I like daisies." Cara's voice was soft. "Such a friendly, unassuming flower."

"A loyal flower." Lauren was thinking more of Cara than of daisies. "Remember the laundromat? You said you wanted something green."

Cara didn't say anything.

"Do you remember? You said something like a spring meadow or a summer forest."

"I remember. I was kidding."

"I took you at your word. And you said we could give our possessions, and I've had this for a long time. Over the years, I've collected some things I love for my future home. They're in storage for when my apartment is finished. The artist is Harald Sohlberg and the piece is titled *Flower Meadow in the North*. But it's a copy. The original hangs in the Nasjonalgalleriet in Oslo."

"Wow."

"Between my junior and senior years in undergrad, I did an internship at the National Gallery there. It wasn't long enough to really learn much, but it was long enough for me to fall in love with that painting. Like you just said, there's something about it that makes me want to be where that is, so calming, so beautiful. My copy has been sitting in a storage facility in Queens ever since, and I called and had them ship it to you. I actually can't wait to see it again. Will you invite me over?"

"I can't accept something that means so much to you." Cara's voice was somber.

"I hope you will. It would mean a lot to me for you to have it." Lauren couldn't, and probably shouldn't, articulate what Cara was coming to mean to her. Making a present of something she loved seemed like the best way to demonstrate her feelings.

Cara was quiet for a few long moments. "I can honestly say this is the best gift I have ever received. Thank you, Lauren."

"You're welcome. I'm happy you like it." Lauren breathed a sigh of relief. Things had gotten a bit heavy, and Cara seemed to think so, too.

"So I guess you've recovered from last night's wine drinking contest, huh?"

Lauren heard the laughter in Cara's voice. "There was a contest? Where's my prize because I obviously won. I am fully recovered, thanks. And thanks for taking care of me. I'm sorry if I was a pain."

"Sure. Whatever. You were a cute drunk. And I got to hear your singing voice."

"We are so not talking about that." Lauren tried to ignore her embarrassment. "I'm also sorry I missed stripping you out of that tuxedo."

"I guess that's two outfits I should keep at the ready for you."

"Two?"

"That and my school uniform."

Lauren's mouth went dry. "Yes, both."

Cara said ultra-casually, "Maybe you could wear the uniform for me sometime."

"I stand ready to fulfill any and all school uniform fantasies. Whatever your heart desires." Lauren's voice descended a full octave lower than normal.

"Oh my God." Cara sounded like she couldn't get air into her lungs. "How do you do that with your voice? I wish you were here. Or I was there. I'm still thinking about that kiss from this morning."

"I had to do something to make you not forget me while I'm gone."

"As if." Cara scoffed. "And now I know you're capable of kissing the life out of me while you're still a little drunk."

"I was not still drunk."

"Mmm. Not even a little bit?"

Lauren was quiet. She knew Cara was kidding but she didn't want to be reminded of her foolish behavior.

"What? No phone sex now? No making up for not getting any last night?"

This was not how she wanted to end the conversation. "Can we pretend my little drunken episode didn't happen?"

"Oh, I wish I could, but there's photographic evidence to the contrary." Cara said, faux disappointment coming through loud and clear.

"No."

"Yes."

"Delete them," Lauren demanded.

"There's only one, and I'm not going to do that." Her voice was serious. "I like it too much."

"I want to see it, please."

"Fair enough. I'll text it in a minute. Now what were we talking about before this? Oh yeah, that awesome kiss from this morning." Cara sighed dramatically. "Amazing."

"You're laying it on a bit thick. It was just a kiss."

"That's where you're wrong. It was different. I felt that kiss from the soles of my feet to the tips of my split ends. You managed to make me feel really special this morning even if you weren't feeling your best."

Lauren could feel herself blushing and was glad Cara couldn't see it. "You don't have split ends. Your hair is very healthy."

"Thank you again for my present. I really love it." Cara was wrapping up but Lauren didn't want to say good-bye.

"I love my present, too."

"Good. I'm a bit sleepy. We'll talk again soon, okay? Good night. Oh. The photo. I'll send it now. Bye, Lauren."

And she was gone. Five seconds later, a text came through. *Two human carrots,* it said, and then a photo attached. It wasn't that bad. Taken from inside the limousine from last night, the arrangement of their limbs was somehow reminiscent of the carrots in the framed image beside her. Lauren opened the emoji keyboard, and for the first time since they had been seeing each other, sent an emoji, two carrot emojis in fact, to Cara. She was rewarded a moment later when Cara texted a single red heart. Her breath left her in giddy gratitude for the tiny digital symbol she had finally earned.

Lauren examined the image Cara had sent again. Her eyes were closed and her head rested heavily on Cara's shoulder, and she was clearly down for the count. Cara's arm was wrapped around her, and she looked at the camera with fierce solemnity. Lauren was mildly embarrassed at her sweaty drunken state, and her hair wouldn't be winning any awards, but she kept coming back to Cara's expression. And most of all, she couldn't stop looking at the defiance in Cara's eyes, as if she were daring Lauren to figure out a way to not care about her.

CHAPTER TWENTY-TWO

L auren's wide, arcing turns at the end of her run decreased her speed as she approached the base of the mountain. Instead of heading right back to the chair lift, she looked in the direction of the après patio where people were enjoying food and drink and music in the last hours of daylight. Preston, head and shoulders above the crowd, waved his arms in her direction, signaling to her like she was a plane coming in for a landing. Skiing was done for the day.

"I had a feeling you were going to stop early." Lauren dropped her weary butt beside him and eyed his plate of fries and almost empty beer.

"Can't help it if I'm faster than you. I've done at least three more runs than you have today. You're out of practice." Preston's warm grin took the sting out of his boasting, but he was right. She hadn't skied since undergrad, and sometime in the intervening years she had gone from barreling down the slopes to approaching each run with caution.

Lauren stole a few fries before grabbing a menu. "Have you seen Dad?"

"He texted from the top. He'll be here soon." Preston's phone started to ring. "Sorry, I have to take this."

While he took the work call, Lauren pulled out her own phone and saw the text from her father, as well as a sequence of dirty emojis from Cara, a daily occurrence since they had been apart. She understood most of it, but couldn't figure out what one of them signified.

Preston became agitated as she openly listened to his end of the conversation. "I can't meet with them Saturday, bro. I told you, I'll still be away." He paused to listen, then let out a frustrated sigh. "Set me up to conference in. That's the best I can do. Right. Later."

"A busy venture capitalist's work is never done."

"Sorry. People are going a little nuts at the office, but it's good to get away. I'm having fun with you and Dad."

"I am too." Lauren understood. While they had made it a priority to be together for the holidays, most evenings after dinner saw all three of them catching up on their laptops for at least an hour or two. Havemayers were workers. They got it from their father.

Preston put his phone away and zipped up the pocket in a pointed way, looking at Lauren's phone still in her hand. She beheld Cara's string of suggestive emojis, covering all of the images with her fingers except for the one she couldn't identify, and then angled her phone toward Preston. "What is that?"

He barked out a laugh. "A honey pot."

Of course. Lauren should have known. That's exactly what it looked like, and Winnie the Pooh would have been all over it. The honey pot juxtaposed with the tongue emoji short-circuited her brain and she wasn't ready when Preston plucked the phone from her hand and looked at the screen. She made a grab for it but he held it out of reach. "Give it back."

"Damn, she's creative. I've never seen the rocket ship used like that." Preston laughed and returned her phone.

She glowered at him, but owned her part in it. "I am so stupid. Why didn't I just Google it?" Lauren sat back, putting her phone away as a server approached. She ordered a charcuterie plate and a pitcher of Wasatch Ale.

The sinking sun cast a golden glow over the base of the mountain. As she gazed at the sun-kissed view, her thoughts turned once again to Cara, wondering what she would think of this beautiful place.

"Miles away again. She must be a bobcat in the sack."

"Shut up, dingus." She topped up Preston's glass with the pitcher their server delivered before filling her own. Actually, he hadn't razzed her too badly over Cara when she would sneak away most evenings for a clandestine phone call. She knew he was happy she was seeing someone.

"Are you ever going to tell me about her? What's her name? What's she like?"

Lauren didn't know why she was reluctant to talk about Cara. Maybe she was afraid that if she started talking, her mouth would become like a boulder rolling down a hill, endlessly praising Cara's good qualities with no way to stop itself. "Her name is Cara."

"She was a classmate of yours. Isn't that what Dad said?"

"Yeah, but we weren't friends. I barely knew her back then."

"But she's caught your attention now, that's for sure." Preston gulped down half his beer in one go. "Has she changed since school? What's different about her?"

"Not much, I don't think. She's probably always been this amazing, kind, empathetic person." Lauren let herself warm to the topic. "She's steady, good-hearted. A real idealist. Trying to make the world a better place while knowing how thankless the task is. Intelligent, a bit of a goofball. Really good at making fun of me. God, she makes me laugh." She snuck a look at Preston and was surprised to find he wasn't getting ready to lob another zinger at her. He was listening, his face inscrutable. "She likes literature and bathroom tile and chopped cheese sandwiches," Lauren said with a fond grin. "No, I don't think she's much different than she was in high school. It's me. I'm the one who's changed."

"How?"

"I don't know. Maybe because I can see now how great she is when back then I only cared about the girls who lived in the dorm with me." Lauren held up her beer so it eclipsed the waning sun behind it, turning it into a molten ingot of fire. "She's undiluted. She fills me up, makes me feel a little unsteady. Sweet, a little salty, and golden. She nourishes me." She took a sip and set her glass down with a thump, flicking embarrassed eyes at Preston. "Tell me to shut up already."

He slid his glass along the table and clinked Lauren's with it. "I have to meet this woman. Not many people could make a poet out of you."

"Yeah, she might secretly love to hear me talk like that, but she'd also be quick to tell me I'm being ridiculous."

"What does she look like?"

Lauren retrieved her phone and scrolled to the photo of them from before the gala.

"Paloma took that before we went out last week."

Preston took it from her. "Hot."

"Yup." She looked over his shoulder at the image. "Smoking."

"You don't look so bad, either." He handed her phone back.

"Thanks, Pres." She scrolled to the limousine picture and stared at Cara's intense gaze, turning pensive. "It's not going to last."

"Why not?"

"She wants it all: wife, kids, hers and hers minivans sitting in a suburban driveway somewhere. Your basic happily ever after. I can't give her that."

"Do you even want that?"

Lauren sat back and thought about it. She did, she realized. Somewhere in some dead-end chamber of her heart burned the candle of her thwarted desire for a forever love. Her attempts to starve it of oxygen and light hadn't worked. Dashed relationships and broken hopes had seen the flame gutter and smoke, but it had never gone completely out. That scrappy little light seemed inextinguishable, but locating it amidst all that came after was the hard part. If she allowed herself to even go looking for that candle, she imagined she would find Cara already there, tending its flame. But she had no idea how to get to that place of love and trust and hope anymore, no matter how much she wanted to be consumed by its fire. She stared morosely into her beer, not bothering to answer.

Preston scooted his chair closer. "You can have it if you want it. You're just not letting yourself."

Lauren gave an unamused laugh. "Weren't you the one advising me to find a girl, etcetera, move on?"

"I thought that was the right thing to say at the time, but things change. Etcetera feels like the wrong application for your situation. Maybe she's a keeper."

She shook her head. It wasn't that easy.

"You're letting yesterday take too much of your today. You need to get over Saffron. She's never going to hurt you again."

"I know."

"Then what's the problem?"

Lauren didn't want to say it. Voicing what had until now been a shadowy ghost of a thought would give it weight. But Preston's gaze pinned her as he waited for an answer. "She has debt. Student loans."

Preston reared back as if it was the last thing he expected her to say. "So you think, after all those terrific things you just said about her, that this chick is a gold digger?"

"No," Lauren said, putting a muscular vehemence into the single syllable.

"Then what? She doesn't sound like Saffron or that other girl from college. Do you think you haven't learned to judge a person's character after those two prizes?"

"I know she's a good person. I know it. She actually seems really suspicious of the money, at least most of the time. But what if, subconsciously, that's why she's attracted to me? That's something I'll never know, and I couldn't bear it if it were true."

He leaned in. "I get that you've been burned in the past, but if you can't learn to trust that someone loves you for you, you're going to be lonely."

Lauren seethed with annoyance. This was nothing she hadn't been reckoning with for the past three years. What made him the expert anyway? "What about you? Why haven't you settled down yet? Why isn't Paloma asking you when you're going to start having babies?"

Preston sat up straight. For a moment Lauren thought he was going to get up and leave. He shook his head and chuckled although it was clear he found nothing funny. "I wish I'd filmed you when you were talking about your girl before. You lit up like a Christmas tree. You had this silly grin on your face and you weren't seeing anything but her just then. I was jealous. I'd give a lot to have a baby for Paloma to admire."

Her jaw dropped. "You would?"

"Don't you think I want that, too? It's really hard to find. Why do you think I spend so much time working? I'm so sick of the apps and the small talk and the game of it all. When I find her, I'm going to grab her and never let her go."

Lauren gripped her brother's wrist. "I thought you were happy playing."

"I've been ready for a while, but she hasn't shown up yet. I'm beginning to lose faith she's out there at all."

They separated while a server placed a board of cured meats between them.

"And you're lucky enough to bump into someone great at your reunion, and you're willing to throw that away." He snorted. "At least that's a lesson for me to go to mine."

Lauren wanted to be supportive. Lord knew he had been a brick during her romantic troubles. "She has to be out there, Pres."

He loaded some bresaola onto a chunk of bread. "Hope so. If you know any straight women who will make me look like a dorky, googly-eyed teenager when I talk about them, send them my way."

Lauren smacked him in the arm.

"Why don't you just pay off her loans? Then it won't be an issue anymore."

She rejected that immediately. Lauren wouldn't miss the money, but she knew it would be wrong. "So then I've paid for the pleasure of her company? Doesn't sound right to me. Anyway, she gets prickly when I try to buy her breakfast. I can't imagine she would accept." She grabbed a slice of mortadella before her brother ate it all and chewed thoughtfully. "I think I'm okay with it not being a forever thing. I'd rather have a perfect little jewel of time with her. Something that for once doesn't end with someone valuing what I have over who I am, that ends amicably instead of me feeling my heart's being torn from my chest."

"Dramatic much?" Preston muttered around a mouthful of food. "You're an idiot. Why should it end?"

"Everything ends, but this way I get to dictate the terms of dissolution."

Preston shook his head. "Idiot."

Lauren didn't bother trying to change his mind. The shadows were lengthening across the base of the mountain and her father was heading their way, talking on the phone. Whoever he was speaking to was getting an ass chewing. "Look, there's Dad."

"Something ruined his last run of the day."

If Lauren had to guess, the São Paolo project had hit another snag. "How do you feel about going home early?" She waved as her father stood amid a sea of occupied tables looking for them.

"Yeah, it's looking like I'll be able to make that Saturday meeting after all."

Before he arrived and the topic inevitably changed, Lauren pulled on Preston's sleeve. "You deserve somebody great. I would find her for you if I could."

"You deserve that, too. If you've found her, don't let her slip away."

❖

"Open up that can of tomato paste, will you?" Cara's mom shook the sauté pan on the stove. They were using one of the lazy days between Christmas and New Year's to cook up a bunch of Italian dishes for Cara to take back to the city. Madonna kept them company on the radio in the background, urging them to express themselves.

Cara returned to the table to start rolling meatballs. The kitchen was redolent with the earthy fragrance of simmering white beans, mellowing the bite of raw onions and garlic in the skillet next to it as they alchemized into something sweet. Cara thought about how her Irish mom was such a good Italian cook. "It was Nana who taught you how to cook Italian food, wasn't it?"

"Uh-huh. And not just Italian, she taught me everything. The roast beef we always have on Christmas? The Thanksgiving turkey and all the sides? All Nana."

"Really?" Cara was five when her father's mother died suddenly of a heart attack. She only remembered her through pictures.

"Yep. She could make that dishtowel taste like the food of the gods."

"Was she trying to make sure you knew how to cook all of Dad's favorite foods?"

"Maybe it started that way, and I wanted to make your father happy, so I was a willing student." She stood five feet from Cara but she was far away in that moment. "It's what people do when they love each other."

Cara sniffed in response, not wanting to be rude. She felt no loyalty toward her father. Apropos of nothing except the hollowness of being without Lauren this week and her uncertainty about their relationship, she asked, "How did you know Dad was the one?"

"I just knew. Every moment I spent with him felt exactly right."

Cara frowned. Is that how she would describe her time with Lauren? "How did you and Dad get to the point where you agreed you wanted to be together?"

"We loved each other. We didn't want to be apart. It was the natural next step." She looked up. "Is this about you and Lauren?"

Her mom knew they were seeing each other, but she wasn't aware of their friends with benefits arrangement. Cara didn't think she would approve, and her evolving feelings for Lauren made her embarrassed to confess it now. Cara gave her a slight nod to telegraph her ambivalence.

"You want to be with her, but she doesn't return your feelings?"

"I think she likes me." Cara believed it to be true. "But when we started seeing each other, we agreed we weren't looking for anything serious."

"Hang on. You don't want to settle down?"

"Sure I do, someday. But now is not the time. I'm busy and broke, and she's busy and not broke. I thought it would be a few fun dates and then it would fizzle out. I've been curious about her ever since high school, but as adults we were coming from such different places that I didn't think we would click."

"But you're clicking?" Her mom turned the heat down on the beans and the sauce and came to sit at the table with Cara.

"Like high heels sprinting across a hardwood floor." Cara grinned at her tray of meatballs. That was putting it mildly.

"I've been waiting for you to become serious about someone. I'm happy for you."

"No, Mom. She's not looking for anything serious, and you know I have a plan for my life and it wasn't supposed to include settling down until I'm more than a couple of paychecks away from bankruptcy. But…I've changed my mind." She didn't quite know how to express it. Was it love? It seemed ridiculous to feel so strongly about Lauren after less than two months, but her heart seemed to know what it wanted. "I really like her."

"Then you should tell her," her mother urged her. "You can't control when that connection happens, and you can't neatly schedule it into the calendar app of your life. Love is going to show up whenever it wants to and you have to be ready to make that leap whether it's convenient or not."

"I didn't say it was love." Giving voice to it made her feel superstitious. It was too fragile an idea to even acknowledge.

"Maybe she feels the same way. Maybe she's changed her mind like you have and she's just as worried about letting you know. I'm surprised you're hesitating. You're usually not shy about saying exactly what you feel."

"I know, but I'm afraid it'll be over." Cara looked at her mom, trying to make sense of it. "If I tell her my feelings have changed, she may end it. She was pretty clear about not wanting anything serious. If I don't say anything, at least we could stay in this holding pattern for a while."

"A holding pattern doesn't sound like you."

Indecisiveness was an unfamiliar feeling for her.

Her mom squeezed Cara's shoulder. "If you want the fruit to fall, you have to give the tree a shake."

Cara nodded. One of her mother's sayings that had served her well, but this was not writing essays for scholarship competitions when she was a teenager.

The benefits from laying it all out there with Lauren were clear, but the risk was just as obvious. What would happen if she shook the tree only to knock the entire thing over?

An hour later, the pasta e fagioli was almost done, the meatballs had come out of the oven, and Cara and her mom were readying two trays of baked ziti to go in. Starving and willing to eat whatever was ready first, she had shaken herself free from her hefty earlier thoughts. Conversation topics had turned lighthearted, and there may have been some dancing and singing into the wooden spoon as Cara went about her kitchen chores and listened to her mom's favorite oldies radio station. Cara barely heard when the doorbell sounded.

"Are you expecting anyone?" Her mom wiped her hands on a dishtowel and went to the front door.

"Nope." A Wham! song was making her bop around the kitchen like she was in an eighties music video. She turned the radio up and tried to do the running man and the sprinkler at the same time, hitting it old school while waiting for the lyrics to start back up with her wooden spoon microphone in hand. She thought she heard a giggle under the pounding drumbeat, a giggle that distinctly sounded like....

She whirled around to see Lauren and her mother watching her from the kitchen doorway, both grinning at the spectacle she was making of herself. Cara lunged for the radio and snapped it off. Breathing heavily, she blinked a few times just in case she was hallucinating, but no, Lauren was standing in her kitchen, looking gorgeous in a sky blue ski parka, jeans, and some serious winter boots with a tread that looked like it belonged on a tractor.

"Surprise," Lauren said into the abrupt silence, her eyes sparkling with affection and amusement. "I'm sorry to interrupt while you were bringing to life that old saying, *dance like no one's watching.*"

"No one *was* watching five seconds ago." Cara was mortified but inordinately happy to see her. She expected her heart to stop beating so rapidly with her arrested movement, but it continued to pound while she willed herself to stay where she was and not leap to Lauren and cover her with kisses. "What are you doing here? Aren't you supposed to be whizzing down a mountain in Utah right now?"

"We had a change of plans. Did you know your mom's house is only fifteen minutes from Teterboro?"

"I did not." And she didn't really care. All that mattered was Lauren was here. "Would you like some lunch? We were just about to eat."

"Where are my manners? Let me take your coat." Her mom went to the table and pulled out a chair. "Sit down. We'll have some soup ready in a minute."

Lauren didn't move, suddenly looking uncertain. "I don't want to intrude on your family time. Maybe I should have called first."

"You're not intruding." Cara got right into Lauren's space and unzipped her parka, sliding her arms under it and pulling her into a hug. Static electricity coursed over her fingers as she slid them over Lauren's soft sweater, and electricity of another kind surged throughout her body as she pressed herself against Lauren. "I'm really happy you're here. Eat with us," she murmured into Lauren's neck, relishing the warmth of her, the scent of her. She pushed Lauren's jacket from her shoulders and handed it to her mother, who left the kitchen to hang it in the hall closet. A quick kiss was all she could manage before Lauren drew back.

"Was this a bad idea? We came back early and I hoped you might want to spend some time together while you're still on your school holiday."

"Yes. Absolutely." A thought came to her. "Is that why you texted this morning? To get my whereabouts?"

"Guilty." Lauren's cheeks flushed pink. "I really wanted to surprise you."

"You succeeded, stalker." She sat Lauren down at the table and ladled generous portions of soup into three bowls. Her mom brought out some crusty bread and arranged a few thick slices on a plate for them.

"This is delicious, Mrs. Talarico."

"Call me Joanne, and thank you. How was your Christmas?"

"It was pretty great. I spent time with family, which we don't often get to do since we're all so busy. How was your Christmas?"

"Very similar to Thanksgiving, with less football. The same guests, different main attraction," she said dryly.

Lauren gave Cara a bewildered look.

"We had roast beef instead of turkey. It's my uncle's favorite."

"And how are things at the museum?" her mom asked.

"Things were fine when I left." Lauren frowned a bit, and Cara wondered if she was thinking about the gala and her aunt. "I'm not expected back until after New Year's Day. I haven't taken a vacation this long in years. I hardly know what to do with myself."

Cara could think of a few things, all of them on a horizontal surface.

Her mom finished her soup quickly and sat back. "I bet Cara feels the same way. I think she's become a little tired of the suburban life. Itching to get back to the city, aren't you, honey?"

She snuck a look at Lauren. "Maybe." She wanted to be with Lauren but she had planned to spend this time with her mother. Upping and leaving might be construed as a little rude.

"Could she get a ride back with you, Lauren?"

Or maybe not. "Nice, Mom. Are you trying to get rid of me?"

"Of course not, but why shouldn't you girls go back together? It makes sense." Her mother shot her a meaningful look before turning to Lauren, her expression now guileless. "How did you get here anyway? Did you drive?" She nodded to Cara and raised her eyebrows, apparently trying to convey some kind of telepathic message, as Cara inwardly cringed and tried to get her mom to cool it with slight cutting motions at her throat.

"I used a car service, and that's how I'm getting back. You're welcome to come with me if you want, Cara."

"You know what? I just remembered there were a few things I need to pick up at the store," Cara's mom said. "You'll be all right here on your own, wont' you, girls?"

Cara was incredulous. "What are you talking about? I went to the store this morning—"

"Not that store, the other one," she said in a hurry. "Don't forget the zitis are still in the oven. Take one with you, and all the soup and half the meatballs. Call me tonight to let me know you're back safe and sound." She was now bustling around the kitchen, locating her purse and keys. "Lauren, give me a hug good-bye. It was good to see you."

Lauren crossed the room and received a long, affectionate hug. "It was nice to see you too, Mrs. Talarico. Thanks for lunch."

Cara remained seated and crossed her arms, miffed at her mother's unseemly exit.

Her mom returned to the table and bent to kiss Cara on the cheek and pulled her chin to her so they were eye to eye. She whispered, "Be happy, Cara, baby. Talk to her. Maybe it's time for the fruit to fall."

Cara rolled her eyes, but she couldn't help smiling a little at her mother's antics. Her heart was in the right place. In another moment, she was gone.

Lauren was still standing, holding on to the back of her chair. "If I didn't know any better, I'd think your mom was giving us some privacy."

"It's either that or she really needed to get to the other store."

Lauren laughed. "She's sweet."

"Yeah, and about as subtle as a sledgehammer." She reached over and pulled Lauren down onto her lap. The low thrum of desire coursed through her as her thighs took Lauren's weight.

"You smell good." Lauren circled her arms around her neck, buried her face in her hair, and breathed in. They sat quietly for a minute. "So, do you want to hang out with me since we're both off from work? Do you have any plans?"

"I only have one thing in my calendar—Samantha Cruz's New Year's Eve party. Any interest in going with me?" This was the closest Cara had come to asking Lauren on a date and she was unaccountably nervous.

Lauren made a noncommittal noise. "Does she live in East Harlem, too?"

"No, Brooklyn. Fort Greene."

She pulled a face. "You mean we'd have to go out of town?"

"No." Cara looked at her like she was nuts. "I just said she lives in Brooklyn."

"Anything outside of Manhattan is out of town."

Cara gave her a look. "Don't be dramatic, Princess Havemayer. It's a subway ride away."

Lauren pressed her lips to Cara's temple. "If we go, we'll take the car. I'm not riding the subway home from Brooklyn at God knows o'clock on New Year's Eve." She paused before she gave her decision. "Okay. I'll go with you to Brooklyn if you come to brunch with me and my aunt and Barb on Sunday. You know they love you."

"Barb does," Cara said. "Not sure about Genevra."

"Do we have a deal?"

"Yes."

"Good. On to the next order of business." Lauren didn't hesitate. She angled her face and pressed her mouth against Cara's, her lips soft but insistent.

Cara relaxed into it, heat already pooling within her, but there was something itching at her. She pulled back abruptly. "Wait, if we're hanging out for a bunch of days, who owns the time?"

"Does it matter?" Lauren barely took a second to think about it. "What if we co-own it?" She went in for another kiss.

Cara resisted. "How's that supposed to work?"

"I don't know, Cara. All I know is that it's been a week since I've kissed you and I need this. Can we figure it out later?"

She gave in. If Lauren wasn't worried about it, it probably wasn't worth worrying about. She met Lauren's lips and pulled her hips closer. Who knew how much time had passed as they sat there, making out like teenagers until the kitchen timer went off?

Lauren recoiled in surprise. "That scared me."

Cara had a hard time surfacing from the haze of arousal that made cogent thought impossible. Was it wrong to want to stay right where she was, hands plunged beneath Lauren's sweater, getting reacquainted with her lips, tongue, and skin? She felt bereft as Lauren lifted her warm weight from her lap.

She pulled out two steaming trays of baked ziti. As Lauren sidled up next to her, she grabbed a fork and speared a browned, crisp, cheese-covered tube of pasta from the crusty top layer. "Here, taste this. It's the best part."

Lauren blew on it and accepted the bite. "Yum. That is so good."

Cara pulled Lauren toward her by her belt loops. "We have to give these a little time to cool before we can travel with them, so I'd like to issue an invitation. How would you like to be the first ever guest in my childhood bed?" Cara waggled her eyebrows in the cheesiest way she knew how.

"We're gonna do it in your twin bed?" Lauren said with faux awe in her voice. "I get to be the first? I'm so honored."

"Let's go, smart-ass." Cara took her by the hand. There would be no tree shaking today.

CHAPTER TWENTY-THREE

The mahogany door to Genevra's imposing townhouse featured an old and tarnished doorknocker—a brass fish riding a bicycle. "That's so cool," Cara said, lifting the fish's tail and rapping it a few times.

"Yeah, it's distinctive." Lauren nodded. "I remember it from when I came here as a kid."

"That's proof we're dealing with some old school feminists."

Lauren's expression was uncomprehending.

Cara gestured to the doorknocker. "You know—a woman needs a man like a fish needs a bicycle? It's an old saying from back in the seventies, I think."

Before Lauren could respond, the door swung open and Aunt Genevra stood there, her flowing turquoise palazzo pants and matching oversized top billowing in the open doorway. "Welcome. Come in."

Barb came up behind her in jeans and a purple Hunter College sweatshirt. "Gen's so glad you're here."

Genevra ushered them into a large, high-ceilinged drawing room where paintings covered the walls. Lauren approached the largest piece, hung above the mantel. It was a portrait of a well-dressed society woman. "Oh my God. Is that a Cecilia Beaux?"

"Yes!" Genevra said. "You've discerned that so quickly! She's always compared to John Singer Sargent, but I think she bested him here."

The picture showed the seated formal pose of a wealthy-looking lady with a closed parasol. "Look at how she uses pinks and grays. And the brush strokes are so uncontrolled here." Lauren pointed to a portion of the subject's gown, glancing at her aunt. "There's a stillness to her, but it's infused with so much life."

Genevra had the biggest smile on her face and seemed at a loss for words. Lauren stepped closer to the painting.

Barb elbowed Cara where they stood at the threshold of the room. "You into the art show?"

Cara shrugged, not really understanding what she was being asked.

Barb nodded. "Gen, why don't you show Lauren around? I'm sure she wants to see everything on the walls. In the meantime, Cara and I will find something to occupy us. Right, Cara? Text me when you want to eat."

Cara looked to Lauren first to see if it was okay, and when Lauren smiled, Barb whisked her down the hallway and out of sight. After they had descended two floors to the basement, she was astonished to see what could only be described as a mini bowling alley, one long lane of blond wood, complete with a ball return and automatic pinsetter. "Wow," was about all Cara could manage.

"Yessiree. Regulation length." Barb seemed delighted by Cara's response.

"You and Genevra are big bowlers?"

"Not at all. It came with the place when she bought it in 'eighty-two. The previous owners were Nixon supporters, and when they heard ol' Dick had one installed under the North Portico of the White House, they couldn't build their own fast enough." Barb stepped behind a tiki-style wet bar installed alongside the lane and ran her hand lovingly over the bamboo countertop. "Now this is definitely me. We put this in about twenty years ago to make the occasional bowling party a bit more fun. What'll you have? I've got the makings for Bloody Marys. Want one?"

"Okay." Cara settled on a stool at the bar while Barb made their drinks. "Do your guests have to wear special shoes?"

"Only if they bring their own." Barb popped the top on a can of tomato juice. "Do you like it spicy?"

"Sure."

"Atta girl." Barb gave her one of those corny winks Cara remembered from the night of the gala. "Sorry if you wanted a tour of the walls, but I would much rather be down here. Gen's been agonizing over this visit for days, and the firm we hired to move the paintings around only left about twenty minutes ago. I needed a break."

"Move the paintings around? Why would you do that?"

"She has a large collection. When she buys something new, she wants to enjoy it for a while so we usually have only the most recent stuff here and what doesn't fit goes into storage. But sometimes she'll do a redesign according to what results she's trying to achieve." Barb set the cocktail on a coaster in front of Cara.

"What do you mean?"

"Like if we're having a benefit here, she might hang the heavy hitters—Monet, Renoir, Picasso, Warhol—the recognizable stuff people can pat themselves on the back for knowing."

"And what results is she trying to achieve now?"

"To impress Lauren, of course. She knows Lauren's area of professional interest so she curated her collection to show she understands that."

Cara raised her eyebrows. "Right." It was hard to imagine people with a large enough collection that they could rotate it on a whim.

"What's the matter? You don't approve?"

The last thing Cara wanted was to offend Lauren's relations. "It's not my place to approve or disapprove. Lauren won't ask my opinion anyway. I don't know much about art."

"That doesn't matter. You've got eyes, don't you? And you told me you're an English teacher, right? I'm sure your interpretation skills are as fine as anyone's." Barb eyed her. "Or maybe you don't care. Maybe you think caring about art is beneath someone like you with the serious business of educating the city's disadvantaged youth to worry about? Too frivolous? A rich people hobby?"

"No," Cara said hotly. "I care, and I think my students should care about it as well."

Barb laughed and clinked her glass with Cara's. "I'm just busting your chops."

"I'm not that confident about expressing my opinions," Cara tried to explain. "I'm not an expert like you and Genevra. I wouldn't be able to hold up my end of a conversation about art."

"Me? An expert? Honey, you've got me all wrong. I hadn't even been in an art museum until after I met Genevra. My collar is as blue as they come, born in a tenement apartment in Flatbush and retired from the US Postal Service. The only thing I collect is a civil servant's pension, going on twelve years now."

"Really?" Cara had assumed Barb came from money just like Genevra.

"Had a route in Midtown East for twenty-eight years before I went indoors for another dozen," Barb said proudly. "So you see, youngster, speaking from one government employee to another, I seem to have more in common with you than with my partner of forty-six years."

How in the world did Monets and mail delivery fit together? She took a gulp of her cocktail and her eyes watered at how strong and spicy it was. "Good," she rasped, taking another much smaller sip.

Barb turned shrewd eyes upon her. "I know what you're thinking. You're pondering how two very different gals like Genevra and me managed to make it work. She had cash coming out of her ears and I didn't have a pot to piss in."

"I'm sorry. I didn't mean to offend. That's a long partnership." Cara hoped her smile would mask her confusion. She couldn't help projecting her relationship with Lauren onto Barb and Genevra's experience.

"Look, I don't know much about you, but I can see the way you and Lauren look at each other. It reminds me of Gen and me at the beginning. Our feelings were so big we didn't know how to get our arms around them, and aside from the stigma of being gay and out back then, there were so many other things working against us—me, a working-class dyke with a Park Avenue society lady? Come on."

"Sounds familiar."

"I thought so. I'm sure your social circles don't overlap much. How did you even find each other, anyway? Dating app?"

"We went to the same high school. I was a scholarship student and she was the queen of our class. We reconnected at our reunion in November."

"Ah, still early days, huh? Intensity and uncertainty and delirious lust all swirled together like some crazy confusing delicious ice cream sundae."

"Yeah." Maybe Barb could offer a little insight. "Can I ask you something personal?"

"Shoot."

"I feel like the money thing is like this big hulking thing in the corner during all our time together, and I'm wondering if that ever goes away. I mean, I'm worrying about how I'm going to pay my bills next month and she's showing me the million-dollar apartment she just bought. I like her so much, but I'm always thinking about how unequal things are between us." Cara didn't mean to be that naked. "Sorry. That wasn't really a question."

Barb's expression was all amused sympathy. "I know how a gal's insecurities can loom pretty large when she's feeling out of her depth, but I want you to picture something for me: It's the end of a long day, and the two of you have been apart from each other because of work or whatever, but now you're together, talking about something mundane or having a glass of wine. Normal end of day stuff. Can you see it?"

"Yes." Cara saw herself and Lauren in her dad's kitchen yesterday, eating a frittata and laughing at the weirdness of the word *frittata*. She smiled at the recent pleasant memory.

"Do you feel unequal to her in that moment?"

Of course she didn't, but the problem wasn't in the everyday stuff. "No, but that doesn't change the fact that I can't take her out to fancy restaurants or buy her nice clothes."

"She doesn't need you to! She can do that herself. I don't know about Lauren, but Genevra wouldn't want me to buy her clothes anyway. She would hate anything I picked out for her."

"I feel uncomfortable when she spends money on me. I can't reciprocate."

"Does Lauren seem bothered by it?"

Cara thought about it. "No."

"I know where you're coming from. I felt the same way at the start of my relationship with Gen. But one thing that was always clear between us was that I may not be rich, but that didn't mean I wasn't valuable to her."

Cara frowned.

"What I give her, what you give Lauren, can't be bought with money. Know what you're worth and you'll never feel insecure again. You let her be who she is, accept her, be there for her, support her. And you should expect the same in return. You don't have to know everything she knows, have everything she has, or love everything she loves, but you do have to love *her*, unreservedly and unconditionally."

Cara was concentrating fiercely on what Barb was saying, but pulled back at this. "Whoa, who said anything about love?"

"Too soon? Sorry, but you seemed to be hanging on my every word."

She felt the heat rise in her cheeks, and didn't mention Lauren's allergy to long-term relationships. Barb's description sounded a little too wonderful for her to immediately knock it down with reality. "I think I'm a little ahead of her when it comes to that word, but I'm still approaching it with the wariness of the person who disarms bombs for the NYPD."

Barb laughed. "Someday the two of you will laugh about these early speed bumps."

She wished she could believe that, but Barb didn't know what Cara knew. The whole thing was an exercise in futility. She gestured to the long wooden lane. "Can I throw a few balls? I can't remember the last time I bowled, and I can't pass up this opportunity right here in front of me."

"Sure." Barb hit a panel of switches behind her that turned on some funky flashing lights. "That *strikes* me as a great idea. I think we have some time to *spare*."

Cara smiled as Barb cackled at her terrible puns.

❖

After touring the parlor level, Lauren followed Genevra into a solarium at the rear of the house. She was thoroughly impressed by the collection of women artists her aunt had curated. Focusing on women artists of the mid-nineteenth to the early twentieth century, at least in what was on view, Genevra had a truly discerning eye, and the funds to satisfy it.

"Here is the last picture I want to show you, and I apologize that it clashes with what has gone before, but I thought you would want to see it." Genevra pivoted to the facing wall and stood to the side while Lauren examined the Pissarro the museum wanted for its exhibition. It was a view Lauren knew well from her visits to Paris, of the central fountain in the Tuileries Garden, captured on a cloudy spring day. It was a perfect example of what the show was trying to demonstrate. They had to have it. The reminder of why she was there deflated her exuberance over the previous works.

"Do you still want the Pissarro for the show?" Genevra asked from behind her.

Lauren sighed. "Please, if you would like to loan it."

"Come sit." Genevra indicated a pair of cozy chairs situated in the sunlight. "It's true. I engineered our meeting. Once I knew you were going to make art your career, I wanted to renew our familial connection. You have to understand that I never thought you would want to speak to me after all that discord between my brother and me had trickled down to you."

"Did you have anything to do with my getting the appointment at the Met?" She had to know.

"No, Lauren. I have a few friends on the board, which was how I knew about the Pissarro show, but I was never approached about your fitness for a position, nor did I approach anyone. If you're worried that I had a hand in your employment, you can rest assured that you got there on your own merit."

It seemed that was all the explanation Lauren was going to get. The haziness of it was something she would have to live with.

"In hindsight I can see how you would feel manipulated, and I'm very sorry for that. I hope I haven't ruined my chance to get to know you better."

She had to let it go. It wasn't the main thing that was bothering her, anyway. "No, I'm glad we've reconnected."

"You still look slightly put out, if I may say."

She reached out a hand and Genevra quickly took it. "I appreciate you explaining this to me. But even if you weren't involved with my appointment, it feels like I'm never going to be able to stand apart from our family. No matter what I do, the Havemayer name is going to precede me into any room I walk into."

"Some would think that a very beneficial thing."

"Yes, but our name, the money and status that goes along with it, those will always be what people will see first and want to use for themselves. Nobody—not even my job—wants me for me."

"You don't know that." Genevra's voice was stern. "This is my fault for putting the idea in your head. I can make inquiries with the board if you like—"

"No," Lauren interrupted. "God, no. It's not really about that." The rumble of distant thunder distracted her for a moment, and she looked out the window. But the winter sun was shining.

Her aunt's voice softened with concern. "Then what is it about, my dear? How can I help you?"

"I don't think you can," Lauren said. This was about Saffron. Bloody fucking Saffron. Years later, she still had the power to make Lauren doubt herself, still had the ability to ruin anything good. How she would probably laugh to know the specter of her was still darkening Lauren's life: her job, her relationship with Cara, her damn sanity. But now was not the time to dwell. She took a deep breath. "It's something I have to figure out on my own."

"Are you sure?"

"I am." Lauren reached again for her aunt's hand and squeezed it. "Didn't you say you had some plans you wanted to discuss over brunch?"

"Yes, I did, if you're still willing." The sound of thunder again, and Genevra tilted her head to listen. "Barbie and your partner are bowling. There's a lane in the basement. Can you hear it?"

Lauren smiled. "I thought we were having a winter thunderstorm in full sunlight. You like to bowl?"

"Not really. I'll have to interrupt their fun." She took out her phone and sent a message. "You must be thirsty. How about a mimosa?"

❖

After two of Barb's potent Bloody Marys, Cara switched to coffee. She made a plate for herself at the loaded sideboard and listened to Lauren and Genevra talk about the paintings Genevra had chosen to display. Upon entering the dining room, she and Lauren had communicated silently. Her raised eyebrows were met with Lauren's reassuring nod. Everything was okay, and some things had been cleared up. Lauren's relaxed posture and their easy conversation told her that much. It was an enjoyable meal, made more enjoyable by Lauren reaching for her hand at the end of it.

"Lauren," Barb said, as she sat back with another Bloody Mary, "do you know anything about opening a museum?"

Before Lauren could say anything, Genevra interjected, "Why do you keep insisting on this museum idea? It's ludicrous."

"What's ludicrous about it? You have plenty of art, and after we've both shuffled off this mortal coil, what could be a better place for a museum than right here?" Barb pressed her index finger into the dining table. "It could be like the John Soane Museum in London. People come and see how you lived as well as all the beautiful works you've collected. How great would that be?"

"No one cares about how I live, and there's not enough room for everything that should be displayed. This place is too small to be a museum."

"Not necessarily," Barb said.

"What would you like to do with your collection, Aunt Genevra?" Lauren broke in.

"I have a few options I'm entertaining, but I wanted to get your input."

Lauren paused before speaking. "First, I'd like to know what you're trying to say through your collection, if anything."

"I'm not sure what you mean, dear."

"From what you've told me, not only do you have this incredibly granular slice of women in art from a defined period that we've looked at today, but you also have pieces from many movements, from a variety of artists, lots of whom would be of interest to both private collectors and the general public."

Cara leaned forward. This was like being in the room where it happened.

Lauren continued, "Without actually seeing everything you have... What is the size of your collection by the way? A rough estimate?"

"The database has records for just under twelve hundred pieces," Barb said.

Cara nearly choked on her coffee. *Twelve hundred? Christ.*

"Here are a few ways forward, just off the top of my head." Lauren rubbed her chin. "If you were considering a museum in a small space such as your home, you would have to distill your collection so it reflects a specific point of view, like what we've seen today. On the other hand, it's also robust enough that any museum would be eager to showcase it, either as a loan or as a parceled acquisition. Either way, it would generate lots of interest from both the critical world and the general public."

"You really think the public would be interested in a collection of only women artists?" Genevra said. "I always thought I would have to include some of the more notable works in my collection as a draw to the lesser-seen artists."

"But then you'd be diluting the objective of the museum," Barb argued.

"Barbie, you have to let go of the museum idea. I simply don't have it in me to take on a task of that magnitude."

"Maybe not you, but these two are full of youthful energy." Barb gestured to Cara and Lauren. "Let them do it. What are you going to do? Auction it all? You've worked a lifetime to put this collection together, and you and I are the only ones who have seen it."

Cara couldn't see why she would be included in this. She had nothing relevant to add to the conversation, but she was enjoying listening to it.

"Barb brings up a third option," Lauren said. "You could divest yourself of the works in any permutation of ways: auction them on the open market and add the proceeds to your estate, or donate them to museums and reap a substantial tax benefit."

There was silence at the table. Cara considered whether to go back to the buffet for another bagel. Just as she was about to get up, Genevra spoke.

"How would you feel if I left the decision up to you, Lauren? I could leave you all my assets when I die, and you could do with it what you will, but I won't do that without your consent. It's quite a considerable ask."

"I don't know what to say." Lauren glanced at Barb. "Wouldn't that be your role?"

Barb smiled. "I know I look good for my age, but, honey, I'm almost ten years older than Genevra. It makes no sense to hand it all off to me."

"I realize this is not the easiest subject to talk about. Nobody wants to dwell on death, but it's high time Barbie and I got our affairs in order. You and your brother are the only people we could imagine as heirs. It was never a consideration for us to have our own children."

"Well, maybe we considered it for about five minutes," Barb said. "Turkey basters were available, but society wouldn't have been kind to a family we created. I don't envy much about the generations who've come after ours, but I am a little jealous about how easy and acceptable it is for Lauren and Cara to start a family."

Cara felt Lauren go still next to her. She couldn't think what to say either, so the uncomfortable silence lengthened until Barb realized her misstep and changed the topic, putting Cara in the hot seat.

"What would you do if you were in our shoes, Cara? As an educator, I bet you see the benefit in opening a museum, don't you?"

"As an educator, I know not to venture an opinion on a subject in which I have no expertise."

"Come on." Barb gave her a knowing smile. "Those wheels have been turning the whole time we've been sitting here. You've just been too polite to say anything."

"I'm not judging anyone." Cara was horrified to think she'd been rude.

"I didn't say you were," Barb said kindly. "You're allowed to have an opinion. Tell us what you think."

If Cara thought she would be saved from answering by Lauren, she was mistaken. Lauren appeared just as curious as Barb. Genevra did too. They were all waiting for her to answer.

"I'm not a very regular consumer of art." She let go of Lauren's hand and rubbed both of hers on her jeans, thinking about having the responsibility of such a collection. "But after hearing all the discussion, I would take the portion of the collection that was most important to me and keep it together. It seems like what you showed Lauren today is significant as a grouping, and wouldn't be as meaningful if it were scattered across various museums and collectors." The three women were listening closely. "Then I would sell the rest, probably to museums so the public would have access to it." She turned to Barb. "I think you used the expression *heavy-hitters* to reference the more valuable pieces."

"I did," Barb said.

"Well, they would fetch large sums, right? I would amass as large an amount as I could and do something good with it."

"Like what, Cara?" It was the first time Genevra had used her name.

"As a teacher, I see many students who abandon their educational aspirations due to a lack of funds, and I also have some experience with that. I would start a foundation to help deserving high school students advance their educations through college and any further degrees they want to pursue."

"I like it." Barb tapped the table.

"What do you mean, you have some experience with it?" Genevra's eyes were riveted on Cara's.

"It's nothing." Cara backpedaled. "I had to make some choices that I probably wouldn't have if I'd had the money to do what I wanted."

"Such as?" Genevra asked.

Cara couldn't see a way of avoiding discussing it since she had stupidly brought it up. "I got into a great school, and I accumulated a pile of debt while I attended, despite the scholarships and aid and work study I cobbled together. I studied international economics and loved it. I wanted to become a diplomat."

"I thought you got your degree in English. I thought you loved literature," Lauren said.

"I did. I double-majored. And I do love literature."

"You didn't want to be a teacher?" she asked, her expression bewildered.

Cara waggled her head to show her ambivalence. "I loved English class, but I also loved Model UN. It showed me what could be possible.

I wanted to live abroad, work with other nations, represent our country. I pursued that goal all through undergrad, and I was accepted to a grad program at Georgetown where they have a school of foreign service."

"But you couldn't afford to go?" Barb asked.

"No. After my acceptance, during my senior year, I sat down and really went over all my finances. I didn't get as much aid as I had hoped for from Georgetown, and I would be adding so much more debt, I became kind of frozen with fear that I would never get out from under it. So poof. The end of a dream."

Lauren's hand rested on her forearm, and it took all the strength she had not to pull it away. The waves of sympathy coming from the others sitting at the table made her want to end this little sob story immediately. "But everything worked out. I applied to the Teaching Fellows and got in. And teaching has been the hardest thing I've ever attempted while sometimes being pretty damn cool. I'd like to think I'm good at it, too."

She leveled a frank gaze at them. "But you can bet your ass that if I could have applied for a scholarship that would have underwritten all of the educational expenses I racked up, I would have. And I know about ten seniors right now who are applying to schools based on tuition costs over every other criteria, and that's pretty sad."

Barb clapped her on the shoulder. "For not having an opinion, you can be pretty damn persuasive. I still think we should open a museum, though."

"Thank you, Cara," Genevra said, giving her a warm smile before throwing Barb a look of frustration. "Barbie, I want you to quit it."

"We don't need to worry about this for a long time anyway, Aunt Genevra," Lauren said. "And we'll have plenty of other occasions to talk about it. How about I host next time?"

"I would absolutely love that," Genevra gushed. "Maybe we could invite your dad, too?"

By some unspoken decree, brunch was over. As they made their way toward the door, Cara stopped at one of the paintings. It depicted a group of women, each holding babies who were dressed in white christening gowns. She had never seen a painting of this subject before and was drawn to the domesticity of it.

Genevra stood next to her and gazed at it. "This is by an artist named Anna Ancher, more famous in Denmark, where she's from, than here. I feel lucky to have found it. Do you like it?"

"A lot," Cara replied. "Maybe you should think about opening a museum. There is so much out there people don't know about, and your collection could teach them. I would definitely come, and I would bring my students, too."

"I certainly do have some big choices to make about all this. You know," Genevra said, "sometimes when we make a choice it may seem like a door closing, but sometimes it's a blessing in disguise, and we can't realize that until we have some distance from it. I bet there are any number of students who've benefited from your decision back then."

"That's awfully nice of you to say." Cara was held for a moment in Genevra's arresting blue gaze, so similar to Lauren's. Was it asking too much to know what Lauren would look like at Genevra's age?

CHAPTER TWENTY-FOUR

Lauren couldn't start the car fast enough. The temperature had plunged on New Year's Eve, and as much as Lauren wanted to stay home, cuddled up on the couch, she knew Cara was excited for tonight's party. She set her seat warmer to max, then turned Cara's off with a little flourish designed to draw Cara's attention.

"You can turn that back on, smarty," Cara said. "I'll turn it off if it gets too warm."

"Wouldn't want you to contract another scorching case of hot butt."

Cara laughed. "Got your driver's license?"

"Yes, Officer." Lauren headed for the FDR, and although it was cold, the night was clear with a waning moon hanging low over Roosevelt Island. "Besides Samantha, will there be anyone there tonight from Perry Bidwell?"

"Lisa will be there. I'm not sure about anyone else."

It wasn't that Lauren was nervous about the party. Celebrations used to be right up there on her list of favorite things, but the last time she had enjoyed herself at a house party had been with Saffron, before her duplicity ruined most enjoyable things for Lauren.

"What did you think of what your aunt showed you yesterday?" Cara placed her hands closer to the vents to warm them.

"She must have some excellent people scouring the market for her. I was impressed. What did you think?"

"I didn't get to see much, but what I saw, I liked. I was busy trying not to get too drunk with Barb. She's an interesting woman."

Lauren smiled. "Now there's a diplomatic assessment. Tell me how you really feel."

"I like her a lot," Cara protested. "She's probably the coolest senior citizen I know."

"I guess I shouldn't be surprised at your diplomacy since you intended to make it your career. I didn't know that."

"Why would you? It was a long time ago."

Lauren didn't say she wanted to know everything about Cara, every last thought and feeling and memory. If there were ever a class on Cara Talarico, she wanted to ace it.

"Have your worries been put to rest about your aunt's part in you getting your job?"

"I don't think she did anything directly to impact any hiring decisions, but I'm never going to know for sure. I just have to get over it and not let it bother me."

Cara nodded. "It's your pigeon."

"My what?" Lauren checked her blind spot.

"Your pigeon. It's the obstacle that gets in the way of your success and that you can't do anything about."

"And that's called a pigeon? I've never heard of that."

"Of course you haven't. I made it up." Cara set her seat warmer a degree lower. "One day I was teaching and a pigeon flew in the classroom. It completely disrupted the lesson and was just one more frustration in a day filled with them, and it kind of represented all the things that get in the way of me succeeding at my job, like fire drills, absences, bad behavior, kids not doing homework, and a pigeon flying in to spy on me for the principal, and you know, causing avian mayhem."

Lauren laughed, but Cara was thoughtful.

"But I can't let the pigeon stop me from trying, you know? I have to go in every day knowing there's a pigeon. And so do you, whatever your particular pigeon happens to be."

"You're right." It was nice to have Cara to talk about the things that would normally rattle around in her head and make her anxious. "That really happened? A pigeon really flew into your classroom?"

"Yup."

"What happened to it?"

"It flew away. Pigeons can do that. I can't."

"Do you want to?" Lauren thought Cara enjoyed her job, despite now knowing it wasn't her first choice.

"The question is immaterial."

Something about Cara's tone warned Lauren not to push, and Cara seemed to shake off her mood, slapping her hands on her knees to the rhythm of a song only she could hear.

"Look at this view. How could anyone want to be anywhere else? These vagabond shoes are staying right here." Crossing the East River gave them an incredible view of the bridges and roadways unfurling to the south, and the lighted Brooklyn Bridge was a diamond necklace draped between the sequined shoulders of Brooklyn and Manhattan.

"I thought they were longing to stray." Lauren now heard the song as well.

"Nope. What gave you that idea?"

So many things. "You said you wanted to travel."

"Yeah, of course, but those will be temporary trips, and they're still off in some whatever someday. Until I can afford to go to the world, N-Y-C will bring the world to me. It'll always be my home."

"Really?" Lauren couldn't keep the doubt from her voice.

"Absolutely. Why do you sound like you don't believe me?"

"I remember you talking about white picket fences, which are in short supply around here." Why was she poking this particular bear?

"You think I want a house in the suburbs enclosed by a literal white fence? I want what that cliché represents." Cara twisted in her seat to enjoy the last of the view as they descended from the Manhattan Bridge onto the surface streets of Brooklyn. "If that was what I wanted, I could already be there, living outside the city and saving a ton on rent and living expenses. But even within my limited means, I can still participate in the joyous planetary microcosm that is New York City life."

"I'm glad you'll be sticking around." Lauren smiled at Cara.

"One day soon when I own the time, we'll go out to Queens on an eating expedition. We can stuff ourselves silly on multiple cultures for about ten bucks each. I know some really good places." Her voice became less buoyant. "There is one really terrible thing about living in New York, though."

"What?"

"Parking. I hope we won't have to look for a spot for ten hours." Cara wiggled her fingers. "I'll start praying to the parking gods now."

❖

Samantha swung her apartment door open with a smile so big Cara thought it was like coming home. She accepted Sam's hug before she could get a word out.

"Happy New Year, Sam," Cara said as they parted. "You remember Lauren, right?"

"Of course." Samantha pulled her into a hug and dragged her through the crowded living room to the tiny galley kitchen. "How are you, Lauren? I'm psyched you and Cara have been hanging out, and totally bummed I missed the reunion."

"Lauren brought champagne and I have—" Cara pulled a jar of her mother's giardiniera out her bag. "Direct from Mom. Merry late Christmas."

"Ooh, thanks. You know how I love me some of this. I'll put it out right now. Or maybe I should hide it and save it for myself." Sam took the bottles out of the bag. "And this looks like the good stuff. Thanks, Lauren. I'm definitely hiding this. Honey, come here," she called out to seemingly no one.

Cara shrugged out of her coat and took Lauren's from her. The apartment had that swampy house party atmosphere where the alcohol had already done a good job of raising both the decibel and humidity levels.

A slight, curly haired man entered, and the tiny kitchen reached maximum capacity. "Hector." Cara hugged him. "It's so good to see you."

Samantha grabbed his arm. "Lauren, this is my husband. Hector, Lauren is an old classmate of ours. She and Cara have recently started da—" Her eyes widened at Cara's death stare, and she finished weakly, "Being friends."

Lauren ignored the gaffe and smoothly greeted Hector and shook his hand.

"It's the Perry Bidwell reunion, part two. Go Beaves!" Lisa shouted as she pushed into the kitchen belly first. "Watch out, fetus life support coming through. Cara, Lauren. How've you two been? Never mind, don't tell me. I can guess. You've probably been scissoring since Christmas. I bet your pubes have all but fallen out."

"Lisa." Cara didn't think her face could feel any hotter.

"You're nearly right, Lisa," Lauren said easily. "It's been since Thanksgiving. The chafing is unbelievable." She turned to Cara. "We should really figure out an easier way to maintain our Brazilians."

Lisa and Samantha laughed in shocked surprise, and Hector went beet red. "Um, I'm leaving now," he said. "How about I take your coats?"

Lauren took them from Cara and gave her a private, teasing smile. "I've got it, Hector. Why don't you show me where they go?"

Cara watched them leave, unable to stop grinning.

"Observe the expression," Lisa said to Sam, attempting the hushed voice of David Attenborough as if he were describing the behavior of some exotic wild animal. "That's some textbook sap right there. Ooey-gooey love with a capital L."

"Yeah," Samantha agreed. "I bet she even thinks Lauren's farts smell great, too."

"Zee finest perfume," Lisa said with a chef's kiss.

"All right, knock it off," Cara said. "We're friends."

"So are Sam and me. Doesn't mean I want to lie down and hug her with my legs." Lisa's smug smile changed to a grimace, and she grabbed onto the countertop with both hands.

"What's wrong?" Cara put a hand on her back. "Are you okay?"

"Is it the baby?" Samantha said.

"No. I still have two weeks until my due date. It's just one of those Braxton Hicks contractions. They've been happening all day. It'll go away in a minute."

"Are you sure?" Cara asked. "Where's Burt? Should I go get him?"

Lisa shook her head. "He's not here. You know how he doesn't like social gatherings. I let him off the hook for this one."

"Well, let's at least get you a place to sit." Samantha led her into the living room, saying as she left, "Cara, you want to do a pass with the champagne?"

She opened two bottles of Lauren's champagne and grumbled, "Just put me to work the minute I get here."

Hector reentered the kitchen. "Let me help. There are some plastic cups somewhere. How long has it been since I've seen you? You have to come out to Brooklyn more often. We miss you."

"Back atcha. Our little building is not the same without you two."

Hector paused in his search through the bags of party supplies. "You look happy, Cara. I'm happy for you. And from what little I've seen, I like Lauren."

"Thanks, I like her too."

"But Sam and Lisa have pulled her into their tractor beam, and while she seems like she can hold her own, you might want to see what's going on there." He handed her a sleeve of cups.

"Thanks for the tip." Cara poured champagne as quickly as she could while keeping an eye on Lauren sitting between Lisa and Sam, their heads bent and talking. She crossed the living room to join them only to have Lisa stand up with effort and intercept her.

"Gotta pee. Come with? I hate to say it, but sometimes I need a little help getting up from the toilet. I should just live in the bathroom, I have to go so often."

Cara followed her to the bathroom, looking over her shoulder at Lauren and Samantha, engrossed in a conversation where Lauren was doing the talking, and Samantha was listening, her expression more serious than it should be for a party. She leaned against the sink as Lisa situated herself. "How are you feeling really? The final stretch can't be easy."

"Trust. This is not for the faint of heart, and I will make sure the offspring knows how much I'm suffering right now. I mean, how can a person have insomnia and exhaustion at the same time?" Lisa grunted in surprise and Cara looked over to see her usual aggrieved expression mutate into something more apprehensive and uncertain.

"What's wrong?"

"This is not peeing. Not to gross you out or anything, but it's coming from the wrong hole."

"You mean…"

"I think my water is breaking." Lisa's blank expression didn't help Cara figure out how to respond. "I don't think those were Braxton Hicks contractions. I think I've been in labor all day," Lisa said, a tremor in her voice.

"Oh shit."

"Yeah, I need to go right now." Lisa did not move.

"Where is the closest hospital? There's a bunch in Manhattan, but there's gotta be something closer."

Lisa's eyes filled with tears. "I want my hospital. I want my doctor. I want Burt."

"You want to go back to Jersey? That's over an hour away." Cara was processing as fast as she could, but this didn't seem like a good idea. She needed help. She opened the bathroom door and yelled for Samantha. "You can't go by yourself. Did you drive here?"

"No," Lisa wailed. "I took the train and the subway."

Samantha and Lauren appeared at the door.

"Hey, what's up? Did the toilet back up ag—"

"Lisa's having her baby," Cara blurted.

"This isn't pee," Lisa moaned.

"Wait," Samantha said. "What's happening right now?"

"Are you having contractions?" Lauren asked.

Cara felt a calm overcome her as she brought the others up to speed. The plan materialized in her mind. "Lisa wants her doctor and Burt, so she wants to go home, but obviously she can't take public transportation, and an Uber isn't a good idea either." She gazed into Lauren's eyes and prayed for her to recognize what Lisa needed.

"I'll get the car," Lauren said. "It's only a few blocks away. Meet me downstairs?"

Cara nodded with gratitude, and they shared a moment of understanding before Lauren disappeared.

"Lauren and I will take you to your hospital," Cara said to Lisa with more confidence than she felt, "and we'll ring in the new year with you and Burt and your baby."

"Thanks, Cara. Now help me up so we can get the hell out of here."

❖

Burt's bulky frame waited at the entrance of the hospital after the longest two hours of Cara's life. They did their best, but it was obvious who Lisa wanted as she hurled herself into Burt's barrel chest after Cara helped her out of the car.

"I'm sorry I wasn't there, babe. Why did I let you go to that party alone?" He held her close in a moment of intimacy that made Cara want to look away. She glanced over to where Lauren stood at the driver's door of the car.

"You didn't know." Lisa's voice was muffled against his chest. She sagged against him, renewing her tears for a minute before she pulled back and punched him on the arm. "You're totally going to be my nonstop escort until this child can drive."

Burt's smile held relief as Lisa rallied. "You got it. They're all ready for you. Let's go inside." He gestured for them all to enter. "Cara, I can't thank you two enough."

"My rescuers have to stay." A porter arrived with a wheelchair and Lisa sank gratefully into it as another contraction threatened to overwhelm her. "Honey, tell them I want the epidural as soon as I get off the elevator."

Moments later, Cara and Burt were stationed at Lisa's shoulders as she moaned and wailed through a contraction of increasing intensity. They were now only a few minutes apart, barely giving her a moment to rest between them. Lisa's doctor arrived and things began happening really fast. Lisa's expression resolved into one of determination and Cara knew the baby would be here any second. Lauren reappeared at Cara's side, settling a mask over her face.

"Where were you?" Cara hadn't realized Lauren was gone until she saw her again.

"Parking the car. Where's your phone? I'll document it."

"Oh, good idea." Cara handed her phone to Lauren and retook her position near Lisa's head. Controlled chaos reigned for the next twenty minutes. Cara had never seen anyone work as hard as Lisa did that night, and felt helpless that all she could offer were words of encouragement while her friend brought a life into the world.

And then, after one more big push—the wail of a newborn.

Burt's eyes looking toward the doctor had lit up like the lights in a football stadium. "It's a boy!"

Lisa's exhaustion was a palpable thing, but so was the wonder and elation on her tear-stained face as one of the nurses placed the baby in her arms. He was a scrawny, red-faced, squalling turnip, and Cara had never seen anything so beautiful.

"Burton Jr., meet your daddy."

Burt burst into tears, and so did Cara, great wracking sobs that surprised the hell out of her. Something broke inside her, seismic in scale and force and magnitude. Their image of nuclear happiness was everything she wanted for herself, and the weak structure that supported her stupid rules crumbled. This was what was important. This was what she wanted. This was the boom at the fault line, cracks tearing down into her foundation. Everything else was the stuff that tumbled from the shelves far away from the epicenter.

She dragged her eyes away from Lisa and her family to Lauren as she snapped pictures of them on Cara's phone, her smile wide and tears in her own eyes. Sweet, sexy, wonderful Lauren. She didn't want to hold Lauren at arm's length anymore, carefully compartmentalizing her thoughts and feelings so they never got too unseemly. She wanted all of life's joyful, tremendous, problematic, overwhelming mess, and she wanted it with Lauren.

❖

Lauren wrapped an arm around Cara's shoulders and guided her into the elevator of her building after they returned from the hospital. The journey back to the city had been mostly silent. It was approaching four a.m. on the first day of January, and Lauren had no idea whether the past hours boded well or ill for the upcoming year. The midnight kiss she had been looking forward to had been swept aside due to the arrival of Burton Jr., but now she wanted to rectify that oversight.

The terrace was a perfect setting for a belated welcome to the New Year, but Cara's solemn gaze across the darkened park, at the black reservoir in front of them and the indigo sky above, had Lauren worried.

"Happy New Year," she said tentatively, hoping to recapture some of their closeness from the past few days.

Cara finally turned to her. "Happy New Year, Lauren. I can't thank you enough for what you did tonight. You were so generous to drive us, and calm and capable, and just so amazing. You're really wonderful. I'm sorry it wasn't the New Year's celebration you thought you were going to get." Cara pulled her into a long hug of such fierceness it almost took Lauren's breath. Something was off.

Lauren tried to brush it off. "How could I have said no to a mother-to-be in need? And everything is great now. Baby is healthy, parents are happy. We can celebrate." She went in for a kiss, but Cara stopped her.

"We need to talk."

Nothing good ever came from that sentence. Apprehension radiated from low in Lauren's belly. She didn't want to know what was behind

Cara's unsmiling expression, or why it caused a shiver of unease to creep down her spine. "It's late. Why don't we catch a few hours of sleep and talk in the morning?"

"No." Cara was taking deep breaths, like she was about to do something scary. "I have to do this now. If I don't, I may never get up the nerve again."

"Cara, what is going on?" Lauren took a step back, her hackles well and truly raised. It was okay. Whatever she said, Lauren would be able to protect herself. She hadn't allowed their relationship to progress beyond the physical. *Lies.*

Cara held Lauren's hands gently in her own. "We witnessed the birth of something tonight, and it was more than seeing Burt Jr. come into the world. Lisa and Burt have become a real family now who will have each other for the rest of their lives. They produced a life, and he's a living testament to their commitment to each other."

Lauren couldn't look away from the intensity in Cara's eyes.

"You know I set rules for myself about getting out of debt and not getting involved in anything serious, but I want to start the new year with no limits and no restrictions. I want the freedom to pursue something lasting and meaningful. You also know the end game for me is a wife, a family, something that will endure." Cara's smile was hesitant and hopeful, and it cut at Lauren despite knowing this was Cara's plan all along.

"You want to find your wife? You're not waiting anymore?"

"I don't want to wait. I've already found someone special and I want to see where it goes with her. I think we could have it all." Cara waited for her to say something.

Confusion hampered Lauren's understanding until her meaning penetrated. Cara wanted her? "But we're friends. We agreed."

"I know. I feel differently now. I'm hoping you do, too. You and I, we're so good together. Just think what we could be…"

Lauren closed her eyes and thought about all the things she knew Cara wanted and how she had shut the door on the possibility of wanting them for herself. It was impossible. But what if? What if she could have all that with Cara, who made her heart race every time she walked in the room? She kind of wanted to find out if her heart would still be racing in ten years. Twenty years. Fifty years?

But she had been here before. Despite the rosy rockets of joy Cara's words conjured, an equally dark image of Old Bailey in London replaced them, and she knew she couldn't risk it. Her heart wouldn't survive it again.

She opened her eyes to see that Cara's tremulous smile had compressed into a less hopeful straight line. She pulled her hands from Cara's and turned so her earnest eyes were no longer cutting into her.

"I'm sensing you don't feel the same," Cara said. "I guess the miracle of childbirth doesn't make you want to change your life plan the way it did for me."

"It was amazing and affirming and all that, but I don't see what it has to do with us. I'm happy with the way things are going. We both said we wanted to keep it light, right?"

"I said that in the beginning, but I've changed my mind. I know I'm springing this on you with no warning, but I want the chance to see what we could be for each other if we forget about the limitations we put on ourselves at the start. I know you have reservations. I know something happened with your ex-fiancée that scarred you, that you're having trouble coming back from, but I'm not her."

"We're not talking about that." Lauren's voice was clipped.

"Okay." Cara backed off. "Although I think you might feel better if you could talk through it with someone. Doesn't have to be me, but I can be a good listener."

Lauren didn't reply. Why was Cara doing this? This was not what they agreed. They had a good thing going. Why mess with it? The silence lingered between them until Lauren heard a heavy sigh from Cara.

"Maybe I'm wrong. Maybe you're just not made for something long term, but I've never been with someone I feel so connected to. Name a cylinder and we're firing on it, in all the ways. You make me happy. All the worries I had in the beginning have pretty much melted away." A small smile returned to Cara's lips as Lauren turned to face her again. "And I don't want you to be a placeholder for some other mystery woman in the future. I want to know if you *are* that woman. My forever woman."

Forever. It sounded so tempting. Was she making a mistake? Could it be that easy? In her mind she went over what Cara had said. "Wait a minute. What worries did you have?"

"You know, differences in our upbringings and certain hang-ups you or I may have about that. I'm not saying our issues magically disappear if we decide to open ourselves up to something lasting. We'll have to talk about things that come up, but knowing there may be bumps along the way is not stopping me from putting myself out there like this and asking you to change the parameters of our relationship a little." Cara paused. "Well, a lot. I hope you can appreciate how scary this is right now," she added in a small voice.

"My experiences with relationships so far have led to disappointment. Our friendship is working. Why change it?"

The hesitancy disappeared from Cara's demeanor and she became the direct person Lauren knew her to be. "I don't want to be just friends who fuck. I want more than that."

She winced. Was that really how Cara would describe what they had? She needed to salvage this somehow. How could she get them back to the place they were when they walked in her front door? "I don't understand what the *more* part is."

"I think you do, but I want to be absolutely clear. Friends don't get forever. They don't get everything. I want the chance of forever with you, the possibility of everything. Lauren, I think I'm falling in love with you."

Whatever Lauren was about to say was eclipsed by Cara's declaration. She had heard these words before and they had been counterfeit. And there was no way Cara could prove they were genuine. She closed her mouth, unable to have a hand in steering her own destiny.

Cara waited, but then pressed on. "I know it's fast. I know it's too soon, but I don't think I can continue if we can't at least redefine what we are to each other."

Why couldn't they just rewind the night to before any of this? An awful silence opened between them. Cara's chin crumpled with the effort of holding her emotion in, and she pushed off the railing and back toward the French doors.

She finally found her voice. "Cara, wait. I think we need to get some sleep and figure this out tomorrow."

Cara didn't turn as she replied, voice thick with emotion. "I'm going to get my stuff and go. I think it's best."

Lauren found her in her bedroom, collecting her clothes from the past few days and throwing them into her duffel. She sat on the bed and watched, grasping at anything that might make Cara stay, that might lead to their lying in bed and ignoring this whole conversation. "Don't I own the time? Our time isn't over. I don't release you."

Cara gave her a withering look on her way into the bathroom. "You suspended our time owning arrangement. You said it didn't matter." She was gone a long time, and when she came back out, her face was scrubbed of the remnants of party makeup and tears and she was more composed.

"Please don't go. Can we please go back to the way it was? Nothing has to change."

Cara sat down, leaving space between them. "Everything has changed."

"I know what you want me to say." Her voice was halting and low. "But I can't say it. I feel it, but I can't say it. The minute I say it everything will turn to shit. I put my heart out there twice, and both times I discovered it wasn't me they loved. It was the money. I can't say it, can't even think it. I couldn't bear it. You mean too much."

"But what do they have to do with me?" She waited for Lauren to say something, and then the penny dropped. "Oh God. You're lumping me in with them? You think I want your money?"

She didn't want to believe it, but how could she ever be sure?

"I think I'm a little bit insulted." Cara looked away, her brows drawn in distress. "No, a lot insulted. Have I ever given you the slightest indication that I want your money?"

She had to assert herself even though she was beginning to feel foolish. "No, but it might be there in your subconscious. Maybe you have these feelings for me only because of who my family is."

"I don't believe this. I need you to tell me what I ever did to give you the idea that I want your money more than I want you."

"You have loans." Lauren's weak justification sounded wrong to her own ears.

Cara gaped at her. "You think I want you to pay back my student loans?" She sat there, and Lauren could see her attempting to understand, trying to make it compute, but she also saw the moment Cara rejected it. "Wow. Okay, I guess you really don't know me at all. And what does that say about you, that you're willing to fuck me, thinking I'm only after your money?"

Lauren flinched, the words landing on her like blows.

Cara waited for her to respond, and when she didn't, she took control of the conversation. "I want you to know that the thought of you paying off my loans would never in a million years occur to me. Yes, they're a pretty big consideration for me. They're blocking me from pursuing my goals, life goals I want you to be a part of, despite *my* reservations about *your* money."

Lauren braced herself for what might come after these words.

"Yeah, you heard me. I honestly never thought we would get here. I thought it would be a few dates and I could finally get to know the mysterious Lauren Havemayer, who I'd wondered about since the tenth grade, and I could ignore all the weirdness of being with someone with more money than God because this was just a temporary thing. While you were thinking I was congratulating myself for getting a ride on your gravy train, I was actually trying to get over the idea of your family's insane wealth."

"You managed to let me know that with your occasional snide comments. Don't think I didn't hear them." Lauren wanted to crawl into bed and end this. It was getting ugly and she couldn't take it.

"So how could you think I wanted you to pay off my loans?" Cara asked. "You know what? Don't answer that. Never mind. I guess it's a good thing we had this conversation now, before I allowed myself any more delusions about what we could have meant to each other."

Lauren felt like a gaping hole had opened up in the center of her chest. They were supposed to be friends. They could do this if they stuck to the agreement. Cara got up and shouldered her bag. She was leaving. The absolute desolation on her face and the way she moved with slow determination tore at Lauren. How had they even gotten here? "Is this over? I don't want this to be over."

"I don't know." Cara turned to face her but kept her eyes downcast. "I'm not saying we can't ever be friends, but I'm going to need some time." She laughed without humor. "Maybe by the next reunion."

"You're not serious? We can still talk and text, can't we?"

"Why would you want to continue being friends with someone you think is a gold digger?" Cara asked, her face a picture of weary bewilderment. She turned to go.

It was a reasonable question, one Lauren didn't have an answer to. She followed Cara to the elevator and watched as she pressed the call button.

Cara came close and rested her hands lightly on Lauren's shoulders. She kissed each cheek in turn. "Our time together is now over. Take care of yourself, Lauren." The elevator arrived and Cara stepped in.

Lauren turned so they faced each other, and as the door slid closed and slowly removed Cara from her field of vision, she wondered if she hadn't just made the biggest mistake of her life.

CHAPTER TWENTY-FIVE

Y ou look like you need this."
Cara lifted her head from its position, propped on the very acute angle her arm made on the café table as she ignored her laptop and the lessons that needed to be completed. "I've already had one today." But she reached for the steaming macchiato Manny placed before her all the same.

He sat down across from her with the look of the intervention in his eyes. "Where is my Cara? Lately, you're like one of those knock-off Louis Vuitton bags those sketchy guys sell on a Hun' Twenty-Fifth. You look okay from a distance, but when you get up close you can tell something's not right."

Great. I'm a cheap counterfeit purse. Thanks, Manny. "I'm fine. Just a little low energy."

"You've been low energy and mopey for too long, and I've had it."

Manny had been trying to buck her up for weeks, but this visible frustration was a new approach. Didn't matter. She wasn't in the mood. "Do you want me to leave?"

"No! You need to get it out. I think you need to talk about Daisy."

"We *have* talked about her, and her name is Lauren, not Daisy. We went out a few times, but now it's over. I was curious about my crush. Former crush. Now I know." Cara's phone buzzed. She barely looked at it before turning it over. Lauren had been texting pretty regularly, but Cara hadn't responded. Her feelings were still raw. Sadness and embarrassment and indignation all sloshed around inside her like she was a walking rain barrel.

Manny did have a point. All this wallowing in her misery wasn't helping. She needed to do something to exorcise Lauren from her life.

"She was just like Daisy Buchanan, wasn't she? Cold and heartless, skipping town in the middle of the night just when you need her the most."

"I'm not Gatsby, Manny. And she's not Daisy. She's still in town, as far as I know. This is reality. It just wasn't meant to be."

"Then why are your eyes all glassy right now?"

Damn him, asking all the hard questions. "I guess because I thought it was meant to be for a minute. But like I said, this is reality."

"Reality stinks."

Cara sighed. "Yeah, it does."

❖

"Ms. Havemayer."

Walking across the lobby toward the gray morning, Lauren adjusted the gift boxes in her arms and turned back toward the concierge desk. "Good morning, Raoul."

"Good morning. Your friend dropped off that package for you. She said you would know what it was."

"Package?" She wasn't expecting anything.

Raoul pointed to a large flat package securely wrapped in a several layers of bubble wrap. There was a white piece of paper taped to it with her name written on it in black Sharpie. It was Cara's handwriting. An invisible wind knocked her a tiny bit sideways when she realized it was the copy of the Sohlberg painting she had given to her for Christmas. The rejection of her gift cut her to the quick and she blinked a few times in order to master her emotions.

"When did she leave, Raoul?" Maybe she was still nearby. Maybe Lauren could run out to the sidewalk and see that navy-blue peacoat walking away. Maybe it wasn't too late to catch up to her and somehow change the outcome of their last conversation now over a month ago.

"Must be about an hour or so. I asked if she wanted me to call up and let you know she was here, but she said no, it was too early for company on a Saturday morning." Raoul smiled at the memory of a conversation that had probably included more than he was saying. Cara had undoubtedly been her cheery self, joking with him about the weather, asking about his kids, and Lauren could barely speak past her envy and sorrow that Raoul had been the recipient of her attention rather than her.

"Thanks for letting me know. I'll bring it up on my way back in."

"Your car is waiting out front. May I help you with your packages?"

"No thanks, I can manage." Lauren made her exit and tried to put it out of her mind. She was due at Sasha's baby shower in Connecticut in an hour and already late. Perhaps when she was able to think about it again, the sting of it would have faded.

❖

"I don't know. Milky Way? Snickers?" Lauren quickly passed the diaper to the woman on her left, an anesthesiologist at Stamford Hospital she had just met.

"Definitely Snickers. There's nuts!" The woman buried her nose in the diaper and sniffed it, then actually stuck out her tongue and licked it.

Attempting to disguise the revulsion she felt by the actions of her partner and the foulness of participating in a game called Name that Poop, Lauren averted her eyes and saw her school chum Sasha had observed the entire exchange, and was trying to hold back her laughter. She mouthed the word, "Really?" to her friend, and passed the next diaper on without looking at it.

Amid these strangers in Sasha's living room, trying to determine what type of candy bar had been melted into a diaper, Lauren wanted to shake the despondence that had come on with a vengeance as she drove out of the city. Supporting Sasha was the primary goal today, but it was time to concede that baby shower games were not going to cheer her up.

In the five weeks since New Year's Eve, Lauren had been rowing as hard as she could through the currents of her life, maintaining her work commitments, and trying to understand what had happened with Cara. All of her olive-branchy texts had gone unanswered, and she was starting to accept that Cara was ghosting her. Although it hurt, she couldn't blame her. Deep in her bones, she knew Cara wasn't using her for financial gain, and she was appalled at herself for taking her oars out of the water and letting her fears unravel so messily during their last conversation.

Cara returning the painting had the potential to send her listing aimlessly through treacherous waters, but for Sasha's sake, she couldn't allow herself to capsize right now. She would pretend excitement over the color-coordinated onesies, burp cloths, and bibs her friend was now unwrapping with abandon, mindful of the pledge she had made at the reunion to be a better friend now that she was back in New York.

A few hours later, she retrieved her coat and returned to the living room to sit beside an uncomfortably large and exhausted Sasha on the sofa. The dishes were done, the gift-wrapping debris vanquished, and the gifts neatly piled on the dining room table. "Where's Colin while we're performing this archaic fertility rite? Doesn't seem fair he gets to avoid it."

"He's at a bar watching football with his dad and brothers. He gets hot wings and beer while we make a fucking hat out of gift bows. I just texted him. He'll be home in a while. You don't have to stay, my precious pet. You were a pillar of strength. Thanks for everything."

"Happy to do it, Sash. What can I get for you before I go? Do you want some herbal tea? Coffee? Wine? Sushi? Unpasteurized cheese?"

Sasha laughed. "God, you are such a bitch." She hoisted her feet up onto the sofa. "Be a dear and rub my feet for a minute, will you?"

"Are you kidding?" Lauren looked askance at Sasha's feet. It seemed a bit beyond the purview of a recently renewed friendship.

"What? It's not like I've been walking around with chocolate soiled diapers strapped to them. I'm even wearing socks. Never mind. I forgot you're not Colin for a second."

Lauren pulled her leather gloves from the pocket of her overcoat and put them on. She began to rub Sasha's feet.

Sasha let her head fall back on the couch and groaned in ecstasy. "Lord, that feels good. What is that? Calfskin leather? You sure know how to give a girl a good time. This could've been your present. No need for the Calder mobile for the crib."

"A Calder-esque mobile. Not the real thing."

"Duh. I hardly thought you would be spending millions on my offspring."

"Do you think it's appropriate for a baby? I could return it and get something else. Something with duckies or whatever."

"It's fine. We love it."

"I got one for Lisa Jankowski's baby, too."

Sasha lifted her head. "You did?"

"Oh, I haven't told you. I was there for her son's birth."

Her eyes widened. "No, you did not tell me. This sounds like a story."

"Yeah, I was at Samantha Cruz's place for a New Year's Eve party and—"

"You were at Samantha Cruz's place?" Sasha was incredulous. "Who are you and what have you done with my friend Lauren?"

She looked down at herself. "Same old Lauren."

"You hanging out with day students ten years after graduation is definitely not the same old Lauren. Connect these dots, if you please."

"It's not a big deal. I started seeing Cara Talarico a little bit— remember I gave her a ride back to the city after the reunion." Lauren told Sasha what happened at Sam's party. "And that's where we witnessed the blessed event. Let me tell you, you're in for a real treat." Lauren felt the dishonesty of labeling her time with Cara as no big deal and couldn't meet Sasha's eyes.

Incredibly, Sasha didn't care to know the birthing details. "What do you mean seeing her? Are you dating?"

"We were for about a minute. It was fun while it lasted. Now it's over." Lauren was mortified to realize her throat was convulsing with the effort of holding back her emotion. She turned away from Sasha, hearing the unspoken invitation to pour her guts out to her kindhearted friend, but Lauren wanted desperately to avoid that. "I don't want to talk about it."

"Okay, help me up."

Lauren pulled Sasha to a standing position.

"Walk with me. Did you know we have a library in this house? What a waste for a pair of non-readers." Sasha opened a set of pocket doors off the foyer to reveal a wood paneled room with built-in bookcases on almost every wall, books occupying about half the shelves, mostly medical and finance texts. "We dumped every book we own in here and still haven't filled it up." She pulled their Perry Bidwell yearbook from a shelf that included two copies of *The Da Vinci Code* and volumes D, M, and T of an old *World Book Encyclopedia*. "Let's give this a look, shall we?"

"I haven't the faintest notion of where my yearbook could be," Lauren said. They sank into the leather settee, the only piece of furniture in the room. Passing over the personal messages scrawled across the inside cover and the photos of underclasswomen and faculty, she turned to the senior portraits. She went to the back of the alphabet and gazed at Sasha, ten years younger and visibly less stressed out. "Aw, look at young Sasha, before her medical residency and pregnancy turned her into a scraggly hag."

"Again. You are a bitch, I say." But Sasha was smiling with nostalgia.

It was like falling off a log, being with Sasha again, and Lauren was grateful for their friendship. The quote beneath Sasha's photo read: *Luck is what happens when planning meets preparation.* "Seneca? How'd you come up with that?"

"No idea. There was no *Hamilton* back then so who knows where people found inspirational quotes. Not that I've seen it. What was yours?"

"I can't remember." Lauren found her own portrait and saw that her quote was from the sculptor Auguste Rodin: *The main thing is to be moved, to love, to hope, to tremble, to live.* She now remembered being obsessed with Rodin and taping the quote to the wall of her dorm room after reading his biography.

Sasha read it over her shoulder. "Not bad, Lauren. Definitely more heartfelt than mine. And look at your photo. You were so damned cute. So innocent. Not." Sasha chuckled. "So how much loving, hoping, trembling, and living have you done lately?"

"Not a lot," was Lauren's distracted reply. "You know we don't do much of that in the scraggly hag club." She barely looked at herself before she was flipping forward in the alphabet, consumed with the desire to see Cara's portrait. And there she was, those same warm eyes and big smile in a face with slightly chubbier cheeks. Her long dark hair was not the usual riot of waves Lauren loved touching but was pin straight and parted on one side. She looked young and hopeful, with all of the possibilities of life ahead of her, before its realities started shaping her into the woman Lauren knew—still hopeful, but also wiser from her disappointments. Lauren had disappointed her, and the young girl in the photograph didn't deserve that.

"Forever is composed of nows." Sasha recited the quote beneath Cara's picture. "Emily Dickinson. That's a good one. It sounds smart."

"Her favorite poet." Lauren closed the book, avoiding Sasha's eyes, now gazing at her with questions and concern. She might as well get it out with a sympathetic audience to listen. "I just enjoyed the hell out of her. She was so much fun, and she understood me, and she was a good person. And now I don't get to be around her anymore, and it sucks."

"I didn't know Cara very well in school, but I do have this very clear memory of her from around ninth grade or so." Sasha took the yearbook back and paged through it. "You know how the newly arrived girls are hazed a bit when they get to school? Older girls telling them wrong directions and bossing them around and stuff?"

"Yeah, I remember."

"There was a group of them in the cafeteria looking at some celebrity gossip magazine, and you know how prized that kind of thing was to us back then. It was like a lifeline to the outside world. Anyway, this senior girl walked by and just plucked the magazine out of their hands and walked off with it."

Lauren rolled her eyes, remembering well the power games of some of the girls. "Who was it?"

"Willow Driscoll, remember her?"

"Of course. She was a nightmare."

"And these younger girls were not going to confront Willow 'Wildebeest' Driscoll and get their magazine back, but Cara did. She stood at Willow's table and calmly asked for it back, and Willow ignored her. She just stood there and stood there and waited, and Willow started in with the verbal abuse, calling her day trash and welfare princess and everything else, but Cara wouldn't budge. Finally, Willow could see that Cara wasn't going to back down and flung the magazine at her. Those seventh graders must have worshipped her after that."

"That's so her." Lauren's shoulders drooped. "Fighting for the little guy."

"You know that saying, when someone shows you who they are, believe them? That was Cara showing me who she is." Sasha slapped the yearbook. "Damn, that should have been my yearbook quote. Who said that?"

"How come I never knew how incredible she was while we were at school?"

"We must have had a different definition of incredible back then." Sasha pointed to the Model UN photo, where Cara, Samantha Cruz, and two other students stood smiling, basking in their geekitude, each brandishing a certificate that Lauren had seen recently in Cara's childhood bedroom. "Not really our idea of incredible, shallow bitches that we were."

"We were idiots." Lauren took the book back and looked for the field hockey team picture.

"Isn't everyone in high school?" Sasha asked.

There was the proof. Cara was in the third row, all the way over on the right, far from Lauren in the center of the front row. As she leafed through the other pages commemorating clubs, activities, and teams, Cara's youthful smile leapt out at her several more times.

"If she's so incredible, why are you two already Donesville?"

"It's complicated."

Sasha waited for more.

"We want different things." Then she couldn't help adding, "And I fucked up."

"Can you fix it? Do you want to fix it?"

"I don't think there's a way to fix this mistake."

"I know we haven't been close for a while now, but I could tell at the reunion you weren't happy, and right now you're positively glum, chum. But I'm guessing there was a little interval between today and the last time I saw you when you smiled more? While you were *enjoying the hell out of her*?"

"Yeah, she was terrific."

Sasha nudged her. "You keep referring to her in the past tense. She's not dead, girl."

"Okay, she's great, but she offered me something valuable and I turned her down in a pretty gross way. I don't think I can walk it back." Lauren knew she was being vague, and she waited for the usually inquisitive Sasha to ask for more details, but she didn't.

Instead, Sasha held up the yearbook, open to Lauren's senior portrait. "Look at that girl. She was a good friend to me and lots of other girls, and she was sometimes smart and sometimes a dumbass, just like any other kid figuring out how to grow up. And she had a hard time for a while because her mom died and she was super sad most of senior year, but she recovered, and she deserves happiness. And I know she has the courage to go out and find her happiness if she knows where to find it, and I'm guessing you know where to find it."

"Maybe I don't have the courage." Lauren believed it had been stolen along with a good amount of her property three years ago.

"Maybe. But this girl—" Sasha tapped Lauren's picture. "She definitely had courage, and I don't think you've changed so much since then that you've lost something that important."

The task seemed insurmountable. "How do I do it?"

"I find sharing your honest, open heart usually forgives almost every sin. At least that's what's been getting Colin and me over the rough spots. But if that doesn't work..." Sasha pulled her lips down in the terrible impression of Marlon Brando she'd been doing since they were roommates and spoke in a hoarse, old man voice. "You make her an offer she can't refuse."

Lauren didn't want to reward Sasha's awful impression with a giggle, but she couldn't help it. "You were almost in Oprah territory there, Sash. So good with the advice, and then you had to go and ruin it."

"Yeah, well, sometimes laughter is better than tears."

She couldn't disagree. "You sure you want to be a surgeon? You would make a great psychiatrist."

Sasha tilted her head and thought about it. "Psychiatrists do get to sit down a lot, but they have to listen to people's boring problems all day long, and they don't get to play with the innards of the human body. I'll stick with surgery."

Lauren felt her stomach heave a little bit when Sasha said innards. "You think my problems are boring?"

"Never, sweetling. Only strangers' problems are boring. When will we see each other again? I've missed you, and this past half hour has been so fun. The shower? Not so much, but I got a lot of loot."

"You and Colin deserve it. You know you can call me anytime and I'll come running to help with the baby. I want to see you more now that I'm back."

"I'll hold you to that. Now go on back to the city and—" Sasha held up her fingers in air quotes. "'Screw your courage to the sticking place.'" She waited for Lauren to acknowledge the quote.

Lauren shrugged. "*Hamilton*?"

"No. *Macbeth*, ding-dong! You tell Cara that only ten years too late, I am coming up with way better yearbook quotes. Literary ones!"

CHAPTER TWENTY-SIX

Cara didn't recognize the number that was ringing on her phone. It wouldn't be a student, they texted exclusively. Maybe a parent, but the area code was Manhattan. Against her better judgment, she answered it. "Hello?" Her tone was clipped and suspicious.

"Hi, Cara. It's Lauren. I know you don't want to talk to me, but please don't hang up."

"Hi." Cara paused, trying not to react to the sound of Lauren's familiar voice. Her heart was a little betraying bastard and reacted anyway and pounded away as she waited for Lauren to say something. The silence lengthened. "I'm not hanging up."

"Right." Lauren sounded embarrassed. "I guess I should just get on with it."

"Did you change your number?"

"No, I'm calling from my desk at work. I thought I'd have a better chance of you answering if I used my work number."

She always knew Lauren was smart. "It's nine o'clock. What are you still doing at work?"

"I'm, uh, working."

Cara shook her head. "I guess I walked right into that one."

"The reason I'm calling is…Do you remember that day in the laundromat? You showed me an image called *The Great Wave*. Your student found a poem about it?" Lauren's words came out in a rush.

"I remember." Of all the things Lauren could be calling about, Cara would never have chosen this as their first post-breakup—or whatever their last interaction could be called since they hadn't ever been officially together—conversation.

"I've arranged an appointment for your students to see it a week from tomorrow, February nineteenth. Is ten a.m. okay?"

Visiting the museum? Seeing Lauren again in front of her students? "I don't…I'm not sure. I'd have to clear it with my principal first."

"How about I schedule it and you let me know if it's doable?"

She couldn't really say no. Her students deserved this. "I guess that sounds fine."

"I'm assuming the poem is by Donald Finkel, and its title is the same as the work?"

"I—I don't know. I can ask Miguel tomorrow."

"Great. It's the only poem I found, but let's confirm that. I have to tell you, it's very different from the Anne Sexton one, but I'm sure you'll find some value to it."

"Hold on, let me get a pen. I have to write this down." Before Cara got the pen, she gripped the phone in both hands and breathed in and out a few times. Lauren's demeanor was so businesslike, and her bastard heart was still doing the conga inside her chest. *Pull yourself together.*

"You know what?" Lauren said when Cara returned to the line. "I'll just email you all these details. I found a few more poems too. I'll include links for those."

"Thank you, Lauren. It's kind of you to go to all this trouble." And it was, but Cara didn't know why Lauren would bother after the collapse of their friendship.

"Not at all. I forgot I told you I would check up on this. I'm just following through."

Was it really just Lauren tidying up loose ends? "I appreciate it."

"It's nothing." There was another pause, then Lauren said, "I don't have your email address."

Cara let the irony roll over her. Lauren knew so many things about her. She knew how Cara took her bodega coffee, and how she felt about her father, and the exact spot on her neck that could make her shudder every time Lauren pressed her tongue there. But she didn't know Cara's email address. She recited it slowly and said, "Thanks again, Lauren."

"You can either email me or call back on this number. I won't ask you to return a text."

Her fingers tensed around her phone as she absorbed the dig.

"I'm sorry," Lauren said before she could respond. "I shouldn't have said that."

She didn't acknowledge Lauren's comment or the apology. "I'll get back to you as soon as I can. It's getting late. Be careful getting home." In an alternate reality, she would have asked Lauren to text her so she knew she had arrived safely, but it was an impossibility in this one.

❖

Lauren waited in the vestibule of the education entrance as Cara and her students went through the bag check. She nervously smoothed her hands down the jacket of one of her favorite suits, a wool, navy, chalk stripe with an ivory silk blouse beneath it. It was perfect for the frigid weather and made her feel confident, which was what she needed today.

A few of Cara's students drifted over as they finished with security. She had wracked her brain the night before to remember their names, but there was one girl whose name escaped her. Fortunately, the ones she remembered, Yenifer and Fatoumata, approached her and she greeted them by name.

"Hi, Miss," Yenifer replied, and Fatoumata smiled at her.

"Welcome to the Met." Lauren's eyes found Cara, bringing up the rear, stuffing her scarf and Peruvian hat into her satchel. The enormity of the task ahead became clear when she took in Cara's smiling mouth and solemn eyes. "Come this way, everyone. Let's find a quieter place to talk."

The seminar room had an arrangement of chairs in front of the easel where the Hokusai woodblock print sat. The students gathered around it while Cara stood behind them.

"It's smaller than I thought it would be." Miguel scooted his chair closer to the print, which was a little larger than a legal-sized piece of paper, surrounded by a simple white mat and thin timber frame. "I thought it was going to be giant."

"Why did you think that?" Lauren asked.

Miguel shrugged.

"Because waves are big," Rashard said.

"It looks like the wave emoji, and that thing is tiny," said the girl whose name Lauren couldn't remember.

"The wave emoji is based on this image, and I'm sure you've all seen it before somewhere," Lauren said. "It's one of the most reproduced works of art in history. I've seen it on all kinds of products: clothing, household goods, countless memes, and you wouldn't believe how many people tattoo this image somewhere on their body and then post it to the internet."

Miguel and Rashard pulled out their phones, presumably to look up the tattoos.

"You can fact-check Ms. Havemayer's claims later," Cara said. "Please put your phones away."

Lauren waited until she had their attention. "Why do you think this image—which is entitled *Under the Wave off Kanagawa*, but commonly known as *The Great Wave*—why is it so popular?"

Yenifer put her hand up. "Wait, Miss. Why is it called under the wave and not just the wave? Is it because the wave isn't in the middle of the picture?"

"I'm so glad you asked that question, Yenifer. I'm getting ahead of myself. Why don't we take a minute or two to look at this woodcut print, like we did with *Starry Night*. And while you're taking it in, think about why it's named *Under the Wave off Kanagawa*."

"What's Kana-whatever you just said?" Fatoumata asked.

"Another good question, Fatoumata. Kanagawa is the coastal area in Japan that is the setting for the print. Any other questions before we take a moment to look?" Lauren paused and then took a position next to Cara, who was engrossed in the print as well. Lauren nudged her with her elbow. "What's her name?" she mouthed and nodded toward the girl in the black coat.

"Maritza," Cara whispered.

Lauren took a pen from her pocket and added the name to her notes so she wouldn't forget. She could feel Cara watching her.

"What's all that?" She pointed with her chin at the thick sheaf of handwritten notes Lauren had generated for the class's visit.

Lauren always over prepared, but had really gone overboard this time. "I wanted to be ready for whatever questions they might have. Woodblock prints aren't my specialty."

"So you hand wrote your own fifty page dissertation about it?" The low-grade twinkle in Cara's eye made Lauren flustered and absurdly happy.

"Stop. It's twenty pages at most." Lauren couldn't help drinking in Cara's flesh and blood appearance. She wore her usual teacher uniform of cords, sneakers, and polo shirt. The one difference was the pumpkin-colored puffer jacket instead of the peacoat she usually wore. When had that change happened? "I like your new coat."

The hint of amusement in Cara's expression faded and she turned away to continue examining the picture before them.

Lauren swallowed her disappointment. She shouldn't even attempt small talk until they had large, serious, repairing-the-damage-done talk, which she had built into Cara's visit, if all went according to her plan.

Thankfully, Maritza rescued her. "Are those people in those boats?"

Lauren returned to the easel. "Those are fishermen returning home after bringing their catch to sell in the city of Edo, which is now Tokyo."

"So that's what's under the wave," Rashard said. "People."

Yenifer said, "And a volcano."

"Where?" he asked.

"Here." Lauren indicated with her pen the mountain just off center, dwarfed by the rogue wave in the foreground. "That's Mount Fuji, and that's what's *Under the Wave off Kanagawa*. Katsushika Hokusai did a series of thirty-six woodblock prints on the topic of Mount Fuji, and this is one of them."

"Why did he care so much about the volcano?" Miguel asked.

"Mount Fuji is a sacred site and source of inspiration to Japanese people, which is why Hokusai created the series, and why it was such a success." She had all their attention now. "And one of the most remarkable things is that it was mass-produced. The image was turned into a woodcut, which made it reproducible. You could buy one of these prints for what it cost to buy your lunch back in the 1830s."

"How much would one cost now?" Miguel asked.

"That's a question with a complicated answer." And maybe not very interesting. "Another cool thing is the impact of Hokusai's art on other artists' work. Does this blue color and the swirly motion depicted in the wave remind you of anything else you might have seen?"

"Yeah," said Rashard. "It's kind of like the van Gogh." Yenifer and Fatoumata nodded.

"Exactly," Lauren said. "Van Gogh was influenced by Hokusai's work. Many French Impressionists were also. See how one period has a direct correlation to others?"

"But how much does it cost?" Miguel was not going to let it go.

Lauren exhaled, disappointed that cost was all he seemed to care about. "You could go into the gift shop right now and buy a jigsaw puzzle or some socks with this image on it for ten bucks, but I don't think that's what you mean."

"No, how much for an original from back in the day?"

"Does it matter, bruh?" Rashard laughed. "You can't even afford the socks."

"I'm sure Ms. Havemayer knows the value of this piece and is willing to share it," Cara said quietly.

Lauren surrendered. "If you were alive in 1832 you could buy an original for about the equivalent of five dollars, but if you want one today in good condition, you would have to be prepared to pay anywhere from half a million to a million dollars."

"Deadass?" Rashard exclaimed, and the rest of the students burst into chattering disbelief about the value of the print.

It was what Lauren disliked most when talking about art. All the students laughed and joked while Cara passed out the poem, all except Miguel, who knelt down so his face was inches from the easel.

Lauren crouched next to him, genuinely curious. "What's so important about its cost?"

His eyes slid toward her before gazing at the image again. "Nothing, I guess. I just want to know everything about it." Lauren was about to stand and give him some space when he continued. "I don't know how to swim, and I've only ever been in the ocean once. It didn't have big blue waves like this. It was warm and flat and green."

"Where was this?"

"In DR, where my family is from. This is so different. Those waves look like they could kill somebody, but they also look like a ride, you know? Like they could carry you away from everything, and then you would wash up somewhere new." Miguel's voice had become dreamy, and Lauren knew he wasn't talking to her.

She recognized the experience he was having. She had been slightly younger than Miguel, in this very museum, in a gallery two floors above where they now stood, when she had first fallen into a piece of art. She stood up and took the poem handout from Cara, allowing Miguel more time in his moment with the wave.

Cara's eyes lingered over the two of them before she asked Yenifer to read the poem aloud. In a matter of moments, their heads were bent and they were focused on the rhyme and meter of the lines in front of them. Miguel came out of his reverie, joining his classmates in their analysis of the poem, and Lauren sat outside the intimate grouping they made and listened as Cara facilitated their discussion.

When they were close to wrapping up, Yenifer turned to Cara. "Miss, can we stay and look at some more art?"

Cara let Lauren do the honors.

"Of course you may, and Ms. Talarico and I found a few more connections between poetry and art here at the museum, so we're going to send you on a scavenger hunt."

"Ms. Havemayer is lying. She did all the work today. I'll be scavenging right along with you all."

So, Cara was planning on avoiding her. Lauren had thought about this visit for over a week. Her apology was locked and loaded and she was going to fix things.

❖

Cara followed her students and Lauren up the Grand Staircase to the second floor of the museum, counting heads to make sure everyone was present. Some class trips produced the inevitable headache at day's end, but today's excursion with her five most mature students was almost a gift. It was pleasant to be in the museum instead of the classroom, and she had to admit that observing Lauren in her element, in that gorgeous suit, was more uplifting than depressing. Despite everything, Cara was mostly content to participate in Lauren's planned activities. So far, Lauren had been nothing but professional.

They assembled just inside a large arched doorway, and Lauren distributed a handout and a map to each student. "We are currently here." Lauren pointed on the map she held in front of her. "I've circled it in red on all your maps. You see the four blue Xs? Those are where the Met has artworks that have been memorialized with poetry. They're all here on the second floor."

Cara held up the handout. "The poems are here. Your mission is to find each piece of art and study it and the accompanying poem. Take pictures of the art with your phone, make sketches if you like, discuss with your classmates, and choose one art-poem combo to analyze. And yes, you will be writing an essay about it." She ignored the groans.

"You'll have an hour to visit these artworks and wander around the European Paintings galleries on this floor," Lauren added.

"But if you don't feel like writing an essay, we have an alternative for you." Cara flipped the handout. "Find an artwork that speaks to you, that you fall in love with. You may write a poem about that piece of art instead. The requirements for that are listed on the back."

"All we have to do is write a poem?" Rashard looked suspicious.

"Check the requirements first. You won't be able to get away with writing a haiku."

"At least fourteen lines, six examples of figurative language, four musical devices? Typed?" Maritza complained.

"And the rubric for grading is there, too," Cara said. "You'll have to put some effort in if you want a decent grade. I'm talking a multi-layered, deeply felt work of emotional resonance. Got it, everyone?"

"And don't forget to record the title and artist of the artwork you choose," Lauren said.

Cara flapped her arms at them. "Okay, off with you. We meet back here in an hour. I'll be wandering around too if you have questions."

The girls departed, forming a trio, while Rashard and Miguel each set off in a different direction.

"I can't believe you found all these poems," Cara said to Lauren. "Are you sure you're not an English teacher in curator's clothing?"

"Pretty sure." Lauren's tour guide energy diminished into something that seemed more intimate and grave.

She avoided her eyes. "Well, you did a great job. Look at them all going off to learn something. I'm not sure why you did it, but I'm happy you did."

"I saw Sasha Weikert from school a few weeks ago. She said I should make you an offer you couldn't refuse."

"Sasha, huh?" This confused Cara. What did Sasha have to do with anything? "She's turning you into the Godfather?"

"Whatever you think of me, I knew you would come today for your students. You wouldn't pass up a teachable moment for them even if it meant spending time with a fool."

Cara looked down at her map. She was the fool for thinking they wouldn't have to rehash what had happened. Lauren placed a hand on her arm. Her body only stiffened after her brain registered how comforting it felt resting there.

"Thanks for coming today." Lauren's quiet sincerity was at odds with the cacophony of noise and people around them.

She stepped back and Lauren's hand slid down her forearm and hung at her side, and Cara tried to get them back to distant cordiality. "Are you kidding? I should be thanking you. You've put so much effort into this. They don't even realize how great it is."

"I'm glad you think so, but I didn't do it for them. I did it for me." Lauren cleared her throat. "It's step one in my multi-layered, deeply felt, emotionally resonant apology to you." There was a ghost of a smile on her face, but her eyes were as intense as Cara had ever seen them.

"How many steps are there?"

"Thirty-seven," Lauren said promptly.

"Sounds very thorough." Cara chuckled. "But unnecessary. I thought I saw something that wasn't there." She shrugged. "No harm done." Playing it off as something casual was the only way she would be able to get through this.

The anguish that passed over Lauren's features surprised her. "Please don't say that. I know I did you harm. Otherwise you would still be talking to me."

"Lauren—"

"Before you say anything else, can we just move on to step two?"

Cara rocked back on her heels. "Okay, I'll bite. What's step two?"

"Come with me. I want to show you something."

"Oh, I can't. I have to stick around here where they can find me if they need me."

"It's not far. Why do you think I planned it so we would have an hour to talk?"

"We have fifteen minutes tops. They get bored quickly."

Lauren frowned at that. "Then come on. Please." She held out her hand but awkwardly morphed it into a walk-this-way motion.

Cara followed Lauren through several crowded galleries of European paintings, which then gave way to the hushed and far less occupied space that held Islamic art. Objects made with precious metals and multi-colored ceramics sat in vitrines, and aged and muted textiles were displayed in cases, but what Lauren wanted her to see was on the wall in front of her. An enormous tile installation of an arabesque arch embellished with mosaics in multiple harmonizing patterns of white and every shade of blue took up a good portion of the wall. It was obviously created as the focal point of something, and it was stunning.

"It's called a mihrab, and it's from the fourteenth century." Lauren stood next to her in front of the competing yet complementary patterns of tile.

"What does mihrab mean?" Cara's eyes roamed over the intricately designed patterns of glazed tile. She pointed to the inset words that framed the installation. "That's Arabic, right?"

"It's a prayer niche, and yes, it's Arabic, a phrase from the Quran."

"Was this taken from a mosque?"

"A madrasa, I believe." Lauren bent toward the label. "In Isfahan."

"The Blue City." Cara backed up so she could take in the whole of it, marveling at its balance and symmetry. She noticed Lauren's surprise. "What? I may not travel, but I read."

"I didn't say anything."

The various shades of blue were magnificent—from a bright aqua to a deep midnight and every shade between. "Between this and *The Great Wave*, so much amazing blue today."

"Kind of like my mood lately."

"Mine too." Cara took out her phone and snapped several pictures. "Thanks. This is tremendous, but we should go back." When Cara turned to go back to the galleries where her students were, Lauren stopped her again.

"Just one more, it's right over here."

Cara helplessly felt herself drawn toward more exquisite tile.

A part of the gallery had been constructed into a facsimile of a Moroccan courtyard, and Cara imagined them transported to a sunlit afternoon in medieval Fez, with its carved plaster and timber, and colorful, intricately patterned tile. The serene space had a water feature in the center and was surrounded by low benches, and it was empty.

"The museum installed this a while back. I thought you might want to see it." Lauren sat on one of the benches.

Cara followed her, but instead of facing the water feature in the center of the space, she faced the wall and its inset tile, this time in shades of green, blue, ochre, and white. With her finger she traced the narrow pieces that made up an eight-pointed star. "You are the only person in the world who remembers and understands and enables my obsession with tile."

"I know you like it. I wanted you to see it." Lauren gazed at Cara. "I'm so sorry. I'm so embarrassed and sad that I hurt you, especially when you said such lovely things to me that day. I don't know why I said any of it."

She nodded, not taking her eyes from the tile. It was nice to hear, but it didn't really change anything. "I said some not-so-nice things, too. I apologize for that."

It was as if Lauren hadn't heard her. "Actually, I do know why I said it. I want to tell you about Saffron. It doesn't excuse it, but maybe it could explain it a little."

"I should go back."

Lauren slid closer to her on the bench. "If you could give me a minute to explain—"

Cara scooted back. "What were you and Miguel talking about?"

"What?" Lauren seemed unsettled by the interruption.

"When you were bonding over the painting. What were you talking about?"

"Oh." Lauren visibly tried to shift gears.

Cara saw she didn't want to be deterred from delivering whatever speech she had prepared, but she didn't want to hear it.

"He was telling me how the woodcut made him feel. The danger of it but also the thrill and the potential for being swept away." Lauren's expression changed, like a realization had dawned on her. "That's you for me."

Now Cara was the one who didn't understand. "Huh?"

"This is going to sound so dumb, but you're my great wave, Cara. You arrived in my life out of nowhere and you loom so large—you're dangerous."

"I'm dangerous now?" Cara repeated incredulously. Anger shot through her so quickly it almost made her dizzy. Why did she keep allowing herself to be hurt by Lauren's words? She needed to get out of here.

Lauren nodded. "I know that sounds bad, but hear me out—"

"No thanks. You couldn't be any clearer. I'm a freeloading, opportunistic, dangerous person who wants to rip you off." Cara stood, and Lauren got up, too.

"That's not what I'm saying. Please, wait."

No, she was done with this. Trying to clamp down on the anger rising in her, Cara took a step back and put her hands up, which thankfully stopped Lauren from talking. "I'm grateful for the experience you gave my students today, but if the price of admission is you once again telling me why I'm not good enough for you, just save it. I don't want to hear it. Now I'm going back. You've done enough. I'll say your good-byes to them. Thanks for everything."

❖

Cara stormed off, farther into Islamic Arts and the wrong way from the European galleries. Lauren sat there for five minutes or so, steeping in despair at Cara's curt dismissal. Her bungled apology had only made things worse. She considered taking Cara's suggestion and slinking back to her office to avoid the students' departure, but she couldn't be that cowardly.

At their meeting point, Lauren saw the girls sitting together on a bench in the middle of the room and Miguel gazing at a Cézanne landscape. Cara was not there. Rashard entered the gallery and made a beeline for her with his phone in his outstretched hand.

"Miss, can you explain this?" He showed her the image on his phone. It was Charles Demuth's abstract portrait entitled *I Saw the Figure 5 in Gold*, one of the works on their handout that had a poem connected with it.

She smiled at Rashard. "You've got an interesting one there. This is the only artwork inspired by a poem and not the other way around."

"Okay, but I read the poem, it's the shortest, and I looked at the painting and I don't get it."

"You've read William Carlos William before, so you know he's a poet of few words. What do you think it means?"

Rashard frowned. "How do you know I've read him before?"

Lauren took a step back in surprise when Cara suddenly appeared next to them, looking squarely at Rashard. "The Brueghel. He wrote the poem about the Icarus painting. Remember?"

"Oh." Rashard clearly did not.

In that moment, Lauren saw the difficulty in Cara's job. But she didn't seem to mind as she pretended Lauren wasn't there, patiently reminding Rashard of the past lesson.

Miguel ambled over to where the girls were still sitting, and Cara stepped toward the group. "How did everybody do?"

Lauren didn't hear any of their replies. She was too busy noticing the way Cara was ignoring her.

"We'll stop and have lunch before we go back. Everyone ready for McDonald's?"

Lauren faked her Met guide enthusiasm. "There's a cafeteria downstairs. You could get your lunch there."

Cara was barely able to meet her eyes. "It's on the permission slip and it's on our way back to the subway."

"Would you like to come with us, Miss?" Yenifer asked.

"She's way too busy, Yeni. Everyone say thank you to Ms. Havemayer."

The students mumbled their thanks, and Maritza said, "Thanks for making me write another essay," but she was smiling when she said it.

"I have time. I'll join you for lunch." Lauren didn't pick up the excuse Cara had dropped for her. She had to go. For all she knew, it might be the last time she could reasonably occupy the same space as Cara, and maybe there would be an opportunity for her to salvage the day somehow. Lauren saw disbelief and annoyance on Cara's face.

They moved as one organism down through the Great Hall and out onto Fifth Avenue, where Lauren realized she didn't have her coat. Nor her wallet. Returning for them meant being separated from Cara and her students, and she couldn't bear for that to happen. She wrapped her arms around herself and struck up a conversation with Fatoumata as they followed the rest of the students down the frigid sidewalk.

McDonald's was a zoo, and Lauren couldn't tell where the lines ended or began. She and Cara brought up the rear, and she stood silently as Cara kept a close eye on her students and told them to get a few tables together as they collected their lunches. When only the two of them were left, Lauren decided it was as good a time as any to plead her case again. She covered Cara's hand with her own where it rested on the aluminum countertop. "I just want to say—"

"Your hand is freezing." Cara picked up her hand and pressed both of hers around it, trying to convey warmth to it. Her eyes roamed over her, and Lauren's body temperature rose several degrees at the way Cara was really seeing her right now. "Why aren't you wearing a coat?"

If Lauren could have stayed in this moment, with Cara tenderly chafing Lauren's hand between hers, she gladly would have. In this moment, Cara hadn't dismissed her from her life, there was kindness in her eyes, and she still cared about her. But the moment dissolved when the cashier called for the next customer and Cara dropped her hand.

"What would you like?" Cara asked.

"Nothing. I'm not hungry."

"Well, I am." She turned to the cashier. "Six cheeseburgers please, and a large coffee with milk and sugar."

Six? Class trips must make her hungry for many burgers and sugar. Cara never added sugar to her coffee.

The coffee came quickly and Cara pressed the cup into Lauren's hands. "Here. This will warm you up."

Oh. It was her coffee order. Lauren wrapped her fingers around the cup in gratitude. While she preferred Cara's hands, the coffee would do as a heat generating proxy. She was about to continue groveling when Cara said abruptly, "I'm mad at you."

"I know. You have good reason to be."

"But I'm glad you're ready to talk about your ex. You need to find someone qualified to listen to you about it."

Lauren didn't think she needed a shrink, she'd been down that road before and it hadn't helped. "I'd like to tell *you* about it."

Cara's order was ready and she grabbed the sack of burgers and led them upstairs where the girls were seated together, chowing down on what looked like every McDonald's menu item between them. Rashard and Miguel were sitting at an adjacent table. Neither had gotten anything to eat. They simply stared at their phones.

"Got room for two more?" Cara slid onto the molded plastic bench and left the chair next to Rashard for Lauren. It was unlikely that two teenage boys weren't hungry, so Lauren surmised they didn't have the money for their lunch. She was about to offer to get them something when she remembered she didn't have any money herself.

Cara opened her bag. "You know, I thought I was super hungry, but I'm not really. Will you help me eat these? It would be a shame for them to go to waste."

"Yeah," said Rashard, and Miguel inclined his head so slightly it might not have happened.

Cara distributed two cheeseburgers to each boy and then passed one over to Lauren, not looking at her. "Can't have you eating cashews for dinner."

Lauren ate and maintained a nominal part in the conversation, but in truth, she was deep in thought. It was possible that Cara possessed a gene Lauren didn't have, one that expressed kindness in every situation, and tried to convey it in such a subtle way that the recipients of it were not meant to feel self-conscious, or uncomfortable, or less than. How often had she been on the receiving end of Cara's kindness without realizing it? And in their too-brief time together, had she ever deserved it?

Emotion welled up in her as she recognized that Cara bestowed her kindnesses on everyone she met, and Lauren, if she ever had been, was nothing special to her anymore. Both the understanding of it and its loss came upon her at once and she quickly stood before her composure was obliterated.

Her three tablemates gazed at her.

She struggled to produce an excuse. "I just remembered. I have to get back for a meeting."

Cara stood as well. "Are you all right? Your face is a little splotchy."

Lauren put her hands to her cheeks and felt the heat emanating from them. "I'm fine." She pivoted to the students. "Thanks for coming today. Come back anytime. Ms. Talarico has my contact information if you have questions about the art."

She made the mistake of meeting Cara's concerned gaze one last time before turning to go. The kindness she saw there was killing her. She made it to the sidewalk before the tears started to fall.

Around four o'clock, a text from Cara came through. *Thanks again for today. They couldn't stop talking about it on the train ride back.*

Lauren replied: *There was so much more I wanted to say.* The double meaning was intentional, and Cara could interpret it however she liked.

Didn't get through all fifty pages of your dissertation? Two smiley emojis.

Cara opting to respond to the less personal interpretation didn't surprise her. She waited when she saw Cara was still typing.

Still think you should seek a professional, but if you want to tell me about your ex, I'm willing to listen. You can usually find me here after 6PM most weekdays. Cara pinned the address for Café Mi Vida, a coffee shop in East Harlem.

Lauren's plan had utterly failed, yet Cara's kindness had left a door open for her.

CHAPTER TWENTY-SEVEN

Cara sat in Café Mi Vida attempting and failing to create a lesson that made citing sources interesting. She leaned away from the table and stretched.

"You need a break? Let's watch this makeup tutorial." Manny was suddenly at her side, pushing his phone in front of her. The place was empty and he obviously was bored. His application of super long fake eyelashes since she had arrived a half hour ago said that much.

She was tempted, and in need of distraction.

"What's wrong, boo? You never take this long to say no to a makeup tutorial. Is it Daisy again?"

It had been a few days since the museum and Cara had gone back and forth about whether sending that text had been a good idea. She had worked hard to put her feelings behind her and return her life to the industriousness that marked her pre-Lauren existence. She worried now that her new, hard-won serenity would be upended by thoughts of her. That spike of anger Cara felt at the museum had felt alien to her and produced almost immediate guilt. "You know her name is Lauren."

"At least I'm not calling her Evil Daisy." The phone rang and he bustled away. "Who da fuck calls a landline anymore?"

She tried to refocus on her schoolwork, but less than a minute later, she felt a presence beside her. "I really need to finish this lesson, Manny."

"Who's Manny?"

Lauren stood there in a camel hair overcoat with a leather briefcase in her hand, looking like a bajillion bucks. Cara's heart leapt into her throat but she tried to be casual. "I thought you were someone else."

"Manny, I gather. May I sit?"

Cara gestured to the chair opposite.

Lauren looked a little harried as she sat and rooted around in her briefcase. "I'm going to get something to drink. Do you want anything?"

"No, thanks." Cara's eyes followed her across the coffee shop. She was glad for the chance to watch her unobserved. As put together and beautiful as she always was, Lauren's head drooped and the shoulders beneath her coat sagged while Manny made her drink.

When she returned to the table, Lauren said, "I would have come earlier, but I've had some stuff going on after work the past couple of nights."

"Oh?" Cara closed her laptop and sat back, letting Lauren's presence fill her up. Even though they were at odds, she felt peaceful as she watched Lauren do something as mundane as add a packet of raw sugar to her cappuccino.

"I had dinner with my aunt and Barb last night. They asked after you, by the way. And I had drinks with some coworkers the night before."

"Look at you, going out and being all social on the weeknights." Cara was strangely proud of her. "How are your aunts?"

"They're fine. It was nice, actually. My dad was there too and they talked about my parents' wedding and lots of things I never knew about." Lauren tried to hide a yawn and quickly took a sip of her cappuccino. "Oh, that's good."

"That's Manny. He's the best." Should she say what she saw? *Hell with it.* "You look tired."

"I've been running all day and this is the first moment I've had to slow down." Lauren grimaced. "And I haven't been sleeping well."

Cara hadn't been sleeping that great either.

Lauren leaned forward and launched right into it. "I'm so sorry for—"

"Please don't apologize anymore. I get it. I understand that you're sorry. Let's just move on."

"May I at least explain what I meant when I said you were—"

"No," Cara interrupted again. "I'd rather you didn't." There was nothing to be gained from rehashing what had already happened.

"Don't you think we should clear the air? You invited me here, after all."

"Because you wanted to tell me about your ex and I cut you off. I had been urging you to talk to someone about it. I would be a total hypocrite if I refused to listen." *And once I've met the obligation of hearing about your ex, we can really stick a fork in this friendship.*

"Is that the only reason? I was hoping we could talk through our issues and put them behind us. It's not crazy to think we could get back on track, is it?"

Get back on track? Their train had been permanently derailed. Rail cars lay like a kinked necklace across the landscape, smoke rising from the debris, luggage and limbs scattered everywhere. There was no getting back on track. Still, she could not be that blunt with Lauren, gazing at her with so much hope in her eyes. Hope that Cara had no idea what to do with. "I'm ready to listen," was all she said.

Lauren rolled her lips inward and didn't speak.

Cara had effectively shut her down, and now she looked miserable. Yes, it was probably difficult for her, but Cara was feeling pretty wretched herself and wanted to get this over with.

Finally, Lauren sat a little straighter in her chair and began her story. "I met Saffron at a party about a year into my coursework in London. She wasn't in my program but she was always hanging around with people from the Courtauld. She was this exciting, gregarious, posh woman and she locked onto me like a heat-seeking missile."

"She sounds delightful," Cara deadpanned.

"You'd think, right?" Lauren said. "She had charm, a great smile, and sex appeal. Got me out of my shell, showed me all these great places in London. Took me out to expensive dinners, dancing, West End shows, you name it. We'd ride horses in Hyde Park, spend hours in the National Gallery. She brought me to her family home, which was this amazing country house in Wiltshire. I met her brother there, who was also charming and welcoming. He took us trap shooting. So British, right?"

Cara nodded even though she didn't know what trap shooting was.

"She had me fully caught in her gravitational pull and I began to trust her. Early on, probably the first time I visited her flat, she left some bank statements conspicuously lying around on her coffee table, and of course I looked at them. They showed accounts that had lots of cash in them. It should have been a red flag. I mean, who does that?" She shook her head. "I fell right into it. Call me gauche, but I always figured if I ever found someone I liked again, she would have to have money so I could avoid being hurt the way Terri hurt me. How could she be after my money if she had her own, right?"

"Right," Cara agreed faintly. It sounded like a horrible criterion for a relationship, but she could understand why Lauren wanted to avoid the pain.

Lauren turned her chair slightly, so she looked out onto Second Avenue and avoided Cara's gaze. "You would think. But you would be wrong. Terri was out for a quick cash payoff, but with Saffron, it was a long con. She was going to get her hooks in me and bleed me dry." The detachment in Lauren's delivery of these words troubled Cara. "Bank statements? Fake. Country home? Rented for the weekend. The first time Saffron was in my flat she found enough information to steal my identity and open up three credit accounts. All those good times? The dinners and plays and weekends away? My money. And the worst of it? The brother was really her husband."

Cara's jaw dropped. "She was fucking married? God, Lauren. I'm so sorry."

"Actually, no, that wasn't the worst of it. The worst part of it was that she made me fall in love with her." Lauren heaved a shuddering breath and lapsed into silence.

Understanding and agony burbled up in Cara, and she wanted to touch Lauren, wanted to reassure her, make her feel better, but Lauren was still looking out at the street, her hands white and tense in her lap.

"She proposed at the top of the London Eye with a ring she said had been in her family for generations but had actually been bought the day before with a credit card in my name." Lauren looked down at her left hand as if she were looking at that phantom ring. "And I said yes."

They sat in silence while Cara absorbed all Lauren had said. "But how could she..." Her question might have been inappropriate and was probably irrelevant, so she didn't finish it, but Lauren knew what she was thinking.

"Bigamy was nothing compared to all the other crimes she was willing to commit."

"Obviously, you found out what she was doing."

"This was a time when I was becoming more independent financially. I came into a part of my trust that year. Ordinarily, any new credit cards would have to be approved by my dad's personal team, but things got a little bit lost in the shuffle as I transitioned to my own wealth manager. Preston recommended someone he used, but it took time for her to familiarize herself with my holdings and also to get the appointment coordinated between San Francisco and London. I was busy and having fun and I admit it wasn't a priority to take care of it. During our initial teleconference, we discovered the credit accounts that had been opened without my knowledge. She started listing the transactions on those and they were all familiar and...I knew." Lauren turned her face and Cara could finally see her eyes. The bleakness in them took her breath away.

"I could not believe it had happened again. The most harrowing part? I had to keep seeing her so she wouldn't know that we knew. My father flew in, the police got involved, and we made a case against them pretty quickly. For a month, I pretended I was the happiest woman alive until the authorities had all the evidence they needed to put them away. She and her husband are in prison now. Her name wasn't Saffron. I can still hear her screaming that I ruined her life after they read the verdict and she was taken from the dock."

"Irony of all ironies," Cara muttered.

Lauren nodded. "I lost my way for a little while after that, depression and anxiety." She made a motion with her hand that Cara guessed was supposed to sum up the mental health ramifications. "My father stayed with me while I put my life back together. I was lucky I had my degree to worry about. I immersed myself in research and eventually things got better. I revisited many of the places I went with her so I could reclaim them, and not have her memory attached to them. And I found other places of my own that weren't tainted by her. I couldn't bear to let her ruin London for me. I love that city so much, and getting lost in its anonymous embrace was one of the things that saved me. Art and London saved me."

Cara couldn't imagine the betrayal of it, the loss of confidence in the world and in herself, but it hurt that Lauren had put her in that same category. She understood, but she didn't like that Lauren believed she had so little integrity. Still, she was willing to put it all aside in the face of Lauren's pain. She reached her hand across the table but Lauren only stared at it.

"I'm messed up, Cara. I only want what everyone else wants. I want to love and trust and share my life with someone, but I think maybe I'm incapable of it now."

"Don't say that," Cara implored her.

"I want to be completely honest. I didn't plan to get so attached to you, but like I said before and I'm going to say again now even if it makes you angry, you're dangerous. You hit me like a tsunami, and now I'm entirely at sea. I should be kicking for the surface, but all I want is to stay submerged in you. You're not like Saffron. You never could be. My bad experiences made me believe everyone would be the same. You're not the same. You're not like anyone else I've ever met."

Compelled to comfort her, Cara opened her palm.

"And I'm looking at your hand and there is nothing I want more than to take it, but I know what you want, and I don't think I can give it to you, no matter how much I may want to." Lauren had remained stoic throughout the whole of her story, but now her eyes were wet and her breath started coming in gasps. "Oh God, this was the opposite of what I came here to do. I wanted to apologize and get back together, but I can't do that to you. I'm not going to hold you back from getting what you want."

Cara pushed her chair around the table and sat next to Lauren, drawing her into her arms as the emotions broke through the surface and erupted in rafts of tears. Lauren's forehead rested against Cara's neck and moisture saturated her collar as Lauren quietly sobbed. Cara's arms tightened around Lauren's shoulders, and she pressed light, protective kisses into her hair.

She heard a discreet cough and looked up to see Manny behind the counter across the room, his face etched in alarm. *Is she okay?* he mouthed, and she nodded, waving him off. They sat like that for a while and her hands smoothed over the vulnerable arch of Lauren's spine as she slowly became calm.

Eventually, Lauren excused herself to the restroom and Cara began packing her things. Her heart was heavy about the end of their friendship, but this was a good thing for Lauren. It was a step in the right direction for her anyway. And Cara had to move past what had been said on New Year's Eve. Understanding it didn't make her feel any better, and she was now resigned to her Lauren-less fate.

When Lauren returned to the table her eyes were red-rimmed but she gave a slight smile. "I'm sorry about that." She sat down and searched Cara's face like she was trying to memorize it.

Cara gave her an exasperated look that was meant to be comical. "When are you going to stop apologizing?" When in doubt, try to lighten the mood.

"So now you know. I guess I shouldn't do the friends-with-benefits thing. I regret you happened to be my guinea pig for this disaster of an experiment."

If Lauren wasn't going to attempt a relationship like theirs again, she would most likely return to the reclusive state she had just emerged from, which was an injustice that made Cara itch. No matter how bad she felt about Lauren's rejection, letting her become a hermit again was unthinkable. Without thinking of the cost to her emotional well-being, Cara said, "We can still be friends though, right?"

Lauren looked bewildered. "I'm not...Would you even want that?"

"I'll always be your friend," she said with the sincerity of a solemn oath, and then she smiled. "And I'll return a text, I promise. And you always know where to find me." Cara gestured at the coffee shop around her. "Most weekday evenings. Keeping Manny company after all the normal people have gone home."

Lauren stood. "Thank you, Cara. You made me feel like a human being again for a while."

Cara stood too and felt the tectonic shift occurring between them. However ill-defined their time together had been before, it was changing into something else now. "You're already a pretty great human. You don't need me for that."

Lauren opened her arms and Cara stepped into them, crushing herself against her. It wasn't until Cara felt Lauren's diaphragm expanding, capturing the scent of her like she always did, that she lost her grip on her own emotions, tears pooling in her eyes as Lauren turned and fled the coffee shop.

CHAPTER TWENTY-EIGHT

Lauren made it a week before returning to Café Mi Vida. Selfish. That's what she was. She'd spent the past week feeling by turns mortified and sanguine about her tearful breakdown with Cara, but dragging into the light all of the shame associated with that time had the opposite effect than she was expecting. Instead of riding a downward spiral into depression like before, sharing her burden with Cara helped her see how much better her life currently was.

Transitioning to a platonic friendship with Cara felt selfish. It was doable in the abstract, but how was she supposed to stifle her intense feelings? Putting all that toothpaste back in the tube seemed impossible, yet she couldn't resist being with Cara again.

She hadn't texted for fear of not getting a response, and Cara hadn't texted either. When she entered the coffee shop, Cara was at her usual table, laughing riotously with the person sitting across from her, a woman with long pink hair and unusually broad shoulders. Lauren froze at the sight and felt a searing hurt in her chest. Nope. She couldn't do this. She turned around and headed right back out the door.

"Lauren!"

She looked back to see Cara on her feet and moving toward her, and the other occupant of the table turned to face her. It was the barista in a really bad wig.

"Hey, it's good to see you. Where are you going? Get in here."

Lauren allowed herself to be led to the table. The barista stood and made a big production of flapping his table rag over the chair and gestured for her to sit.

Cara curled her arm around his. "Lauren, this is Manny. You might not recognize him from the last time you were here with his new 'do."

"Hi, Lauren." Manny lifted his wig like he was tipping a hat. "Decaf nonfat cappuccino, right?"

"Great memory, and it was a great cup of coffee."

"It brought you to tears, if I'm not mistaken."

Lauren felt her cheeks flame.

"Manny, shut up!" Cara gave him a gentle shove. "Apologize, asshole."

"Sorry! I was kidding. I got you, girl." She found herself wrapped in his arms, awash in pink synthetic hair and feminine perfume. Just as quickly, he let her go. "Cara? You want to go crazy and have a second today?"

"Why not?" Cara smiled at Lauren. "Seems like a special occasion."

"Go off, sis! Living your best life on a Thursday." He pushed strands of pink hair behind his ears and returned to the counter.

Lauren took off her coat and set her bag to the side, cognizant of Cara's eyes following her every move. It was unnerving. "What?"

"Nothing. I'm sorry about him. I'm really happy to see you." Her smile faded, her eyes turned thoughtful. "I was going to text you today. Tonight, actually."

"You were?"

Cara nodded. "I was waiting, letting you have some time. But it's a week today and I wanted to make sure you were okay. I'm glad you came."

"I'm all right. Talking to you was a good thing, I have to admit." The week had been full. Work kept her busy, and her aunts were inserting themselves into her life with a frequency that Lauren welcomed, but even among the fullness of the hours, she felt empty. Seeing Cara again brought back all she had missed about her. She missed their phone calls. She even missed the too-numerous emojis Cara added to a simple text message.

Since their conversation, Lauren wondered how their shared time could have been different if she had told Cara about Saffron right at the start, but it was something she would never know. All she could do now was focus on creating a new normal with her. "How is school?"

"It never stops." Cara eyed the stack of papers in front of her. "It's hard to motivate myself to do work, you know? That's why I come here. Once I go home, nothing comes out of my bag."

"How did the essays from the museum assignment turn out?"

"They're in this pile somewhere. Three of them wrote poems. You can have a look if you want, but I'll tell you right now, lower your expectations."

"I'd love to see them." The bell attached to the front door jangled and some people entered the shop. Lauren looked over at Manny, now stuck behind the counter, steam rising from their coffee drinks as he dealt with new customers. She went to retrieve them and left a twenty on the counter as she caught Manny's eye and pointed to the tip cup. She set the cups down at their table and took her seat. "I got these. I guess that means I own the time today."

Cara's small macchiato cup halted on its way to her mouth. "No, I don't think that's a good idea. I'll pay for my own." She looked pained. "And I don't think we should do that anymore."

"What?"

"The owning the time stuff. It kind of heightened things. I don't think we should do that now that we've taken the benefits off the table."

"What do you mean, heightened things?"

"It led to these expectations and plans we were responsible for, and I know I felt like I had to give you a fun experience with my allotted time. It was a work-around. It was a date without calling it a date."

"It was your idea." Lauren had to point that out.

"I know, and it worked for a while, but things are different now. Friends don't plan elaborate ice-skating excursions or rent a limo to go to a gala together. They hang out. They keep things casual."

"Okay. So..." What exactly was Cara saying here?

"So I pay for me. You pay for you. Let's keep it simple." Cara reached into her pocket and passed a few bills across the table to her.

"But friends do things together. Maybe not galas, but they go to movies, have dinner, take walks in the park, etcetera." Etcetera? Now why had she used that word?

"We can't do any of that, and we definitely can't do etcetera."

Did everyone know etcetera meant sex? When did that get added to the dictionary? Her frustration level rose. Everything was a negotiation with Cara. All these self-imposed rules. They tried it last time and what did it get them? Nothing. She gazed at her, at a complete loss for how to pick up the strands of whatever this now was between them and weave them into something meaningful.

Etcetera did not mean sex. Not for her. It was practically the opposite of that. It was all the ephemera that didn't fit into an easy category, and it was what she wanted with Cara.

It wasn't sex. It was all the little moments she got to witness because Cara had shared her life with her, and it was exactly what she needed to preserve. It was watching her dance with abandon in her mom's kitchen, or laughing with her in a cozy car on a dark highway. It was Cara teasing her about anything at all. It was silly inside jokes, dirty emoji texts, and phone calls at bedtime. It was that thunderclap of recognition on a cellular level that she had never known with anyone else.

"I know I'm being kind of high-handed right now." Cara's voice was pleading. "But I'm trying to figure out how I can do this, and I need a sort of structure to it, I need some…"

"Rules?" Lauren supplied.

"Yes." Cara seemed to sag with relief.

Lauren understood. All of those bits of meaning that sheltered under the umbrella of etcetera were worth holding on to. If she wanted any part of Cara, if she wanted her new definition of etcetera, she would have to abide by the rules. Because Cara really liked to cling to her rules. She made rules for exchanging Christmas presents, for God's sake. Lauren didn't exactly like it, but she understood, and she accepted it. "Okay. What are the rules?"

❖

Cara didn't know what the rules were. Why was she once again trying to impose order over being with Lauren? It hadn't worked before. She hadn't thought Lauren would agree, but there she was, boundless blue eyes gazing steadily at her, waiting for her to say something. "How about this? We use this place as our neutral territory. We can meet here and hang out, and there's no financial pressure, and we can enjoy each other's company as friends, and…that's it. Simple, and only one rule."

Lauren considered. "We don't see each other anywhere but here?"

"Is here okay? I know it's kind of out of the way for you."

"No, that's fine. I can get a cab here, no problem. And you're here every day?"

"Usually Monday through Thursday. I go home early on Fridays."

"But didn't you say you use this place to get work done? How's that going to happen if you're socializing with me?"

"Oh yeah. Maybe this won't work."

"No, never mind," Lauren hastily said. "It'll be fine. I have work I need to do, too. We can share a table and a coffee and each do our work. Objection retracted." Lauren took a sip of her cappuccino, seemingly unperturbed by the new rule.

Now that Cara was thinking about it, it was awfully limiting. Maybe Lauren was avoiding more conflict. Maybe she had no intention of observing any rules and was just biding her time until she could reasonably leave and never come back. There was no way she was going to sit with Cara while she graded papers and planned lessons. Lauren was not going to travel by cab every day to sit in a coffee shop in East Harlem when there were much better options between her home and work. No, she would not be coming back. In creating this crazy rule, Cara had finally found a way to drive Lauren away from her. Just when she wanted her to stay.

❖

Lauren came back on Monday. She went to the counter and ordered her decaf cappuccino from Manny, and spent a good five minutes chatting with him, only relinquishing the counter space when new customers lined up behind her.

She set her cup down and added sugar like always, reached down to her briefcase and brought her laptop out, but paused when she noticed Cara staring. She smiled as her eyes locked with Cara's. Lauren seemed to be enjoying their affable staring contest.

Warmth seeped into Cara that had nothing to do with the baseboard radiator under the window. It was probably time to say something before the staring got weird. She cleared her throat. "You're back. I didn't think you would come."

"You didn't?" Lauren looked surprised. "Why not?"

Cara didn't want to admit she'd thought Lauren wouldn't want to observe her rule. "I'm sure you're busy."

Lauren frowned. "You came up with this new rule for us and now you don't want me here?"

"No, that's not it. I'm glad you're here. I just didn't think you would want to come."

"Well, I did. I do." The aggressive yet confused response made Cara melt a little more.

"Good. Like I said, I'm glad." Cara sat back. "How was your weekend?"

Lauren shrugged. "Boring. Yours?"

"Same."

"Genevra and Barb want to have brunch again this Saturday. My aunt said specifically to invite you." Lauren smiled. "I think she took a shine to you."

"That's nice to hear, but there's the rule. And anyway, I have plans on Saturday." Cara had no plans on Saturday.

"Okay, I'll let them know." Lauren's smile faded and she directed her attention to her laptop, which she opened and turned on. She nodded toward Cara's open laptop. "What are you doing?"

"Finalizing my lessons for tomorrow. Then I have to make a worksheet on how to use conjunctive adverbs to connect independent clauses."

Lauren winced. "Sounds fun."

"This may seem bizarre, but it really is fun for me. I love grammar."

"Yeah? How do your students feel about it?"

"Oh, they hate it."

Lauren laughed, hearty and open-mouthed, and Cara laughed with her. There was nothing like extracting an unexpected laugh out of Lauren. It was the best.

"I think you are contractually obligated to love grammar, and they, as teenagers, are supposed to hate it."

"Yup. I love everything about it. It makes so much sense. Grammar is nothing but a set of clearly defined rules that govern language." She paused, thoughtful. "But sometimes, they're not so clear. There are a few exceptions to the rules of English grammar."

"There are a ton of exceptions."

"Doesn't matter. I still love it. And I have opinions, deeply felt opinions, about the sort of grammatical dilemmas that no one but other English teachers care about. Oxford commas, split infinitives, prepositions at the ends of sentences, you name it, I have a stance."

"Okay, what's your stance on people putting prepositions at the end of their sentences?"

"Well, that's the sort of nonsense up with which I will not put."

Lauren laughed. "So you're pro-prepositions at the end of sentences?"

"I'm pro-clarity, in whatever form that looks like."

"You're just lucky I appreciate a good grammar joke." Lauren sipped her cappuccino, her eyes lively and happy. God, she was beautiful.

"I guess I am." Cara cleared her throat. "I'm sorry whatever you'll be doing has no chance of being as fun and interesting as conjunctive adverbs. *However*, I'll let you know when my worksheet is finished. *Thereafter*, you can practice your sentence construction skills."

"Please do that. I look forward to it." The crooked smile Lauren was trying to hide was pretty darn cute.

Cara grinned back at her. "See what I did there?"

"Conjunctive adverbs, I presume?"

"You presume correctly. I always knew you were smart. What are you working on, anyway?"

Lauren raked a hand through her hair. "I've been invited to speak at a symposium in New Haven in April. I've known about it for months, but I still haven't figured out what I'm going to present."

She pretended to think about it. "Hey, I know. Why don't you do something about art?"

Lauren stuck her tongue out, but she looked amused.

She was about to say something naughty about Lauren's tongue but stopped herself—they had already drifted too close to flirting for a platonic friendship. When would the urge to take their conversation toward sex subside?

Lauren seemed not to notice her internal struggle. "It's actually kind of stressful since I'll be returning to the University Art Gallery where I spent a *lot* of time during undergrad."

"What's the topic of the symposium?"

"Women in Art."

"That sounds right up your street. *Accordingly*, you should be able to think of something. *Furthermore*, I bet it will be great. *Nevertheless*, you could—"

"Oh my God, please stop." Lauren looked both exasperated and charmed at the same time. "Maybe we should do some work."

She mimed zipping her lips and got to work, and Lauren buckled down to her own task. Cara couldn't help peeking over her laptop at regular intervals to marvel at the sight of Lauren following the cockamamie rule she had set down between them and trying to repair the broken mechanisms within their friendship.

CHAPTER TWENTY-NINE

Snow in New York City did not age well, particularly in mid-March when the whole city was impatiently awaiting spring's arrival. The couple of inches that had fallen the night before had been pushed to the gutters of Second Avenue and was already crusted over with a sickly gray sheen. It didn't bother Lauren in the slightest. She was heading toward Café Mi Vida and the best part of her day, where the surroundings were warm, the coffee was hot, the work got done, and the company was amazing.

Over the past weeks, the ramshackle East Harlem coffee shop had become a haven. She really liked Manny, and not only for his stellar barista-ing. She understood why Cara called him a friend.

And Cara.

Spending time with Cara these days was like being in the kitchen while Paloma baked her incredible homemade bread. She could see it in the oven, expanding into something light, airy, and hopeful, and she could smell it, the promise of sustenance—warmth and satiety permeating everything around her. But this was bread she would never get to taste.

Sometimes when Cara was absorbed in her grading, muttering to herself and swiping at homework papers with her marking pen, Lauren got to watch her for a little while, feasting with her eyes, not having to hide the depth of emotion Cara stirred in her, and she would remember what it was like during that brief time when all of her senses were satisfied—the sight, the smell and the flavor. Sure, their new normal, the conversation and jokes and laughter at the coffee shop, was not nothing, but neither was it everything, and Lauren wondered how long she could last before she starved.

But today was a good day because she was back after work conflicts prevented her for the past two evenings, and as she pushed through the door and heard the jingle of the bell that announced her presence, her heart felt a little bit more at home.

Manny waved with his whole body from behind the counter. "Lauren! We thought you'd never get here. I thought Cara was gonna go cross-eyed staring through the window and watching for you."

"Don't you have work to do, Manny?" Cara stood while Lauren took off her coat, and for a second, she thought Cara was going to hug her, but she didn't. She remained standing while Lauren stood, and sat when she sat. "How did your work stuff go?"

"It was good. The member event was packed. Who knew so many people were into Frans Hals?" Lauren gratefully accepted her cappuccino from Manny, and he dashed off again even though he usually stayed to chat with her when she first arrived.

"And did you share your Yale presentation ideas with your boss? Which one did she go for?"

"The same one you liked. She said she was glad the presentations would be recorded so she would get to see it. So just a little bit of added pressure now."

"You're going to be filmed? That's awesome. Can the general public watch?"

Oh. That was probably the wrong thing to say. The last thing her nerves needed was Cara watching as well. "I'm not sure. I'll check."

Manny came back to the table and placed a narrow triangular slice of creamy something between them. "My niece made a flan. Want to try?" He presented two plastic forks.

"Yum." Cara grabbed a fork. "This looks great. Osmara made this?" She dug in and groaned with delight.

A stab of lust plunged into Lauren just below her belly. She had heard that groan before in a much different context. She took a bite and the creamy texture of the flan contrasting with the sweet caramel sauce was the perfect distraction to her senses. "Wow, that's good."

"Right?" Cara commandeered the plate and took another bite, lifting her chin and closing her eyes in enjoyment. The sight of her captivated Lauren, the column of her neck framed by those dark curls reminding her of another time when she could have leaned in and tasted that smooth skin.

Manny brought a chair over and sat with them, resting his forearms on the table and nudging Lauren's wrist with his elbow. The knowing smile he gave her when she dragged her eyes away from Cara made her blush. "We missed you around here."

"It's only been two days."

"Seems longer." Cara scraped her fork across the plate to get every last bit of flan into her mouth. "That was delicious. My compliments to Osmara."

"Can you believe she made it in school? She's in a cooking club."

"That's a good idea for a club," Lauren said. "We didn't have one of those at our school, did we, Cara?"

"Nope." She was busy licking the fork.

"Cara was the queen of clubs. She was in all of them."

"Not all of them."

"Most of them," Lauren said to Manny. "She was so cute back in high school. I mean, she's still cute, look at her, but back then…" She shook her head. "Cara was in all the club pictures in the yearbook with this gigantic smile."

The tips of Cara's ears were fiery red. "How do you know this? You can't possibly remember—"

"Sasha and I looked through our yearbook after her baby shower. Your senior portrait is stunning." Lauren turned from Cara and grabbed Manny's arm. "She used to straighten her hair, Manny. All that beautiful curl and she straightened it."

"No." Manny clutched imaginary pearls.

"Yes." Lauren knew she was getting carried away, but it felt good to let out some of her pent-up admiration for Cara. "And she had a perfect yearbook quote, too. Do you remember?" her eyes flew to Cara, who nodded. "'Forever is composed of nows.'"

"Ooh, I like that." Manny raised his fist and Cara bumped it.

"My girl Emily Dickinson."

"I'm sure your senior portrait was stunning, too." Manny raised his fist for Lauren to bump, which she did in a half-hearted way.

"It was," Cara said.

"What was your yearbook quote?" he asked.

"I don't remember. It was dumb." Lauren didn't care about her quote. She just wanted to gush about Cara.

"'The main thing is to be moved, to love, to hope, to tremble, to live,'" Cara recited. "Rodin."

Lauren's mouth dropped open. "How did you know that?"

"I have an excellent memory. And it wasn't dumb." Cara pulled her laptop out of her satchel. "I have to write up a vocabulary quiz for tomorrow, so I have to cut short our trip down memory lane or Manny might be here until midnight."

He got up and walked toward the counter. "I'm closing at nine, ready or not. I got places to be, bitches."

❖

Ever since April had arrived, Cara was loving the additional sunlight that streamed into Café Mi Vida's windows in the late afternoons. But with the longer days and the nicer weather, it was becoming harder to concentrate on getting her schoolwork done. Another major distraction was Lauren's presence across from her on a daily basis, but Lauren never seemed to have trouble focusing, always lost to whatever was on her laptop screen.

Today brought a distraction of an unlikely nature—a physical impediment. The sun was reflecting off a truck parked across the street and right into the coffee shop. It was blinding her. She bent her head to avoid the piercing rays, but that didn't help. Adjusting her chair, repositioning her body, shielding her face with her hand didn't work either. Lauren watched her with an amused expression.

"Want to trade seats?" Cara asked.

Lauren stifled a laugh. "Nope."

"I can't work like this." Cara scooched her chair over so she and Lauren were at right angles to each other at the tiny table, their forearms nearly touching. Lauren tried to shield her laptop from view, but Cara saw it. "Shoes? You're shopping? I thought you were working on your presentation."

"I was." Lauren's defensive scowl was adorable. "I'm taking a break. It's finished, anyway."

"Do what you want. I'm not the boss of you." Cara smiled to show she was kidding. "I like the sparkly ones."

"I'll keep that in mind." Lauren minimized her browser.

Cara propped her chin in her hand and ogled Lauren's screen, now very willing to be distracted. "Don't let my nosiness stop you. What else are you shopping for?"

"Nothing."

"Come on. Let me help. I don't want to do any work either." She waited for Lauren to say something. "What about stuff for your new place? You have to need some new things there." She rarely shopped for herself. It would be fun helping Lauren pick out items for her new home.

"No, but thanks for the offer." Lauren smiled at her briefly and then directed her gaze back to her laptop, opening a few documents on her screen.

"How's that going, anyway? The renovations must be coming along. When will it be finished?"

Lauren seemed reluctant to talk, but Cara was dying for conversation. Lauren had been here for a half-hour, and they hadn't had their usual chatfest yet. She had mainlined her cappuccino and gotten right to work, which Cara now knew wasn't work at all.

"I bet you can't wait to get in there." She tried to elicit any kind of response.

Lauren surrendered to Cara's pestering. "Nothing's been done since you saw it. I fired Sheldon."

"Who's Sheldon?"

"The architect. You met him that one day. When you came to the apartment."

"Oh, right. I'm sorry to hear that. It wasn't working out?" Cara also remembered the pretty, fashionable decorator. Were they a package deal?

"He wasn't the problem. This was in January. I wasn't in the right frame of mind to be making a lot of irreversible decisions."

That shut Cara up. Silence lengthened between them.

"But I've been thinking about it again lately. I think I'll call him and see if we can work together again. Not Stacy, though. I'll have to find a different interior designer."

"Why? Your tastes didn't mesh?"

"It never got that far. At that last meeting I had with them in January, I brought a few pieces of art to show her my aesthetic. She tried to persuade me not to include something I had recently acquired so I knew we were not on the same page. We weren't even in the same library."

Cara couldn't figure out what the expression on Lauren's face meant. She looked pensive and agitated at the same time.

"Turns out, I have a strong affinity for pictures of carrots. Don't try to tell me it doesn't go with the *essence of the space*." She used finger quotes for the condescending phrase.

Cara smiled.

"And you—" Lauren pointed at her with an attitude she could only define as anger-lite. "I hope you don't expect me to give the carrots back because I already know exactly where I'm going to hang them."

Cara felt her breath leave her, so wounded was she by the thought of it. "I can't believe you would say that. Of course I don't expect you to give it back. It was a gift. I wanted you to have it."

A sudden desolation arose in Lauren's expression. "How about that? Now you know how I feel."

Remorse flooded Cara. It never occurred to her how Lauren might feel about her returning the painting. "Lauren, I don't want you to think—"

Lauren's phone started to ring. "Sorry, it's my aunt. Do you mind if I take it?" She couldn't get up because Cara was practically sitting on top of her, so she turned a bit to give herself the illusion of privacy while Cara brazenly listened to Lauren's side of the conversation.

"Hi, Aunt Gen...Yes, I remember. The reception at the Frick...I'm sorry to hear she's not feeling well...Tonight? Now? I think I could do that...No, I'm not at work...At that café I told you about...Yes, she's here." Lauren's eyes flicked toward Cara and then down again.

Dusk had arrived, so Cara moved back to her original spot, still listening closely.

"I'll ask her but I think she still has some schoolwork to do. Hold on." Lauren pulled the phone from her ear and said, "Do you want to come to a reception at the Frick Collection right now?" while she emphatically shook her head no.

Cara answered the way Lauren wanted her to. "No, I still have some schoolwork to do." It was what she would have said anyway, but she was tempted to say yes to see how Lauren would react.

"I'm sorry, Aunt Gen, she can't make it…What? No, really, she's just busy…You want to talk to her?"

Cara gestured for Lauren to pass the phone to her.

"It's just a boring event with a lot of boring people," Lauren whispered with her hand over the phone.

"Let me talk to her." She reached for the phone, which Lauren handed over with reluctance. "Hello, Genevra, how are you? It's been a while, hasn't it?"

"Yes, it has, Cara. I'm beginning to think you don't like Barb and me. I've extended several invitations through Lauren. Why won't you accept any of them?"

Cara only knew of one invitation to brunch but that had been weeks ago. "I'm sorry. Spring is a busy time at school."

"There's something we want to talk to you about, dear. I'll let you off the hook for tonight since it's such short notice, but do make an effort to come next time. I'd like to see you soon."

"I'll do my best. Please give my regards to Barb." She gave the phone back to Lauren, who was getting ready to leave. Even though she had no desire to go to a fancy reception at a museum tonight, the knowledge that Lauren didn't want her there stung. "Have fun at the Frick."

Lauren wouldn't meet her gaze. "I'm following your rule."

"I know." Cara shouldn't be upset, but she was.

"I'll see you next week."

She looked up in confusion. It was only Tuesday.

"I have to get ready and pack tomorrow. I'm catching a train early on Thursday."

"The symposium?"

"Yes."

"I thought you said it was only a two-day thing."

"It is, but we don't see each other on the weekends, remember?"

"I remember." Cara had the irrational desire to make Lauren stay. Next week seemed a million years away, and she only got a half-hour of Lauren's time today. It wasn't fair. "Good luck. You've worked really hard. I know you're going to kill it."

The smile Lauren gave her as she left looked anatomically correct, but it had no life behind it. In her head, Cara had a catalog of all of Lauren's smiles, but she had never seen this poor excuse for one before, and she never wanted to see it again.

CHAPTER THIRTY

Cara needed distraction, but Manny was busy serving a line of customers. Where had they come from? They were horning in on her private time with him. Coming to the coffee shop on a Friday was something she rarely did, but after the last few days, she knew the only place worse than a Lauren-less Café Mi Vida was her own Lauren-less apartment. At least Manny was here to distract her, but he wasn't fulfilling his duty right now.

She ought to be getting a ton of work done. With all the time she had on her hands, Cara ought to have finished grading the junior argument essays and the AP literary analyses. But nothing was getting done. She put her head down on her folded arms and groaned.

Some time later, she felt the table quake as Manny sat in Lauren's seat. She raised bleary eyes to his less than sympathetic face. "Maybe I need another macchiato."

"That's not what you need, and you know it." Even Manny was moody because of Lauren's absence.

"What do I need, then?"

"Just text her. See how it's going."

Cara wanted to, but they didn't text anymore. Somewhere along the way, that very vital component of their relationship had withered to nothingness. Whatever they needed to say was said at the coffee shop. At least when Lauren was here, Cara knew she wanted to be here. The boundaries she had set for this new iteration of their friendship made texting feel too personal, too intimate. She shook her head.

"Why not? What's stopping you?"

"I don't know. I don't want to bother her." She knew how ridiculous it sounded.

"Don't you think she'd like to hear from you?"

"I actually have no idea." Misery made her sink lower in her seat.

"Cara, mija." There was disbelief in Manny's voice. "You can't be seeing what I see. If I put a plate of pasta between you two puppies, you'd be chomping on the same strand of spaghetti in five seconds."

"No, we wouldn't."

Something in the finality of her response made Manny really look at her. "This math ain't mathing, mami. What am I not getting? You're back together, right?"

"No." Cara slapped her hands over her eyes. "Every night we leave here and I watch her get in a cab before I walk home. The time we're together here is the only time I have with her." When she brought her hands down, she saw Manny's confusion. "We're just friends."

"But what about the way you look at each other?"

"What do you mean?"

"You're a little better at hiding it, but sometimes Lauren stares at you like she's three-D printing you with her eyes so she can take home a copy of you to do kinky shit to."

Cara had no response to that.

Then he reconsidered. "Or maybe it's not sex. Maybe she's crushing on you bad." Manny's eyes narrowed. "But she was your high school crush. How did this get turned around? Wait. Are you Daisy now? And she's Gatsby. Girl, she loves you!"

"Knock it off, Manny. Neither of us are fictional characters in this scenario."

"You're right. I got a little carried away. But, Cara, why do you only see each other here?"

Cara felt stupid. "Because I made a rule that we could only see each other here."

"Why?"

How could she explain this in a way that would make sense? "Remember that day when she cried?"

Manny nodded.

"She was crying because of something from her past. We had already ended things and I thought I was ready to let her go, but I couldn't stand seeing her like that so I offered to be friends."

"And she wanted to stay friends, too? Seems like neither of you was ready to end it."

"She has trust issues. And although I understand her reasons for it now, she didn't trust me." Cara looked away. "Also, she doesn't believe in a forever kind of relationship, and I do, so…"

"You want that with her?"

"I wanted the possibility of it, but she couldn't do that." It still hurt to think about. "It probably would have been better just to end it."

"I still don't understand how this rule comes into it."

"She had finally opened up to me about a really harsh thing that happened to her. I couldn't just say *see ya* and let her walk away forever. I wanted to be there for her, but there had to be boundaries. I needed the rule so we both understood our limits."

Comprehension dawned in Manny's eyes. "That totally makes sense. If there's one thing I know about you, you're all about limitations."

"You think?"

"Hello?" Manny adopted the voice of a robot. "My name is Cara. I must come to Café Mi Vida, sit at this table, and drink exactly one macchiato."

"I guess I do find comfort in making rules for myself." Cara thought about the various times she had forced Lauren to follow rules of her making. "And others."

"And Lauren must know that about you."

"She does?"

"Totally. Why else would she follow your crazy rule and go out of her way to get a cup of coffee in East Harlem? It's worth it to her, so she's meeting you where you are."

He was right. Lauren had accepted Cara's need for rules since the beginning. What else was their owning time agreement but another set of rules? When had she become so inflexible? Lauren had probably found it frustrating as hell, but she had always let Cara be who she was.

"Are you meeting her where she is?"

No, she wasn't. If she were, she would have forgiven Lauren for what happened on New Year's Eve. She would have supported her in whatever way she needed.

She needed to meet Lauren where she was.

Which was where, exactly?

She glanced at Manny before pulling her phone from her pocket.

"You're gonna text her?" He clapped his hands with delight.

"I'm going to meet her where she is." Determination flowed through every part of Cara's body, but mostly her thumbs. "And, Manny? You are the wisest person I know."

"Girl, tell me something I don't know."

❖

Lauren sagged with fatigue against the window as her Metro North train trundled southward back to New York. Toward home. On this sunny early spring evening, she realized she once again associated the city with a feeling of home: familiar surroundings, meaningful work, and someone important in her life.

Someone important. Cara had become vitally important to her, but she doubted whether the reverse was true. Lauren had stupidly refused to hear her on New Year's Eve. Now, it seemed Cara had been able to throttle back her emotions and make the transition to friendship easily, while Lauren's feelings had increased in intensity. It was becoming painful to sit across from her and stifle the love she felt.

She had to own up to it. It was love. Deep and inexorable, and so different from what she had felt for anyone else ever. But this feeling, which the movies, songs, and greeting cards assured would solve all her problems, had only made her more conflicted.

Lauren used the rule as an excuse, but the truth was she'd never told her aunts about how their relationship had changed. When she was with them, she could pretend to be the kind of person who deserved to love Cara. If she'd accompanied her to the reception at the Frick that night, there would have been a lot of explaining to do, and concealing her love of Cara would have been impossible.

And now, she had concluded that the best way to express her love would be to end it, to stop visiting the coffee shop and let Cara live her life and eventually find the woman of her dreams. It wouldn't be her.

Her phone chimed with an incoming text, and she fished in her bag for it.

As if summoned by her thoughts, it was Cara. *Hey! Couldn't wait until Monday. Had to hear how your presentation went. Was it so good that they're making you the queen of art now?* Five smiley emojis.

Lauren smiled in spite of herself. When they repaired their friendship, Cara had said she would return a text, but Lauren had never dared test that claim. The last message she had received from Cara had been back in February, and the degree of happiness she now derived from a stupid text only reinforced how much she needed to deal with this. *Who's they?* she replied.

The symposium people! Surely they must have that kind of power. Can I come to your coronation? How far is New Haven? I'll come right now. Three plane emojis.

Don't bother. I just got on a train home. And don't call me surely! Cara wasn't serious. She wouldn't break her own rule. It was a silly text, and Lauren couldn't help being silly right back. Cara inspired that in her.

Three laughing emojis. *How did it go really?*

It went well. I'll tell you all about it on Monday.

The gray ellipsis appeared and disappeared. Then came one frowny face emoji and *OK. I expect a full report then.*

She put her phone away, too tempted to continue texting with Cara. On Monday, she would go to Café Mi Vida for the last time and end it. Then this all too brief chapter would end, and they both could move on with their lives.

❖

Lauren was roused from a deep sleep by the clanging of a bell somewhere. Once the sun had set and the view turned monotonous, keeping her eyes open had been a losing battle. The reduced speed of the train and the quiet rustling of her fellow passengers signaled that she had nearly arrived back in Grand Central. Still groggy, she brushed off her trousers and straightened her rumpled blazer. Then she and her wheely suitcase disembarked and made their way up the platform.

The sheer scale of Grand Central, with its soaring ceiling of cerulean blue, hosting a starry night of constellations and zodiac signs, never failed to put the insignificance of her existence into perspective. She was a tiny being in the universe, ricocheting and recoiling against other tiny beings, trying not to do too much damage to herself or others. Boy, was she in a strange mood.

Entering the great hall, her eye was drawn to a woman who looked like Cara standing nearby, clearly searching for someone arriving on Lauren's train. *Good grief, now you're imagining her everywhere.* She took a second look, sure she was wrong and her mind was playing tricks on her. Gazing at the woman, Lauren slowed down, and then stopped altogether.

It really was Cara.

And in that moment, with a scattering of commuters surrounding and bypassing them, Cara's eyes locked onto hers and the smile that broke over her face just about tore Lauren's heart in two. Why was Cara here?

"Hi." Cara rushed over to her but stopped a few feet away, running her hand over her ponytail in a familiar gesture of nervousness.

"What are you doing here?" *What happened to the fucking rule?* She didn't have enough of her wits about her right now to handle this, and she felt robbed of the weekend she should have had to prepare for letting go of Cara. She wasn't ready, but the moment had arrived anyway.

"I'm breaking the rule, I know. How are you? How was it? I couldn't wait for Monday."

Lauren drank Cara in, her scruffy jeans and tennis shoes, the frayed collar of a white button-down shirt peeking out from the neck of the navy crewneck sweater she wore with the sleeves pushed up to her elbows. Another thing Lauren would miss—Cara was so authentically and adorably herself. It was not fair of Cara to break her own rule and barge into Lauren's bubble of glum by being so endearing.

"I hope it's all right that I came here." Cara filled the silence with more nervous talk. "Coming from Jersey, I usually enter the city through Penn Station, which is a dump you try to get through as quickly as possible without catching a disease, but this place…" Cara shook her head. "I've actually been hanging around for a little while and I learned some things about it. It's really amazing, isn't it? I mean, look at that ceiling."

They both looked up at the ceiling, seventy feet above them. It was still there in its colossal, comforting, cerulean glory.

Cara couldn't seem to stop talking. "And there is some terrific tile here. Guastavino tile." She pointed to the information booth below the famous clock. "There's a woman named Rhonda who answered all my questions. She's fantastic. She told me at what gate your train would arrive, but she also knew about the tile when I asked her."

"Did she?" Maybe Lauren didn't need to do anything drastic right now. Maybe she could just float along on the reassuring sound of Cara's voice as she told her about where her love of tile intersected with her newfound appreciation for Grand Central Terminal. She was a tiny insignificant speck, after all. Maybe this was what the universe wanted of her right now.

"Yes! And I have to show you this. I don't know if it's legit, but I have to try it out. Will you come with me? It'll only take a minute. I know you must be tired." Cara paused, trying to gauge Lauren's reaction. "You know what? Maybe I should get out of your hair. I haven't even let you get a word in."

"It's okay." Lauren was now content to be led by Cara to something that might or might not be legit. "Show me what you want to show me."

Cara took the handle of Lauren's suitcase and left a wide gap as she walked beside her, telling her facts about Grand Central as they navigated the sparsely populated main concourse, the day's rush hour long over. As Lauren half-listened, she imagined another reality where she and Cara had been together for a long time, and Cara would meet her like she always did after Lauren arrived from out of town, and they would walk closely, arms entwined, their heads angled toward each other as they caught each other up on their time apart. And Lauren was secure in the knowledge that Cara would always be there and Cara was satisfied with what Lauren could offer.

Cara led her down a wide, sloping ramp and stopped in front of the Grand Central Oyster Bar.

"Oysters?" Lauren shook herself out of her pleasant reverie and rejoined her less perfect reality.

Cara frowned. "What?"

Lauren nodded at the glass-fronted entrance to the oyster bar. "Did you want oysters?"

Cara looked at the restaurant as if seeing it for the first time. "Oh. No. But look, the tile is in there, too." She looked up and that's when Lauren noticed that they were in the middle of a sort of rotunda with a low vaulted ceiling, which was anchored by four pillars. The curved surface above them was encased in handsome tawny-colored tile laid in a herringbone pattern.

"The tile is very striking." Lauren gazed at a woman standing at one of the pillars, strangely facing it like she was a child sent to the naughty corner. After a moment the woman turned around and met with a man approaching from the other corner. They laughed and continued up the ramp where she and Cara had just come from.

"I know. It's awesome. But here's what I wanted to show you. Apparently, this place is called the Whispering Gallery, and it's some kind of acoustic phenomenon."

"Really?" Lauren tried to concentrate on Cara's tourism spiel, but it was hard when she was busy observing how everything about Cara brightened when she was excited about something.

"Yeah. If I stand in that corner, and you stand in the opposite one, we'll be able to hear each other even if we whisper."

"Impossible." Lauren judged the distance between the corner the woman just vacated and its opposite. "There's got to be at least thirty feet between those two corners."

"I know! An auditory marvel right here next to the six train. That's why we have to try it, right? I guess the sound is supposed to travel up and along the rounded arch in some crazy way. You have to get close to the surface and whisper. I'll try to hear what you say."

"I didn't say anything."

"Not yet, you haven't." Cara laughed and then flung her hand out like she was reaching for Lauren, but drew it back. "I can't do this alone. It has to be two people. I need a partner. You'll be my partner, won't you?"

Was Cara even talking about this whispering thing now? Lauren's instinct was to step away. Participation seemed risky. "There's no way it'll work. It's just a way to make people look like idiots. There's probably a hidden camera somewhere recording it all." Lauren got her objections on the record while she looked around for the cameras.

Cara was already walking backward toward the far corner. "Let's just try it. Say anything that comes to mind. Sing the 'Star Spangled Banner' if you want. No, wait. Forget I said that. Do not sing." She gave Lauren a teasing smile.

She watched Cara back away from her, and couldn't help smiling in return. Why did it have to be so easy with her? So good? Of course she would be Cara's partner. Of course she would. But this was not going to work. It was crazy to think that a whisper could be heard from such a great distance.

She pulled her bag with her and stood in the corner, and turned to where Cara stood thirty feet away, her back to her, patiently waiting for Lauren to say something that she would never hear. And if she would never hear it, maybe Lauren could pretend that other more pleasant reality was true for one minute and give voice to what she could never say out loud to Cara.

She rested her forehead against the cool stone for a moment, then whispered, "Cara, I love you with all my heart. I want to spend every last one of my nows with you."

Almost immediately, she heard an intake of breath. How could she hear that?

And then, quiet but unmistakable, "Me too. I love you too, Lauren." She heard it. Cara said it. Didn't she?

"What?" Lauren needed confirmation. She had to hear it again. "Hello? Cara? What did you say?" She shouted at the wall.

"Lauren."

She whirled around to see Cara closing the distance between them, almost bumping into an older man as he crossed her path. They met in the middle of the gallery, and this time Cara didn't stop a few feet away. She got so close Lauren could smell her, and nothing could stop her from collecting as much air into her lungs as possible. She smelled like faith and courage and everything that was right. "What did you say?"

"It worked." Cara took the lapels of Lauren's blazer in her hands, eyes alight with happiness. "I know you heard me. And I heard you."

"Say it again. Please." Lauren needed to hear it.

"I love you. I love you! So much."

Lauren expelled a breath. "I love you, too. Oh God, I do." She cast her eyes downward, focusing on the navy yarn of Cara's sweater. She couldn't look at Cara.

"Then why am I the only one smiling? You look like you're in pain."

She was in pain. "Nothing has changed."

"Everything has changed."

Lauren shook her head. "No."

"Yes. That's all I need to hear. Please, Lauren, look at me. We can make this work."

Lauren lifted her head and gazed into eyes brimming with tenderness. "But you want forever."

"I want you. The rest is negotiable."

"What about your rule?"

Cara slid one hand over so that it covered Lauren's heart. "You are the exception to every rule."

Under Cara's hand, Lauren felt something shift. It was like the stone rolling back from the cave, letting the light in.

"Plus, my rules are terrible. I won't say I'll stop making them. It's kind of how I do. But I think you're going to have to put your foot down once in a while if it gets too crazy."

"Cara," Lauren said, barely believing it to be within her reach, still hesitating, unsure.

She smoothed her hands over Lauren's blazer to rest on her shoulders. "Yes?"

"I really want this. I really want you. I love you, but..."

Cara waited. The calm in her eyes calmed Lauren.

"I'm scared."

"Are you scared because placing your trust in another person is a new and terrifying thing for you, or because you're afraid I'm going to steal your money?"

"The first one."

The tension in Cara's face—which Lauren hadn't noticed until it left—dissipated and was replaced by a look of determination. "I'm scared too. We can be scared together. But we can't let that stop us from trying. Do you want to try with me?"

"I do. I can't think of anything I want more." She let herself touch Cara, settling her hands on her waist, and got lost in the warmth and strength in Cara's brown eyes, feeling more hopeful now than she could ever remember being. Everywhere else, life was traveling at the breakneck speed of the city, but here on the lower level of Grand Central, it felt like time had slowed to allow her to recognize, to savor, to settle into this. Eventually, the world began to intrude, and Lauren noticed late evening commuters noticing them as they passed by. "What should we do now?"

"Well, the first thing you should do is kiss me." Cara said it like it was the most obvious thing ever. "Because I've been waiting for ages. Then we should get your suitcase. It's been hard for me to look at you and keep an eye on it at the same time, but I don't want anyone to walk off with it."

Lauren grinned. "Thank you for doing that. I forgot about it completely. And after that?"

"Take your pick: Fifth Avenue or 118th Street."

Lauren didn't even have to think about it. "Your place. The bed is smaller." She didn't plan on letting Cara stray more than a few inches from her side until Monday morning.

Cara nodded, her smile more beautiful than any piece of art. "So are you going to kiss me or what?" Her eyes widened in delight as Lauren immediately yanked Cara's hips against her, and Lauren welcomed the inevitable surge of desire that bloomed from her center. She pressed her lips against that smile, wanting it to fill her up with more of the joy that was now washing away sadness and pain. She wanted an overload of joy, an overflowing fountain of joy burbling up and saturating their whole lives. Cara wrapped her arms around Lauren's neck and kissed her back with a fierceness that took her breath away, or maybe her breath had simply left her over the kiss's duration. She gulped air so that she could lose herself once again and—

"Get a room, ladies!"

Cara pulled away slightly and chuckled, flicking her eyes toward the random commuter who had the audacity to comment on their very public display of affection as he walked by. "I intend to," she murmured, touching her nose to Lauren's before letting her go.

"Let's go home." Lauren left Cara's side for a moment to retrieve her bag. As they walked together up the ramp that led to the six train, their arms were linked and their heads were bent toward each other. Lauren could barely contain her wonder at how radically life could change, and Cara seemed positively giddy.

"I love you, New York," Cara threw her head back and called out, "but you sure do know how to ruin a moment!

CHAPTER THIRTY-ONE

Cara pressed her intercom buzzer and heard "Champagne delivery!" in Lauren's breathless voice. She clicked the entry button to let her in and left the front door open a crack, knowing she had about three minutes before Lauren appeared at her door. After two straight weeks of spending the night in Cara's studio, Lauren had shaved almost a minute off her stair-climbing time. Girl was quick.

Most nights they came home together after an hour or so at the café, where less and less schoolwork was getting done, but Lauren had an event at the museum tonight, so Manny had seen the old Cara today, grading assignments like a demon possessed.

On her way home, she bought ingredients for a big pot of chili, now simmering on the stove. Eating dinner at nearly ten p.m. on a weeknight was not normal, and meal prep for the week was supposed to happen on Sundays, but life was different now and she was breaking her rules with abandon.

"What smells so good?" Lauren burst into the apartment, sucking in lungsful of air as she took off her suit jacket and pulled a bottle of champagne from her bag. "Look! The catering manager slipped me this because I was able to smooth over their delay in the kitchen. It's not the best in the world, but it's drinkable, and still cold. Want some?"

Champagne on a random Tuesday. This was Lauren in a nutshell. "Yes, I do. Are you hungry? I made chili."

Lauren came to stand next to her and looked in the pot. "You made a lot of chili."

"Yup." Cara ladled some into a bowl and handed it to her. "Lunch for the rest of the week. For you too, if you want."

"Of course I want." Lauren took the two steps to put her bowl on the table and then returned to Cara's side. Cara put another bowl in her hands and Lauren dutifully put it on the table, and then did the same with the napkins and spoons, and the salt and pepper. After slamming two plastic tumblers on the table, she lunged for Cara. "No. No more setting the table until I get the sugar."

Cara laughed. "It's right there in the cabinet. Want me to get it for you?"

"Shut up, sugar," Lauren growled, before planting a good one on Cara.

They stood there and drank each other in like two thirsty women who hadn't done this same thing before leaving this morning, and it ranked right up there as one of the best moments of the day, right after waking up next to Lauren and falling asleep wrapped in her arms.

Cara pulled away first and forced them to the table. "I can't go to bed without eating again. I'm really hungry."

"I am too." Lauren looked happy to be off her feet. She popped the champagne cork and sloshed some into each tumbler, not seeming to mind that Cara didn't have fancy flutes to drink from. "What shall we drink to?" She held up her cup.

Cara clicked hers to Lauren's. "To chili and champagne. A classy combo."

"I love chili," Lauren said, all suggestive and sexy.

"And I love champagne." They grinned at each other and started shoveling their dinner as fast as they could. Cara knew what would come next, but she had to talk to Lauren first. "You got mail today."

Lauren paused. "Sorry?"

"You got a piece of mail, with your name on it, delivered to my mailbox." Cara grabbed two cream-colored envelopes from the counter and handed one to Lauren. "I got one, too. Do you know anyone who uses the law firm of Medeski, Martin, and Wood?"

"Why would I get mail here?" Lauren frowned and opened it.

"Does yours say that your presence is required at a meeting tomorrow at four p.m.?" Cara asked.

"Yes."

"Mine too."

"Who could've sent this?" Lauren looked mystified.

"Who knows you've been staying here?"

"My father. Nobody else, I don't think." She put the letter down. "It's probably some family thing. No biggie. I'll call him tomorrow."

"But why would I get one?"

Lauren was silent. "I guess we'll find out tomorrow. Can you be there at four?"

"I'll get someone to cover Homework Help for me and leave right after eighth period."

Lauren dropped the envelope and pushed her bowl away. She got up and settled herself on Cara's lap. She held her cup of champagne precariously as she bent to Cara's neck and kissed her. "Today was such a long day. I missed you."

"I missed you, too." Cara's breathing quickened. This was going to be a ravishing, and she sat back to enjoy it.

Lauren bent her body lower, and Cara felt her begin to slide off her lap. She grabbed Lauren around the rear and yanked her back up, but her cup went flying, saturating Cara's shirt in champagne. "Oops. Sorry." Lauren looked like she was trying to stifle a laugh, but it came out anyway.

Cara's words were as dry as her beverage. "I like champagne, but I don't want to take a bath in it."

"Oh, honey. Let me take this off you. This wasn't my intention, but I can't say I'm sorry we got here." Lauren unbuttoned Cara's shirt, dropping kisses where each button revealed more skin. "You taste even better than usual."

As Lauren adjusted her position from sidesaddle to astride, Cara gazed into her eyes, already hazy with arousal. "If you wanted me drenched in champagne, all you had to do was ask. I'd pour the whole thing all over me." She unhooked her bra and Lauren's hands were beneath it almost instantly, covering her nipples, making them stand at attention. Lauren buried her face in the soft spot where her shoulder met her neck, licking, kissing, sniffing.

"God, I love you." Lauren came up for air and sat back while Cara rid herself and Lauren of their tops and bras. "You know what else I love? The fact that your bed is never more than four steps away from anywhere in your apartment."

"I bet we could make it in two."

❖

The offices of Medeski, Martin, and Wood were located in the Seagram Building on Park Avenue in midtown, an icon of midcentury modern design that Cara had always been curious about, but tension about whatever would befall her at this meeting had eclipsed her interest in architecture at the moment. She was relieved to see Lauren in the lobby and they were quickly ushered into a hushed waiting room.

"Did you talk to your father? Did you find out what this is about?" Cara asked.

"No, his texts were cryptic and I couldn't get hold of him directly."

This was one well-heeled waiting room, replete with black leather, glass, and chrome, and some intriguing stuff on the walls. Cara got close to one wall, where an enormous glass-fronted cabinet was hung, filled with very shallow shelves that showcased individual pills, capsules, and caplets, hundreds of them in a myriad of colors and varieties. It was kind of mesmerizing. She turned to Lauren. "This is kind of cool. They must represent a bunch of pharmaceutical companies."

"Nope. That's art."

"It is?"

Lauren nodded. "Remember the shark? Same artist."

"Lauren, what the hell am I doing here?"

"I'm not sure, but I don't think this is my dad's meeting. I'm willing to bet these are Aunt Gen's lawyers."

Before Cara could say anything, a well-dressed young man came to guide them to the conference room, where Lauren's hunch proved correct. Genevra and Barb sat at a large conference table with a man and a woman who were probably attorneys. The fifth occupant was Lauren's father. Everyone stood.

Cara hung back and let Lauren take the lead.

"Hi, everybody. What's this about?" Lauren greeted her father and aunts with kisses on their cheeks, her voice careful. "Dad, you remember Cara, don't you?"

Cara came forward with her hand outstretched. "Hello, sir."

"It's nice to see you again." He held her hand a little bit longer than expected, looking her dead in the eye.

Barb welcomed her with an effusive hug. "Hey, Cara. Where you been? Long time no see, bowling buddy."

Genevra was more reserved but looked equally pleased to see her. "We meet again, finally, Cara. You're a slippery one, aren't you?"

"I'm really glad everyone is so happy to see Cara, but what is going on? Why are we here?" Lauren stood with her hands on her hips.

Everyone turned to watch the same young gentleman set up a screen at one end of the conference table, and a face that shared the same genetic material as the other Havemayers in the room appeared via videoconferencing software.

"Oh good. Preston is here. Now we can start," Genevra said.

"Hi, everyone," Preston said. "Anyone want to tell me why I've been summoned?"

"Preston." Lauren dragged Cara over to the screen, clutching her around the shoulders. "This is Cara."

"Hello, Emoji-girl. I've heard a few things about you. Nice to meet you."

Lauren glanced at her, her face reddening. "Don't call her that."

Cara offered a small wave at the screen. "Nice to meet you, too."

"Maybe later we can talk about why I haven't heard from you in a while, Lauren," Preston said. "I was getting worried. Had to get reports from Dad."

"She's fine. Everything is fine," Malcolm said. "Sending the letters to Cara's address was another unnecessary bit of drama, Genevra." He turned to Lauren. "When you stopped returning your aunt's calls, she asked me to get hold of you. Apparently I didn't do that quickly enough for her."

"The meeting was already scheduled and we needed her to know about it," Genevra said. "And Cara, too. If she was with her, why not send the letters there?"

"It's been two weeks. I'm an adult living my life. I've been busy." Lauren threw up her hands. "Why am I justifying myself?"

"I hadn't heard from you since the night I saw you at the Frick. I was concerned. But now you're here, we're all here, so let's sit and talk a bit." At Genevra's command, everyone sat.

"Barb and I have called this meeting because we have decided on the disposition of the largest asset in my estate, the collection. It probably won't be a surprise to Lauren and Cara, since Cara gave us the idea. We intend to liquidate the majority of the collection and use the proceeds to create a scholarship fund for New York City public school students, which will underwrite all education expenses for any number of degrees recipients wish to undertake."

Cara broke into a wide smile and looked around. She could tell Mr. Havemayer knew this already. Lauren and Preston looked mildly surprised. "Genevra, Barb, this is—it's astounding. It's going to do so much good, and the ripple effect—it'll be unbelievable how much it will do for generations of New York City students and their families."

Barb smiled a sneaky smile. "I'm glad you think so, Cara, because you're the one who's going to run it."

"You're hilarious, Barb." Cara laughed and threw a look of disbelief at Lauren, but she gazed back with a thoughtful expression.

Genevra rapped the table to get their attention. "That's the headline, but there are a few more bullet points to go through. The three of you will be a leadership triumvirate. Cara will design, develop, and administer the scholarship, Preston will handle the finances, and Lauren will, of course, oversee the collection. Now—"

"Hold on, Aunt Genevra," Preston said. "I have no background in philanthropic finance. Not to mention this will be a charity based in New York and I live in California."

Cara was surprised by her inclusion in Genevra's plans. "And while I'm grateful for your vote of confidence in me, I don't think I'm the best candidate for that job. Aren't there professionals who run non-profits? I don't have the experience you'd need. Not with scholarships, not in art. I didn't even know those pills out there were art." She said to Lauren, "I think I should be going and let you and your family have your meeting."

Lauren grabbed her hand and gave her a reassuring smile. "You don't have to go."

"Never mind that now, Cara," Genevra said. "Now, one condition I have is that Lauren must be allowed to go through the collection and put aside anything that will further her area of study, and to curate a collection of women artists to donate to the museum of her choosing. I have some ideas about how we can word the bequest, so it has maximum impact for whatever institution is lucky enough to receive it."

Cara insisted on being heard. "Genevra, Barb, thank you for the compliment you pay me in thinking I am capable of a challenge like this, but you've met me twice. With all due respect, you don't know me at all."

"Lauren knows you," Mr. Havemayer said, and everyone turned to him. "Not that you need it, Genevra, but Cara meets with my approval. We've only met once, Cara, and you're right, that's not long enough to know your character. I have to tell you I had you investigated."

Cara's mouth dropped open.

"Oh my God, Dad," Lauren said.

"I'm sorry, honey, and I'm sorry to you too, Cara, but I was not willing to let Lauren get involved with anyone again without checking into their background. And when Genevra and Barb told me their plans, it was equally important that they know more about the financial history of a potential employee who would have access to millions."

"Dad, you could have asked her permission. That's a serious invasion of privacy," Preston said.

"I'm aware, but I had only Lauren's best interests in mind."

Lauren said to Cara, "I didn't know about this."

"There's nothing to suggest Cara would be unfit for this position, but Lauren knows her best. What do you think? Could Cara do the job, honey?" Mr. Havemayer asked.

Lauren turned so she was looking at Cara, who was still poised to leave. Her eyes shone with love and respect. "There's not a doubt in my mind that she could. She's brilliant. And she has the biggest and kindest heart of anyone I've ever met. But I guess the question is, does she want to? She's an excellent teacher. She's already doing a lot of good in her classroom, Aunt Genevra, and you would be asking her to give that up."

"God knows, the city can't afford to lose a good teacher," Barb said.
"You're not helping, Barbie," Genevra said. "Of course, we would compensate you generously, Cara."

"While I appreciate that, it's not the point. Again, this is a terrific idea and I wish you luck with it, but this seems more like a family matter. I think I should step outside." Cara spared a quick, apologetic glance at Lauren before she stood and pushed through the heavy door.

She walked in the direction of the elevator bank, past several closed office doors toward a floor-to-ceiling window at the end of the corridor, drawn to the view. She raised her forearm and leaned it against the glass, gazing at thousands of office windows in neighboring high-rises. This was Mr. Havemayer's world. No wonder it seemed like the window was tinted green. It was surreal to listen to a bunch of rich people decide if she was suitable for a job she didn't want.

"Cara."

She turned to see Lauren standing a few feet behind, her face etched with an expression of misery so pronounced it made Cara reach out to her.

Lauren curled into Cara's side. "I didn't know," she murmured. "You have to believe me."

"I do believe you." Cara hushed her, brushing a hand over her hair, feeling Lauren sag against her.

"I thought you'd be gone."

She hadn't planned to leave, only to remove herself from their meeting. But maybe she hadn't been very clear about that. "I'm not going anywhere. I'll wait out here for you. I won't leave."

"I've said my good-byes. Let's go."

Cara pulled back so she could look at Lauren. "That sounds ominous."

"He doesn't get to do that. They don't get to do that." Her face was hard.

"Sometimes family does get to do that. That's why they're called family." Cara was realizing something that should have been clear from pretty much day one. God, she was an idiot. This is who Lauren was. Her family's wealth, her father's protectiveness, her aunts' kooky meddling—even her past experiences—none of that could be separated from her. If she wanted Lauren, she had to take all of her, as she was. And Cara wanted all of Lauren. Every last imperfect, confounding, lovable bit of her.

When she thought about it like that, it wasn't a decision. It was acceptance. All those compartments she had been stuffing her thoughts and feelings into sprang open at once, and the emotion that welled up in her released itself in a not-quite-appropriate belly laugh. The solution was so simple. She felt so much lighter now.

"You're laughing?" Lauren raised her voice. "He crossed a line."

"You're right, he did." Cara shrugged. "I'm okay with it."

Lauren gaped at her. "You are?"

"He did it out of love for you, and if there's one thing I can understand, it's love for you. And I guess he's okay with my negative bank balance. I'm kind of glad to know that." She pressed a gentle kiss to Lauren's lips. "I don't want to come between you and your family. You should be a part of whatever your aunts want to do. Now go back in there and listen to their plan for scholarship domination."

Lauren looked unsure.

She raised a hand. "I promise. I'll be sitting on one of those big black sofas waiting for you when you finish."

It looked as if Cara's reassurances were sinking in, and Lauren gave her a tentative smile. "Are you sure you won't come with me? In a bizarre way, I think they're trying to welcome you into the family." She gave her best jazz hands. "Hey! We like you! How about a new job?"

Cara's giggle contained a note of hysteria. "It's kind of nice, but also a bit insane, too. You have to admit, it's a little overwhelming for this to be my first real introduction to my girlfriend's family."

Lauren's good humor seemed to return, along with relief. "I've graduated from friend-with-benefits? I'm your girlfriend now?"

"I have your diploma around here somewhere." She slapped her pockets. Cara led Lauren back toward the conference room, stopping at the waiting area and its arrangement of chrome and leather seating.

"Why don't you come in with me? Just sit and listen and nod and say you'll think about it, and think about it if you want to, or don't, and then you can politely decline later. It doesn't matter to me either way. But for what it's worth, I think you would be tremendous at that job."

Cara pretended to consider for a moment. "I probably would be with some decent training videos, but I'm not sure I'm done with the classroom."

Lauren nodded, looking disappointed. "Cara?"

She waited.

"What if I said I want you to come in there with me?" Lauren asked, then shook her head. "No. Scratch the what if part. I want you in there with me. It feels wrong to go in without you, whether you want to give away scholarships or not. I love you, and even when they're interfering pains in the ass, I love my family, too. I want my family to love you. I want you to love them. If we're really going to try, like you said, then I think we need to start here and now."

Lauren was absolutely right. Were more logical, more perfect words ever spoken? Cara thought she heard choirs of angels singing and saw shafts of golden sunlight slanting down over Lauren as she stood before her in a lawyer's office in midtown. She returned to Lauren's side and walked with her to the closed door that separated them from Lauren's family. "I don't think I'm ever going to be able to say no to you." Cara gave her a kiss before opening the door. "I probably shouldn't have told you that. Just forget I said it, okay?"

The smile that broke over Lauren's face was as big as the island of Manhattan. "My memory has improved a lot since school. I'm not going to forget a second of being with you."

EPILOGUE

Thirty-one monthly student loan payments later

"I think we need a new rule for tomorrow," Cara announced as they strolled arm-in-arm through Central Park. There had been rain earlier and the leaves on the ground were sodden brown mounds they had to occasionally step around, but there were still gorgeous bits of red and yellow clinging to the trees. "Let's have a no football Thanksgiving."

"Doesn't seem so difficult to achieve since we don't own a football." Lauren avoided the issue, angling her face toward the late afternoon November sunlight.

"I'm being serious. I don't want my uncles sitting around watching it or making everyone talk about it during dinner. No way would your family stand for that."

Lauren wanted all her loved ones to share the same Thanksgiving table this year, so she had proposed a gathering of the families. She and Cara would host. Preston was flying in, her father and aunts would attend, and Cara's mom and the McNamaras were coming from Paterson. "How much do you think your uncles are going to enjoy themselves if they can't watch football?"

Cara countered with, "How much will your aunts enjoy themselves if they're forced to talk about weaknesses in the Giants' defensive line over dinner?"

"I'd think you'd want them distracted by anything that would let you avoid their usual plea for you to run the foundation."

"They're doing just fine on their own. They don't need me."

"It seems like they do need you." Lauren felt protective of Cara. Her aunts hadn't enticed her into accepting a job, but that didn't stop them from picking her brain as if she were a paid consultant. "If they try to corner you tomorrow with another list of questions, you won't be able to drop everything to research, I don't know, New York State non-profit tax codes or whatever."

"I know. Tomorrow, my first priority is providing a delicious meal for our guests."

"They should be paying you for all the free labor you do for them," Lauren grumbled. She did a lot for her aunts, too, but working with Aunt Genevra's collection didn't seem like labor to her.

"I don't mind. It's for a good cause. Maybe one of these days I'll say yes to their offer."

That surprised Lauren, but Cara didn't say anything else. They continued to walk in comfortable silence, and Lauren wanted to hang on to this peacefulness with Cara right now for as long as possible, before the chaos of entertaining both their families descended over them.

"How about we move a few more comfy chairs into the study and make that the football-watching room?" Cara suggested. "And we let the conversational chips fall where they may at the dinner table."

Lauren exhaled. "Very sensible, as usual, dear." She leaned over and kissed Cara, her reward for resolving the issue that had never been an issue to begin with. The look Cara gave her in return, the combination eye-roll-rueful smile, was one of her favorites.

They were nearing the western edge of the park, and the pathway they traversed spit them out onto Central Park West somewhere in the high seventies. Turning northward, both of them stopped at the sight of an enormous crowd in front of the Museum of Natural History.

Cara said, "Holy moly, that's a lot of people."

"Maybe this isn't such a good idea."

"Of course it is." She began walking again, dragging Lauren along with her. "You've been saying how much you enjoyed doing this when you were a kid. Let's go see these balloons get blown up!"

"I don't remember it being so crowded when my family used to do this all those years ago."

"It's free and highly Instagrammable. I'm not surprised it's crowded."

There seemed to be an orderly flow to the way the crowds ambled past the enormous balloons laid out in the park surrounding the museum, as they slowly expanded with helium in preparation for the Macy's parade the next day. Cara and Lauren joined the procession of gawkers, skirting the large crowd that gathered in front of an uninflated SpongeBob SquarePants.

Lauren hadn't watched the parade in forever. She found herself wanting to establish little customs and traditions with Cara, and if they already had some connection to one of their families, so much the better. It felt important somehow. She felt on the verge of something big, at a stepping off place, and she wanted Cara beside her. She had been waiting for Cara to finish paying off her loans because that was a milestone for her.

Cara slipped her hand into Lauren's. "Oh. I have to tell you something."

"What?" Here it was.

Now Cara was going to tell her she had made her last loan payment. She was such a creature of habit. Every third Sunday evening of the month she sat at the dining room table with her laptop to pay her bills. Their phones. Her share of the household expenses they had argued and debated and discussed and finally compromised on. Her loans. Did she think Lauren wouldn't remember her saying she only had one payment left last month? That third Sunday was three days ago.

"Aunt Deedee is bringing her pumpkin chiffon pie. I tried to talk her out of it, but she wouldn't be swayed."

"Okay." Lauren frowned. Had she gotten the Sunday wrong?

Cara nudged her. "You don't have to eat it, Lauren. It's not the end of the world."

Lauren chuckled. "All right, I won't. Anything else?"

"Nope." Cara smiled at a family posing by the Baby Yoda balloon, then swung back to Lauren. "Yes. I forgot to tell you. Samantha and Hector don't have any plans for Thanksgiving. I invited them to come tomorrow. Is that okay? Even more people in your home?"

"Our home," she gently corrected her.

"Our home," Cara repeated.

Cara was like Lauren's mom, inviting all the strays so they had somewhere to be on Thanksgiving. They hadn't seen Sam and her husband since their housewarming party. Lauren and Cara had made all the interior design decisions together, and they had finally moved into a home that was an expression of both their personalities, and featured a little more tile than was typical for the Upper East Side.

"I don't know if they'll come. Sam was kind of noncommittal, but I put it out there."

"I hope they do. You're very welcoming to people who have nowhere to go on Thanksgiving."

Cara wrapped both arms around Lauren's and bent her head closer. "They won't get the extra special, post dinner, childhood bedroom, teenage crush, sex proposition, premium deluxe package. There's only one of those, and it's already sold."

"To a very lucky buyer."

"A satisfied customer."

"From a super sexy seller."

Cara started to laugh. "Are we the corniest people alive?"

Lauren laughed, too. She liked that they were corny. She didn't want to be corny with anyone else.

Cara lapsed into silence and seemed to be doing some heavy-duty cogitating as they continued to walk along. She gave Lauren a considering sidelong glance.

"What?" Lauren asked, and gripped Cara's hand tighter. Now she would tell her about making the last loan payment.

"Do you think we should make two kinds of stuffing? Everyone loves stuffing."

Stuffing? When was Cara going to tell her? "Sure. Whatever you want. If you're happy, I'm happy." In that moment, the *if* in that sentence became impossible to ignore. It felt to Lauren as if those two tiny letters had ballooned to gargantuan proportions and separated her from Cara, and would continue to separate them until she knew why Cara hadn't told her about her loans. Lauren stopped in the middle of the footpath, prompting Cara to stop, too. "Are you?"

"Am I what?"

Lauren's throat was incredibly dry, but she pushed the word out. "Happy?"

Cara's eyebrows drew downward. "About two stuffings?"

"No. About...everything. About...with me?" People moved around them like water flowing around a river stone.

"Lauren, what's going on? Wait, let's move over." Cara led her toward the side of the path, where they replaced a family who was vacating a bench. She gazed at Lauren with those kind, concerned eyes. "Tell me what's wrong."

Lauren put her hand in her coat pocket. "Did you pay your bills on Sunday?"

"Oh." Cara sat up straighter. "I was going to make a toast tomorrow in front of everyone. It's finally done. All paid off." She made a dusting off her hands gesture.

How ironic. Lauren wanted to say something tomorrow, too. But this had to come first, and she couldn't possibly wait anymore. She had to do this now. There was no way she could wait another moment.

But Cara continued speaking. "I wanted to raise my glass to you because I did it so much faster with you in my life. Thirty-five is still a few years off, and that's something to be thankful for. I'm so grateful to you. But I should have said something. You were probably waiting, weren't you?"

"Only because you once said when your loans were paid, you would be free to look for your forever woman."

"But I found you." Cara smiled. Her smile had grown so necessary, so precious, Lauren didn't know if she could live without it. Refused to live without it.

"And there were things you said you wanted. I remember those things you said."

Cara's eyes looked steadily into hers. "Things change."

Lauren pulled from her pocket a red leather jeweler's box from Cartier. It was slightly larger than a typical ring box. "If you still want those things, I want to give them to you."

She eyed the box and then looked at Lauren, her eyes wide with wonder. "What is that?"

"I can't ask you in the usual way, Cara, because that way is kind of tainted for me, and it would make it less special for me. So I'm going to ask you a different way, but I hope it's just as meaningful and special."

"Ask me." Cara's eyes were already damp, and her smile of encouragement made Lauren brave.

She took a breath. "Cara Talarico, with these random New Yorkers walking by and this half-inflated giant red Mighty Morphin Power Ranger as our witnesses, will you agree to officially keep trying with me for as long as we both shall live?"

Cara was nodding before she had even finished asking, tears streaming down her face. "Yes, Lauren Havemayer, I will!"

Lauren opened the box to reveal two identical marquise-shaped diamond rings. She plucked one from the silk inset and eased it onto Cara's left ring finger. "Thank God it fits! I've had these for weeks. If you don't like it we can take it back and get you something else." It felt like the weight of ten worlds had been lifted from her as she gazed at Cara, the woman who had shown her what real and lasting love was, the woman who healed her heart and would have it forever.

"It's beautiful. You made a perfect choice." Cara wiped a hand over her face. "I'm sorry. I'm so surprised. You really got me."

Lauren took Cara's face in her hands and kissed her before she brushed away her tears with her thumbs. "I was ready to whip these babies out as soon as you told me about your loans. I've been in agony since Sunday. Whew! I feel so much better now."

"Me too." Cara gave her a watery smile. She took the other ring and slid it onto Lauren's finger. "A perfect fit." She laced their fingers together. "You're so prepared. Coming to a proposal with *both* rings. You are such a catch."

Lauren's laughter was giddy with relief and elation. She couldn't believe she got to spend the rest of her life with Cara.

"But I already love our life, and I'm happy. I don't need this"—Cara held up her hand with its shiny ring—"to be happy with you. What made you decide to propose?"

"Part of it was loving you enough to want to give you whatever you wanted, and I knew this was what you wanted. And over time, as we got closer and stronger and better together, it became something I wanted, too." She gripped their interlaced fingers tightly. "I don't want yours and mine. I want to share all that I am and all that I have with you. Our home. Our family. Our life. Can we do that?"

Cara's eyes were flooded with tears again. "Yes, starting right now and for all the nows to come."

About the Author

Nan Campbell grew up on the Jersey Shore, where she first discovered her love of romance novels as a kid, spending her summers at the beach reading stories that were wholly inappropriate for her age. She was, and continues to be, a sucker for a happy ending.

She is a seasoned traveler, having visited many countries across six continents, and hopes to make it to the seventh someday. She hates to cook but loves to practice her cocktail-making skills. She also loves karaoke, which is unfortunate for anyone within range of her singing voice.

Nan and her wife live in New York City, where they struggle to balance their natural homebody tendencies with all the amazing things the city has to offer.

Books Available from Bold Strokes Books

A Good Chance by Ali Vali. Harry, Desi, and Desi's sister Rachel are so close to getting everything they've ever wanted, but Desi's ex-husband is coming back to get his revenge and rip apart their chance at happiness. (978-1-63679-023-7)

A Perfect Fifth by Jaycie Morrison. Streetwise pianist Zara Keller and Lady Jillian Stansfield couldn't be more different; yet their connection brings a new awareness of who they are and what they truly want in their lives—including each other. (978-1-63679-132-6)

Catching Feelings by Ana Hartnett Reichardt. Andrea Foster expected to catch a lot of pitches from the Alder Lion's star pitcher, Maya, but she didn't expect to catch feelings. (978-1-63679-227-9)

Defiant Hearts by Lee Lynch. In these stories, you'll find your lovers, friends, and lesbians you wish you knew—maybe even yourself. (978-1-63679-237-8)

Love and Duty by Catherine Young. All Princess Roseli wants is to marry her three lovers, but with war looming, she must instead marry Princess Lucia to establish a military alliance between their planets. (978-1-63679-256-9)

Murder at Union Station by David S. Pederson. Private Detective Mason Adler struggles to determine who killed a woman found in a trunk without getting himself killed in the process. (978-1-63679-269-9)

Serendipity by Kris Bryant. Serendipity brings jingle writer Annie Foster and celebrity pop star Bristol Baines together, and their undeniable attraction keeps them close, but will their different paths drive them apart? (978-1-63679-224-8)

The Haunted Heart by Jane Kolven. A ghost, a ring, and a quest to find a missing psychic—it's a spell for love. (978-1-63679-245-3)

The Rules of Forever by Nan Campbell. After reconnecting at their high school reunion, Cara and Lauren agree to embark on a textbook definition friends-with-benefits relationship, but trying to keep it uncomplicated is harder than it seems. (978-1-63679-248-4)

Vision of Virtue by Brey Willows. When virtue and desire come together, be prepared for sparks in this next installment of the Memory's Muses series. (978-1-63679-118-0)

Cherry on Top by Georgia Beers. A chance meeting leaves Cherry and Ellis longing for a different life, but when Ellis's search for truth crashes into Cherry's insta-filter world, do they have any hope at all of a happily ever after? (978-1-63679-158-6)

Love and Other Rare Birds by Angie Williams. Ornithologist Dr. Jamie Martin and park ranger Rowan Fleming are searching the Alaskan wilderness for a bird thought to be extinct and they're about to discover opposites really do attract. (978-1-63679-108-1)

Parallel Paradise by Mayapee Chowdhury. When their love affair is put to the test by the homophobia of their family, community, and culture, Bindi and Rimli will need to fight for a chance at love. (978-1-63679-204-0)

Perfectly Matched by Toni Logan. A beautiful Cupid named Hannah, a runaway arrow, and just seventy-two hours to fix a mishap that could be the best mistake she has ever made. (978-1-63679-120-3)

Royal Exposé by Jenny Frame. When they're grouped together for a class assignment, Poppy's enthusiasm for life and love may just save Casey's soul, but will she ever forgive Casey for using her to expose royal secrets? (978-1-63679-165-4)

Slow Burn by Missouri Vaun. A wounded wildland firefighter from California and a struggling artist find solace and love in a small southern town. (978-1-63679-098-5)

The Artist by Sheri Lewis Wohl. Detective Casey Wilson and reclusive artist Tula Crane are drawn together in a web of passion, intrigue, and art that might just hold the key to stopping a killer. (978-1-63679-150-0)

The Inconvenient Heiress by Jane Walsh. An unlikely heiress and a spinster evade the Marriage Mart only to discover true love together. (978-1-63679-173-9)

A Champion for Tinker Creek by D.C. Robeline. Lyle James has rescued his dad's auto repair business, but when city hall condemns his neighborhood, Lyle learns only trusting will save his life and help him find love. (978-1-63679-213-2)

Closed-Door Policy by Erin Zak. Going back to college is never easy, but Caroline Stevens is prepared to work hard and change her life for the better. What she's not prepared for is Dr. Atlanta Morris, her gorgeous new professor. (978-1-63679-181-4)

Homeworld by Gun Brooke. Headed by Captain Holly Crowe, the spaceship Velocity's crew journeys toward their alien ancestors' homeworld, and what they find is completely unexpected—and they're not safe. (978-1-63679-177-7)

Outland by Kristin Keppler & Allisa Bahney. Danielle Clark and Katelyn Turner can't seem to stay away from one another even as the war for the wastelands tests their loyalty to each other and to their people. (978-1-63679-154-8)

Secret Sanctuary by Nance Sparks. US Deputy Marshal Alex Trenton specializes in protecting those awaiting trial, but when danger threatens the woman she's falling for, Alex is in for the fight of her life. (978-1-63679-148-7)

Stranded Hearts by Kris Bryant, Amanda Radley, Emily Smith. In these novellas from award winning authors, fate intervenes on behalf of love when characters are unexpectedly stuck together. With too much time and an irresistible attraction, anything could happen. (978-1-63679-182-1)

The Last Lavender Sister by Melissa Brayden. Aster Lavender sells her gourmet doughnuts and keeps a low profile; she never plans on the town's temporary veterinarian swooping in and making her feel like anything but a wallflower. (978-1-63679-130-2)

The Probability of Love by Dena Blake. As Blair and Rachel keep ending up in the same place despite the odds, can a one-night stand turn into forever? Or will the bet Blair never intended to make ruin their happily ever after? (978-1-63679-188-3)

Worth a Fortune by Sam Ledel. After placing a want ad for a personal secretary, a New York heiress is surprised when the woman who got away is the one interested in the position. (978-1-63679-175-3)

A Fox in Shadow by Jane Fletcher. Cassie's mission is to add new territory to the Kavillian empire—murder, betrayal, war, and the clash of cultures ensue. (978-1-63679-142-5)

Embracing the Moon by Jeannie Levig. Just as Gwen and Taylor are exploring the new love they've found, the present and past collide, threatening the future they long to share. (978-1-63555-462-5)

Forever Comes in Threes by D. Jackson Leigh. Efficiency expert Perry Chandler's ordered life is upended when she inherits three busy terriers, and the woman she's referred to for help turns out to be her bitter podcast rival, the very sexy Dr. Ming Lee. (978-1-63679-169-2)

Heckin' Lewd: Trans and Nonbinary Erotica by Mx. Nillin Lore. If you want smutty, fearless, gender diverse erotica written by affirming own-voices folks who get it, then this is the book you've been looking for! (978-1-63679-240-8)

Missed Conception by Joy Argento. Maggie Walsh wants a relationship with Cassidy, the daughter she's only just discovered she has due to an in vitro mix-up. Heat kindles between Maggie and Cassidy's mother in a way neither expects. (978-1-63679-146-3)

Private Equity by Elle Spencer. Cassidy Bennett spends an unexpected evening at a lesbian nightclub with her notoriously reserved and demanding boss, Julia. After seeing a different side of Julia, Cassidy can't seem to shake her desire to know more. (978-1-63679-180-7)

Racing the Dawn by Sandra Barrett. After narrowly escaping a house fire, vampire Jade Murphy is unexpectedly intrigued by gorgeous firefighter Beth Jenssen, and her undead existence might just be perking up a bit. (978-1-63679-271-2)

Reclaiming Love by Amanda Radley. Sarah's tiny white lie means somehow convincing Pippa to pretend to be her girlfriend. Only the more time they spend faking it, the more real it feels. (978-1-63679-144-9)

Sol Cycle by Kimberly Cooper Griffin. An encounter in a park brings Ang and Krista together, but when Ang's attempts to help Krista go spectacularly wrong, their passion for each other might not be enough. (978-1-63679-137-1)

Trial and Error by Carsen Taite. Attorney Franco Rossi and Judge Nina Aguilar's reunion is fraught with courtroom conflict, undeniable chemistry, and danger. (978-1-63555-863-0)

A Long Way to Fall by Elle Spencer. A ski lodge, two strong-willed women, and a family feud that brings them together, but will it also tear them apart? (978-1-63679-005-3)

Barnabas Bopwright Saves the City by J. Marshall Freeman. When he uncovers a terror plot to destroy the city he loves, 15-year-old Barnabas Bopwright realizes it's up to him to save his home and bring deadly secrets into the light before it's too late. (978-1-63679-152-4)

Forever by Kris Bryant. When Savannah Edwards is invited to be the next bachelorette on the dating show When Sparks Fly, she'll show the world that finding true love on television can happen. (978-1-63679-029-9)

Ice on Wheels by Aurora Rey. All's fair in love and roller derby. That's Riley Fauchet's motto, until a new job lands her at the same company—and on the same team—as her rival Brooke Landry, the frosty jammer for the Big Easy Bruisers. (978-1-63679-179-1)

Inherit the Lightning by Bud Gundy. Darcy O'Brien and his sisters learn they are about to inherit an immense fortune, but a family mystery about to unravel after seventy years threatens to destroy everything. (978-1-63679-199-9)

Perfect Rivalry by Radclyffe. Two women set out to win the same career-making goal, but it's love that may turn out to be the final prize. (978-1-63679-216-3)

Something to Talk About by Ronica Black. Can quiet ranch owner Corey Durand give up her peaceful life and allow her feisty new neighbor into her heart? Or will past loss, present suitors, and town gossip ruin a long-awaited chance at love? (978-1-63679-114-2)

With a Minor in Murder by Karis Walsh. In the world of academia, police officer Clare Sawyer and professor Libby Hart team up to solve a murder. (978-1-63679-186-9)

Writer's Block by Ali Vali. Wyatt and Hayley might be made for each other if only they can get through nosy neighbors, the historic society, at-odds future plans, and all the secrets hidden in Wyatt's walls. (978-1-63679-021-3)